Also by L. J. Hutton

Fantasy:
The Power & Empire series:
Chasing Sorcery
The Darkening Storm
Fleeting Victories
Summoning Spectres

The Menaced by Magic Series:
Menaced by Magic
No Human Hunter
Shards of Sorcery
The Rite to Rule


Historical series:
Heaven's Kingdom – prequel
Crusades
Outlawed
Broken Arrow

# UNLEASHING
# THE
# POWER

# L. J. HUTTON

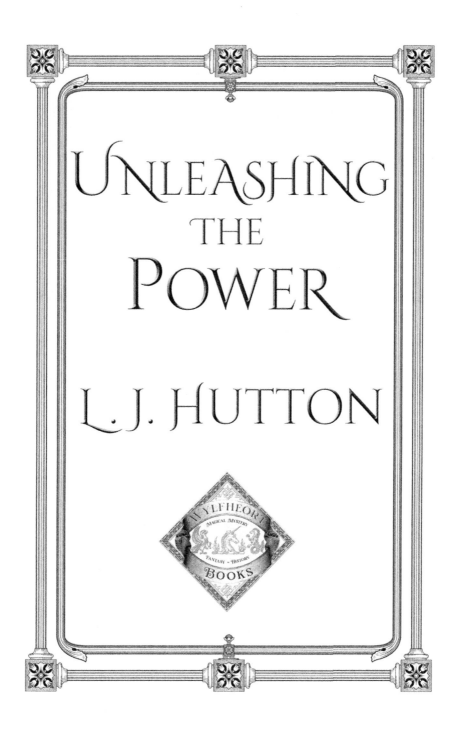

ISBN 13: 9781719932653

First published 2013
This edition 2021

## Copyright

## Acknowledgements

As ever there are people whom I need to thank

Once again, thanks to Karen Murray for her stalwart support right from the very first page of this series. She has been the best first reader a fledgling writer could hope to have, always encouraging but never backwards in telling me when things weren't working. Everyone needs someone who can put things into perspective from a distance and she has done this admirably.

My husband John has had to cope with a very absent wife during the writing phases but has somehow survived! And of course my lovely lurchers, Blue, Raffles and Minnie have been companionable sleepers at my side while I've worked.

And finally, thanks to you the readers who have stayed with this series through to its completion. I hope you enjoy the final book!

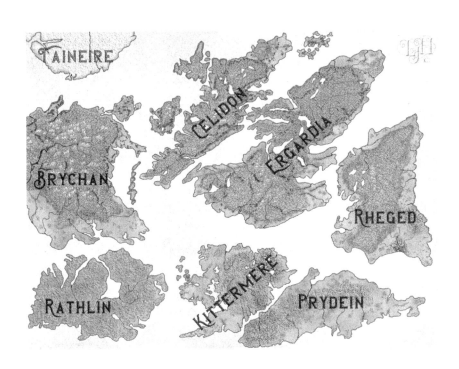

# The whole of Brychan

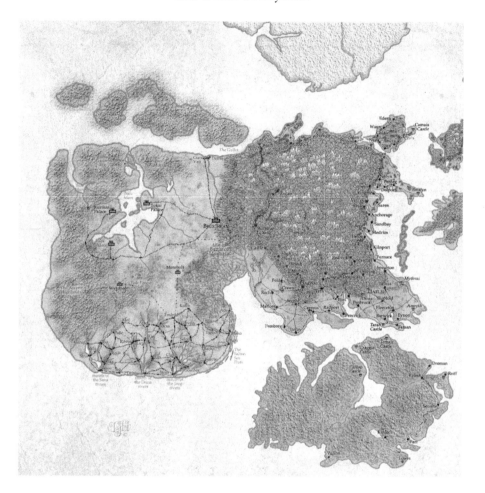

# Chapter 1

## *Crossing the First Bridge*

### Brychan: Beltane

Berengar spent the first couple of days back at Garway analysing the reports which had flooded in in his absence. The first good news was that, while the floodwaters were still extraordinarily high for the time of year, they had peaked – although many feared that this was only temporary, and might change again once the snow deeper within the mountains began to head their way. Word had come through from Laon that, after two weeks of incredibly high floods, the river there also was now only a little higher than a normal spate for a melt after a hard winter and a spring thaw. High but steady, they all prayed, and unlikely to make any sudden deluges which might be a risk to life, even if this time the full thaw might take weeks longer than normal.

By MacSorley's reckoning, the road from Laon down onto the plain and Foel should be passable any day now, although the sodden mass of farmland immediately west of it (which lay lower than the Tern's east bank and the road) would still be underwater for at least another week, and impassable for two more at a minimum – possibly even a month. And that was discounting the normal water meadows along the western banks, which might just about dry out by midsummer at this rate. The DeÁine were therefore still securely trapped in eastern Brychan with no way of marching westwards yet.

Other waiting news included reports from ealdormen Allainn at Blass and Eoghan at Wolfscar. The tunnel up to Wolfscar had been accessed with Nettie's help, and together they had begun scouting westwards. As Sioncaet's message had suggested, they had found the New Lochlainn side of the range much clearer of snow than expected, and had been able to start checking out DeÁine troop movements. However, the heavy snows must have been driven so hard at the mountains that the western slopes had not escaped by as much as the Knights had hoped, and if the lower slopes were snow free, the same could not be said of the higher ridges and peaks. When the Water of Sgair had risen alarmingly, they had been forced to remain indoors for a couple of weeks for fear of men becoming trapped and isolated by the fast flowing and unpredictable floods, but even so, they were confident that they would soon be able to be on the move again.

The only worrying news was that the Ertigun family might have been the last, rather than the first, of the lesser DeÁine families to commit their house forces to the take-over of Brychan. Allainn wrote that there might be four or more other families ahead of the Ertiguns, going by the absence of armed forces observed west of the mountains. All that could be said on a positive note was that they might barely scrap a full Jundis each, and that none of those would be of the calibre of the great families' forces who had taken Arlei. Mercifully there was no sign, Allainn said, of those families who had holdings in the wealthy south of New Lochlainn, the Souk'ir. For which Berengar was heartily glad, since those wealthy merchant-trader families could afford to purchase the pick of the soldiers from the training camps once the royals had taken their share.

The next good news came from a company of men he had detoured east from the main force, under Esclados' command, to scout for where Tancostyl had disappeared to. The older Knight had accepted the mission willingly, for he knew what Berengar could never say out loud in front of others. The Grand Master was desperate to know if Cwen's family had survived and if they had had word from her at all. Only a few days behind Berengar in getting back, Esclados reported that Radport had suffered no new deprivations after its harrowing occupation by King Edward. However, they had had word up from Pencrick telling of sightings of a

DeÁine force embarking on ships beyond the estuary closer to Tarah, which worried Berengar although he could not show it.

Esclados was able to whisper to him, "I've seen Roger and Jane! They're all well!" as they walked side by side to the debriefing, but had no chance to say more before they were again in the presence of others. However, it was not the last of the good news. In the formal debriefing, Esclados reported back to the collected senior officers that the folk of Radport had had contact with a senior captain named Iolo, formerly of the Kiln grange.

"He was there lending expertise to the ordinary folk," Esclados told the assembly. "They've done a good job of keeping the people safe, but better still, they've had contact with a captain called Emlyn. He was from Penbrook, but has since taken charge of the evacuation of the folk of the far south-east."

"Evacuation?" Warwick was staggered. "What? All of them?"

Esclados grinned. "Pretty close! Apparently he had some help from a determined young lady called Cwen and a young man named Swein, both of whom the Master and I know very well!"

If Esclados' joy was clear for all to see, the effect on Berengar was as blatant as it was unexpected to those who knew nothing of their Master's recent past.

"She's alive?" Berengar asked, his eyes shining and a dark weight clearly lifting from him.

"Very much so, apparently," Esclados said happily. "Between Emlyn, Iolo and our two they got a flotilla of ships going. All the folk from Penbrook, Barwick and Farsan are safely over on Rathlin, along with quite a few from Eynon and stragglers from the outlying hamlets. But here's a written report addressed to you from Emlyn himself."

Esclados handed over a sealed roll and stood back as Berengar opened it and sat back and read. The others in the room were clearly itching to find out what all this meant but dared not ask outright. Unfortunately Warwick's inscrutable expression as he watched Berengar, did nothing to dispel any ideas that something was going on outside of the overriding emergency.

"Sacred Root and Branch," Berengar muttered as he read, shaking his head in bemusement, but clearly pleased rather than distraught at the scrolls contents. When he placed it down on his desk, he raised his eyes to find everyone watching him expectantly.

"Well now, that's news indeed!" he told them with a smile. "As you know, we lost Commander Jathan of Tarah and Commander Seisyll of Kiln in mysterious circumstances. It now appears that they never got my messages, but went after King Edward thinking he was going to join up *with* us to fight an unknown DeÁine force. It was their dreadful misfortune to have completely misread the situation, albeit with the best of intentions. However, the orders I gave while on my way to Garway to take over as Grand Master have been acted upon in the best possible way. Not only did the folk of Kiln get away in time to avoid the DeÁine, but those captains who assembled down at Tarah acted with great resourcefulness. Sadly Emlyn acknowledges that there was nothing he could do for the folk of Shipfold or Fleeceston, and I'm sure when the tally of dead gets made there'll be a high number from those towns.

"Against that, though – as Esclados just said – the folk of the other towns have virtually all escaped unscathed. And it doesn't end there! Emlyn and his helpers guessed that they might still be vulnerable if they simply waited out the disaster at Temair. So they've moved all the people around the Rathlin coast, and down along Loch Canisp. Emlyn says they've even started ploughing and planting crops on the protected western shore in case they're there for some time. And they've taken the boats with them. That's how they got this message to Iolo to hand on when he next saw someone. They've been keeping in touch with the folk of Radport and Pencrick by boat."

"And I can add something to that," Esclados chipped in. "We asked that Iolo send word back to them that we found Trefin and Pembrey untouched, so they can keep in touch with them now too."

"Oh this is all good!" Warwick enthused. "That means that we don't have to worry about driving the DeÁine south onto our own population! Even on Rathlin they're far enough away not to be in danger if the DeÁine march west along the coast."

Berengar was positively beaming now. "No we don't! Gentlemen, I think it's time we took our Island back! The DeÁine are still stuck east of the Tern and Tarth rivers. We have the far north secured, although they don't know it. Warwick, now's the time you should ride for Bere with all haste through the tunnels! For once we'll risk taking horses through, because you'll need them at the other end for the speed they'll give you."

"I'll give the order and we'll start tomorrow morning," Warwick enthused.

4

For the rest of that day they worked out the necessary details of who was going where and when, but the next day they were on the move. In the bright spring dawn men were queuing, not to ride out over the castle's drawbridges as they had done a couple of weeks back, but to head deep under the mountains. In the vanguard was Warwick. He was riding virtually alone, for he and Berengar had decided that since he had further to go, he would ride at speed to Laon without trying to have men keep up with him, then with a battalion of Foresters he would head straight on to Redrock. Only then would he round up those battalions there, and they would join with Ealdorman Corin's men presently still defending the north road. Eight and a half thousand, plus a few stragglers, coming down the north road at the DeÁine was a good number, the two leaders thought, to draw them out with.

With the DeÁine already having sent a portion of their army north and which had clearly been defeated, these Order-men could be presumed to be around two-thirds the size of the remaining DeÁine force in Arlei. A force which hopefully those DeÁine would think needed to be shown a lesson, and one the Donns would want to show their strength against. Big enough not to ignore, but small enough to tempt them into thinking they could crush it decisively with their superior numbers. But with Warwick and Corin's force plus the men Berengar would lead from Laon, the Order actually had close to fourteen thousand men going into the field, and *that* was something the DeÁine should be really surprised by!

Riding as fast as they dared for the horses' sake on the bare rock, Berengar and Warwick's party were surprised the following day to hear lighter hooves heading towards them at a substantially faster pace.

"Lost Souls, that idiot will kill his horse," growled Esclados.

"Unless its news that won't wait," Warwick suggested and all three felt their hearts sinking.

They did not have long to wait. A rider mounted on a short and stocky hill pony, sure-footed and used to treacherous terrain, came belting along the tunnel towards them. Whoever had sent him had clearly deliberately chosen his smallest and lightest man to ease the pony's burden, but the man was not downcast. As he spotted Berengar in his distinctive Grand Master's surcoat, the man cried out.

"Sire! Sire! Great news!"

"What in the Islands can have happened?" Berengar wondered to his friends, reining in his horse and waiting for the rider who slithered to a halt in front of them moments later.

"A message for you, sire," the man beamed, eyes glinting joyfully, "from Ealdorman Corin!"

He thrust the scrolled message at Berengar but then could contain the good news no longer.

"They've come, sire!"

"Who have?" demanded Warwick, unable to bear the suspense any longer.

"The Order from the other Islands!" the messenger revealed. "Grand Master Brego got your message, sire! He called the muster and now his ealdorman has landed at Anchorage. Those shiploads were mainly the horses. Each man has a whole string of them! Even now they're riding south to meet the next shipment!"

"By the Rowan! Is this true?" Esclados gasped in delight. One look at Berengar's face as he read told him it was. "So that's what our foxy friend meant about help coming!"

"Praise the Trees!" Berengar sighed from the heart. "And bless Brego! This is a message forwarded from him through Corin – whom his men must clearly have never expected to find quite so easily." Then his face fell as he read further. "But I'm afraid, my friends, it's far from all good news. Sweet Rowan, this is bad! Brego writes that at least one of the Abend has managed to get to Prydein and retake the Scabbard," Warwick winced and Esclados shuddered, "and that the Helm was seized by Tancostyl from Rheged – well we knew about that the hard way! May the Trees protect us! We may have to fight a DeÁine army with Abend amongst them *and* armed with at least two of their infernal weapons. Oh this isn't good! This isn't good at all!"

Then he read more and groaned in disbelief, making his friends hold their breath in fear of what was coming.

"May the Trees look to us and aid us in our hour of need, for we shall surely have great need of them! ...Brego has had word that *more* DeÁine are coming in a great fleet! Great Oak protect us and the great Yew deflect their evil magic!"

"In you we trust," everyone around automatically responded, many still not sure what possible further catastrophe could be coming being out of hearing, but all worried by the way Berengar was shaking his head as he read and then reported the news on to them.

"He'd already sent his commander, Dana, out to make the muster after my message got to him, which is why his men are here so quickly. But like us he thought back then that we were simply going to drive the DeÁine west once more and then clear New Lochlainn. Now he tells me that it's confirmed, more DeÁine are on the way from over the sea. Apparently more of them lived in their last place of exile than we'd ever imagined. Quintillean had long since summoned them, and they could be landing on one of our south coasts as early as the end of *this* month."

"How many men has he brought?" wondered Warwick, his elation fading as swiftly as it had appeared and the old sense of dread seeping back into his stomach. "This must be some mighty DeÁine fleet if *Brego*'s fretting."

It was the messenger who answered. "It's not good news, sire, I'll not give you false hope over that. The Ergardian Commander I saw said that estimates put the number of possible new DeÁine troops maybe as high as a hundred thousand." The men who had by now clustered all around them collectively openly groaned in despair, many crossing themselves and uttering silent prayers. "But it isn't just the Ergardia men who're coming!" the messenger added quickly before everyone succumbed to gloom. "Commander Dana says that the men from Prydein are coming! They're coming through Kittermere and Rathlin."

"Master Hugh!" Berengar breathed. "Thank the Maker for that! The master tactician and Brego, our greatest war leader, fighting together again. Flaming Trees we're going to need them!"

The messenger assumed an air of intense concentration as he tried to recall perfectly everything he had heard and been told. "No ...no, it's not him who leads the Prydein men. Apparently the ancients who helped our ancestors are on the move again."

"Ah ha!" Esclados exclaimed. "Yes! We've seen one of those! The fox!"

The messenger nodded. "Well something happened and they're a bit stronger now. They've been acting as messengers between Master Hugh and Master Brego. It was them who brought the news about the fleet and the Scabbard to Master Brego, because he was already out of Ergardia by then. If I've got it right, they haven't appeared to you because you're so close to the DeÁine and they've been trying to keep their presence secret from the Abend. They want their appearance to be a shock when it comes, because they've been working on resurrecting some kind of ancient weapons ...I think that's what was said. Something about the advantage of surprise."

"That would make sense," Warwick confirmed. "So what else?"

"Well Master *Hugh* is staying on Ergardia in Master Brego's place for some reason – but it's important whatever it is. Master Brego is coming, though, with some of the later men, and these ancients will keep them in touch with one another. Apparently this means we can get messages back and forth almost instantly! No waiting for birds and not knowing what's happened for days."

"So who commands the Prydein men, then?" Berengar asked.

"The man who should have been Master in Rheged...?" he was told tentatively.

Berengar racked his brains then looked up hopefully. "MacBeth? Would it be Ruari MacBeth?"

"Yes, that was the name!"

"Yes!" Berengar shouted and punched the air.

"I take it that's good news," Warwick said wryly, smiling at his friend's undisguised relief, and the somewhat shocked expressions of some of the men at such un-Masterly actions.

"Sacred Root and Branch, yes!" Berengar chortled. "Oh yes! MacBeth commanded the Rheged Order's forces in the east when they went to fight the raiders. Dare I say it, but in a way he's an even better option than Master Hugh. For a start off he's a good twenty years younger and in his prime. If we have Master Hugh's tactical advice easily available through these ancients, then we'll want for nothing if Ruari's the man in the field."

"You've met him?" Warwick asked.

"Indeed I have. He was the one who moved the DeÁine Gorget from Brychan over to Ergardia. I was closely involved with him then and I'd met him before that, albeit briefly. He's a real soldier's soldier. And I know how he thinks and how he'll fight! Which is an extra blessing. I've never fought beside Master Hugh, and only really know Master Brego from a distance. To have someone I'm much more in touch with will make things much easier for me."

"Then I think we're all glad he's coming," Esclados said fondly. Anything which eased the intolerable burden Berengar was labouring under was a good thing in his eyes.

"So how many men will he be bringing?" Warwick asked, bringing them all back to the practicalities of the matter.

The messenger took a deep breath. "I believe they said twelve thousand from Prydein. But that's just coming up through the southern Islands. Among those who showed up at Bere there were about three and a half thousand Foresters' men and others who took every fishing boat they could commandeer from Celidon. There're very few Knight amongst them but a lot of veteran sergeants."

"The Celidon sept?" Warwick demanded, almost unable to believe what he was hearing. "They've been reformed?"

The man shook his head in awe and shrugged helplessly. "Again, something to do with Master Brego. They somehow managed to get their horses into all manner of craft and landed up on the coast by Breslyn, then marched down to Bere. Something to do with the fact that there weren't enough ships for them to go with the Ergardian Foresters. At the moment they're helping the Ergardia men with all their horses. I can't tell you how many of those there were in that first wave of ships, but Ealdorman Corin was saying that by the time they have the third wave of men landed they'll have just short of twenty thousand at a muster at Shipton including the Celidon men."

"Fuck me!" someone gasped.

"Twenty thousand!" another chuckled. "Shit we can wipe out the DeÁine here with no trouble!"

Berengar laughed with them, but held up a restraining hand when the wave of relief had passed. "Yes, we can wipe out the DeÁine here, but don't forget that the Abend are here with these DeÁine too. They'll help even the odds substantially, and we daren't be reckless if there are more DeÁine on the way." He paused and did some quick reckoning which the messenger interrupted apologetically,

"Oh by the way, sire, that twenty thousand doesn't include the Ergardian Foresters under someone called Ealdorman Sion... something. They're being shipped straight to Kittermere. ...or was it Rathlin? Oh Trees, you'll have to ask them when you see them, sire, I'm sorry but I'm stuffed with information and it's getting a bit jumbled."

"Sionnachan?" Now it was Warwick's turn to be jubilant. "By the Trees, Berengar, this is a good day!"

Berengar chuckled. "I suppose this is where I say 'I suppose *you* know *him*'?"

Warwick nodded happily, grinning as broadly as Berengar now. "He's the second-in-command of the Foresters in Ergardia. Their Master is a scholar of formidable learning but truly ancient. Sionnachan is the man who leads them in the field, and like MacBeth he's a veteran who knows his stuff. If I could hear that the man who should've led the Celidon Foresters was around I'd be downright ecstatic. Maelbrigt and Sionnachan together saved the day at Gavra."

"I did hear that name!" the messenger chipped in quickly. "He's somewhere in all of this too! Just please don't ask me how because I'm struggling to keep up with all this."

"Maelbrigt's back in action?" Warwick gasped. "He's come out of the Celidon hills? It wasn't just a passing reference to him?"

"Oh no! Whatever it is he's doing, he's been doing it with Master Brego and this Sionnachan, and he's coming here too. Or he'll be with Sionnachan on Rathlin, maybe, but don't quote me on that either."

Warwick gave a yip of delight and did a small dance on the spot, raising even more eyebrows than Berengar's outburst had caused. It was so out of character for the restrained Forester, but it hammered it home to those around the two leaders that this really might be the saving of Brychan that they had all prayed for. The other Islands had not left them to their fate but had come in force. Meanwhile Berengar was reading Corin's message again now that he could take it in properly.

"This changes everything," he declared. "Corin says he's taken it upon himself to order all of his men to Redrock. All the Ergardia men should be at Spearton on the twenty-second – that's …oh Great Maker! That's in six days time! They'll march for Beluss on the twenty-third, all being well. On the twenty-second Corin will lead the men at Redrock out in support of them, hoping to meet them at Arlei. Men, we must *ride* out straight from Laon! We can't march. We must empty your stables, Warwick!"

"Be my guest! I'm guessing MacSorley will have all the horses from the granges up in secure stables away from the floods so they'll be close at hand."

The word was passed back along the line of men in the tunnel and suddenly everyone was quick-marching. The elation filled the air and everyone was buzzing with excitement. Although Berengar and Warwick hurried on ahead, leaving the Garway men with Commander Barber at their head, the men made an epic march. Not only did Warwick and Berengar get to Laon by the next day, but before the break of the following dawn so had the rest of the men. Warwick immediately despatched Foresters who knew the locations of the more distant stables even in the dark, and they hurried off as soon as they had packed to reach those horses. Other messengers rode out to summon more mounts for daybreak of the day after.

Early on a cool late-spring morning, a long snake of mounted men began to wind its way down out of the mountains. Four abreast they rode, full colours flying and armed to the teeth. For Berengar it was an emotional moment. He had never in his wildest dreams ever thought he would be the one riding at the head of a muster of the Brychan sept – or as near a one as was possible in the current circumstances and given that none of them were on foot. He was torn between immense pride in the men and what they had achieved so far, and desperately nervousness that he might not be up to the job after all and let them down. He had offered Esclados a command of his own, for his old friend was more than competent and had seen more action than almost anyone else present. However, to his secret relief, Esclados had declined, saying that he would rather serve as Berengar's personal aide. So now Berengar was able to cast the odd sideways glance at his friend who rode beside him, carrying the Grand Master's personal banner, and received encouraging looks back – Esclados knew him well enough to guess what was going through his mind.

The horses had picked up on the adrenaline burning through their riders, and the whole column was soon moving at the briskest of trots. It was the eighteenth of Beltane and only four days remained before Corin would lead his men out of Redrock and the Ergardian muster would have massed at Spearton. Warwick was going to have to cut a whole day off the march if he was to get there in time, but pruning a five day march to four through the tunnels was more attainable than what Berengar had to do. Yet there was no way, Berengar knew, that he could have marched any more men through the tunnels either. There was a point when it simply was not possible to shoehorn more men into such a confined space. And there was also the other problem to do with the horses. Up in the mountains at Redrock there would be only be horses for the commanders, and Berengar had no wish to fight without any cavalry at all. So what he had now was the only cavalry he could field, and he cursed the Abend for the floods and snow which had robbed him of horses he could have used from closer to Garway.

Yet it was also the worst of luck that the high, switchback, east-west road through the hill passes from Tarth to Deepscar was gone, forcing him to go the long way around from Laon, right down to the deep estuary at

Foel before he could sweep back to close the trap with Warwick and Brego. And if it nonetheless had the bonus of allowing him to check for stray DeÁine, it would still normally be an eight day ride by that route to go down and then get back up to Deepscar or on to Arlei.

"We'll have to risk the bridge above Kiln now if we're to fight the DeÁine on the plain by Arlei," Berengar muttered to himself worriedly. He looked to Esclados. "I keep trying to find a way to shorten the journey time and it just isn't possible. Above Kiln the land rises so sharply we'd be building bridges to cross the ravine let alone the river. We have to risk going down almost to the coast."

"I know," Esclados said calmly. "Stop fretting Berengar. You've done all that any man could."

"Yes, but will it be enough?" worried the newest Grand Master, who had never felt so overwhelmed by his rank as he did now.

However, when they stopped to rest the horses at midday they were surprised to be visited by the fox once more. His outline appeared to be far more solid than the last time and he was also more positive.

"I'm Owein. I'm not going to risk showing my true form yet," he said without preamble. "That would take too much energy for the Abend not to notice. However, I bring you word which may help you. Master Brego said to tell you that he estimates that the final wave of his men won't be able to leave Ergardia until the twenty-eight of this month. These will be the Foresters, who'll therefore sail directly for the southern Islands, and support the Prydein men in case this new threat of DeÁine troops should land earlier than expected. Master Brego says that if the worst comes to the worst, they'll still be able to keep these newcomers off your back for a short while.

"He also asked me to tell you that the ships which will be taking Commander Sionnachan across will then come to act as ferries for you and your men to get you to Rathlin, but that this cannot take place before the fourteenth of Solstice. He's planning on massing all the armies of the Islands there. There's therefore no need for you to rush. You still have time to drive these DeÁine out before you can possibly embark, and anyway Master Brego has a plan for the others he wishes to talk in person to you about. I've been asked to get a sensible estimate from you as to when you'll be able to reach Arlei – or at least nearby – because Master Brego will delay his strike to match yours. When I know your answer, I shall visit your other force and inform them of your decision for you. So don't fear on that score, either."

Berengar felt the tension drain out of him as though it were water running off. "Oh thank you!" he sighed. "I've been worrying about all this none stop for the last couple of days!" He stopped to gather his thoughts. "Very well. By my estimate we can't make Deepscar in less than eight days." He stopped and massaged his temples again for a moment. "We only picked up the pace again because we heard of the Ergardia men and thought they would be at Spearton and leaving around the twenty-third. By my reckoning that means – if they march fast – that they'll reach Beluss by the twenty-sixth and the DeÁine around the twenty-ninth. Warwick and Corin can just about make the plain outside Arlei for then too ...aach no, but I can't be at Deepscar for the twenty-fourth to rendezvous with them..."

The fox shimmered and then formed into a man's shape. He held up his hand, the fox shape being no good for this and clearly he thought it worth the risk.

"No, no, Berengar! You misunderstood the message! Master Brego has no intention of you fighting a pitched battle! He's intent on *driving* them out of Brychan. He certainly doesn't want to incur heavy losses fighting the Abend, and then have to try to pull everyone together to fight the new DeÁine! No, he and Master Hugh plan to chase the Abend out. Out and down to Rathlin to where the terrain favours you, not their big battalions." He gestured to Berengar's map which had been dropped on the ground and temporarily forgotten. "That's why Brego wants to wait for you! He wants to present them with the sight of a huge army. One they'll think twice about fighting with the numbers they have this side of the floods. He wants them to retreat. To drive them across these moors." His airy finger traced a line down from Arlei on the straight road down to Barwick and Tarah.

"Oh that's better!" Berengar enthused as relief flooded through him. "We've had word that most of the ordinary folk have been evacuated from that area, which was why we were willing to risk a battle with the Abend there even before this news."

"Excellent!" Owein agreed. "So ...when can you *reasonably* get to Dinas ...and in a fit state appear to be ready to fight well?"

Berengar thought about and then looked to Esclados and other senior men who had by now hurried up to them. "I think we should safely be at

Dinas by the twenty-fifth – but that's providing that the bridge at Kiln hasn't been swept away in the floods."

"I will go and scout for you," Owein offered. "Now then, if you can be at Dinas by then there's no problem. In fact it would be better if you could arrive, or at least make yourselves seen, around the twenty-sixth. Brego says that then all three directions – north, east and west – will seem unpalatable to the DeÁine Donns. You will all then drive them south beyond Arlei. Does that sound like a plan?"

"Oh yes!" Berengar agreed thankfully. "We'll make our best time to Kiln in case you find out that we have a problem."

Owein nodded and began to fade. "I must go now before I'm spotted, but I'll report back to Brego and then go and look at this bridge for you."

As he winked out by Berengar, Owein took only seconds to reappear by Brego. The Grand Master of Ergardia was currently using a pleasant inn just north of Spearton as his headquarters as he directed his men. The whole of his first and second waves had arrived on Brychan's soil without mishap and they were currently only waiting for the third shipment. A vast herd of horses were contentedly cropping the bright new spring grass in every possible field in the area, carefully watched over by armed men. The men themselves were being sensibly frugal with their supplies, but for the moment there were no major worries there either. In the corner of the room, the four tame DeÁine agents were sitting deciphering the latest missive from Arlei and had just informed Brego that, as far as they could see, the Donns were still buying the stories of persistent and irritating raids by Islanders and that these reports were from their own. The surprise had not been discovered.

Appearing in his human form, Owein told Brego, "Berengar will be able to match your timing if the bridge north of Kiln holds. Apparently other men under his Master Forester will begin marching from Redrock on the twenty-second, which I presume is still the day you expect the rest of your men to land?"

Brego nodded. "Peredur just checked on them for me, and from the co-ordinates the lead captain sent back, they're right on schedule, although with the spring tides actually docking may take a few hours more. How is Berengar?"

Owein frowned. "He seems very stressed. Are you sure he'll be all right?"

Dana snorted. "Humph! Stressed? I'm not bloody surprised! Give the man a break! This time last year he was just one more ealdorman, running his own area, checking for DeÁine raids, and probably thinking that ealdorman was as high as he was ever going to get. As far as anyone knew, Rainer was young enough that they could've expect him to run the Order for years yet. I doubt that anyone had given so much as a passing thought as to who might succeed him. After all, the last few years since Gavra Pass have seen the DeÁine backing off from the worst of their raids. The Brychan Knights could hardly have anticipated any of this, let alone a full-scale war. Berengar has my every sympathy! It'd be like me suddenly having to take over from Master Brego without any warning, and in the same circumstances!"

"Exactly," Brego agreed. "It isn't even like when Hugh took over during the Battle of Moytirra. He'd already been the tactical advisor to his Master, and all the organising and sorting out had already been done. All he had to do was move the men around to secure the best advantage, and he was already in training to take over as it was. So no, I'm not in the least worried about Berengar. To have come this far is proof enough that he's up to the job. I'm only sorry we weren't able to come and help sooner."

Owein nodded. "In that case I shall go and pass the message to this Forester Warwick and then check on the bridge." He looked faintly harassed. "It would be nice if Vanadis or Aneirin would share some of this running about!" he grumbled, making Brego and Dana feel rather sorry for their most obliging ancient.

"They clearly don't see the tactical necessity like you do," sympathised Brego. "For what it's worth, we're deeply appreciative of what you're doing for us."

Sooty looked up from the pile of walnuts he was devouring and chirruped his agreement. Owein could not be sure, but he had the distinct impression that the black squint was getting fatter. Every time he saw him the beast was happily munching on something. Catching Brego's eye Owein gestured to Sooty, who was back extracting another kernel from a shell, and drew his hands apart to indicate Sooty's expansion. Brego smiled but shrugged and whispered,

"What can we do? He's discovering all these new tastes! It seems cruel to deprive him so soon after all he's been through. Don't worry. Once we come on the DeÁine, my men won't have time to go foraging for him every day. He'll soon burn it all off with all the messages that'll be going backwards and forwards to Hugh."

Owein rolled his eyes and disappeared, surprising Warwick mightily moments later when he appeared in front of him. When that was complete, the ancient took himself south and followed the short but fast flowing river down to the sea north of Kiln and Foel. What he saw there troubled him greatly. He had felt Berengar's skirmish with Tancostyl, but what he saw of the bridge confirmed that this member of the Abend at last was learning just how much Power could be channelled through one of the master pieces. The tatters of the bridge would only hold one person at a time out to either of the first arches. After that there was nothing but a void.

However, the scorching on the stone work showed that Tancostyl had managed to anchor a weaving of Power to either side and create something substantial enough to allow both him and his escort to ride over it. The scarred and battered remnants of the slaves still milled disconsolately on the western banks, only held together by the remaining slave-masters and the fact that there was clearly nowhere else to go. The survivors within the Jundis, however, had gone with Tancostyl, as evidenced by the footprints in the damp earth on the eastern bank. More pressingly, though, Owein could not see how Berengar was going to cross with all his horses and men. There was nothing for it, he would have to go back to Berengar and see if he had any ideas.

In the end it was Esclados not Berengar who had the idea.

"What about the ships down at Pencrick," the older Knight speculated. "If we line them up alongside one another across the river, then put heavy planks over them, we could make a pontoon bridge."

And so Owein was sent on yet another mission. He caused quite a stir when he appeared amongst the hidden folk of Radport and Pencrick. By now he had given up hope of keeping fully hidden from the Abend, but just hoped like mad that they would think he was one on his own and of no consequence, since he had shown no sign of using any energy in an aggressive way. Luckily the men of the southern coast had a good idea of what was needed and he had no need to try to explain in details.

"You leave it to us," Cwen's father said firmly with Captain Iolo nodding his agreement by his right shoulder. "You tell Berengar that when he gets to the Kiln River, not to go to the bridge at all. There's a short spur on the road that goes down to a broad beach where a lot of the fishing boats over-winter. We'll bring the boats up as far as we can on the high tide and then anchor them there. Tell him to get rid of those slaves you've told us about and we'll have his pontoon bridge ready and waiting for him."

Come the morning of the twenty-fourth, the sullen Seljuqs of slaves, or rather the tattered remains of them, woke up to a nasty shock. There in the spring dawn stood a silent force, ghostly in their white surcoats like avenging spirits come to torment and terrify. The cries of alarm were already masking the occasional jangle of a horse's bit from the long line of Order troops, and the very stillness of these alarming apparitions did more to panic the slaves than any other action Berengar's men could have taken. The slave-masters hurried to their beasts and began trying to chivvy the terrified slaves into some kind of order, while the two Donns who had remained with the Seljuqs mounted up on their horses and sat there waiting – useless and ineffectual, which was why Tancostyl had left these two behind in the first place.

This was all that Berengar had been waiting for. Lifting a horn whistle to his lips he blew on it sharply. From along the line a fearsome groaning and hissing rose up for a moment or two and then a sound like no other the DeÁine had ever heard began. It was a nerve-wrenching ululating, eerie and discordant to their ears.

"Aach, they have no ear for the pipes," a highland Forester sergeant observed sagely to his friend. "Fancy not knowing that's Sorley's Lament that they're playing!"

Many slaves clamped their hands over their ears and whimpered, but the horror was not over, it was just beginning. Out of the damp rolling grass rose arcs of arrows, which flew with whistling flights into the air and then plunged down again to pick off the slave-masters and their beasts, leaving the huge creatures writhing in the grass like vast, ungainly pincushions. The archers skirmished forwards again and chose new targets, picking out those men who seemed to have some idea of what should be done. With those men on the ground it was too much for many of the slaves. Despite there being the best part of a thousand in the camp, several hundred simply broke ranks and ran. They had no idea where they were running to, they were just running.

A small core of around five hundred had pulled themselves together, and were belatedly arming themselves, and it was these whom Berengar now focussed on. With perfect timing the front rank of the Knights heeled their horses into movement and began to build up speed, closely followed by the ranks behind. Those in the lead charged down upon the five hundred who had formed into an ungainly clump. Once more those on the leading horses did not bother to close fully on the enemy, but instead launched a hail of spears into their midst. As these riders peeled off to the left and right, those behind swooped down on the slaves who were still standing, and cut them down where they stood. Like scythes through a cornfield, the riders reaped death. Without a single injury to the Order's force every one of the resisting slaves was slaughtered. It was not an order Berengar had been happy about giving, but he dared not have any who might offer resistance behind him.

However, those who had thrown themselves on the ground in surrender were herded up by the rear ranks of Knights, and driven past the bloody corpses in the wake of the fearsome leading riders. Within the hour the coast came into view and Berengar could hardly contain his delight and relief. There, swaying gently at the tide's edge, ran a long line of fishing boats lashed side by side. Over the top ran a broad walkway of overlapping boards and many men were hammering the last nails in to hold them secure. As Berengar rode down to where the first of the wooden causeway touched land, a familiar figure rose to his feet and stepped up to his horse.

"Berengar!" Roger said with genuine warmth. "It's good to see you again!"

Dismounting, Berengar greeted Roger equally as warmly. He had liked Cwen's father immensely when they had first met and it gave him heart that these people, among them many others of whom he had met while staying at *The Brace of Brachets*, had survived unscathed.

"Can we cross?" Berengar asked when the greetings had been exchanged, and enquiries about everyone made.

"How're we doing, Alf?" Roger called out, and a stout man out in the centre got to his feet, whistled to get the attention of someone on the far side.

"All done!" Alf called back a moment later, and waved his arm in a beckoning movement.

"There you go then *Master* Berengar!" Roger said proudly. "Two at a time should be fine if you take it steady and spaced out. I'd keep a good horse's length between each pair, but it'll certainly take that."

With a grin he could not suppress, Berengar took his horse's reins and alongside Esclados led the dismounted men with their horses out onto the bridge. Some senior captains stayed at the bridge head to keep the spacing correct, but soon there was a stead line making their way to the east bank of the estuary.

"We're going to do it!" Berengar said softly to Esclados, his eyes shining with new found energy and optimism. "I almost didn't dare hope too much until now, but by the Trees, we're going to do it! We'll be in place to support Brego's troops and Warwick's, and then we're going to take back Brychan!"

# Chapter 2

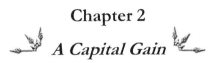

## *A Capital Gain*

### Brychan: late Beltane

Brego sat on his war-horse, desperately trying to force himself to an inner calm as his massed troops assembled behind him. It was not that they were doing it badly – far from it! The Ergardian Order were doing him proud with the way they were performing, every man the true professional soldier in everything he did. Nor was he worried about engaging the DeÁine. Or at least not the ordinary troops under the Donns. Brego had every confidence that his men would acquit themselves well when that fight came, and some of his lack of calm was the old thrill of impending battle – he was still enough of a soldier for that! The presence of the Abend was what sent shivers down his spine at unexpected moments. For all the years that he had fought the DeÁine en masse, he could count the number of times he had come up against the Abend or their acolytes on one hand – and none of them had been experiences he wanted to repeat! Since the dreadful fight eight years ago at Gavra Pass, he knew that the number of acolytes was severely reduced. Yet that might count for nothing if the Abend decided to use the two Treasures they now had back in their possession.

"We're ready, sire," his aide, Commander Dana, said softly and breaking his train of thoughts.

"Thank you," Brego breathed back equally quietly, then raised his mailed fist in the air.

A sudden hush fell over the ranks in the early morning haze, rippling back through them from the front as everyone waited for Brego to give the signal to advance. Taking a deep breath to steady his own racing pulse, Brego spread the fingers on his upraised hand and then clenched them back into a fist as he thrust his arm forwards. With a jingling of reins and spurs the horses stepped forward but every man was silent – this was too momentous an occasion for words.

It was dawn on the twenty-seventh of Beltane. They were less than half a day's march from Arlei, and the ancients had informed Brego that both Berengar coming in from the west, and Warwick and Corin leading the men down out of Redrock, would be able to converge in unison with his troops today. Three and a half thousand from Celidon marched in Brego's wake –

that all by itself gave him a thrill, a sense of joy that he should be able to restore their pride and reward their faith after so long. Those loyal Forester men-at-arms, recruits and auxiliaries who had waited and waited for this day to return to active service, were riding with shining eyes and heads held high today.

With them rode the sixteen thousand Knights and soldiers of the regular sept on Ergardia – the nine thousand Foresters of Ergardia being due to embark from that Island's southern port, minus horses, the very next day to sail direct to Kittermere to act as Brego's watchdogs against the new DeÁine threat. Yet even without them, if you counted the Foresters of Brychan who had stayed to act as guides for Brego and his men, nearly twenty thousand armed and battle-ready men were currently sweeping westwards. That was impressive given the speed with which they had had to respond, Brego thought, his heart giving another excited skip.

It was all down to timing he reflected, and thank the Trees that they had the ancients to communicate back and forth with. The difference that alone made was worth putting up with the ancients' more eccentric ways for. Ealdormen Warwick and Corin would dangle the first bait, appearing out of the morning mist with their ten and a half thousand men – that force having been swollen by the men whom Berengar had not had time to lead out of Laon as he had originally intended. Brego wanted to entice the Donns in their arrogance out from behind the stout walls of Arlei. Yes, the Brychan Knights had eliminated the force the Donns had sent north, and that, combined with the slaves they must have lost in the fighting coming into Brychan, should have left a noticeable hole in the DeÁine army's original twenty thousand.

Except, of course, that the ancients now said that the minor houses had come along in their wake, dragging their less experienced but still dangerous troops with them. Not enough veterans to cause desperate concern, but a cursed nuisance for restoring the main DeÁine army back up to near twenty thousand again. It would all depend on the Donns in charge as to how much of a real threat they became. Well used and spread amongst the major families, the minor ones could absorb a lot of punishment and leave the real veterans to do some serious damage. So for this ruse he hoped Warwick's approximate ten thousand, against their twenty, would seem like second, nice easy victory of the kind the Donns had been longing for for nearly thirty years.

Only when the Donns and their force had cleared the gates would Berengar bring his four thousand cavalry into view out of the west. But even then the Donns would hopefully be capable of the simple calculations to work out that they still outnumbered the Islanders by good odds – or so they would think! What Brego prayed they would then think was that the arrogant Knights on horseback to the west were there to stop the DeÁine getting back home; maybe even that the Islanders were attacking with irrational arrogance or even panic, not careful deliberation. For Berengar, whose men had hidden overnight in the ruins of Dinas, would sit in full sight and wait, making no provocative moves. Only when the DeÁine army were well out on the plain would Warwick wheel his men towards Berengar.

Even then, Trees willing, the trap might not be apparent. After all, Warwick's men would have to manoeuvre around to get down from the last of the highlands and onto the plain to be able to fight, so from the DeÁine's angle it might not seem so likely the two could join up. Indeed the Donns might never even look to the east behind them. The most natural thing for the Donns to do would be to swing their army westwards in turn to face this tempting target, thinking that they were crushing just one Island's massed Order; and leave the security of Arlei in the mistaken belief that there was no-one else to take that stronghold. Twenty thousand, albeit made up of a huge number of inexpert fighters, should still seem more than enough to take out the Islanders decisively. Then and only then, when there was no time to retreat to Arlei, would Brego's force advance with speed, more than doubling the Brychan force and trapping the Donns between them.

The ancients had come up trumps for them in another way too. Although this was barely the start of summer, and here the temperatures were still more like early spring due to the chill airs still wafting down from the vast quantities of late snow in the mountains, a misty heat-haze was lurking over the River Lei. It was nicely done. Not enough to make the Abend twitchy, but just enough to cloud the horizon from view. And Warwick was taking advantage of it from the distant sounds Brego could hear. All of a sudden on the morning air there came the sound of the Foresters' pipers, and Brego needed little imagination to picture the consternation that ghostly ululating would have set up in the opposition as it appeared from out of the mist. Those amongst the DeÁine who had heard that sound before would recall the bitter blows Foresters had inflicted on them in the past, and hopefully their qualms would spread. From the quiet chuckles coming from behind him, several of his men were thinking along the same lines.

With only the sound of the horses' hooves and the jangling of bits, Brego's men continued to move silently towards Arlei. Then to his horror he heard sounds of fighting breaking out. What in the Islands had happened? Surely Warwick had not started something on his own? Or had they missed some scouting party of the DeÁine's? He kneed his horse to a trot and those behind him followed suit. The River Lei, in spate and on their left, provided a drumming of its own that kept them company as they hurried onwards, but hopefully also disguised the sound of the massed horses' hooves. All of Brego's instincts were telling him to sound the charge and to engage with the enemy, yet he did not dare until he had made more sense of what was going on. The ancients must have been having similar thoughts, because suddenly the mist began to rapidly lift and clear in a light breeze.

Sure enough, on the higher ground of the north bank, Warwick's party was engaged with what looked like several Seljuqs of slaves and some Jundises of veterans. Yet there were by no means enough to account for all of the troops who should have been in Arlei. Was this some rash tactic of an inexperienced Donn from one of the minor families? And if so, where were the Donns of the major families and their men?

Dana tapped his arm and pointed towards the city. "Look! The gates are open! We can take the capital!"

Brego grimaced. It was almost too good to be true. What if the Abend were in there waiting for them? He would be sending good men to be slaughtered. Then the light seemed to bend in front of him and one of the ancients appeared.

"Send your men in!" he instructed. "The Abend have already left! They're at Farsan now, and with the pick of the experienced troops. These are just the minor families and some overconfident junior Donns from the others. The Abend seem to have left them here to make sure that your people didn't take the city back."

"What in the name of the infernal Wild Hunt did they go south for?" Brego fumed. "We thought we'd be driving them! Not chasing to catch up!"

"I'll tell you when you can get your other leaders together," Owein said reassuringly. "For now, take advantage of this chance and get to meet Berengar before he goes white-haired with worry!"

The reminder of the strain the new Master of Brychan would be under halted Brego's frustrated rejoinder, and he swiftly ordered his men to set about taking Arlei.

His men spread out in battle formation and without a sound they followed the signal to bring the horses to the trot. In the distance, Brego could now see, Warwick had his men engaged with what looked like two Jundises and two Seljuqs, although these four thousand troops were being very badly lead. In patches the DeÁine had some kind of battle line set up, and there seemed to be an order of sorts. The problem was that in between them there were areas of pure chaos. A chaos which Brego guessed stemmed from the presence of inexperienced youngsters of the noble DeÁine families. Young Donns who had no doubt been sent westwards in the wake of the others to join in what had surely seemed like a foregone victory after the ease with which they had rolled into Brychan. It must have seemed like such a prime opportunity to give a new generation their first taste of blood.

To his right, a bemused Dana muttered, "Is this it?"

Brego knew what he meant. Surely the Abend had not left their newest conquest to be defended by just four thousand second-rate troops? Then he heard a distant trumpet call which must be coming from Berengar's men. It was an alert and it signalled that Berengar wanted help.

"Shit! How many is Berengar facing?" Again Dana voiced Brego's thoughts as well as his own. Had the missing DeÁine troops not engaged with Warwick because they were already on the move and had run into Berengar?

Brego raised his arm once more and signalled to speed up the advance, and the Ergardian sept picked up speed as one sweeping line of men and horses several wide. The earth began to drum with the thundering of hooves and they swept around the city walls of Arlei, past the north gates which stood open and deserted except for a few terrified looking sentries. Even as Brego was about to detail some men to take the gate he saw that there was no need. The citizens of Arlei had needed no further encouragement than the sight of the Order in its might sweeping to their aid. Armed with clubs, hammers, and any other kind of makeshift weapon they could lay their hands on, the people were beating the living daylights out of the few hapless DeÁine left inside the city.

Hammering on, the horses were now fully extended to a gallop and eating up the ground as they tore past the city. They swung into columns as they funnelled over the two wide bridges which were more like great causeways over the Lei than arched spans, then spread out again over the western water meadows. There they saw the remaining DeÁine troops. Some six thousand were engaged with Berengar's cavalry.

"Bloody cowards!" someone yelled off to Brego's left, and it certainly looked that way. Were they just going for the easy victory first? Six thousand to four, giving them good odds? Or had they not seen Warwick's men, let alone Brego's force? Or had they seen the full extent of what was facing them and decided that they would make a break and try to get back to the homeland?

"You won't get far that way!" Brego snarled through gritted teeth, as he momentarily steered his horse with his knees as he twisted his sword's lanyard around his wrist – there was nothing worse than losing a sword mid-battle, and the Grand Master's sword was no ordinary piece of weaponry. It had been handed down through generations and was a masterpiece of pattern-welding which had never yet been broken by a DeÁine weapon. *Like us*, the thought flittered through Brego's mind. *Stamp on us, entrap us, but you won't break us!*

Too late the DeÁine realised that something was happening behind them, even as Brego took in that these troops were far better organised than those facing Warwick. With some semblance of order the troops of these Jundises ceased their attacks and grouped into large squares, weapons facing outwards. Against cavalry it was a classic defence, but Brego had no intention of sacrificing his precious horses in what was rapidly becoming a minor if important engagement. He signalled the two men who rode close beside him, and who carried long pennants on tall poles with which they now conveyed his order by a series of sweeping motions. From here he had to trust to his individual commanders to implement tactics as befitted each situation. One man alone could never hope to command such a huge force as a single entity on the move, especially without being able to get some distance from the field to see who was going where.

Taking a sweeping cut at the back of a slave, Brego hacked his way on deeper into the Seljuqs, not out of some kind of misplaced heroism, but because he had spotted where Berengar must be in the line beyond, and he knew there were only a few ranks of men between them. With his personal guard still tight around him Brego exploded out of the other side of the Seljuqs, and reined in his horse before he collided with the Brychan men. With the pressure suddenly off as the surprised DeÁine frantically tried to fight on all sides, the Brychan men were leaning on swords and panting but grinning mightily.

A tall man with cropped dark-haired, and a long scar down the side of his face, shoved his helmet back to mop his brow and then heeled his horse towards Brego. Several others were sticking to him like glue, including a big veteran Knight who was practically on his heels and a banner bearer with the Brychan Master's flag, making it clear that this was the new Master of the Brychan sept. He rode straight to Brego and then extended a mailed hand.

"Master Brego! Blessed Rowan, it's good to see you!" he said with feeling. "I can't begin to tell you how grateful I am that you've come."

"*Master* Berengar, I presume?" Brego responded with a grin, taking the hand and shaking it warmly. "Congratulations on your elevation! ...Right! Let's get this lots of thugs wiped out and then we can speak properly!"

He turned back to the fight and saw that his ealdormen were doing a grand job of taking out the DeÁine. The slaves had all but given up the fight already and some of the Order men were herding them away. Most of the others of the Order were dismounted and forming up to take the Jundises' squares. At a signal the nearest Order archers, under Commander Dana's orders, let fly a volley of arrows into the packed ranks of DeÁine veterans. With a speed which eternally stunned their enemies, the archers reloaded and loosed another volley, then another, and another. At that range, and with their enemies packed so close, there was no way anyone could fail to hit some kind of target, as agonised screams testified. Men began falling like rag-dolls in untidy heaps stained scarlet with blood, leaving gaps in the defences and the hedge of weapons slowly disintegrated. The DeÁine had never been good archers except with smaller mechanical bows, although they excelled in larger war machines. Luckily these were not anywhere to be seen, so the Order's men were in little danger of being on the end of a returned volley.

Already the other ealdormen had their archers doing the same, and once their opponents had begun to waver, the troops moved in. These were the experienced DeÁine troops they were facing, and men who had no intention of surrendering, but surrounded and with their movements also hampered by their own fallen, they were never going to inflict any serious damage on the Islanders. The fighting was bloody but short, and here there was no chance of taking prisoners. The men of the Jundises fought to the bitter end – an end which came far faster than they anticipated, for the

Islanders had no mind to give quarter, quite apart from their enemies having no intention of giving up. There was a fury amongst the Islanders which saw men hacking viciously at those who had already received a killing blow, the sight of which only heightened the DeÁine's panic. Small groups of remaining slaves tried to make a break from where they were held and were cut down with equal ferocity, until the remainder huddled together in abject terror.

As a kind of stillness finally descended on the river bank, Berengar earned even more respect from Brego. Without hesitation he called one of his commanders to him.

"Get those slaves round up and imprison them in Dinas," he ordered. "Pass the word to our friends! I don't want these anywhere near Arlei! And I want them behind some stout walls! Give them food. The wells are usable. Then seal them in and post just enough guards to be able to patrol the circuits."

"Good thinking," Brego congratulated Berengar, but got a wry smile in return.

"I knew we'd not have the men to spend guarding them as they are. So we ripped the place to bits last night! Anything burnable, or which could be used to make ladders to get out with, is already stacked outside the walls. It's spring time! They can make do sheltering in the lee of the burnt stone walls. I expected we might have at least a few prisoners, and with the new threat on its way I felt it imperative that I had some kind of plan in place."

"Speaking of the threat, let's go and meet your Forester Warwick and find out what it is that the ancients want to tell us." Brego rolled his eyes in despair. "Great Maker, I know they're a boon at times, but I'm beginning to wonder what kind of experience of war they can possibly have had. They certainly don't seem to have much idea about the realities as we know them."

Just after noon he entered the old palace at Arlei with Warwick and Berengar at his side, and the three of them went to the great hall followed closely by Dana, Esclados and General Tully, along with a substantial bodyguard of Foresters. After all the Abend had been here. Who knew what nasty surprises they might have left behind? However, it transpired that there was nothing arcane left, although evidence of some of the Abend's nastier pastimes still lingered and had to be dealt with. Once the room was declared safe, Sooty was brought up from his litter in which he had travelled at the back of the column.

"Sooty, would you tell the ancients that we'd really like some kind of explanation, please?" Brego requested politely, but his human companions could see that he was starting to lose patience with the game of cat and mouse they seemed to be playing. Sooty must have sensed it too and conveyed it in his message because the ancients came quickly.

"Sorry about that!" Cynddylan immediately apologised.

"They rather caught us on the hop, too," Peredur added. "We'd been trying to stay clear of here in case we tipped the Abend to the fact that something was about to happen by them sensing our presence. Especially with Owein needing to be active to relay messages for you. We've had to keep a very low profile. So it was only when we started to feel their absence here that we became aware that they were on the move."

"Why?" All Brego's frustration was injected into the one word.

"Well when we felt them take the Scabbard," Cynddylan said, "we were initially tracking that. At first when they were on the sea, we were sure those two must be heading back to New Lochlainn by sea since they wouldn't be able to go by land due to the flooding. The Abend have all been communicating with one another on the Power a lot – another reason we've had to play things softly. When they're riding the weaves of Power they can sense us much faster because we're in the Power too, albeit in a different layer. So once they'd split up they were communicating far more than normal and that curtailed us badly.

"We didn't bother telling you the little details because you had enough to cope with as it was. Now, though, I can tell you that something very odd has been happening in the Abend. Geitla has met with some kind of accident which involves the Power. She isn't dead, but she isn't truly alive either. Nothing confirms that more than the fact that new a member has been elevated to the nine."

"What?" Brego and the others all exclaimed in unison.

"You call that *nothing*!" Warwick spat in fury. "Bastard Hounds of the Hunt! It's a fucking *big* difference! Geitla gone would mean we were only facing Tancostyl, Magda and Helga here. We knew Calatin was gone and thought that we'd be facing one less because of that anyway, and according to you Masanae and Quintillean were still west of the mountains. With Eliavres and Anarawd across the water we *thought* we were in with a chance. So how many cursed Abend *are* we dealing with *here*?"

The ancients had the grace to look faintly abashed, and Owein cleared his ghostly throat self-consciously before answering. "Well put like that I suppose we should have told you."

"I told you we should have defied Vanadis and told them!" muttered Peredur darkly.

Owein sighed. "Rather too late to be arguing about it now, though, isn't it? Very well, around seven days ago Masanae and Quintillean landed on Rathlin. I think Masanae found out that Quintillean had summoned the other DeÁine without informing her, because there were some high powered spats going on at Pahi before they boarded the ships – and they nearly took separate ships which is a sure sign that they've had a falling out! As near as we can tell, the other Abend have aligned against them, which is a new and unexpected dynamic. Even more intriguingly, the two Abend with the Scabbard, Eliavres and Anarawd, landed at the old castle at Temair then took off again barely days later, we think purposely to avoid the two leaders. As of this morning all nine of them are at Farsan."

"*Nine?* Fuck!" Warwick exploded. He, after all, would be the one dealing with them and their summoning. "Nine including Geitla or as well as her?"

"The newcomers..." Peredur began but got interrupted by Berengar's,

"Newcom*ers?* In the plural?" he spat angrily, the detail having sunk in. "So there's another? They really are up to nine Abend again? And that's not just Geitla being replaced is it?"

"No it isn't," Peredur sighed, giving his fellow ancients dirty looks which said as clearly as if he spoken 'I told you so!' "Their first recruit was actually to replace Calatin, we think, because it was a war-mage who appeared out of the elevation ceremony – which is something our own Power-based equipment here on Taineire picks up because they use a very ancient device to force open the minds of those elevated to the nine. At that ceremony there was almost nobody there, and we think Magda supervised it."

"Isn't she a little mentally unstable for that?" Brego could not help himself asking, curiosity getting the better of his irritability.

"Well we'd have said so too," admitted Cynddylan, "but by then Geitla had been incapacitated for several days, and it seems to have made a difference to Magda. We felt something go from within the Power, and after much very careful searching, we think it was the essence of one called Othinn. That was a tangled affair, but as near as we can unravel it, Othinn went into the Power in a way no-one else has done. Unfortunately it doesn't seem to have brought him what he wanted, and so he's targeted Geitla and seems to be using her body in some way. If we could see her in the flesh we might be able to tell you more, but scouting around the fringes of the Power does have its limitations. What we can tell you is that the personality of Geitla seems to be totally severed from using the Power, although she's trapped within it, while Magda's weavings are more stable than they've been ever since Othinn went into the Power – he was her acolyte and lover, by the way."

"So do you think he was trying to attach himself to her in some way, and that's what made her unstable?" Warwick asked, for as a Forester anything to do with the Power impacted on his men and what they might be called upon to do. "Was he attacking her through the Power, is what I suppose I'm asking?"

Cynddylan's ghostly head nodded. "It's what we've been thinking, although we can't say for certain. So as far as your situation goes, you no longer have to face Geitla's enormous drawings of Power. Unfortunately, though, after Magda elevated this new war-mage, Helga returned to Arlei and with Magda and this new Abend, elevated another to replace Geitla. Another new female Abend who is a totally unknown quantity, I'm afraid. Since then these two newcomers have been in close communication with Anarawd and Eliavres in company with Magda and Helga, and also Tancostyl once he got back after your skirmish with him."

Brego turned to Warwick. "In the absence of Sionnachan I'm afraid I have to lean on you as the one and only Forester leader I have with me. What are our chances up against the whole Abend with two of the ancient Treasures?"

The ancients made as if to answer but Brego silenced them with a terse wave of the hand. "I want an appraisal from someone who fights with us and knows *our* strengths!" he said firmly. "We have time here and now to make some serious decisions. Decisions we might not have the time to deeply consider once we head south and face them."

Warwick turned and walked down the hall a little, arms folded and head bowed in thought. Everyone left him in silence and waited patiently until he came back to them.

"I've got to be honest and say that I don't like the fact that they have this Helm thing back," he admitted. "I'm worried more about that than the Scabbard. If anything I've heard of the Helm is true then it will magnify the user's ability several fold. Given that it's in the hands of one of the two most powerful of the war-mages means that it's a formidable weapon indeed. If we were doing nothing more than driving the DeÁine out of our homelands, then we could take the risk and attack him, as long as we made the men aware of the dangers. We'd be likely to take severe casualties with the rest of the nine backing him up, but it could be done. However, if the numbers of incoming DeÁine are anything like correct, then we'll need every man we have to fight again in a few weeks' time again. We daren't risk taking massive casualties to overthrow the Abend and their men, only to find we've no choice but to fall back in the face of the threat of vast numbers from across the sea. One DeÁine overlord being exchanged for another – and that's no kind of victory.

"If you want my opinion, I'd say that the best option we have is to follow them with all speed, but just harry their rear. My men can protect you from a fair amount of low level stuff if we keep our distance. The kind of things the acolytes might throw at us. Take out their stragglers. Attack the outlying camps at night and destroy their troops' morale. That sort of thing. I honestly don't think I could recommend a set battle in the circumstances. Not against Tancostyl with the Helm, not yet. It might come to that in the end, but not until we've seen how desperate things are when these new ships arrive. And by then we'll have more Foresters and more men. Let's see if the Abend are as eager to fight when they've only got ten thousand against our number. See if they'll risk us taking back their two Treasures by sheer force and make a stand at Farsan. Or if they head south towards these newcomers and the force they have with them. That might tell us as much about the Abend's situation as anything else, and give us a clue as to how to fight them best."

Brego looked to Berengar. "Are you happy with that analysis? After all, you know the terrain and the people hereabouts."

"The people aren't a problem," Berengar was able to say with some pride. "Some of our men and two amazing civilians – whom I shall have to tell you about at some point – managed to evacuate huge numbers of the local population. What we mustn't do is drive the DeÁine towards the west of Rathlin because that's where our people have taken refuge."

"That's not a problem yet," Brego informed him, "not least because it will be another two weeks at least before the ships I've commandeered will be able to come to transport us across to Rathlin." His chin came up and he addressed the ancients as very much the senior war leader of the Islanders giving them his decision, not asking their permission.

"We shall swing eastwards and fan out, then begin harassing the Donns in earnest. At any given time we will never show all of our force at one go. We have in excess of thirty-three thousand men here with our combined force. It would be foolish to expect the Abend to *not* know that there are barely thirty thousand in the entire Brychan sept, and that not all would be able to get here from the far north to fight. We must therefore not show them more men than they can logically account for, thereby tipping our hand that men from the other Islands are uniting behind Brychan. That must be saved for the larger battle as a vital element of surprise.

"If we've driven them out of Brychan before the ships can come to take us off, it will actually be a good thing. We can patrol up and down the coast shaking our spears at them, so to speak, and make them think that we're satisfied having chased them off our territory. It'll look all the more convincing since we won't appear to have the means to follow them. Having said that, do you actually *know* what will happen with the DeÁine on the south coast? From what you've said I would take it as a foregone conclusion that there will be a ship waiting at somewhere like Farsan for the Abend to go across to Rathlin and meet the new fleet. I'm also assuming they'll have ships for a substantial bodyguard for the Treasures, for a display of force to show the newcomers if nothing else. But what of the rest of the Donns and their armies?"

The three ancients looked to one another.

"They've certainly summoned ships from the eastern three ports south of the Brychan Mere," Peredur volunteered.

"How many?" Brego demanded. "Sacred Trees, man! It's no bloody use telling me 'ships'! I need to know how many and how big they are! ...Well? ...How many? And are there already additional troops on board, or are they expecting to pick up the Donns from here? If we wipe these men out are there others, or will we be chasing the Abend on their own down to the south coast and this new army?"

The three looked like school children caught out by an exasperated teacher for not having done their work.

"I think you'd better go and find out, don't you?" Commander Dana said politely but pointedly, his gaze travelling to Brego and back.

After the chastened ancients had disappeared, the leading men went and found chairs and collapsed into them.

"I still can't make up my mind whether they're as much help to us as they think they are," General Tully said, thankfully taking a goblet of wine off an aide, who had been given a small barrel to bring up to the hall after some enterprising looting had taken place.

"They don't seem to have much idea about warfare as we have to fight it," Esclados agreed, holding out his goblet for a refill.

"That's often been the case," Dana told the Brychan men. "When it came to sorting out the Island Treasures, more often than not it was our men who came up with the really useful ideas. The squints are a real boon, though!" and he leaned across to stroke Sooty's fur as the black squint buried his nose in a wide bowl of spring water and guzzled noisily.

For the first time the Brychan men had a chance to observe the squint. The first meeting had been a shock to them – finding yourself in the presence of beasts from legends was hardly an everyday event, even for men of the Order. Now Berengar levered himself to his feet and came forward to crouch in front of Sooty. Suddenly the squint stopped drinking and his big eyes opened wide as he saw Berengar lean closer. His whiskers began quivering, flicking drops of water off, and he made a soft mewing noise almost as if in distress.

"That's weird! He's never done that before," Dana said, taking the water bowl off Sooty before he dropped it.

However, Esclados was wearing an almost pained expression.

"Looks like your family secret is going to come out after all," he said sadly to Berengar, who got to his feet and stepped back from Sooty.

"It's alright, little chap. I won't hurt you," he said gently, then turned to Brego. "He's picked up on the fact that I've got DeÁine blood in me," he said simply.

"*You* have?" Warwick gasped in shock.

"Yes, me," Berengar answered with a tired smile. "Sorry Warwick, I suppose I should have told you before, but there was never any need before now. It's why I could never be in the Foresters! You can, with your slave ancestors, but I can't because my father, or possibly my grandfather or both of them, were the full thing. A real DeÁine."

"You don't sound sure," Brego said calmly. "Would I be right in guessing that you don't even know their identity?"

"No I don't," admitted Berengar. "My mother was raped when a girl and I'm the result. She got out and spent her later years far from the border, but her mother in turn had been another pretty girl in the wrong place when opposing armies went through. It's a common enough story, and there were men on both sides who acted without honour towards the local people in the Brychan Gap."

Brego called Sooty to him and took hold of both the squint's forepaws. "Do you remember Eric and Dylan telling us about Talorcan? About how he's part DeÁine but fighting with us?" Sooty gave a whistle, then chirruped and waggled his ears, suddenly looking brighter again. "Yes, Berengar is the same."

Sooty's eyes seemed to glaze and he stared off into the distance, giving faint chirps and whistles.

"What's he doing," Esclados asked, fascinated.

"Talking to the other squints," Dana told him. "I expect he's telling them all about Berengar. When Eric – that's Ivain's squint – touched Talorcan, he seemed almost able to see into his soul. I'd be prepared for him to try and touch you," Dana warned Berengar. "According to what Peredur and Cynddylan said, Talorcan found it uncomfortable but not painful."

Moments later Sooty focused on them again and then went to stand in front of Berengar, but whistled at him as though he was asking him something.

"I'm sorry, Sooty, but I don't understand," Berengar apologised.

The squint repeated his chirrups much slower but everyone was still in the dark until Peredur arrived in their midst. Sooty repeated his questions again, and a rather surprised Peredur asked,

"Are you the Berengar who's Swein and Cwen's friend?"

"Yes! Yes I am!" Berengar exclaimed, confused but delighted. "How ever did he know?"

"Well he was once partnered with a squint we've called Daisy, and together they should've helped us use the Bowl and Knife," Brego explained, "but when we were rescuing them from the void it got a bit complicated. The ancient who should've been working with Sooty has died altogether. Together Sooty and Daisy should have linked the portable Knife – which I have – to the fixed power of the Bowl, but then Fin appeared, who's the squint for the Spear. He was in a dreadful state, quite unable to travel – and don't get me or the others started on what we think of *that* situation! So we asked Daisy if she would exchange with Fin, so that he could stay in Ergardia with Hugh. When Cwen got the Spear we…"

"You what?" demanded Esclados, as Berengar let out a yelp of surprise. "Our Cwen is one of the Island Treasure holders?"

"No, no, no!" Berengar protested. "She can't be! That would mean her going into a battle situation! No, it can't be Cwen! She needs to be kept safe!"

"I'm afraid it is her," Brego told him sadly, "and there's nothing you or I can do about it."

"What about Swein? Is he with her? Is he safe?" Esclados asked. "I would hate it if he was to suffer after all he's been through."

"Err... Swein is the holder of the Arrow," Dana broke the news to them. "His squint is Dylan who was the first one to try and make contact with Talorcan."

"I don't know whether to be proud or horrified," Esclados groaned. "For the lad to have come so far that this can happen, is proof of how different he could have been with a decent family around him."

"Who was he, then?" Tully asked.

"One of King Edward's catamites," Esclados replied, "and you should see the scars on his back as a result! When we finally managed to get bits out of him about his home life, it wasn't so surprising he should run away to try to find a better life in the city. It was horrendous bad luck that he should've caught Edward's eye, because after that he was stuck under Edward's crushing power for years. When we first met him he was barely able to think for himself, he'd been so downtrodden, and now look at what he is!"

"And what about Cwen, then?" Brego asked.

"Ah!" said Warwick pointedly, making Berengar turn to look at him and then Esclados.

"You didn't...?" Berengar accused his old friend.

"Well I thought someone had better know in case something nasty happened and I wasn't there," Esclados said ruefully.

"Know what?" Brego asked suspiciously but beginning to guess.

"Well our new Grand Master is very fond of Cwen," was Esclados' tactful comment.

"Oh, I see!" Brego smiled and then said something very softly to Sooty. The squint waggled his ears, which seemed to be his equivalent of nodding, and chirruped in a way which made them think this is what he had been trying to say all along. He then walked over to Berengar and held out a tentative paw. Very gently Berengar extended his fingers until they just touched the tips of Sooty's claws. The squint gave a low whistle, then shuffled forward until he could reach out and touch Berengar's chest with his paw-pad. His eyes lit up and he gave a whistle and a squeak, but of joy rather than any sort of distress, then he began twittering into the distance again. Some kind of conversation was going on and he was becoming happier by the second. Suddenly he chirped wildly in a different way, then began running excitedly in circles. A rather harassed Peredur appeared again.

"You are keeping me busy," he said wearily, but without rancour. "Sooty says to tell you that if Talorcan might be able to use one of the DeÁine pieces, then Berengar too might be able to."

"You're kidding me!" Berengar gulped. "No, surely not?"

Warwick was staring at him intently, then glanced to Peredur. "Can you confirm that? Is it possible that this could happen? An Islander with DeÁine blood use one of the DeÁine Treasures without it killing or severely maiming him?"

"And can you shield him from the Abend's glare if he does try?" Brego added.

Owein and Cynddylan had appeared to join them and, after they had relayed what they had found out about ships and men, a hurried conference took place between the three ancients.

"I think the squints and the Guardians would have been highly unlikely to tell Talorcan that he could use one if it was going to cause him serious harm," Owein then said carefully. "Although I have to say that 'use' might be a little optimistic given that the Abend are the only users we know of. Redirect might be a better word."

"Then we may put that to the test," Brego decided, but addressing the Islanders more than the ancients. "The Gauntlet sails with Sionnachan and Maelbrigt and a brave young DeÁine called Sithfrey. What you from Brychan may not have had chance to catch up on is that Maelbrigt is the chosen user for the Island Sword. Travelling with them is a Rheged lady called Matti Montrose who's been chosen to carry the Shield. Because of that we thought it wiser not to have the DeÁine Gorget travelling with them as well. Sithfrey has in some way already bent the Gauntlet to his will. So he and it are causing no complications sailing in such close proximity to the Sword and Shield. But we've had no way of doing anything like it to the Gorget. And they have a long sea crossing ahead – not a place to have to deal with sparks between Island Treasures and an unturned Gorget! For that reason it has travelled with us.

"Also, after MacBeth brought it out of Brychan, we stored it in a hidden location in western Ergardia. And once we'd started the muster it became increasingly clear that Sionnachan and Sithfrey wouldn't have time to travel across the Island to retrieve it to take it with them. We were very wary of bringing the Gorget back over here, I can tell you! A bit too close to the Abend for comfort! But once we knew of the new fleet arriving, and Sithfrey had changed the Gauntlet's orientation, and on top of that the squints were saying that men like Talorcan might be able to bend another away from the DeÁine, we felt it ought to come with us despite the risks. It might yet help change the course of a fight against the Abend, even if it only smothers some of their sendings. Thanks to our three ancients here, we now have the right kind of casket to transport it in, and the Celidon Foresters were eager to act as its guardians. However, we can have it brought up here."

"You mean to test him *now*?" Esclados protested. "Sacred Trees, Master Brego! Could you not give him a bit of a breathing space?"

But Berengar was smiling quietly and nodding even as Brego made to explain himself to the surprised men and ancients.

"Look, the Abend are down on the south coast thinking that all here is going swimmingly well, apart from an excess of water cutting them off. Well how much do you think they'd be thrown by suddenly feeling someone else using their precious weapon? Even if one of our spectral friends here asked Sithfrey to tweak the Gauntlet it wouldn't have the same effect because they're still too far away, and the Abend will surely feel that. Now, we've all agreed that we don't want to fight a pitched battle here and now, so if Berengar can use the Gorget in some way, then it could force the Abend to make a move. I hope it will be to try and save face with these newcomers, and therefore they'll try to get the two pieces they have out of our grasp as fast as possible."

"And what if they come here full of fire and brimstone?" General Tully said, speaking words others had clearly also been about to say.

"Then at least we fight the nine Abend alone," Brego said firmly. "If they've got to come back that fast then they won't be bringing all the acolytes with them, and they surely can't march their remaining force that fast either. However, for a start I was simply thinking of finding out if Berengar can do anything at all with the piece, which is why I asked you three if you could shield him for a brief moment. Give him a moment to try this thing without the Abend flying down his throat on the Power. Can you do that?"

Another hurried consultation took place, but then Owein answered for them. "I think we can do that. We'll have to be very careful, but we can probably get away without the Abend noticing."

"Good," Brego said decisively. "Then someone go and get that thing brought up here."

When it was brought up and was unpacked from its multi-layered case they all stood looking at it.

"I'm not asking you to put it on," Brego said gently to Berengar – with a gorget going around a man's throat it could literally mean Berengar risking his neck. "For a start, just try touching it. All of us feel horribly sick even handling it with blacksmith's tongs."

"I don't even have to be that close," the strangled voice of Warwick came as he retreated down the hall until he was as far away as possible. "Oh Trees, that feels so disgusting!"

Several others from amongst the senior men also hastily moved away to join Warwick. Esclados, however, remained close by his friend even though he was as white as a sheet. General Tully also stood close by, albeit with gritted teeth and an expression which hinted that he was avoiding being sick by sheer willpower alone. With great caution Berengar extended his hand. When his fingers were almost upon the golden Gorget it began to shimmer slightly. Instantly, at the end of the room the window was flung open and Warwick was hanging out of it, with what was visible of him heaving violently.

"This feels dangerous," Berengar said shakily. "It's almost like it's trying to suck me in. I don't think I'd be the one in control if I actually touch it."

"Blood," said Owein suddenly. "That's what changed it for Sithfrey. They said that the Gauntlet absorbed the blood from wounded Forester and after that it was changed."

Before anyone could speak Esclados had drawn his dagger and, shoving up his sleeve, drew the sharp blade three times across his muscular forearm. Unsteadily he stepped forwards and then flexed his arm over the gorget. He had gone deep enough that the blood flowed easily out of the wounds and down onto the alien metal, thick drops splattering its pristine surface. The thing's glow increased and Berengar shot to his friend and spun him, putting himself between it and Esclados, just as a bolt of light sparked out of it directly at the older Knight.

"No!" Berengar was trying to order Esclados, then grunted with pain as the charge hit him in the back. Yet the spark too seemed to take something from the collision, turning it back onto itself and striking the Gorget too. The air crackled and sizzled, and as Esclados caught his stumbling commander, his blood seemed to boil for a second on the shiny surface and then appeared to seep into it.

"Sacred Rowan!" Esclados exclaimed in shock. "Berengar! Berengar! Are you alright?"

# Chapter 3

## *Absent Enemies*

### Brychan: end Beltane

"Berengar!" Esclados yelled, even more panicked now as his friend and Master slumped further in his arms.

Sooty, who had been taken to the far end of the room with Warwick, shot forwards whistling furiously. He was capable of a surprising turn of speed when he wanted to, and was beside Berengar at the same moment that Brego reached him and put a strong arm under Berengar's to help take the weight from Esclados.

"*Hmpff*! I'm alright!" Berengar panted faintly. "...Sit. ...I need to sit down!"

Dana thrust a chair beneath him and Berengar collapsed into it thankfully. Tully, in the meantime, had hurriedly flipped the lid closed on the first layer of the carrying case which the Gorget lay in. Sooty was making cooing noises like a distraught dove and hugging Berengar as best his short forepaws could manage.

"What happened there?" Brego demanded sharply of the ancients, as he supported the swaying Berengar to prevent him from falling off the seat.

However the ancients, he realised when he turned to see them, were all looking shaken too.

"Ouch! That was interesting!" gulped Peredur, his image shimmering rather erratically.

"Rather a drastic trial," agreed Cynddylan shakily.

"But it changed something," Owein told them, even as his ghostly image swam around as though ripples were radiating from the Gorget.

Before anyone could say anything else, Vanadis blinked into being followed almost instantly by Aneirin.

"What in the Islands are you doing?" he demanded brusquely. "Do you want the Abend to be alerted to us at this critical point?"

"In a way, yes," Brego answered no less tersely. "We deliberately wanted to unsettle them."

"Well you've certainly done that!" Vanadis snapped. "They're all over the Power talking to one another and trying to work out what just happened."

"Then that's exactly what I wanted to happen," Brego told her calmly. "Very well, men, pack that thing back up. Get it insulated against the Power again." He turned again to Berengar who was sitting a touch more upright and taking sips of mead from a glass which someone was holding steady for him. "How do you feel? Do you think you took any lasting harm from that thing?"

Berengar looked up at him, face white as the mountain snows but eyes fully focused once again. "No, I don't think so. ...I feel very shaken, I'll admit. It's not something I would do again in a hurry! But then I don't think I'll have to."

Warwick, almost as pale after the strange surge of Power, had made it back into the room, and after he too took a restorative swig of mead from a flask, spoke.

"I think he's right. You ancients correct me if I'm wrong, but the Gorget was supposed to be a protective device rather than offensive weapon." The wavering forms managed to nod. "Then I believe that when Esclados dropped his Islander blood onto the Gorget it reacted as we should have expected it to. It tried to defend Berengar – as the DeÁine in this situation – against an Islander. So Berengar was never going to receive any lasting harm from it. But he in turn did something to the Treasure."

"Do you think he's managed to turn it as Sithfrey did the Gauntlet?" Tully asked in amazement.

"Not turn it exactly," Owein said. "I don't think anything as definite as that happened, but I think Warwick has the right of it. When it hit him, Berengar's DeÁine blood caused the energy flow meant to harm Esclados to ricochet back to the Gorget. And in doing that, because his intent was only to protect Esclados, it ... 'reoriented' rather than 'changed' is the best word I can think of that you would understand, ...something inside the piece."

Cynddylan was nodding. "And I also think that in some way a bond has now been made between you, Berengar, and the Gorget."

"What kind of bond?" Esclados demanded suspiciously. "He's not going to be manipulated by the Abend if he tries to use it in battle, is he?"

"Actually, rather the opposite, I'd guess," Peredur told him. "Do we agree that the piece is now more firmly bonded to Berengar's intent? And that it will now be far harder for the Abend or one of their acolytes to affect it from a distance?"

Aneirin's scowl had slowly lifted and now he was almost looking enthusiastic. "Definitely! Much harder for them to manipulate it at a distance! Also, Berengar, you and Esclados both acted with the intent of defending someone, and that accords with the primary purpose of the Gorget. It's not so surprising, then, to believe that you will retain the dominant control over the device, even if the Abend get close to it. Since they never think of anyone but themselves, they're already working against its primary function, and that means they have to work much harder to get what they want out of it. With any luck, if it came to a tussle between you and an Abend, it might plausibly end in a stalemate, even though you have no ability or experience in using the Power as they do. It would be a question of an intent to defend, albeit Islanders, versus DeÁine blood-alignment but trying to force it to attack, where they're never going to get the best out of such a piece anyway. You might not be able to do anything with it, but it wouldn't allow itself to be used to do you any harm either."

"Well that's a comfort!" Esclados breathed in relief. He had been suffering desperate pangs of guilt at the thought that his impulsive move to help his oldest friend might nearly have killed him instead.

"Why did you want to provoke the Abend, anyway?" Vanadis demanded despairingly. "I just can't understand you Islanders!"

Brego, his own pulse having returned to something nearer normal, was able to assume the air of confident commander-in-chief once more. "Listen …Owein, Peredur and Cynddylan have told us that Quintillean and Masanae have a small army of their own now, and appear to be chasing after Anarawd and Eliavres back to the south Brychan coast, and at the same time Magda, Helga, Tancostyl and these two unknown Abend are tearing south to meet with Eliavres and Anarawd too. What that says to me is that there's a power struggle going on within the Abend. The two who have led up until now have suddenly begun to lose control, but what I *don't* want is to exchange an Abend led by Quintillean and Masanae for an Abend led by Tancostyl and Magda, who then feel smug and secure in their positions. That achieves nothing.

"By getting Berengar to test his strength against the Gorget just as these two have got the upper hand, I wasn't just seeing what would happen to him. I wanted Magda and Tancostyl to remain off balance. I want them and the others of the Abend to stay reacting to events we provoke, not have them turning the tables on us again and leaving us in the position where all we're doing is turning the DeÁine army away from Brychan once more. This time I want to drive them out for good, and the best way to do that at this early point is to not let them think that they have control of everything."

"A risky tactic, but one which I can appreciate would work," Aneirin mused. "It's not one which I would ever have dared try, but then I was never our best tactician, those were always Myrddin and Artoris' strengths."

"Humph! Artoris wouldn't have been so rash!" Vanadis snorted, defending her deceased lover.

"Forgive me, Vanadis, but I think he would," Owein said firmly. "He would have seen what Brego is trying to do and I think he would have approved. Listen to the Power all of you! ...What do you hear? ...The Abend all over the place, that's what! Can you feel them questing in unison straight for us?" He paused as the other ancients clearly used whatever strange ability it was they possessed to quest along the Power. "No! They're in a flap! Magda accusing Masanae, Masanae accusing the new Abend, and Eliavres and Helga going at one another like cat and dog. Brego's succeeded!"

This sudden confirmation that Brego's gamble had paid off had all the men in the castle room grinning at one another, even Berengar. Then he realised how long Sooty had been hanging on to him and a thought occurred.

"Sooty, are you more comfortable with me now that this has happened? Can't you feel my DeÁine presence so strongly?" He was quietly worried that somehow they had masked the squint's ability to sense a member of the DeÁine, and that that in turn might make it more difficult for Sooty to focus back on the DeÁine as the enemy when the time came to really fight to the bitter end with them.

Sooty, however, was much more specific about what he felt. The black squint loosed his hold on Berengar and trotted a few feet towards the ancients, then let rip a stream of chirps and whistles.

"Did he indeed?" a surprised Cynddylan exclaimed. Then realised that this was a very one-sided conversation for the Knights. "Sooty says that you've made the Power in the Gorget less ...'dirty' is, I think, the best description for what he feels. He says that you aren't changed Berengar, which is a relief because the squints can see such things much better than we can. He says that he feels less of the DeÁine about the place, although I'm not sure what he means by that."

He paused as another stream of whistles and chirps came from Sooty. "Ah, I see! He says that he felt as though Berengar was like a clean person swimming in a dirty river when he touched the Gorget – sooner or later Sooty was worried that he was going to get made dirty ...contaminated ...by it. Now he says that what Berengar and Esclados did was make the 'water' of the Power they were in around the Gorget clean again. Not the whole river, but enough for them to not be in any danger any more. He thinks that if Berengar was able to work with Talorcan, then they would be able to make the part of the river of Power which flows around these Islands – the bit around the pieces – properly clean again in time."

"Well that's very reassuring, Sooty," Brego said fondly to his squint, "but I think we have to do a few more things first before we can start doing cleaning up jobs."

As the ancients disappeared once more to continue observing the Abend from a cautious distance, Brego once more called his men to him and began making plans as to how they would proceed. Between them they decided that they would never openly show the Foresters to the DeÁine, or at least those DeÁine in the army whom the harrying force were likely to come into contact with. If the Abend quested around on the Power and found them despite this, then there was little the Knights could do about that. It was a chance they just had to take. The Foresters would remain in these second ranks, hidden but on hand to counter any arcane summoning the regular army might run into.

The major harassing of the DeÁine rearguard would be done by Berengar's men for two reasons. Firstly, this was personal to them. It was their land which had been so swiftly invaded and there was a burning desire to exact revenge upon the DeÁine. Yet that would have had to be contained had Brego not also agreed that the DeÁine army were likely to be familiar with the uniform insignia of the Brychan sept. There were not that many variations between the Island septs' uniforms, but Brego was not going to risk some sharp-eyed veteran realising that these were not the home-grown troops at their backs, and concluding that the other Islands were now in the game too.

First thing the following morning they marched on again. General Tully was staying behind to secure Arlei and guard the slave prisoners in Dinas. With him were those few men who had taken injuries in the brief fight and were not up to a long march just yet, plus those of his own men who had marched back out of Laon with him and Warwick. All told Brego was leaving a full battalion with Tully, but even with those men gone, there was once again a massed army of thirty-three thousand marching southwards. It brought smiles to the faces of many a man as they looked at the different banners floating on the stiff breeze funnelling down from the mountains. They marched at speed, stopping only when darkness had truly fallen and were up again at the first crack of dawn, but their eagerness paid off after five days. As the men rolled themselves into their blankets they could see, down on the coast, the campfires of the DeÁine army. They had willingly gone without hot food or drink for the pleasure of surprising their enemies, for the few scouts the DeÁine had sent out were now feeding the crows.

"Any signs of the Abend?" Brego asked Cynddylan, when the ancient appeared as he and Berengar and Warwick talked tactics with Dana, Esclados and the other ealdormen.

It was a question Donn Monreux was also asking of his senior Donns too. They had marched south and had finally reunited all the Abend on the same day that Brego and Berengar's armies had taken Arlei, and since then there had been all manner of commotion going on. At first there had been surges and rippling in the Power, and if the gossip coming from those who were having to act as household servants to the Great Ones while on the road was right, not all of it had come from the Abend or their acolytes. Something had happened on that day which had all of them in a flap. Something which also had them tearing at one another like mad dogs for the next two days, caused, the gossip grapevine said, by each thinking it was one of the others making some kind of play for control of the Abend. Then, when they realised it was an external force there was more frantic consultation. If it had not been dangerous to say such a thing out loud, Donn Monreux would have said the Abend were panicking, and going by the expressions on the faces of his fellow young Donns, they were thinking much the same.

Then just two days ago the entire Abend had set sail once more for the southern island. All the Donns got from them was that the Souk'irs' ships would be coming back to collect them too, and that they would be cleansing the southern island. The young Donns were all for that. In their time there had never been a proper cleansing, because the local populations of the places they had stopped at during the Exile had been needed for slaves.

However, young Vir Monreux had seen the distaste on the faces of the older Donns, and wondered whether this would be quite the exhilarating experience his fellow junior leaders were anticipating. It sounded rather more like butchery and slaughter, hardly the kind of noble activity one of the highborn should be sullying their hands with.

And now there was another question – who were the men a blood-drenched scout had seen? He was from an elite Jundis, so when he said that his fellow scouts had been cut down, and that he had only escaped by the desperate measure of jumping off a cliff, then been lucky enough to find enough water to break his fall at the bottom, nobody doubted he spoke the truth. He had not seen enough to be able to tell them just how many men there were, but it was worrying that there were any at all. Where had these armed men come from out of a land where the flooding to the west defeated any sort of travel? They could not have come out of the north. The messages from the Jundises up there had admittedly revealed that it had been harder to subdue than expected, but nothing implied that they had encountered a serious level of resistance. So if not from the north or the west (where all the cursed Knights castles were), then where?

The senior Monreux, Corraine and Telesco Donns were all in council right now, debating what should be done. Once upon a time, if the Abend had said stay here, then nobody would have moved. Now, though, there had been too many disasters to lay at the Abend's door. Some were saying these Abend were nothing like the calibre of their predecessors, and were all too fallible. Others were going further, saying that allegiance came at a price – a price which the Abend had singularly failed to meet – and that the Donns should therefore only back them when it benefited the noble families too.

"I think we'll turn back and root out these dissidents," a young Corraine Donn said to a fellow family member only a decade or two older than him.

"Our family don't like this sudden turning to the Souk'ir either," a Telesco said. "Since when have the Souk'ir been involved in something like a cleansing? If the natives had been any good for slaves they'd have mopped them up decades ago, so they can't have any interest in them."

"I heard from one of the slaves sent to serve the Abend that the Sinut families are on the way," one of Vir Monreux's younger cousins whispered to him. "Won't that mean that the Veroon are with them?"

The Monreux and the Veroon had had a blood-feud going since time immemorial. Just having them on the same island was asking for blood to be shed! Ritual duelling would become laden with matters of family honour, and the priests would be healing wounds and intervening to prevent actual deaths.

Vir nodded and whispered back, "That's why I think we'll fight whoever this is. Never mind what the Abend say. Our families will want to have everything here secure if the vendettas are even remotely likely to flare up again. They'll want the Veroon and the Komanchii and the Soullis to see us in a position of strength which matches what they have in Sinut."

"Here they come!" hissed the younger Monreux.

Their family heads came over to them and the leading families once more separated out into separate groups.

"We shall not be waiting for the Abend or the Souk'ir," the head Monreux announced to his clustered relatives. "We have decided that first we shall deal with this minor uprising. Our hold is not yet so strong in this part of the island that we can afford to let rebel attitudes spread and take hold. They must be nipped in the bud!"

"Where *are* the Abend?" Vir asked his leader. "Are they truly taking part in a cleansing?"

The leader gave an exasperated sigh, the nearest he would risk to any open criticism of ones with such powers as the Abend – you never knew when they were listening in on the Power! "They told us before they left that the Sinuti will be arriving shortly, and that they have gone to make sure of an 'adequate welcome'. That's all I know. As for us, we shall march off tomorrow morning and deal with this inconvenience behind us while we wait for the Souk'ir to recover from their feelings of self-importance, and remember that we do the fighting and they do the transporting."

Yet as the sun rose on the morning of the third of Solstice, many of the lesser men among the DeÁine army were privately wishing that the Souk'ir would show up there and then. Arrayed before them in the morning haze was not just some tatty band of rebels, it was an army. A real proper army, with the dreaded banners of the Order rippling in the breeze coming in off the sea.

"Great Mother Seagang! Where did they come from?" a Corraine gasped to Vir as they hastily pulled on their armour and grabbed their weapons. "Can these cursed Islanders breathe under water? They should be trapped behind the melt-water floods! Or do they have webbed feet like ducks?"

"Quiet you fool!" Vir hissed at him. "Never, ever make the association between folk so base and one of the sacred beasts of the Temples! If one of the Abend were to listen in and hear you they'd fry you to cinders in a heartbeat!"

"I'm not frightened of them!" the youngster snorted.

"Well you should be!" Vir riposted. "If you'd seen them do the things I have then you wouldn't be so bold! Phol's balls, that Helga's ice and steel held together by sheer Power! And I don't ever want to be that close to Masanae!"

They had no further chance to speculate, for from the arrayed troops on the ridge above them, trumpets rang out announcing the advance.

High above the DeÁine on the ridge, Berengar called along the line, "Steady men! Keep in line! Don't break formation!"

With great deliberation the long line of horsemen walked down the hill, the foot soldiers right on their heels. Berengar had chosen to have a full battalion mounted up at the front, and another at the rear – not to attack the main body of the DeÁine but to give chase to any who fled the field. They wanted no word of this getting to the Abend across the water, which was where the ancients again assured them that they were. Between the two mounted lines were all of the rest of the Brychan troops with the exception of Warwick's Foresters. They were just out of sight below the horizon with the Celidon Foresters and the Ergardians. Having not given the DeÁine time to make a good estimate of the numbers facing them, Berengar was presenting them with an army which looked equal to their own. Enough to worry them, not enough to prompt them to turn tail and run, and that included fooling the Abend if they were watching somehow.

It was working too! The DeÁine were spread out around Eynon, which made Berengar's job easier. Had he been fighting them on the congested peninsular across the water around Farsan, his big worry would have been that some might retreat to Tarah and hold that against them. Luckily the Donns had not wanted the Jundises and Seljuqs packed quite so close together, or to be quite so close to the Abend who had rested briefly at Tarah castle. So they had chosen to camp around the eastern port instead, which meant that the nearest castle was distant Amroth, much too far away for any fleeing DeÁine to get past the Ergardians and take refuge in. The Jundises were forming up into squares and the slave drivers had mounted their lumbering beasts and were flaying the slaves into line – all the standard DeÁine tactics.

"No sign of those siege machines," Esclados breathed to Berengar with a touch of relief – a sentiment which Berengar sympathised with. Nobody had mentioned siege engines being used on Arlei, but then there had hardly been any need for them. However, that did not mean the DeÁine had not brought any with them to supplement the Abend's Power with. On previous occasions the huge catapults had been used to fling sacks of flaming oil into their lines, as well as balls of iron which shattered on impact and sprayed all around with lethal shards of flying metal, and these could operate far beyond the reach of their own archers.

"None of the fell beasts, either, thank the Trees!" Berengar whispered back. Apart from the slave drivers' horned and scaled beasts – which the DeÁine called tuatera and rhynungyuli, Warwick informed them – the DeÁine had breeding grounds over the seas for some other strange creatures which had been brought to the Islands at times. At Moytirra the men had had to face flying lizards called jaculi who spat flaming, acidic mucus which ate at flesh, and against which their only defence was their hawks, who could bring the small reptiles down in mid-air.

Other delights included fighting beasts which once might have born a relationship to very large cats, but which now sported vicious beaks and talons, although their puny wings were too feeble to lift the gryphes' mass off the ground. The same wasn't true of a fighting bird which looked very like an immense cockerel, except that it was scaled not feathered and had a powerful pair of legs like a huge feline. Unable to truly fly like a jaculus, a kokatris could still lift itself enough to be able to fall on its prey from more than a man's height in the air. Spears were the best weapon against these terrifying beasts and the gryphes, but not having to fight them at all was better still!

"No," Esclados sighed thankfully, "no kokatrises or gryphes, although a nasty whispering inside of me says that I bet the ones who are coming bring some of their pets with them!"

"Then all the more reason to annihilate this enemy here and now!" Berengar declared, and nodded to his two signallers. With a swirl of the pennants the signal was given, and the archers paused and let fly the first volley.

Now it showed that the more experienced Donns were in charge this time. Instead of standing waiting to be stuck full of arrows, the Donns immediately ordered the Jundises to break ranks and charge. The slave drivers lashed the slaves into a run and the first wave pounded its way towards the Islander line. The archers still had time to let off another volley, and the front cavalry split into two and peeled off to the side, engaging with the flanks of the Seljuqs as they too tore forwards, more frightened of those behind them than the enemy in front.

Berengar swung his sword and severed an arm, then opened another slave's face before he was past the slaves. Now came the hardest part for him, for as the sept's Master he now had to pull up with Esclados and his small bodyguard and let his ealdormen do their job – the job which only months before he would have been doing. His hand clenched the sword as he fought his instinct to return to the fray. Stefan of Hirieth was leading the foot soldiers with the able assistance of Jonas of Merbach, while Corin of Wynlas led the rear cavalry with Nilsen of Bere, and Ranulf of Seigor took over the leading cavalry with Herrin of High Cross. None of them needed any help from him any more than he would have wanted their late Master, Rainer, telling him how to do his job.

The men were doing well, the archers turning their attentions to the slave masters' beasts, for without the masters behind them driving them on, the slaves soon lost their focus and milled around in confusion presenting tempting targets. Several of the great beasts already lay on the ground, covered in arrows, then suddenly one was pounding up the slight incline straight at Berengar. He could have retreated. He probably should have. But Berengar could not change the man he was at heart, and at heart he was a soldier. Without thinking he and Esclados held their horses side by side and then at the last moment separated so that the pounding beast with its lethal horns passed between them. Not before they both made vicious cuts with their swords at the beast and its rider, though. As the beast passed, they swung together behind it and past one another, so that each now came back alongside the beast but on the opposite side to where they had been before.

Sword in his right hand and guiding his horse with his legs, Esclados made a mighty sweeping left-handed cut with his battle-axe and it embedded in the rider's spine. As the rider slumped forward, Berengar drew level and plunged his sword downwards at an angle so that it penetrated between two scaly plates, deep into the charging creature. It gave an ear-piercing scream and tried to toss its head, but could not lift its head now because of the sword-blade. As it wounded itself further, one of Berengar's bodyguards laid open its face by the means of sticking his sword in the screaming maw and sawing sideways. Even as the beast stumbled and fell, Esclados plunged his sword into the wicked red eye which rolled towards him. As it collapsed it drove his sword right into its brain and lay twitching in its death throes.

Turning in his saddle to pull the spare sword he carried from its place strapped behind him, Esclados suddenly espied something and let out a yell, pointing to the horizon. There was no mistaking that eerie glow.

"Power-fire!" he bellowed.

Berengar swung to where he pointed and swore. "So the Abend aren't that far away after all!" he growled, as Esclados pulled a horn whistle from beneath his uniform where it hung on a lanyard and blew the warning. It did not have to carry far. The trumpeters heard the warning and, without need for an order, sounded the alarm. At the same time they saw the Foresters come running over the ridge. At the top they stopped and planted their wands into the ground and began chanting en masse, air now visibly rippling outwards from in front of them. The ball of Power streaked towards them, then as it dropped lower and lower, seemed to hit something which made it fragment into sizzling droplets which vaporised before they got low enough to hit anyone. More bolts followed, but after half a dozen, the assault stopped, successfully fended off by whatever it was that the Foresters had done.

By this time it was clear who was winning this engagement. Not one of the slave-masters was still alive, and the fighting had congealed around the Jundises who were now seriously outnumbered. From his vantage point, Berengar spotted a small knot of figures making their way to the back of the turmoil.

"The senior Donns are making a run for it!" he yelled to Corin, then remembered the signallers and got them to attract Corin's attention for him, for Ranulf was too far to the east now to be signalled to. As he and Corin made distant eye-contact across the bloody field he saw Corin's face split into a wolfish grin, then two companies of cavalry split off from Corin's force and swung around the fighting from the rear towards Berengar, who threw his head back and laughed. Corin knew him too well! He had guessed Berengar would be itching to join in and not sit on the sidelines, and this was his way of showing that he was happy to have a more hands-on Master again.

Berengar pulled out his spare sword, and led his small band to meet the coming companies as they swept around the battle to reach the rear of the DeÁine. Together they reached the southern extent of the mêlée as the Donns and their guards broke out and turned for Eynon. For a moment the Donns' party streamed towards them until they realised just who it was blocking their path. Hauling their horses to a halt there was a momentary stand-off, then a Donn in the centre gave a resigned nod and flipped his face guard back down again.

There was no charge this time. The two groups of horsemen walked their horses towards one another, both watching the other closely for a hint of what tactics might be coming. Berengar and the central Donn were watching one another intently, and he knew that this would be a duel between them while their subordinates fought around them. He forced himself to patience and was rewarded by the Donn being the first to break ranks as he kicked his horse into a burst of speed. It was all the signal any of the others needed, and the two sides suddenly lurched at one another, for there was little ground separating them by now and certainly not enough for a proper charge. Berengar's sword rang against the Donn's, and somewhere in the back of his brain he registered seeing the insignia of the Monreux.

However, he was too busy dealing with the man himself to contemplate familial connections. The Donn had not risen to head of the family in the field without some ability, and like all of the highborn DeÁine soldiers the one thing he had had ample practice at was this kind of one to one fighting. However, Berengar had the advantage of having learned to fight in a style devoid of the multiple conventions which governed DeÁine duelling. As the Donn lifted his sword to make a perfectly arced backwards cut, Berengar drove his sword in beneath his arm and cut him along the ribs, his pattern-welded blade crimping one segment of the Donn's armour plating, and slipping beneath the joint with another. His blade came away wet with blood and still in time to block the coming cut, which had faltered as the Donn felt the pain. Berengar pressed his advantage and got another cut in before he felt the Donn's blade strike his own armour.

It was a well executed strike, but the Donn's full strength was not in it. Berengar knew he would have a bruise where it landed when he took the padded jacket off from under his chainmail, not anything worse. His riposte, on the other hand, bit deeply into the Donn's leg and a jet of blood told of a major vein cut open. The Donn would not last long now and he knew it. He made a valiant attempt to counterattack, a cut which slithered worthlessly off Berengar's vambrace and left him open for Berengar's killing stroke, which cut up under the Donn's gorget and deep into his neck.

As the leading Monreux slid off his horse to the ground, Berengar looked about him and saw that most of the enemy were dead. Two young Donns were struggling in the grip of some burly men-at-arms, which pleased Berengar. It was not just that it was a means of him getting more intelligence about the DeÁine's movements. It also demonstrated that even in such emotionally charged situations, his men were capable of restraint and of not killing when there was no need. *Even here in the dirt and blood we're better than them,* Berengar thought proudly. *We can rise above it and make decisions for ourselves. I didn't have to tell those men, they did it themselves. Find me a DeÁine soldier who'll reinterpret his orders for himself!*

He turned back to the main battle, and saw that there too the Order had taken the day. However, Warwick was watching out to sea intently, and when Berengar looked out to where he was gazing he saw that there was a shimmering in the air in one spot. Heeling his horse to a canter he hurried to Warwick's side.

"Is that the Abend watching us?" he asked the Forester.

"I fear so."

"And can they tell that Brego's with us?"

"I don't think so. He's kept well back. We only came forward with our own Foresters because I was confident of dealing with the Power-fire they were sending. That was coming from a long way off, by the way. The Abend aren't just sitting on the opposite coast, they must be a good day's march inland. It felt very strange, and I guess that it's because one of them was using the Helm to give them more distance with their attack. Lucky for us they'd stretched themselves a bit too far. I'm hoping that's the same for whatever it is they're using to view us with. I think that thing is hovering so far away because that's the nearest they can come without losing control of it. In which case, no, they won't have seen that the Ergardians are with us."

"Then let's keep it that way!" Berengar declared. "Send no messages back over the hill just yet. We'll do it in a while, as if we were simply sending a message back to Arlei or somewhere. Let's get this mess cleaned up before we're knee-deep in rats."

"Rats?" a young archer close by said in surprise.

Berengar could have ignored the comment. A Grand Master did not need to explain his every word to the lower ranks. But Berengar had vowed that he would be a very different Master to the last ones, who had kept themselves quite aloof once they'd taken office.

"Yes, archer, rats," he said. "You come from the mountains by your accent?"

"Aye, sire," the astonished archer gulped, overawed by the fact that he was speaking to his Master.

"Well we're right by a port here," Berengar continued, "and they have trouble with rats at the best of times. This will be like a banquet feast for them if we don't clear it up, and once they've finished we don't want them exploring our camp, do we?"

"No, sire!" the archer gabbled, and then turned to help hoist up a corpse another archer was starting with towards the beginnings of a pile of bodies.

Warwick smiled to himself. Berengar was already making quite a reputation for himself and for all the right reasons. Then he frowned as he looked back out to sea. The Abend spying on them, however, was not something he liked.

Not that the Abend were particularly happy with what they were seeing either.

"Sweet Lotus, how did that happen?" Laufrey groaned. "I thought the Order wasn't supposed to be able to get out of the mountains."

"They weren't!" Tancostyl snapped furiously. "*I* couldn't get across *those* floods! There's no way that they could've come across the southern plain to get there."

"Then how did they get there?" Masanae spat in a fine temper. "Sprouted wings and flew?"

"If you'd let *me* use the Helm I could have annihilated them with the Power," Quintillean growled at Tancostyl, who retorted in similar style,

"Oh, in your dreams! Firstly, after all you've done you're not getting your hands on the Helm, and that's final. And anyway, that's the limit of the Helm. It has nothing to do with your strength as opposed to mine, which I might remind you is not that big a gap! Before you took yourself off into the accursed wilds you might have had the edge on me, Quintillean, but not anymore!"

That was quite true. For all the healing Quintillean had received, that indefinable something extra which he had always had over Tancostyl had disappeared somewhere in the Ergardian soil never to return.

"Enough!" Eliavres said firmly. The others all turned to him, but before anyone could deliver another stream of invective he held up his hand and spoke again. "Great Dragon of Death, listen to you all! Hissing and spitting like children! Stop throwing blame and think! They have ships and can use them with immunity. What was to stop them sending messages to the north and others coming in ships to their aid? This doesn't need to imply betrayal of us by someone within, or a sudden ability of the Islanders to use the Power!"

"But what of that strange surge in the Power a week ago?" chided Helga, still unwilling to let go of her belief that something more had happened, or to let Eliavres be right without her doubting him.

Anarawd fixed her with a steely glare. "We went over that then, Helga. That's why we're on the way to secure the south, remember? Someone used another piece and that can only mean the Emperor. As Eliavres worked out, he must have been forewarned by the Sinuti and took the chance of trying to take it, even from so far away, when some opportunity presented itself. We don't know what that was, and that's a weak point for us. So the important thing is to bloody the Helm and Scabbard well, and empower them fully. *You* agree to that! In fact it was *you* who said that your research agreed with Masanae and Quintillean's, that all those pieces we have which relate to war draw strength from the blood of our enemies."

Helga mentally kicked herself. It had been almost automatic to agree with Masanae once she had been back and standing face to face with her. Such long-standing survival tactics were not so easily shed.

"He's right, sweetling," Magda purred. "You agreed that there wasn't anything like enough blood in the few peasants we found remaining in that hovel of a town. And it was very much you who suggested that it would be easily obtained over here, which was why we moved without the Donns with us. Had we waited we would've been on hand to aid the Donns and could've analysed the situation much closer. Not to mention questioning the prisoners we would've taken! So if I were you I would keep quiet for the moment, because if there's anyone here who might be blamed it's you!"

Helga's expression would have curdled fresh milk, but she took Magda's advice and said nothing. She really could not be seen as too closely allied to Masanae and Quintillean now.

"What do you see?" Eliavres asked Barrax, for the newest war-mage had his hand on Tancostyl's shoulder and was drawing Power, with Tancostyl's consent, to make the far-seer projection.

"There were about the same number of Islander as of ours, as I said before," Barrax reported irritably. Why could they not just accept that this time the Islanders had defeated them? Did there always have to be an ulterior reason for the DeÁine losing at anything? He was struggling to keep his personal fury under control. That was his family over there who had been massacred! The mighty Monreux cut down like cattle! Vengeance for blood-kin screamed within him. Even as Tancostyl began to speak to urge him to calm, his restraint snapped. A bolt of pure energy ran out along the current to the far-seer and transformed it into a spear-like Power-spike.

At a blinding speed it shot towards the Island troops, yet even as the warning was called it was too late. The expanding sickly white blade of light ploughed into the Islanders, killing first some of the Brychan men-at-arms who simply vaporised, and then plunging into a company of female Foresters and the men behind. As the energy was dissipated the damage it did became more tangible. Arms and legs were shorn off, huge rents were torn in bodies, and at the last the residual spike thrust itself explosively into the gut of the women's second-in-command.

Anna did not even have time to scream. Her eyes bulged, and as the fountain of blood gushed out of the hole where her midriff had been, she simply fell like a puppet with its strings cuts. Her captain, Hawise, tried to catch her then fell to her knees sobbing in a mixture of grief and fury.

"Where the fuck did that come from?" Berengar roared as he spun towards the carnage. The bolt of Power had only just missed Warwick, and while no casualty was good, to lose such knowledge and experience would have been even more devastating.

Warwick, however, was on his knees with a wand in each hand, as were several Foresters around him, all chanting softly. The wands were quivering gently, and Esclados pointed to the ground a little beyond the army where the grass was moving in ripples. A moment later Warwick opened his eyes and stood up wearily.

"It's little consolation, but I think that was a one off blast. A parting shot if you care to think of it like that. But it's not good. It's not good at all! That Power signature was the new war-mage, and he's done something with the Helm which we certainly didn't see Tancostyl try. He might be younger and more flexible, and in that case he might be adapting to using this piece quicker than the Abend old-guard are."

Across the water the Abend themselves were looking at Barrax with similar surprise. Tancostyl was torn between annoyance that the younger mage had used the Helm in such a way without asking his permission first, but also intrigue over something he would never have thought of trying. Barrax really was going to be worth cultivating.

"What was that all about, sweetling?" Magda asked cautiously. Barrax had been all restraint so far, so what had tipped him off balance? Even as she said it, though, she remembered that he was a Monreux by birth. "Was it family?" The military families had far more binding ties of loyalty than those highborn of the court.

"You must learn to disregard the loss of a few distant cousins," Helga said snidely, only to find herself suddenly being physically lifted off the ground by Barrax's hand around her throat.

"That was my youngest *grandson* they killed!" he howled. "My *grandson!*"

All were shocked, but Anarawd most of all. Of course it was possible. The senior Donn would have shown his age more than his Power-wielding grandfather, but more surprising was that Barrax should have fathered a child at all. It must have happened before his Power had been awakened, Anarawd reasoned. Somewhere in his passage through puberty while the priests had suppressed his abilities for him to keep him sane, as they did for all who had such potential. Nevertheless, it was the first time he could recall hearing of one with sufficient talent to be elevated also being fecund enough to produce an offspring, whatever the stage of life it happened at. He must watch this one very carefully! It would not do to have Masanae and Quintillean's ritual to gain total power destroyed only to find that Barrax, of all people, could beat him at his own game by having heirs already there and waiting. For now Barrax was very useful, but it would not do to allow him too close!

"You'll get your revenge and more," Magda was saying soothingly to Barrax, as a shaken Helga stood rubbing her swollen and bruised throat. "We'll kill them all, just you wait and see! When there's no sea between them and us, and we show them what Nicos and Othinn can do, they won't find our troops so easy to overrun."

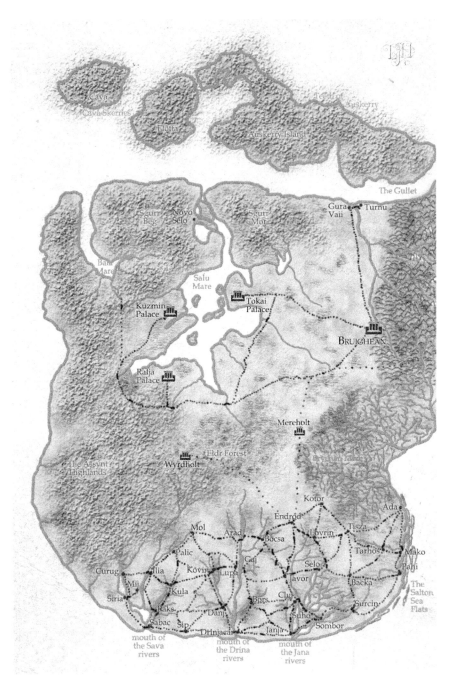

# Chapter 4

 *Beginnings of Resistance*

## New Lochlainn: Beltane

Will stretched his aching joints and groaned, despite the sun warming him as he stood on the long wooden porch outside Wyrdholt Palace. They had arrived three days ago, and had spent the time cleaning out the dusty old place to make it habitable for those they were leaving behind. It had also been necessary for some of the men to go out hunting to provide a stock of meat. Grain was not a problem, for although Wyrdholt had never been favoured by the DeÁine as a royal residence, it was strategically useful and had regularly had the trader families passing through. The Souk'ir appeared to have used Wyrdholt sporadically as some kind of neutral meeting house, going by the scrolled documents they found neatly filed in a series of pigeonholes in a room which had been converted into a massive archive, and which Saul translated for them. So any dry sort of food was plentifully supplied in the cool cellars beneath, and those staying even had quantities of dried fruits and some wine to supplement their diets with. Only fresh vegetables were going to be in short supply.

However none of this was what was giving Will grief. He had even had two whole days to himself to go and sit in the sun and snooze. Something he suspected being down to Sioncaet having quiet words behind his back with all the Knights and Labhran to the effect that he was close to burning out. No sooner had they got here than all of them had ganged up on him and told him to rest, and that they were more than capable of provisioning a camp without his constant supervision. Of course he had made a token protest, it would not have been right not to! But in his heart Will was deeply grateful for the chance to just stop for a while, for he had enough good sense to know that he would be leading with a vengeance once they got down to the maze of small towns in southern New Lochlainn. Then he would need all his faculties about him, and for that to happen he could not get there dog tired and falling asleep on his feet.

So he had relished the soft, late spring sun, swinging in a makeshift hammock someone had strung up for him out on one of the upper balconies, and very nice it had been too. Unfortunately the bubble had burst the night before. Just as everyone had sat down for an evening meal of roast venison, the sentries had sent frantic messages saying that a horseman could be heard riding at speed their way. Every one of the fighting men had grabbed their weapons, and headed out to the long tunnel through the tree canopies and undergrowth which led down to the palace. Diving into the cover of the ferns and small bushes, they had only just managed to get out of sight before the hooves could be heard turning onto the gravelled path from the old flagstone road which ran across the forest to the north of them. Less expected was a voice calling in Islander out for them not to shoot.

"Festering Underworlds! What's he doing here?" fretted Will, for it could only be one of the men he had sent with Sioncaet. "Now what's gone wrong?"

What had gone wrong was that the massive River Vaii, which rose south-east of Bruighean in the mountains near the castle of Wolfscar, was in flood.

"It's chaos," the rider told them as he gratefully drank a hot caff and rested on a soft-cushioned chair. "I've never seen floods like it, and neither have the DeÁine apparently! The trouble is that all of the Vaii's tributaries rise deep in the Brychan mountains. So when the Abend drove all that snow eastwards they forgot that once it melted some of it would come their way."

"Do you think they even bothered to think about the melting?" Jacinto asked tentatively. He was still feeling his way with his new found relationships in this group, and he was now dreadfully aware of how arrogant he had been in the past. He had no desire to alienate his companions by coming across as haughty and all-knowing. However Saul looked at him startled and then vigorously nodded in agreement.

"I think Jacinto has hit the nail on the head," Labhran also agreed. "To my knowledge they've never tried anything like this before, so how would they be able to anticipate the longer consequences?"

Oliver laughed bitterly. "Well I bet they're observing now! So how bad is it?"

The rider grimaced. "Oh we were alright until we got near to Bruighean. We were just about to turn north, to cut the corner of the road off and avoid getting too close to the citadel, when we realised that there were far more people than usual about. We still didn't think too much about it until we were about to come down onto the main road going north from Bruighean to Gura Vaii. Where we'd come out of the higher land was fine, but we could see south and see that the river was threatening to cut the road off. In fact, where it goes very close to Bruighean it might well be over the road, and we certainly thought that was why we'd seen more folks inland.

"Foolishly, we just thought our luck was in and that it would mean there was even less chance of pursuit. It didn't occur to us that we were being trapped too until we saw the next bridge – or rather what was left of the bridge! By then we could see across the Vaii more clearly and it dawned on us that both the big rivers which come out of the Brychan mountains into the Vaii were absolute churning torrents about three or four times their normal size. Hounds of the Wild Hunt, it was terrifying just to look at! It was like the water was boiling!"

"Are you sure it wasn't some trick?" Bertrand wondered. "Some Abend experiment they might then turn unexpectedly onto Brychan itself?"

Yet the man was shaking his head even as Labhran spoke. "No, Bertrand. It's a worthwhile thought, but I don't think so. The Abend aren't known for testing things first when all they want is annihilation! No, I think Jacinto was closer to the truth. This is a force of nature's not the DeÁine's."

"Sioncaet agreed," continued the man, "because what was doing the damage was the sheer force of water coming down. It was incredible! Huge boulders being tossed about like pebbles! Apart from the terrible currents which must be churning around beneath the surface, those boulders would kill anyone and anything which had the misfortune to get into those waters. Well we stopped and had a hurried conference. The men who're locals were convinced that there was no way we would be able to cross the Vaii, no matter which way we went. They said the floods would only get worse once the second big river came in. If it hadn't been wrecked by flooding already, they thought that Gura Vaii would still be cut off from the sea, because the sheer force of water coming out of the river mouth would make it next to impossible for boats to get into port. So we wouldn't even be able to get to the coast and then hope to sail round to northern Brychan.

"At that point Sioncaet made a difficult decision. He sent me back to warn you, but said to tell you that he'll carry on northwards. He's going to leave Kenelm at the first safe place he can find, but if all else fails he'll go to the coast and get a fishing boat, and go around Auskerry Island on the open sea side. He said to tell you that he's hoping to make contact with those ancients again and see if they can carry the warning to Master Brego. He said you'd understand that the master wouldn't ignore a warning from them, if only he can get to them."

Will had agreed with that decision, for it was the right thing to have done, but through the night he had once again found himself waking and worrying whether Brego, or any other leading Knight like Ruari, had any inkling of the new threat coming from across the sea. Even now, in the light of the new morning, he could think of no other way to raise the alarm if the message they had sent by bird had not been found and taken notice of. And with that came the familiar weight of extra responsibility, for if no-one knew about the additional coming DeÁine army from across the sea, then it was up to Will to try to find a way to turn it back.

That meant that he *had* to raise a good sized army from, what he hoped, would be dissatisfied Attacotti settlers in the lattice of waterways in the south. People who had been under the DeÁine heel for decades now and might be ripe for rebellion. However his greatest fear was that they would have already become like the slaves Sioncaet, Labhran and Saul had described – people too suppressed to have the will to fight. And yet they could be the only force he could assemble to fight the new DeÁine threat – not just support for experienced troops, or forming the rearguard. Terrifying though that thought was, Will could see no option but to fight or face eternal slavery, for once the DeÁine were here in such vast numbers, even pockets of resistance would soon be squashed. The only bright spot was that the waterways in the south all rose from well within New Lochlainn, and would actually be lower than normal for the time of the year, having had no snow at all to feed them this winter. A small mercy, but one to be grateful for!

On the fifth of Beltane, Will and his makeshift force lined up along the tunnelled former carriageway, and waved farewell to those they were leaving behind. As well as the women from Tokai, Will had decided to leave all the older men to continue to hunt and guard the place. They were not that many in number – barely fifty in total, compared to four times that of families and rescued persons – but all those he chose were men well into middle age and former farmers, unused to the different kind of strenuous hardship a forced march would impose on them. He now had no time to slow down for stragglers, and he would rather leave them here where they could still do considerable good, than abandon them on the road to an unknown fate.

Wistan was perched in front of Heledd on a large grey mare and was looking positively excited. With the few horses they had now not needed for the pregnant women, it had been decided that Will, Saul, and Labhran at least should always ride. Oliver had been insistent on that.

"You are the ones who'll be crucial to what we're about to do," he had said firmly. "General, we'll need your ability to assess things militarily. I know Lorcan and Bertrand have experience, but it's nothing in comparison to yours. And you other two are the only ones who really know what it's like in DeÁine territory. Of all of us, you're the ones who might spot something wrong, or something out of place which might hide a danger to us. Or you'll spot an opportunity the rest of us would walk straight past. But for that to happen we can't have you half asleep from tiredness because you've walked for miles and miles the day before. The rest of us can alternate among the remaining few horses if we absolutely need to."

In fact they had loaded the other horses with what extra supplies they could manage to pack, and not all food. During the three days' halt, those men not out hunting had been chivvied by Oliver and the enlisted men of the Order into making shafts for arrows and simple spears out of sharpened poles cut from the forest. Without time to build and light a forge they lacked iron heads for both, but Saul was pretty sure that they would be able to find smiths in the southern towns who could fill that need. So with even the other Knights on foot, they marched out of Wyrdholt and headed south, away from the old road and briefly deeper into the forest.

Despite being on the western edge of the Eldr Forest, the trees were packed as densely as at its ancient heart, although the mixed varieties soon gave way to woods of single species. Within an hour or so they found themselves walking through the huge straight trunks of endless beeches. It made for pleasant marching, for the beech mast smothered all undergrowth enabling them to see for quite a distance, and also made a soft, springy matting underfoot which was easy on the legs and feet. Bright green spring growth was everywhere, and it lifted all of their spirits as they heard the birds up above in their excited spring courtship. Maybe it was a sign that things might yet turn out alright?

Will was even more hopeful five days later when they were within striking distance of the first town. They had made good time, for Curug was the most western town on the Sava river network and was the home to as many miners as farmers. Around this area there were bountiful seams of coal, and the countryside was peppered with the wooden timbers of shafts going down into the earth. Labhran was surprised that there were no heaps of detritus around, but as Teryl, himself a miner's son, explained, this was the old way of doing things. The Island way. Those shattered bits of coal no good for going to the forges were soon gathered up by the locals, who used them for home fires since there was little wood any more around these parts.

"I suppose the Eldr Forest once came all the way down here," Friedl mused, "but it must have all been cut down years ago."

"Centuries ago, more like," Toby chipped in. "Don't forget, the first clearing would have been to make farmlands, long before anyone thought about steel for weapons. I bet the forest was cleared by Attacotti way before even our ancestors came to the Islands, let alone the DeÁine."

He certainly seemed to be on the right track, for when they saw the local people they were all very distinctly Attacotti in appearance – dark haired and pale skinned, or the same skin tones but with red hair. Looking at them it now struck Kim, Teryl and the younger Prydein knights just how alien the DeÁine were and why the older men could spot them in an instant. These Attacotti were fair-skinned, but it was not the blood-drained whiteness of the DeÁine, and nonetheless the older men were tanned from years in the fields – something which never happened to a DeÁine. And if these folk were anything but overfed, they were also not of the very tall, skeletal build of the DeÁine either. No, once you knew what you were looking for there was no mistaking a DeÁine.

It was decided, after much argument, that Oliver would go into the town with Saul, along with Lorcan, Jacinto and six of the valuable Order men. Will very much wanted to go himself, but had been convinced by the others that since they had no idea how these people would react, it was wiser for him to stay out of potential harm's way until the town had been checked out.

To afford them a swift retreat if necessary, all of this advance party were mounted, and so they rode into Curug at a leisurely pace.

"Let's give them time to see us and weigh us up," Saul had suggested. "I think we'd be more likely to be attacked if they think we're a threat to them, so let's keep it non-hostile."

The town lacked any sort of walls or a gate, and so they rode at a steady walk straight into the long wide street which seemed to form a major route into the heart of the town. Looking about them they realised that the rest of the buildings were constructed on far more haphazardly patterned streets and lanes. Topher signalled to them to look down, and they could see what looked suspiciously like building timbers hammered into the surface of the road.

"Reckon the DeÁine must have driven this road straight in through people's houses," he observed softly.

"Well let's hope they're still seething over it!" Oliver said with an optimistic smile.

First impressions, however, were not encouraging. By the time the ten horses had congregated in what passed for a central square, but which was more of a crossroad of two of the DeÁine roads, they had gathered a small and distinctly sullen crowd in their wake.

"What now?" Lorcan asked Oliver softly. Oliver raised his eyebrows quizzically, stuck for an answer. However Jacinto decided to take the bull by the horns and vaulted from his horse. Walking over to a bulky middle-aged man, he kept his hands well away from his sides so that it was clear that he held no weapons, and asked politely,

"Can you understand me? Do you speak Islander?"

There was a long pause as the man stared at him, then the briefest of nods,

"Aye, I can understand thee. What doest thou want?"

His speech sounded archaic but it was comprehensible, which was a relief. Their current batch of recruits to Will's army might have understood them, but these folk down here had always been more Attacotti than Islander, and there had been a real concern that after decades of DeÁine suppression there could be whole generations who understood only DeÁine besides their tribal language.

"Who's in charge here then?" Jacinto tried again, still keeping his voice light and friendly. "Are you the head man of the town?"

The townsfolk looked at him like he had suddenly sprouted an extra head.

"Art thou trying to trick us?" the man demanded suspiciously. "Art thou from Maj'ore Inchoo?"

Jacinto looked back to the others for guidance as he shook his head. Luckily Saul understood what was happening, and dismounted to come and stand beside Jacinto.

"We're not from the Inchoo family nor the Bernien," he said calmly. "I know the Bernien have been trying to improve their standing. Have you had trouble with them?"

"Trouble?" a younger man further back in the crowd spat out. "Aye trouble a plenty! Coming with their soldiers and taking what isn't theirs by force!"

"Would you like to be free of them, then?" Jacinto asked, keeping his fingers crossed that being so direct did not backfire on him.

"Phaa!" another snorted. "And how will that happen? Thee and thine? Ten of ye against an army? I don't think so!"

"Where is this army?" Oliver joined in by asking. "Are they close by? Would they come if you called for them now to defend you?"

"Don't be daft, lad!" The older man said, clearly beginning to think that these must be stray fools from some rich family, who were out to make a name for themselves, and a bit simple but harmless. "Be on your way. There's no fight here for thee. No glory, just coal and dirt, and not much of that since the masters came and took the stockpiles to go and trade with."

"How long have they been gone, then?" Topher asked, also dismounting and walking over to the man, so that they could see that he was far from a member of the nobility. The man looked Topher up and down in surprise, then took another look at the party and registered that apart from Oliver and Lorcan, the rest looked distinctly battered and well worn.

"Who *art* thou?" he demanded, now torn between curiosity and fear.

"We're from beyond the mountains," Topher told, him gesturing eastwards. "Your masters and the other DeÁine are fighting against us over there. They think they're going to walk all over us. They aren't! No matter what happens we shall turn them out of our lands. The question is ...do you want them out of here as well?"

"Thou hast no way to offer us such a thing!" the man said derisively. "How could thou few achieve that!"

"Because we aren't just this few," Jacinto said gently. "We aren't trying to trick you or get you into trouble. Think about it. How long is it since you saw a large number of DeÁine troops, or the slave masters herding dozens of poor souls off?" That seemed to make them pause and think. "I bet it was quite some time ago! And that's because the Abend and the Donns are far away, beyond the great marsh. And I'll tell you something else. You haven't had much rain here, have you? We saw the winter crops wilting in the fields as we rode in. Well all that rain was driven by the Abend to the mountains, to snow the Knights over there into their castles so that they couldn't fight. But now it's spring and the snow has started to melt and they'll be trapped in the east by the flooding.

"If you want to find out how things really stand here, then this is the time to do it. You asked us what we want. Well what we want is for you to join us fighting against the DeÁine. We've got a real proper general with us who knows how to train troops. We're not asking you to go up against them bare-handed. We're not even asking you to do anything your masters would object to just yet, except to come with us to the next few towns and see what things are like there."

It was a move they had not rehearsed or talked over, but Oliver and Lorcan made no attempt to correct Jacinto because his words seemed to be finally having some effect. Jacinto himself looked back to them and they signalled encouragingly for him to go on.

"Look, why don't you come with us tomorrow?" he suggested. "I'm afraid anyone who thinks they might be willing to fight to be free will have to come with us now, because we won't be coming back this way again for anyone to have second thoughts over. We only have a limited amount of time to do this in, because sooner or later the floods will go down, and we have to be ready by then. But will you do it? Will you gather all the younger men who are willing to fight and follow us to the next town? You can even stay far enough back that if you see us being challenged, and you fear it's a trap, then you can turn back before anyone knows you're there. Will you come?"

"I'll come," a new voice in the crowd said,

"And me," another called, to be joined by a third hidden speaker, "and me."

Suddenly there were young men shouldering their way out of the crowd, despite urgent tugs of restraint on their sleeves by many of the older folk. Before they knew it the riders were surrounded by a group of about twenty young men, all looking at them in anticipation.

"Great!" Oliver declared with genuine relief. "Very well, if you'll follow us back out of the town to our camp you can see our leader."

Jens and Dusty were already dismounted and shaking hands with the new recruits, and now Busby handed his reins, and those of Topher's horse, to Evans and got down to talk to the men too. Nothing was going to reinforce the newcomers trust quicker than them walking beside them, and talking to them, instead of lording it over them on horseback.

"We aren't leaving the area until the morning," Jacinto said pointedly to the older townsfolk left watching them. "If these lads don't like what they see they can even come home tonight. We don't have any slave masters with us. We only have men who *want* to fight the DeÁine with us."

With that he turned and joined Topher walking at the back of the group of men, where Oliver dropped back to speak to him once they were out of the confines of the streets.

"That was nicely done, Jacinto!" he praised, and Jacinto felt again the new and unaccustomed warm glow of being rewarded for something well done. "I think offering them the chance to go home tonight was what clinched it. That was inspired! Without it I suspect we'd have had more trouble with the older townsmen. You couldn't see it from where you were, but there were a few burly men hidden back in the side streets who might have given us some grief if the others had called for help. That was good negotiating!"

Jacinto was staggered. He had really *done* something right this time! Not just followed orders correctly (something he had to admit he had been appallingly bad at around Esclados and Berengar), or taken his cue from others, as he had done after the fight at Kuzmin. This time he had acted on his own initiative and got it right! Then a worrying thought came to him. Could he do it again? Was it a lonely freak accident? He had not been doing too badly since he had escaped from the Abend with Saul, so he must be doing something right these days, but what had tipped the balance this time?

He thought back and realised that he had looked down at the faces of the townspeople, and had thought how much he hated it when someone looked down on him, in all senses of the word! And then it came to him. All the ways that Esclados and Berengar had tried to make him understand about treating others as you would want to be treated yourself. About putting yourself in someone else's shoes. In that moment he wanted more than ever to get back and be able to tell his old mentors how sorry he was for all their time he had wasted, and also how – finally! – he was grateful for their perseverance, because against the odds he was learning their lessons.

When the small recruiting party got over the brow of the watershed between Curug and the next valley westwards, the new recruits stopped and gasped in amazement. Laid out before them was a neat and orderly camp with hundreds of men in it! Oliver allowed them a moment to gawp before saying gently,

"We've got nearly four hundred of your fellow countrymen down there already, so you see, you're not alone."

One young lad gave a whoop and then turned tail and began running as fast as he could back the other way.

"It's alright!" Jens called to the others. "He said he was going to get his cousins if we were really all we said we were. I think we just convinced him a bit quicker than he expected!"

By the time the rest of them had met and spoken with Will, there were a couple more heading back into town with their news.

"I don't think we'll ever get a whole town following us," Oliver told Will, as they sat with the others of the party in a debriefing session over the evening meal. "The people are just too scared in case their lords and masters come back, and punish them dreadfully for having the effrontery to challenge them."

Will frowned in concentration as he peered at the map of southern New Lochlainn that Saul and Labhran had managed to create for him while they were at Wyrdholt.

"Twenty from each town," he muttered, shaking his head. "It's not enough, lads, it's not enough! I need a couple of thousand men before we'll even begin to be effective against any decent sized DeÁine force, never mind what's coming over the sea at us." He paused and scratched at the three-day stubble on his chin, for he had broken camp early on the last two mornings to get here quicker, and no-one had had time for luxuries like shaving. "I hate to do this, and I've been trying all ways not to, but I think we're going to have to split up. There's just no way we're going to cover enough ground otherwise. I had hoped that there'd be more coming out to fight, but if this is it, then we *have* to go to *every* town. I'd thought to only sweep through the settlement band closer to the coast, but at this rate we'll not get anything like enough men if we only do that."

He looked across the circle of men around him to Labhran who was sat opposite.

"The honest truth now ...where is more dangerous for you? The northern towns closer to the Eldr Forest, or those down on the coast? Where are you likely, if anywhere, to walk into someone from your old life over here?"

Labhran threw his hands up in a questioning gesture. "Your guess is as good as mine, Will. And that's not being deliberately evasive! As Saul will confirm, the Inchoo family of merchants of the Souk'ir cast control from here across to the other side of the Sava River. It might seem a big territory, but the only asset here is coal. That's bulky to transport and the places

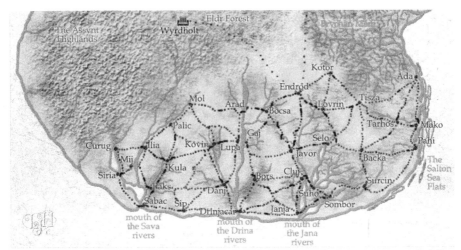

which give the best prices are those where there's iron ore around. The Inchoo do a lot of trading coal for ore across the seas, but they only make a profit on the steel they make, and there's not a lot of that."

"Or to be more precise," Saul added. "They make a lot of spear heads and arrow heads in these delta towns. That's great for us because it's just what we want. But it's not the sort of thing that brings in big profits trade-wise. For that you need to be turning out finely-crafted swords, and those the DeÁine round here can't make, although the men of Kotor have a good reputation in that line."

Labhran nodded. "That's exactly it, and the Inchoo don't go to Bruighean, because the Donns send their quartermasters to make the orders and payments, and their servants do the delivering. I never had contact with the Inchoo themselves because there was never a reason why I should. That's not uncommon either. There aren't many Donns who could name the heads of the leading Souk'ir families without some considerable thought. The two classes just don't mix. As for further on, what Saul told you is actually more than I knew for years.

"The Indiera family have the west bank of the Drina River system, and the Chowlai have the eastern banks and beyond. They back up to the Tabor family's territory, who have most of the Janja River system in their control. Then beyond them are the most powerful Souk'ir family, the Dracma, who have total control of the eastern ports which lie behind what we call the Salton Sea Flats – great mud and sand banks, which shelter the ports from the worst of the currents in winter. Yet for all their power, I've never met any of them, either. Or at least, not knowingly. Who they might have as a guest at any time, is of course, entirely a matter of fate."

Will sighed and gave a faint smile. "Very well, you've made your point. So I can't predict any chance meeting for you." He looked out across the campsite to where Heledd and Briezh sat glowering at him for being excluded. "Unfortunately, I think those two have to stay with me, because I can't in all conscience separate Wistan from me after all he's been through, and the only thing keeping those two out of trouble is looking after him!"

Everyone chuckled at that for the two girls had hardly been easy travelling companions for anyone.

"So tell me," Will said after they had all focused again, "is there one place or more where the girls or Wistan will be in any greater danger?"

It was Labhran who first came up with any sort of deciding factor. "I think that given that Masanae might start questing about with her powers to find Wistan, he would be better staying closer to the sea," he said thoughtfully. "Somewhere where there's a good salty breeze to dispel her powers! And funnily enough, that might go for you too, Will. ...You see it occurs to me that Quintillean might just have got a sight of you back at Kuzmin, and there's always a faint possibility that he connected you with the man Tancostyl was pursuing. If they've exchanged thoughts on this, then Quintillean would know of your appearance from Tancostyl's mental image.

"So remembering what Ruari said about you being better by the sea when Tancostyl was hunting you in Rheged, I think it would be no bad thing if you stayed closer to the sea here too, and out of Quintillean's easy reach. He won't have such a strong sense of you as Tancostyl did, but it might be enough for him to make you feel woozy or a bit sick. And like you said, we don't have time, and that includes time for you to be ill if we can prevent it."

Will looked surprised. "You think I'd still be vulnerable to their probing?"

"If it was aimed at you personally rather than the wider blasts of Power you've encountered lately, then yes, I think you might," Labhran confirmed. "I might be wrong. You might have developed a greater resistance to it by being in the Power rooms at Tokai and Kuzmin, and being on the end of attacks by the Abend. But I honestly can't say for sure, and do you really want to risk it?"

"No, you're right," Will conceded. "Very well. In that case I think I shall divide the force up this way: Labhran, you'll lead the other party and Oliver can go with you. Saul, I'll keep you with me so that I have someone who can speak fluent DeÁine ...just in case! Lorcan, I'd be grateful if you'd go with Labhran, so that means you too, Evans and Waza ...and I think it would be good if you took Topher and Mitch with you so that you have archers as well. That way you might even be able to start some kind of training if there's an opportunity. I'll keep Kym, so that mean you three will stay too," he said gesturing at Newt, Busby and Toby. "I'm not going to start splitting up lances, even if you aren't at full strength. In fact, Colum, you can join them as the other archer. Same goes for you Teryl. You'll be with me, and so will Cody and Trip, so Jens and Dusty can make up your men-at-arms."

"What about us?" asked Friedl, gesturing to himself and Bertrand. "Can we go with Oliver?"

Will knew the young Prydein Knights had found it hard to lose both Hamelin and Theo. "Yes, you're going with Oliver. Don't worry, I'm trying to keep people together in groups they know as much as possible. And that means, Jacinto, that you'll stay with me and Saul. ...There, have I covered everyone?" Nodding heads all round confirmed that they knew which groups they were in.

"Right! ...Then about the territory... My party will go from here to Mij on the middle Sava river, loop back across to Siria, down to Sabac at the mouth of the Sava rivers, then up the eastern Sava to Paks, Kula, and then to Choa. Labhran, you and your group will go as fast as you can to Ilia, right up at the head of the middle Sava, then north again up to Palic, and on to Mol, then come back to meet with us at Choa. We have more towns, but you have the greater distance. We haven't heard of any movement by the Inchoo recently, so that keeps us all within their territory and without risking contact with a different Souk'ir family."

Regarding the newer troops, at Wyrdholt Will had divided them up into a nominal company each for himself, Lorcan, Bertrand and Oliver. Now, though, Kym and Teryl would have to take over Oliver's company so that half of the recruited men went with each party. Not that it would make a huge difference to these men, since they had hardly had chance to get used to their new commanders anyway. Moreover, Will had warned them that as soon as he had enough men, he would be splitting their companies in half to accommodate new men. He had accompanied the news with much praise, warmly congratulating the men on how far they had come since he had met them, and telling them how he had every faith in their ability to help him train the new men they would be getting. Now would be the proof of that, to see if it would actually happen, and whether the training would snowball of its own accord. Will truly hoped so, because without it he would be left with an awful lot of enthusiasm but little skill.

At least come the morning he received a pleasant surprise. Instead of just coming back with one person each, the men who had returned home for the night turned up with far more. And as they broke camp and began to march off, others slowly began to appear out of little lanes and from across fields to slip into the ranks. By the time Labhran gestured his half of their force off onto the east bound road for Ilia, Will reckoned he must have gained nearly fifty men from around Curug. These men he kept with him for the simple reason that Saul believed that Curug probably had quite a bit of contact with the folk of Mij and Siria. There would be no better validation of their cause then the men of those towns seeing their neighbours from Curug amongst the ranks.

For his part, Jacinto was discovering just how much he knew of daily things in the Order, after his mental battering which had left him convinced that he knew nothing of any value. It had never occurred to him that he had learned so much just by being around experienced men like Esclados. Yet now, faced with men who knew absolutely nothing about the military life, he found himself explaining the most basic things over and over again, sometimes to the same person.

Was that what he had been like, he wondered as he fell into his bedroll exhausted at the end of each day? Yes, he had been younger when he had come to the training, as was only natural for someone who was living amongst the Knights, but had he also had two left feet when he had first tried marching? Had he been so uncoordinated that he nearly brained the men next to him when first wielding a wooden sword in practice? He would have loved to think not, but his new found humility nudged him and told him that he probably had been as bad. For the first time, he appreciated that the instructor worked as hard if not harder than the recruits, and his muscles were quick to remind him of it!

The plus for him was that with all the repeated exercises and plentiful food, he was starting to get his old physique back. Not the pristine muscled torso he had once prided himself so much on. It would take longer for that to come back, and Jacinto was not even sure he wanted to go back to being like that, or if he could. In the physical sense his back was a series of ridged scars from when he had been flogged and would never be scar-less, and there were other, less severe but obvious scars on his arms and legs from Edward's torturing. But these were accompanied by internal changes which only Jacinto could see. It was as though he had been stripped down to the bare essence of his soul and then been slowly rebuilt again, with the result being irrevocably different.

Moreover, he liked this new Jacinto far more than the old one, not that he had ever bothered to take a good hard look at himself before. He could do without the nightmares, to be sure, but Labhran and Will had both taken him on one side and assured him that they would pass with time, or at least lessen in strength and frequency. Yet even they seemed a price worth paying if he was going to make something truly worthwhile out of his life – another thought which formerly would never have entered his head.

He was also being used by Will to make the first approaches in the next few towns. At first he could not imagine why, until Will pointed out that, as the dark-skinned member of the party, he was the last person any DeÁine would have allowed to speak for them. Jacinto's obvious slave descent had suddenly become very useful to the cause! And he was even more pleased when Will added that that still would not have counted for much had he not been trustworthy. Him, Jacinto! Trustworthy! It was the first time anyone had ever said the like to him, and it was the biggest incentive yet for him to continue to work at his new found abilities.

Abilities or not, however, they were still struggling to get sufficient troops at the next two towns. Despite the Curug men's appearance being noted in Mij, and Siria at least, being a bigger town than Curug, they had still only just topped the hundred recruits as they marched on Sabac. Even worse, as they crested the rise to look down on the estuary port there were cries of dismay from the local men. There in dock were five great transport ships with men swarming all around them. The Inchoo had come home!

# Chapter 5

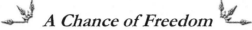 *A Chance of Freedom*

## New Lochlainn: Beltane

"Now what?" Kym said softly to his friend Teryl, but Will heard them despite the fact that he had been cursing quietly and fluently from the moment they had seen the ships. He turned in his saddle and gestured them forwards along with their experienced men. It was the input of men like Toby and Cody that he wanted, but he was tactful enough to include their Knights despite their youth and inexperience in this kind of situation.

"Tell me," he said to the huddle of men he had drawn to one side, "do you think we could take those ships?"

Saul gasped. "Are you serious? Why, in the name of all that's holy, would you want to do that?"

With a flash of insight Jacinto was able to answer that. "To prove we can! If we slink away now, these men will never believe we can be effective against the DeÁine, and if we don't convince them then we'll never get the troops we desperately need. The general needs a big gesture, don't you, sire?"

"Exactly!" Will said with a grin. "Well done, Jacinto, that's exactly it!" He looked at the dubious expressions on the faces of the two young Knights and Saul. "Take a look around you! Those new recruits we've struggled to get are already edging towards the back of the army. We have to prove that we can do what we're saying. *I* have to prove that I'm not lying to them!"

He turned his attention to the Order enlisted men, who thankfully were not showing anything like their officer's scepticism. "I don't give a shit about the cargo, and I'm guessing that that's what those guards down there are for. What I want is to steal those ships out from under the Inchoos' noses."

Toby was squinting against the glare of sunlight coming off the sea as he peered down at the docks with professional detachment. "I reckon they're about halfway through offloading," he mused. "But I can only see seven Hunters down there."

"Hmm, maybe four triads then?" Colum suggested and got general grunts of agreement from the other men, who were now all scrutinising the docks.

"Possibly thirty real seamen to each ship," Jens added. "That'd be a safe minimum to sail something of that size with. Enough men to be able to rotate shifts with in heavy seas, but not so many that they'd be taking up valuable cargo space with themselves and supplies." Nobody argued since Jens' family had been seagoing folk from the very northern isles, and he had spent his youth more on the sea than on dry land.

"Will they be used to fighting?" Jacinto asked deferentially. "I mean, can we send two of our lads up against each one and have a reasonable hope of them besting the sailors? Or are they likely to be professional sailors *and* fighters in case they get boarded on their travels?"

Jens thought for a moment and had a muttered conversation with Dusty, who then answered for the two of them. "We reckon that the Hunters would be the main escort, and that given that the cargoes we've seen so far are ores for smelting, not many pirates would bother with an Inchoo ship. On the other hand, if they've been trading away from DeÁine-conquered lands, then fear of the Hunters alone wouldn't deter any would-be thieves, and so the sailors are probably handy with a cutlass at the least."

"I'd think it would be safer to send this lot in three to one, just to be on the safe side," Jens added.

"So we'll have to go in at night," Cody immediately deduced. "If there are thirty sailors to each of those four ships we'd be using almost all of our force just to subdue the sailors."

"And let's not forget that we're on the wrong side of the river," Newt pointed out.

The entrance to the channel which took shipping up the Sava river system past Sabac, had been narrowed by a great stone edifice. It came out of the nearby sea-cliff in a solid buttress, then made a high archway beneath which small boats could enter the sheltered channel. Another great pier out in the channel then carried one half of a massive drawbridge, echoed on the other side by mirror-image stonework. The central gap would allow the tallest masted ships through into the safety beyond them when the pair of drawbridges were raised up out of the way. A second small arch then connected to a further buttress linking the whole structure to the other steep bank of the estuary. From where they were, the men could see that folded back beneath the drawbridge were also massive sea-gates, which could be swung across the central passage and the two side ones. No Attacotti raider would sail unannounced into this port.

"That might not be guarded on the land ends, you know," Trip broke the silence, as everyone had looked at the way across to the quays. "That looks like a doorway into the fortifications down there, but I can't see any sentries guarding it, can you? It looks to me like the whole thing's intended to stop attacks from the sea. Nobody would land men on the beaches further along because the cliffs are low but too treacherous for climbing up. So the only people walking out over that bridge ought to be folks subdued by the DeÁine, and do we think that they'll be expecting rebellious actions any time this century?"

"Probably not," Will answered with a chuckle. "So can anyone think of a specific problem if we launch a night attack?"

Despite obvious nervousness at the thought, Kym and Teryl kept quiet, deferring to their enlisted men's superior experience. Saul was shaking his head worriedly but said nothing either, and so it was decided.

As dusk loomed, Jacinto found himself with some ten of the men who had attacked Kuzmin, creeping forward on his belly through the bracken, to slide down to the track which ran up to the archway into the stone sea-bastion. His task was to take the entrance and then summon assistance. A task he had no illusions that he had been given because he was one of the more expendable of the Order's fighting men. The men behind him had all shown talent in fighting at close quarters when put to the test, but they looked to him to lead, and he was desperate not to let it show that this was the first time he had been in such a position.

Far below them he suddenly heard the sound of chains clanking and the groan of something big moving. He froze and gestured his men to halt. It took its time but then the noise terminated in a deep, wooden *thunk*. The sea-gates had been closed for the night!

One of his men immediately started to move forward, but Jacinto signalled him back down sharply. His instinct was to wait and it proved right. In the distance they suddenly heard the sound of men's voices coming closer, then out of the archway appeared ten men, all big, dark-skinned men like Jacinto and chained ankle to ankle with one another. Herding them along were four men who must also have come from a land far to the south but further east, going by the different reddish cast to their skins. It was these four, chattering carelessly whom they had heard, men elevated from slave status and entrusted with the defences against casual pirating by the Attacotti.

Jacinto was about to let the men go past before he moved – for one on one odds were not what he wanted with novice soldiers – until one of the four drew back his arm and lashed out with a long leather whip at the slaves. It was done with casual indifference and for no apparent reason, another of the four shouting, "Im*aa*shi! Im*aa*shi!" at them, with gestures of irritation. Jacinto guessed this meant 'get a move on', and was just thinking they would not be lingering, when one of the slaves turned so that Jacinto could see his face. The look of pure hatred which he and two more of the slaves shot at the four changed Jacinto's mind. Here were men who *would* fight the DeÁine if given half a chance!

Swiftly gesturing to his men to go for the four unfettered men, Jacinto levered himself up into a crouch and loosened the knife at his belt. One last glance back to make sure that the others were similarly prepared, and he was off in a sprint. Better than three to one, he thought in near panic as he forced his legs to run even faster. Surely they could not fail ...could they?

Up on the ridge Will and Saul gasped in horror as they saw Jacinto break cover closely followed by his men.

"What the fuck is he doing?" Dusty swore in disbelief, and there were other murmurs of worry, until they saw Jacinto plough into one of the guards and strike upwards with his knife before the man had even registered he was there. Before Jacinto's men had even got to the two men in front, the slaves had taken one look at what was happening to the rear and took action of their own. The leading slave yanked hard on the chain at his wrist which linked him to their persecutors. His fellow leading slaves had shuffled rapidly forward so that two others lent their weight to the tug which nearly took the guard off his feet. As the guard stumbled backwards he was dragged into the clutches of the slaves, and all anyone on the ridge saw was fists battering down on him and his fellow leader, who had been seized by the arm and then hauled in too by the slaves.

From their vantage point, Will and the others saw Jacinto come forward and make pacifying gestures to the slaves, and then bend to start feeding the chain out from the ankle fetters.

"Flaming Underworlds! He got that right!" Teryl exclaimed, while Will's face broke into a grin as he said,

"Now those are the kind of men I want fighting with me!"

They saw Jacinto stop the slaves from running off down the road and gesture up the hill towards their force, after which the ten freed men began to climb up through the bracken towards them.

"Trip, get yourself down to those men!" Will called out. "Try speaking in our tongue first, but use DeÁine if you have to to make yourself understood. I'm guessing that you aren't fluent enough for them to worry that you're the real thing?"

Trip shook his head and called over his shoulder as he set off at a trot with Cody, "No way! I've got an accent as thick as treacle, or so the novices we rescued at Tokai said!"

Will found his vision flicking between Trip and Cody, who seemed to be communicating through a mixture of words and gestures, and Jacinto's party, who had now retraced their steps and were at the archway. Now came the hard bit, for Jacinto's men disappeared from sight into the gloom, and all Will could do was sit and wait and hope that they heard no alarm bells being rung.

Deep in the gloom of the great stone buttress, Jacinto was being very cautious. At each bend he was checking very carefully that there was nobody beyond. Yet to his relief and surprise, they seemed to be alone in the vast edifice. The only men in there appeared to have been the crew to winch the sea-gates shut, and once that was done their duties were over. At the end of a long corridor, with several right-angled bends put in to aid defenders, they first came to a flight of spiral stairs leading downwards. Four men went down to scout it out but reported that it only led to the winch room, and that was deserted. Carefully creeping forward they got to a doorway out onto the drawbridge.

"This can't be right," Jacinto whispered to the two men closest to him. "Surely they would guard this crossing. Look about the place and see if we've missed something."

He stood in the gloom of the doorway watching the opposite tower carefully. If it was a true mirror of the one he was in it might give him a clue, and then as his eyes travelled upwards he saw it. Way up above them, but still well below the top of the tower, there was a gallery. That they had known about from up on the hillside, for it had shown up as a black slit in the stonework. Thick chains dangled down from it and were presumably used for securing the drawbridges when in the upright position. What they had not seen was that there were sentries walking back and forth inside the gallery.

Dipping back into the gloom, Jacinto nearly collided with a man coming to tell him that they had found the stairs leading upwards. Jacinto raced for the stairs, taking them two at a time as he heard the man telling him that they had killed the two sentries above them.

"Quick!" he called out as he panted his way upwards. "Someone get their jackets and helms off them and take their place!"

He bounded into the gallery, and then, keeping well back pushed and shoved the man nearest to the right size into the one sentry's uniform. The other dead sentry was a dark-skinned man and Jacinto realised with a jolt that he would have to take this one's place. Rapidly shrugging into the tunic top and donning the strange helm, he walked right to the edge of the gallery and waved to the two men opposite, who had spotted something was amiss and were now peering at them trying to see into the dark space. In a sudden burst of inspiration, he mimed someone being very sick and then gestured to his other 'sentry', who caught on and leaned theatrically over the parapet as if resting his head on the cool stone.

With shakings of their heads, the other two turned and began their constant pacing to and fro again. Jacinto timed his pacing to match theirs and then began to issue orders.

"You four, get back up to General Montrose as fast as you can, but stay low in the bracken so that those two won't see you. Tell him we have this side secured, but that we'll have to wait until dusk to take the other side. The only way we can get to them is across the drawbridge, so that will have to be when it's dark enough for someone to creep across. Tell him the good thing is that the drawbridge has sides, so it's not totally exposed. I'd guess it's to stop people falling off the edge, but it'll serve us well! The rest of you, except for you," he singled one man out, "get down to the archway and watch for any relief troops coming. Those slaves must have been being taken somewhere on this side of the river, so where there's one lot there might be more.

"Now then," he said to the man who still lurked in the gloom behind himself and the other 'sentry'. "You'll wait here out of sight in case I need to send a message in a hurry. I daren't leave this gallery now without giving the game away, so you'll have to relay messages for me."

The thought that there might be more slaves had already occurred to Will, and for once he had insisted on taking the lead. Using mixed communications, they had elicited from the slaves that there were, indeed, more of them further up the valley. With Will, Trip, Toby and Newt acting in the stead of the slave-drivers, they got the freed slaves to show them the way. They marched in their lines once more but without the shackles. It was taking a chance, but Will could not find a way to ask the slaves to let them chain their ankles again. Nobody would believe someone on such short acquaintance that they would be released again, and it would more likely sour their fragile union. He just hoped the long grass would disguise the fact until it was too late. In the scrubby bracken and stunted shrubs off the path, Kym and Teryl were leading covert parties of twenty men each on either side in support.

Trip and Toby were at the back of the column so that their bows would not be seen until the last minute. It made them no less effective at despatching the two guards who stood at the doorway to a large barn, just over the brow from where they had been, and who were staring at them with some impatience.

"Oh dear, are we making them late for supper?" chuckled Newt. "Never mind, they won't be waiting much longer!"

The two great bows sang out and the guards stopped worrying about everything permanently. Leaving the slaves behind, the Order men now streamed forward and surrounded the stone and wood barn. Once upon a time it must have been used for storing the grain brought in from the fertile fields of the delta, for it stood on land high enough not to flood, and far enough from the town around the port for it not to be in danger of any fire which might catch amongst the crowded houses there. In the near distance they could see a second barn, but there was no danger from that one. Its doors stood open and the roof was partly off, exposing the walls to the elements which in turn had destroyed the in-fill between the oak beams on the seaward side, enabling Will's men to see it was empty.

However, the barn they now surrounded was clearly far from empty going by the sound of men's voices from within.

"I think those are more slaves," Newt whispered to Will. "It sounds like the same language our friends over there were using..."

He got no further because the slaves they had rescued had not stopped, but had walked up to the door and now marched in as though they were returning as usual, heads suddenly dropped and more of a shuffle returning into their steps. Once inside, though, something was called out in an unfamiliar language, and all of a sudden mayhem broke out. Men could be heard screaming in agony, and there was much noise of scuffling and thumping. Before Will's men had got to the door the sounds were stopping, and as they flung the double doors wide open a bloody sight greeted them. The slaves had evidently only needed that small sign to take their fate into their own hands. It was impossible to tell how many must be huddled in the dank conditions which stank dreadfully, but the fate of the guards was easy to see. The near pulverised corpses of eight men lay near the door, unrecognisable as anything human anymore except by their clothing. Slaves crouched around them with feral snarls on their faces as they blinked in the sudden light as the setting sun shone straight into the barn.

"Sacred Root and Branch!" Teryl gulped and looked away fast.

Will grimaced and called over his shoulder in a tight voice, "Newt, Trip, get talking to those we freed and fast! Get them to tell their fellow prisoners we mean them no harm!"

He gestured his own men to retreat to outside the doors and back a way. There was the possibility that the slave men, having been driven to the limits of their endurance and sanity, might not find it easy to distinguish between Islanders and DeÁine. In the brief inspection he had been able to make, Will was also fairly sure that there were over a hundred men crammed into the stinking barn. More than enough to completely overwhelm him and this small party of men by sheer weight of numbers. He looked to where Newt and Trip were in hurried conversation, if you could call it that, with the two men who had appeared to be senior amongst the slaves Jacinto had freed.

They clearly made some headway, for the two slaves and then all ten of the freed men began calling out to their companions. The atmosphere shifted, and although it was far from relaxed, Will sensed that it had moved away from the explosive tension following on from the murder of the guards. He still found himself holding his breath as Trip and Newt walked into the mass of slaves with their hands held high. Both men were accompanied by one of the slaves they had been talking to, and then bent down and seemed to be examining something.

"General? Can you come and have a look at this?" Trip called back to Will. "We seem to have a bit of a problem."

Smothering his instincts to run in the opposite direction, Will squared his shoulders and marched in, hoping he looked too much of the soldier to provoke an unsolicited attack. When he got to Trip, he saw that the archer was holding the end of one of the chains, which was linking more slaves together than he could distinguish, and was embedded in the wall.

"Can you feel if this has been done with DeÁine magic?" Toby asked. "I can't make out how the end is held. It goes straight into this old stone, so it's not like a bolt loop built into a wall."

Will could see what he meant. The iron loop at the end of the chain was projecting at right-angles to the wall, but if it was held there by one of the DeÁine's spells or by something else was impossible to see. He reached out cautiously but could feel nothing. Grasping the ring he could still feel nothing of the swirling sensations and nausea he was coming to associate with proximity to the Power.

"If it was done by the Abend then I can't feel any residue," he told his audience. Straightening, he looked around him at the sea of desperate and expectant faces, some of them gaunt to the point of being skeletal. "Is there a bloody big hammer or a pick around here?" he asked.

It was a question the two Order men had real trouble translating, but Teryl heard and went exploring outside, coming back clutching heavy tools which they guessed must have been used for rock breaking.

"Why in the Islands do they need rock?" Teryl asked, perplexed. "It's not like the DeÁine are known for their building works! Even the roads are going to wrack and ruin!"

"Possibly for ballast in the ships' holds," Will suddenly realised. "It would depend on what they were taking out. Light stuff, like some of the plants that get used in dying wool, fetch a good price, but you could have a whole hold full and have not much weight. So they must put stones in the holds to make the ship steer better, especially in rough weather. I saw ships using stone ballast offloading sometimes in Rheged, and I once asked a captain why we were importing rocks into an island stuffed with mountains – that's how I found out. But never mind that now! Let's see if the picks will shift these bolts."

He picked a good hefty pick with a decent pointed head and weighed it in his hands. "Get them to turn away," he told Trip. "I don't want anyone blinded by flying shards of stone!"

Trip and Newt mimed ducking out of the way of flying bits. The slaves caught on quickly, proving that many must have been doing the backbreaking work and knew the dangers of old, and hurried words in their own tongue prompted those who did not know better.

Swinging the pick up, Will brought it down in a mighty blow. He was half expecting it to bounce off some unseen warding and waited to feel the jarring up his arms. To his surprise the pick bit deep into the stone, and a

83

chunk broke off revealing that the loop had a long spike welded to it which was driven deep into the block of stone. The sigh which went up from the slaves was one of relief, and Will turned back, grinning.

"Get the rest of the tools in here!" he ordered those outside, as an eager slave took the pick out of his hands. "These lads can free themselves now there aren't guards to take the tools off them and whip them if they move. Let them have all the tools but I want every one of you outside. I don't want any of you to end up with a pick embedded in your back because one of these men is teetering on the brink of insanity. Let's wait for them to come to us outside."

When the slave men came stumbling out into the light it was clear that many were in no condition to fight. They hung on to friends, and four had to be actually carried out – these four having dreadful suppurating wounds which stank badly, leading the experienced soldiers to suspect that they might be suffering from gangrene. Toby went to look them over as a gesture of goodwill and concern, but turned back shaking his head regretfully, although the slaves did not seem surprised or upset that their rescuers could do nothing to save their companions. With more negotiating led by Trip and Newt, by virtue of communicating with their own strange mixture of DeÁine and Islander, they finally ended up with some twenty slaves who would stay behind and wait by the barn for now. The rest, some hundred men, to Will's astonishment were all for coming with him to fight.

As they led their newest recruits back to where a very nervous Saul waited with the remaining men, Trip and Newt questioned them further.

"They're all from the same place on the coast of the southern seas," Trip came to tell Will. "It's no wonder they look quite alike. There are men from about six extended families in amongst this lot. Most of them are each related to at least half a dozen others!"

"Will they really fight *with* us?" Will asked softly, just in case some of them understood more Islander than they were letting on. "I don't want them following us to the quays and then buggering off on some killing frenzy against the ordinary townsfolk, or legging it for a ship at the first chance."

"For now, yes, I think they will," Trip answered cautiously. "However, I wouldn't count on them staying to fight the new DeÁine threat. They might offer, but if I can advise you, General, I wouldn't try to force them to stay."

Will flickered a hint of a smile and gave the smallest nod of agreement. "Point taken, and offer advice whenever you want. What about if we offer them a ship when we've taken the quays? Could they cope with that? I don't want them to drown in the excitement of being free."

"Oh I think they'll probably bite your hand off for that. They've already said that many of them were fishermen, so I don't think there'd be much danger of them wrecking a ship."

"Then let's make that a plan. Not the big cargo ships. I have something in mind for them. But there were a couple of middling sized ships in port. They can take one or both of those, and it'll look better if we offer them rather than them feeling they have to fight us for them."

Over in the gatehouse Jacinto was getting very twitchy. As the daylight faded, across in the opposite gallery the guards began to put shutters up, sealing the gallery off.

"Shit! They must shut the whole place up at night!" he fumed. "We daren't let them haul up the drawbridge!" He looked to his fellow acting guard. "I think you should start to behave very sick. Go and stand right by the balcony wall and then when one of them looks at you, clap your hand over your mouth and make a dash back into the gloom. That way it'll be more convincing if I'm slower than them getting these shutters up."

He turned in his prowling up and down and then spoke to the messenger. "Run like mad to General Montrose and tell him to get some extra men down here now! We might have to make a dash across and immobilise those sentries before it gets much darker!"

Stood there alone in view, Jacinto got all of the shutters but the central one in place, each a little behind those on the far side. Suddenly a gong was struck somewhere in the town, its metallic note ringing out in the quiet evening air. Across the way the other sentry now appeared gesturing them to hurry up with signs of considerable annoyance.

"Bugger! That must have been summoning them to the evening meal or something," Jacinto growled, and stuffed the last panel into place. "Come on! We'll have to take them now or never!"

He shoved the last shutter in place and sprinted for the stairs, bounding down with the other man in hot pursuit. At the bottom he whistled to the four men by the archway and with his sword drawn gestured them to follow. As they got to the drawbridge Jacinto grabbed the man in the sentrie's tunic and hauled his arm over his shoulder.

"Go limp, man! Like I'm half carrying you! The rest of you in single file, and stay in my shadow until we're almost at the door."

He set out across the drawbridge with the limp man hanging onto Jacinto and the side rail, keeping his head bowed so that it was not visible that he was far from sickly. They had got two thirds of the way across when an irate man came trotting out of the far doorway, muttering under his breath but showing no signs of seeing anything wrong. Jacinto held his men back until the man was almost upon them and then waved the men forward, dropping his 'sick' friend and bringing his sword up as he leapt forward to run the man through. The others tore into the far tower and after a brief scuffle there was silence.

"How many?" Jacinto demanded, waving his men to be quiet as excited chatter began.

"Only the two up here," someone reported.

"Right. Doesn't mean there's nobody on sentry duty down below," Jacinto pointed out, for the far tower differed in one respect from the one they had come from. Whereas their tower had its opening high up, giving onto the bare hillside, this one had its entrance several floors down, as Jacinto had observed from his vantage point on the balcony. He was just contemplating what to do, when the sound of running feet alerted him to new arrivals coming across the drawbridge.

"Alright?" Trip's familiar voice came at his elbow a moment later.

"Don't know," Jacinto said tersely and explained the situation as Kym arrived with Newt, Busby and Colum.

He had barely finished when an annoyed call came from below.

"What's that?" Jacinto whispered.

"He says why haven't we pulled up the drawbridge," Trip translated.

"Right, we need to get down there and shut them up before they alert the whole town," Kym decided, and without further prompting the Order men flitted past like ghosts and disappeared down the stairs. Signalling the men behind him – of whom there was now a substantial number – to silence, Jacinto began to lead the way down after Kym's men. He gave them time to do their stuff, for nothing would hamper them more than having novices getting in the way. Sure enough, four bodies lay piled into a corner of a small square guardroom by the door out onto a fortified wall. The wall seemed to run around the cliff as some sort of protection for the quays below.

"Let's keep moving," Jacinto said. "I've a nasty feeling that there might be sentries around at the next door we come to too. They seem to lock the place up in some kind of sequence."

With him in the lead still in his borrowed uniform, the Order men hurried around the bend as if men in a hurry for their meal. Someone called out to them from inside the gloom and Trip answered with a couple of words. But there was no time to translate before they were inside and fighting hard again. This was not a long fight, either, but someone down in the town called up and Trip had to hurriedly reply, then reached for the door and slammed it shut turning the key in the lock and sealing himself with Jacinto and Newt on the outside and the rest within.

"He was asking why we were taking so long locking up," he whispered a few seconds later after shouting down again and receiving a reply. "I told him we'd be on our way, and he said he wasn't waiting any longer for his dinner!"

As he was doing this he was gently easing the key in the lock again to unlock it, then swung the door open again very softly. Kym had clearly caught on to what was happening and had everyone inside silent. Very quietly now, they all began to creep along the parapet until it came to a flight of stone steps which led down to the quays through a stone archway. Again the four Order enlisted men went on alone and checked out the arch, Colum then briefly appearing and signalling that there had been only one man inside a small guard room, and he was now dead.

Not daring to go any further until they knew what was expected, the main force huddled along the wall's parapet out of sight. Luckily, Will was not long in coming.

"Well done, lad!" he said, clapping Jacinto on the arm. "Nice work!" He edged past and went down to the archway and then returned. "Right! Kym, lead these lads round to the left, back under this wall. There are two big ships tied up there. Get on board and get them secured. You know what we discussed on the way down – if there are slaves set them free, if there are soldiers kill them unless they surrender straight away."

He pulled Jacinto to one side as Kym and his men took their soldiers out and away, Toby bringing up the rear and exchanging places with Trip to reunite Kym's lance. Now Jacinto heard a second force coming. One less disciplined, even allowing for the new recruits, and it occurred to him that a good hundred men had gone with Kym. Allowing for some experienced men staying to watch their retreat, just in case, there still seemed far more footsteps than he had expect.

"Slaves," Will's bass voice rumbled softly by his ear. "Dead keen on slaughter, so we'll have to direct them away from the townsfolk." A soft bird call came on the breeze and Will nodded. "Right, that's Teryl saying they're all behind us and ready! Come on, let's go and find this evening meal!"

With men of their own army on the outer edges, and the freed slaves forming an inner core to the column, they hurried through the darkening town. Nobody looked out of a window, nobody made a sound. The locals had presumably learned harsh lessons about displaying curiosity over the activities of their DeÁine overlords. Yet this contributed to the DeÁine's men's downfall, for the noise of them gathered in their hall was easily heard through the near-silent town, guiding their slayers to them without diversions. At the hall, all Will did was signal his men to peel off left and right, and then when a press of the slaves was right at the outer doors, he and Busby grabbed the handles and flung them wide open. Jacinto and the others never even got a chance to see inside before the slaves streamed past them, brandishing hammers, axes and picks and any other weapon they could lay their hands on.

Going by the sounds from inside it was utter slaughter, making Jacinto look askance to Will.

"I know, it's brutal," Will admitted, "but they would've gone after their persecutors whatever we'd said or done. This way, at least those who are suffering actively helped the DeÁine nobles subdue the people. I certainly don't have any intention of sending any of our men in there, even after they've done! Clearing that place can wait until tempers have subsided." He glanced briefly into the hall again. "Festering Underworlds!"

He could see the slaves disregarding the bodies, which were everywhere, in order to get to the food. Men were stuffing handfuls of bread into their mouths and shovelling up spoonfuls of the stew from bowls, regardless of whether the former consumer was lying dead across the table beside them. Will beckoned Trip to him.

"You and Jens stay here. I'll leave you about ten men. Just guard this lot. I doubt they'll even think about moving until the food runs out. But if they do, keep them here. Lock the bloody doors if you need to! I don't want them going on the rampage and messing this up now we've got this far. Teryl, bring the rest with me," and Will tapped Jacinto on the arm and beckoned him alongside him at the front.

Moving quickly now, they hurried through the town until they saw the town's land-side gates ahead. Unlike the sea-gate, this was a paltry affair, but Will was taking no chances. He wanted that secure so that nobody would be running off to warn other towns that an enemy was in their midst. As it happened, nobody was there, but Will left Teryl there with some more men for safety's sake. He could now take his time over the ships, time it turned out which he did not need. By the time they had got back to the quays, a beaming Kym greeted them and an amazing sight lay before them. Hundreds of people of every size, shape and colour were being led ashore by his men.

"Slave ship!" Kym said with distaste. "The Inchoo had been on a slaving trip. Some of the seamen are Attacotti. They changed sides in a heartbeat. They're the ones who told us that these folk were picked up in their villages by some of their own and brought to the coast. The one old sailor says that all the DeÁine do is collect them and pay for them. Apparently the DeÁine have made it such a lucrative business that they don't need to get their hands dirty doing the actual taking. We've got a couple of senior men and also the addresses of the Inchoo who are here in the town. The docks are secured already," he could not resist adding with a grin.

"Marvellous!" Will grinned back. "Then I think it's time we called on our Inchoo friends! Get forty of the steady men. I'm going after them with plenty in case there are Hunters about."

"There are," Kym confirmed. "Luckily the Maj'ore and some of the other Inchoo are still at sea, so the family's twenty triads are well spread out. There were two triads on each ship, but one's gone to accompany an Inchoo to Bruighean. Apparently they have to inform the royals of how many slaves they have and pay a tax on them. Another triad has gone with another of the family to the Souk'ir headquarters somewhere east of here to do the same for the Souk'ir taxes. So there are six triads spread out between four Inchoo mansions. Luckily for us, the big man in the family doesn't live here in the town, so he's got two with him about a mile out on the road north. The others will be somewhere in three big town houses up on the hill."

He gestured inland to where the town walls swept away from the water as the land rose. Going by lights now twinkling in windows, it was possible to see where the more prosperous houses lay, up on high ground and distant from the smells and noises of the docks.

"Right," Will said with gleeful savagery, "let's go and get rid of these vermin!"

It was a series of short but violent encounters, but by a turn of the hourglass later Will had control of Sabac and all that lay within it. The Hunters had been overwhelmed by sheer weight of numbers, as ten or twelve of the soldiers piled onto them. The experiences of Kuzmin had taught them just how fearsome the Hunters were, and none felt foolish for shortening the odds by fighting less than honourably. As he sat with his boots up on a beautifully polished table, staring at a quivering Inchoo held by two scowling soldiers, Will felt something like relief. This at least was something like what he had hoped to achieve. If he could hold onto the ships too, then that would really give him something to work with. Now he could sail into Paks with all his men hidden away and really surprise any DeÁine force there. All that remained in doubt now was how many men he would gain in real terms for his army.

He looked at the calendar carved into the wall by some former Attacotti lord who had built this place. He had a week to get to his rendezvous with Labhran at Choa, or at least that was when he had said he should be there. He was now thinking it might take Labhran even longer than he had estimated to get there if they were encountering anything like the same repressed locals as he had. That was not good news. It gave him a month, if he was lucky, before they might see the first of the DeÁine ships. They had to move faster. Much faster! Had to convince people quicker that they should be joining the fight. And somewhere in all of this he had to start training men to fight. He sighed and levered himself up onto his feet to confront this cursed member of the DeÁine, without whose Spirits-forsaken race none of this would be necessary. It was going to be a long month!

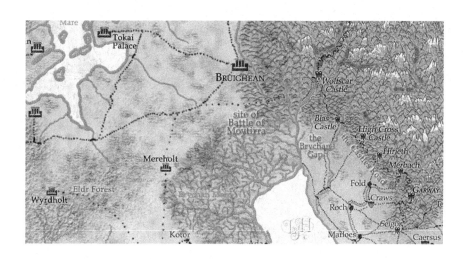

# Chapter 6

## *Beyond the Flood*

### Beltane: New Lochlainn

Ealdorman Eoghan eased his weight on his elbows and privately wished that they were campaigning in slightly warmer conditions. At times like this, age reminded him it was gaining on him through the creaking in his joints. He was currently lying in melting snow alongside his friend and fellow Ealdorman, Allainn, as they stared down at the mighty DeÁine citadel of Bruighean. Once they had heard from Berengar that the Abend were out and about following his encounter with Tancostyl, Allainn had badgered Eoghan into bringing their men out in force westwards.

"Can we take it?" Eoghan's second-in-command, Pirinne, asked softly from another snowy hillock to their right.

"It looks very devoid of any elite Jundises," a young captain commented from the other side, observations which Eoghan was having to rely on younger men's eyesight for. He could see the citadel alright, and movement within it, but not sufficiently well to make those kinds of distinctions.

"So we believe it?" he said quietly to Allainn. "Not only the Abend gone but the Donns' family armies too?"

Allainn turned to him with a savage grin. "Almost too good to be true, isn't it! I say we do it! At least we can retreat into the mountains with all this snow still lying so deep if we have to."

Following the first massive wave of flood waters coming down the valleys, the melt was progressing at a steady rate, but the sheer volume of snow encased in the depths of the mountain range meant that it was going to be a very long time before the mountains were truly free of snow. The Order's fortress in the midst of the mountains at Esgair might well be sealed off for weeks even now – if indeed it had actually survived, for no word had come from the mountain fastness yet, and there was the serious worry that all there might have been buried alive under the weight of snow that had engulfed them. In part, this was what had prompted Allainn to press so hard for getting their men out on manoeuvres. Esgair was their link to the northern fortresses, and without it there was no way of knowing how bad things might be on the frontier at Borth Castle, or even worse, at Clodoch or Peruga. If they could operate on the DeÁine's side of the border, Allainn had argued, then it could solve their vital communications problems.

As a result, the men from both Blass and Wolfscar had donned their woven willow and hazel snowshoes, and made the gruelling four day march over the watershed which separated the Islanders' Water of Sgair river from the tributaries of the DeÁine-held River Vaii. They had come armed and ready to fight – had the DeÁine still been here in numbers – to allow them to get back to the safety of their castles, but as it stood, there was a more optimistic use for all the arrows, spears and swords. The tented city which normally encircled the great citadel had shrunk to a fraction of its normal size, and some time ago going by the way the grass was starting to grow again in patches.

"There might be a lot of people in that place, but the number of fighting men can't be that great," Allainn said with conviction. "Let's go!" and he turned and signalled to those captains who were only a few paces behind him, and who passed the signal on.

Like wolves through the snow, the Knights and their men padded almost noiselessly down the slopes, spread out in informal groups to avoid setting the loose snow cascading beneath them. All were dressed in the pale linen over-jerkins which they used for scouting in during the winter, and as a result, from a distance they were virtually indistinguishable from the snow clad countryside they moved through. As they got down from the last of the foothills and in amongst the scrubby woodland, they paused and took off the snowshoes, which were carefully stacked behind bushes and trees where they could be retrieved if need be. Carrying them further if there was fighting to be done was not practical, and most of the men shed the off-white and grey patched over-jerkins too. Now the white would single them out amid the spring greenery instead of keeping them hidden.

By the time the lead men had reached the edge of the woodland, even the optimistic Allainn was having trouble believing their luck in not being spotted. Not a man spoke, and with hand-signals he directed several companies to investigate the remaining tented encampment. Within minutes a man had scurried back and was whispering his report to Allainn.

"There are probably about three thousand slaves of one kind or another still in the camp," he told the ealdormen. "Commander Ellis says that he can see the insignia of the royal household on most of the slaves closest to the main city gates. Commander Lackland says that over to the right there are slaves of the Propp, Tomasch, Buelna, and the Barthees, but no sign of the Jundises to go with them."

"The little men," Eoghan mused. "Only the most minor of families who have to stick with the royals and can't swim the rougher political tides. Well they shouldn't be too much of a problem. I know our intelligence from right in the citadel isn't wonderful anymore, but we know they struggled in the past to afford a full Jundis each. What's the betting there's only about half a one each in there? Maybe less if the royals have decided to back the Abend and have sent the minors east with their blessing."

"So the palace guards are the main thing we have to worry about," Allainn agreed. He turned back to the messenger. "Tell Ellis and Lackland they can attack when ready. Have Pirinne hold his men ready in case they need support." He turned to where Eoghan's other commander, Niles, waited silently beside him. "Come on, we're going for the gate!"

If they were spotted now nothing would disguise what they were up to, and so Allainn and half of the men from Wolfscar ran openly towards the towering walls. Eoghan had willingly delegated such manoeuvres to the younger Allainn, and stayed back to act as co-ordinator. Once in the lee of the walls it would be much harder for anyone within to see them, and it made sense to minimise the time they were exposed. Allainn dared to hope they had got away with it completely, but just as the final companies were half way across the open space, he heard urgent calls coming from far above in one of the two enormous towers which faced the mountains.

"Crap!" Allainn muttered. "I'd hoped we could get closer to the gates before they caught on. ...Run men! To the gates as fast as you can!"

A thousand men ran like mad, pelting around the part circle from the corner tower and past the three lesser ones in the circuit, until they came to the vast oval gatehouses. The men attacking the camps must have been alerted to their fellows' actions, for there was a sudden outbreak of sounds of fighting as they ceased trying to be subtle about subduing the encampment. Speed was now of the essence not stealth. Somewhere sunk within the complex a deep bell began a monotonous tolling, and as Allainn and his men got to the gates, they heard the creaking of machinery and saw the gates beginning to swing inwards.

Sword in hand, Allainn led his men on an assault of those DeÁine hurriedly assembling in the closing gap. For a brief few minutes it seemed like they would affect an entry into the stronghold, as the less experienced DeÁine fell beneath their swords. However Allainn spotted the palace guards approaching down several streets, and had to make a decision. He could not hope to get all of his battalion inside before the gates closed, and a couple of companies were not enough to fight their way through that many DeÁine and reopen the gates for them. He would be sending them to the slaughter, and just at the moment this was not the only nut they had to crack, even had such a costly gestured ever been acceptable.

"Fall back!" he yelled. "Fall back! Don't get caught behind the gates!"

Slowly but inexorably the enormous copper-plated gates swung to, and finally closed with a decisive thud. An eerie silence descended, punctuated only by cries and groans from the camp behind them.

"Move back in case they start throwing things at us from off what passes for the parapets," Allainn told them. "Just because this thing doesn't have proper battlements doesn't mean they might not get inventive."

Yet nothing happened, and by the time the three other commanders had joined up with him, and Eoghan had come down too, there still had not been a peep from those now holed up inside the citadel.

"Now what?" Niles asked, perplexed. "We can hardly mount a proper siege of a place the size of that. Even if we could get our trebuchets down here from the mountains, they aren't big enough to make an impact on these walls."

It was Eoghan who was now decisive. "I'll stay here with Niles' battalion," he declared. "We can patrol this easily when there's nothing around to threaten us. Pirinne can take his men and go north. A full battalion should have nothing to fear from anything the DeÁine have left here in New Lochlainn. If they can get hold of boats, they can be at the coast in no time and find out how the north fares.

"If all's well there, then I'm sure Errol and Phineus would welcome the chance to come and join the fighting, and with their men we can think about a serious assault on this monster. We can ensure the DeÁine have no place to come back to! I doubt the palace guard will want to try and fight it out with us until then. In fact, I'd suspect that the royal family will want to sit it out in the expectation that the Donns will come and rid them of this pest at their door. They've never been known for their martial skills in the past, so I don't expect young king Ruadan to suddenly take up sabre rattling, or trying to rally his people to deal with us himself. You go and join Berengar, Allainn."

However the younger Ealdorman frowned rather than accepting the chance to flex his muscles in a major battle.

"And which way would I go?" he queried. "Thanks for the thought, Eoghan, but think on this. It would take me the best part of twenty days just to get from here to Laon, which is where we last heard of Berengar. It's the sixth of Beltane today and surely there must be a good melt going on in southern Brychan by now. We know we can't go east overland because of the flooding, but where will the DeÁine go in that case? If there's been the faintest opportunity, I'd bet Berengar's got his force out and in pursuit, but which way? North? South to clear any DeÁine ships? Or down into the far eastern peninsular? I could spend the rest of the month just trying to find him and wearing my men out in the process."

"Well what do you propose doing then? Wait here with me? It seems something of a waste of manpower for our battalions to sit around just watching a fortress we can't take alone. Even if Berengar's got some men from the north, he could still do with you."

Allainn grinned. "I wasn't thinking of sitting around, I was thinking of going south."

"South?" Niles questioned.

Lackland was also looking puzzled, but Ellis' face slowly revealed his understanding even before Allainn explained,

"There's Mereholt for a start. We can reach that in five days' march even with the rivers up! We need to make absolutely sure that no stray member of the Abend has snuck back in there. Berengar thought he had them all accounted for, but we should make sure. Then if there's no trouble there, and I don't have to worry about getting cut off, I shall carry on further south into the townships beyond what was once called the Brychan Mere. Again, we can get to the old northern capital of the fjords in five days. The Maker only knows what remains of Kotor these days, but in the dreadful event of the DeÁine only being driven back to this side of the mountains by Berengar, it would be really good to have some solid intelligence of how things lie in those places we haven't visited in over a generation."

"And they might even be feeling a bit rebellious!" Ellis added with a grin.

"They might indeed!" Allainn agreed and with equal optimism. "I hope we can deny them the New Lochlainn ports to come back to, as well as this place!"

In normal conditions, five days marching might well have taken them to the walls of the ancient palace of Mereholt. However, this time they had to add on two whole days more because they needed to return into the hills to be able to reach a point where they could cross the earliest of the Vaii's tributaries. Luckily, this one rose in the southernmost peaks of the range and had thawed first, so once past the confluence, they were able to rig rope bridges and get across the sodden gorge. Arriving at Mereholt, they discovered that the lovely old building which had once been a great hall of the Attacotti was no longer visible for the excrescent extensions the DeÁine had smothered it in. The scouts sidled up to the walls and made a circuit of them, reporting back that there were just some very bored sentries patrolling outside the main gates. The gates themselves were shut, but the picket gate in the wall beside them was wide open, and someone was handing out food and drink.

"Go!" Allainn ordered, and the scouts spun and signalled to others who were waiting for that sign. Even as Allainn and the leading company hurried out from the scrubby bushes they had lurked behind, another scout was coming back to report on their success. Moments later, Allainn found himself flattened against the side of the double, gated arch, peeking in through the small picket gate. The courtyard beyond was quiet with nothing sounding but some bees buzzing around the blossom on an apple tree. He hand-signed to his men to go in and open the main gates, and an eager young captain with his company slipped inside through the picket into the compound like ghosts. Not only did they get the gates open, but nobody disturbed them in the process. Once in, Allainn had them bolt the gates again. He did not want anyone getting out now and running off with warnings of attacks.

As the men went through the palace with rapid efficiency, it became clear that the only ones here were the resident servants. Most were slaves, but a few others must have been half-breed DeÁine, invested with more authority, and to the last one they put up a spirited fight. It signed their death warrant, and unfortunately also of those slaves who were prodded into resisting along with them. Yet in less than a turn of the hourglass Allainn was in control of the palace, and detailed men off to find somewhere to bury the thirty corpses they had laid out in the central courtyard. The rest of the slaves were herded into another courtyard, and kept under guard until Allainn could be sure that any room he put them in did not have a secret way out.

To their shock, Allainn's men received carefully delivered passwords which marked out three amongst the slaves as remnants of the Covert Brethren. As soon as he knew of this, Allainn arranged to have all the prisoners moved and split into two groups arbitrarily on the way, thus enabling his men to edge the three spies out without it being obvious. One was a woman in the draped robes of a house slave, while the two men had been outside servants. The one had been a gardener and another tended the tame fowl. Allainn kept them separate from one another, for the last thing he wanted was to betray someone who had been loyal to another only masquerading as one of their own. He was alert to the danger of a spy's cover having been compromised, and of someone loyal to the DeÁine thinking that they would take their place, and take other traitors with them to their deaths.

The woman was wizened, made old beyond her years by her long servitude, but there was no mistaking her pride in showing Allainn secret passageway after secret passageway.

"And this one's mine!" she finally declared with pride. She shimmied under the chimney-breast's supporting lintel, and then stood up to take two steps upwards using the decorative brickwork in the side of the hearth. "Follow me!" she called back, as she disappeared from view.

Allainn made to follow her, but Ellis put a restraining hand on his shoulder and ducked under the lintel instead.

"Just in case!" he cautioned. "Anyway, I'm shorter than you. You might get stuck!" and with a cheeky grin disappeared after the woman.

When he returned a few moments later, it was to direct the others to a chamber eight rooms away before disappearing again. As Allainn and twenty men hurried into the room, they heard Ellis' voice calling out,

"I can hear you!"

Allainn looked about him. The room to all intents and purposes appeared to have no windows or anything like a cavity. Through double doors there was a room beyond, with a pool in the centre and the door they had come in by, but that was it.

"Where in the Islands are you?" he called back to Ellis.

"About three feet to your left," the disembodied voice replied. "Woodworm ate through the beams leaving cavities all over the place. Our enterprising lady here chipped away until she'd connected them up to make a big hole she could get through. She says the Abend's head of household used to get his men to tap on the walls to check for cavities, so she left the stuff on the backs of the slabs of marble alone so that it sounded solid still. What she's done is work lots of little holes around the joints of the blocks. Together they're remarkably effective!"

"Why this room?" someone else asked.

"Because it was the room the witches used to come to and do the plotting they wanted no-one to overhear," the woman's voice floated back to them.

"Come back here, you two," Allainn commanded, and when a rather dusty Ellis and the woman reappeared, he looked her straight in the eyes. "How did you get away with this?"

She never flinched away but answered him straight away. "I'm the lowlife who cleans the fireplaces. I do a good job and I can lay a fire that catches first time every time, so I've never been replaced or moved on to another task. I get dirty doing my job and most of the time when the Abend are here I'm working at night. The Maker forbid that one of the Great Ones should see a speck of soot! So I was expected to take myself off somewhere out of sight to sleep, too – just in case there was an inspection of the slave quarters, because they wouldn't have understood why I was being allowed to sleep in the day. I often sat in there all day listening! I was there on the day they decided to move into Brychan. They're after their old Treasures, you know!" She suddenly sighed sadly, reminded by her recollection of that day. "I'd better show you the other graves, too."

Allainn and Ellis exchanged horrified glances. How many might that be? They had already found many small burials within the palace garden walls. They were even more disgusted by the time they had reached the end of her tour. They were facing a large plot of land to the side of the palace, which she told them was the regular burial ground for the slaves. Ellis expressed the view that he was amazed there was anyone left to bury out there after the number they had found inside the palace.

"Don't you believe it," the woman, who by now they knew as Sara, told them. "The slaves buried out here were the lucky ones. The ones who just died through overwork and disease. The ones inside were often tortured. The ones in the last courtyard we went to were the poor lads whom Geitla 'entertained' the last time the witches were here. Helga's pet acolyte killed them all with marsh worms in their ears. I wouldn't dig them up yet if I were you! They'll have become a breeding ground for the worms! That's why they weren't buried too deep. Helga's orders were that sometime around now we were to dig them up and put them into one of the pools, so that the worm's larvae could hatch and she'd have plenty to experiment with. No-one wanted to know who she was going to do the experiments on!"

The older man from the gardens also proved to be the genuine article. His knowledge of the Abend's movements was encyclopaedic, and he was soon sat with one of Lackland's men at a scribe's desk while his information was taken down in the Order's shorthand for future reference. Even if it was only for the record, it would prove valuable as an insight as to how such an enemy thought and reacted once it could be analysed. Nobody even bothered to question whether there would be a later on. If they did not believe in themselves that they could defeat the DeÁine, then they were lost before they started.

Yet the elderly spy was insistent over something quite recent. A message had come in only a handful of days ago which had had the senior servants in a right flap. He was pretty sure it had come from Masanae or Quintillean, and had something to do with someone arriving from the south. He regretted that he could not show them the message, and believed it had been so dangerous that it had been burned – something Sara confirmed independently, having found ashes in a grate she had cleaned out, and which had not had a fire in to account for the small pile of white ashes.

Something about the other man, though, warned Allainn that he was not all he said he was, and they imprisoned him separately until they had time to deal with him. If he was genuine, then he should understand their caution, and part of what niggled at Allainn's instincts was the way the man accepted it without a word, but looked as if he would make a break for freedom at the first chance. No true Covert Brother would be so keen. The pair of Foresters who went to question him also said that they were having to prompt him for information, as though he did not know what would be of interest to the Order.

"What are we going to do about him and the slaves?" Ellis asked Allainn as they sat eating a hearty roast meal, courtesy of the ample supplies the DeÁine had at Mereholt.

Lackland mopped the gravy with a chunk of bread as he spoke. "Given that we're miles from anywhere here, I reckon we could barricade them in and leave them here. They'll have plenty of food and they've got a good clean well – they won't want for anything. I don't see them having the initiative to get themselves out now that the head men are gone."

"I agree," Ellis said. "We can take our two Brethren with us so they'll be safe, but I wouldn't want to be trying to march this lot with us. All they have to do is shamble about and they could delay us endlessly. And as for having them fight, well I for one am not comfortable about that. This lot seem to have been pretty content with their lot. They're more worried about what the Abend will say when they come back and find we've been here, rather than in getting out themselves. They can't seem to conceive of a situation where the Abend *never* come back."

Allainn nodded. "You're only saying what I've been thinking. We'll spend one more day checking this place out in case there's any valuable intelligence we can use. The day after, we'll be gone at dawn, blocking the gates behind us. I want to get down to Kotor and find how things stand with the real people of the south. I'm worried by this message from the Abend. Who or what is coming that has them in such a froth?"

'Wet' was his first impression of how things were in the south when they got there. They had spent a soggy two days marching through the kind of rain which seeped through everything. The steady early summer drizzle which had come in off the southern ocean made their lives uncomfortable in every way possible. It was not helped by the waters of the Brychan Mere being higher than normal, which they guessed was due to the amount of water coming out of the mountains into the bay at the moment and giving the Mere nowhere to drain to, so that they were squelching through mud.

Consequently every man in their battalion was hoping for shelter and the chance to dry out when they got to Kotor, even if it meant taking it by force. The reality was disappointing. The downtrodden folk of the largest town of southern New Lochlainn simply stood in mute resignation as they marched in, which was when it became apparent that they had already lost anything of value a long time ago. Houses leaned ramshackle against one another, and roofs leaked for want of attention, not from laziness but because the poor folk had no means of purchasing the required items to effect even the most basic repairs.

"There has to be somewhere better than this!" the middle-aged archer who was acting as Allainn's personal aide while in the field grumbled, as he looked in vain for a fire to start drying things out in front of. "You can't tell me that these trading DeÁine who control the area live in anywhere like this!"

"No, the Souk'ir will have something far better," Sara confirmed.

Her fellow spy, Moth, agreed as he came back into the house they had temporarily taken shelter in. Being more of a local, he was having greater success in getting information out of the residents than the soldiers, and so Allainn had given him his own guard of a lance and sent them out to discover what they could.

"The locals say that the Souk'ir as a complete DeÁine-cast run Kotor, not one of the families. It's to do with the skilled sword-makers they've got here, apparently. Anyway, there's a Souk'ir guildhouse just outside the town on the south side. We're likely to find several triads of Hunters there, though."

"Hunters?" Lackland perked up. This was more like it!

Allainn looked around at the way everyone had suddenly forgotten about being wet and hungry, and smiled. "A night attack, then, I think, don't you lads?"

The grins and muttered assents were only so muted because they were all ferreting in bags for cloths to dry weapons with as best they could, while the archers dug into inside pockets to check that they could get to the bowstrings they had been careful to keep dry, even if nothing else was.

The entire force crept silently through the streets until they were at the outer limit of the town. There they could see the hall, for it stood in splendour a short way off, a spiteful statement of luxury given the conditions the people lived in. Not that Allainn believed for one second that the DeÁine had thought about what the local folk thought of the hall. The Souk'ir were more likely out to impress the other DeÁine, and they had not spared the expenses, for the hall was huge and ornately decorated. Allainn signalled to his men to surround the place and the men filtered off into the gloom, out of his sight even though he knew where to look. He had no worries that anyone in the hall would spot them either. These DeÁine were far too complacent here to place guards against the ordinary citizens, and besides, with two thousand men at his back, he was vastly over-numbered to take one mansion house, however grand.

Skirmishing forwards, Allainn got up to the walls of the hall. This close to he could feel that beneath the outer white-painted surface there were blocks of local stone, but nothing ragged enough to give a climber purchase. They would have to go in through the doors and windows on the ground floor, and work their way up through the four other floors. He passed the word and heard crashes as the luxurious lead-paned glass windows were smashed. Not something his men were used to doing. Most of the places they attacked would have had stout wooden shutters in place – much harder to burst through! He grinned as he heard the sounds of fighting breaking out, then wasted no time in joining in, once a man had opened the back door he had been waiting by.

Inside, the rooms were lit by chandeliers containing dozens of candles. Another massive statement of wealth, for even in the palaces of the great within the Islands, on a day to day basis such a waste of precious good candles would not have been considered. It made passage across the floor a little hazardous, as the chandeliers were now swaying in the breeze coming in through the smashed windows, and a light rain of molten wax was dripping down as the candles guttered and spluttered as a result. Allainn swore as a hot droplet hit him on the back of the neck, but was then too busy fending off an irate servant armed with a carving knife to worry about any more falling on him. He ran the servant through, then ran towards a door in the far wall which had been flung open, revealing more serious fighting beyond.

He emerged into a dining room where Hunters were slowly being subdued and then killed by his men. It was bloody work and he knew he was going to have some serious casualties amongst his men in here. There was no room for them to overwhelm the Hunters by weight of numbers, although some of the archers had begun to make good use of the height a minstrel's gallery afforded high up on the left-hand wall. It was messy work here, but they did not need him to tell them what to do, and he moved on. Another room revealed more Hunters, who must have quit the dining room and come to play dice and board games, going by the pieces he found himself trampling on as he skirted the fighting. A room beyond again, and he found what he was looking for. A DeÁine in opulent clothing lay sprawled face down in a puddle of blood from where the fighting had passed over him. The torch he had had in his hand had been stamped out, but there was no mistaking his intentions. A huge desk and two cabinets were stuffed with scrolls. No doubt secret papers relating to the Souk'ir which the man had intended to destroy.

Allainn picked his way around to the desk and began sifting through the papers. By the time Lackland came to find him, Allainn had pulled up the great upholstered chair and begun reading in earnest.

"I was going to ask if you'd had any joy, but clearly you have," Lackland observed, picking up a fancy latticework chair from against the wall and coming to sit opposite his ealdorman. Then noticed how worried Allainn looked as he answered.

"Oh yes! Very informative! The DeÁine here are far from pleased about something Quintillean has done. That message we heard about? It's about *more* DeÁine coming from over the sea!"

"What?"

"I know! I can't work out how many, but these traders are pretty horrified. There's no love lost between the families involved, and there are records here of messages sent out to the other Souk'ir from the Dracma and the Tabor. Apparently Masanae and Quintillean have demanded a fighting force to depart with them from the Dracma's ports. These messages say that they aren't happy about it, but have gone along to protect the Souk'ir's interests."

"A fighting force?" Ellis repeated, as he came in to join them too. "Does that mean that there aren't likely to be any of the Souk'ir's Jundises around?"

Allainn's grin was vulpine as he pulled a map out from beneath the papers he had unrolled. "We never knew much about the Souk'ir before because they've always used their fighters for their expeditions abroad, not against us – except at Moytirra, of course. But since then they've stayed away from the frontier, so we have very little intelligence about them, other than what the Covert Brethren were able to glean for us. Since Gavra Pass destroyed that source we've been very much in the dark, but it's good news now! Our two unloved Abend got a pair of Jundises each out of the Tabor and Dracma only a week back, and a Seljuq each too.

"Once upon a time that would have been only half of their force, but we've been making deeper cuts into their armies than we thought. In this area I'll doubt we'll see any others, although if we go west we might not be so lucky with the Chowlai. The Inchoo and Bernien are apparently away! But even then I doubt they'll have as many men as they used to have. You see the royals and the Donns have been making heavy demands on them for replacements to hold the Brychan Line, or whatever they call it. That means that torn between making a profit out of the other DeÁine, and having to spend money on keeping a fighting force for themselves, they've sold the produce of the training camps on every time."

"And the camps?" Ellis asked breathlessly, almost unable to believe their luck. "Are the camps at Endrod as we thought?"

"Endrod and Tisza," Allainn supplied, his grin getting wider. "The two towns nearest to here!"

"We won't be able to let Berengar know that we've eliminated this particular threat," Lackland said with regret. "It would've been nice to take that off his mind, even if we can't do anything else. Dare I ask how many men the Souk'ir have in training there?"

Allainn's enthusiasm waned slightly, but only for a moment. "The good news is that they were expecting several new shipments of slaves any day from the Inchoo and the Bernien. The bad news is that there are about five thousand still in the camps in varying stages of training."

Ellis looked aghast. "You surely don't mean to take us up against five to two odds against us?"

Now Allainn was deadly serious. "If Berengar has to fight the Abend in Brychan without us, what kind of odds do you think he'll be facing? We can't expect him not to suffer casualties going against the Abend around Arlei." Ellis and Lackland looked suitably chastened, but Allainn had not finished. "And what if the Abend survive to fight another day? Now there are these newcomers too. They worry me. They're so much of an unknown quantity. I fear that if we're ever to chisel the DeÁine out of New Lochlainn, then we have to do more than defeat them in Brychan. We have to free New Lochlainn now, while they're distracted and before any reinforcements come. That way we can deny them the chance to land and ever set foot on our shores." However, Allainn was in too good a mood to dwell on the negative for long. "Anyway, we're not going to fight them all in one go, for goodness sake! One camp at a time!"

Ellis blinked and then lost his worried frown. "Of course! They're in two camps!"

"And even better, these papers tell me that the newest recruits are at Tisza."

"Tisza it is, then," Lackland agreed, smiling too now.

However, by the time they had finished scouring the room, and had gathered more information and rejoined their captains out in the hall beyond, there had already been some changes. Men had gone back into the town and started bringing families out to the hall. Families from the worst houses had been scooped up with their few possessions by the Order men, and were currently being instated in rooms at the top of the massive building.

"Most of the servants fought to the death," a bright and enthusiastic young captain reported. "Strangely enough the cook is a local, though, and so are most of the kitchen staff. They're happily getting food ready for these poor souls, although we did leave a few of our own more expert cooks to keep an eye on them, just in case it's all a sham and they stick something noxious into our soup! We thought we'd get the worst affected in first, and they're up at the top because there aren't any bodies or blood to clean up there. Achaid Company are building a pyre out the back and dragging the bodies out as we speak. My men are rounding up all the valuables. We thought we'd wait until everyone was a bit more awake in the morning and then share the spoils out evenly."

With several hundred people inside out of the weather, even a building as big as the Souk'ir's hall began to feel cramped. It made Allainn proud of the way his men made the best of the stables and outbuildings, and willingly left the house to the needy without any order being given. The only use the men made of the place was to take over the large kitchen building which was at the back, well away from the house no doubt so that any fires from the huge bread ovens would not spread to the Souk'irs' luxurious home.

Come the morning, they were able to see more of what they had taken command of. The people of Kotor could not believe their luck at first, and some slunk back to their hovels, too afraid that their tormentors would return and exact some dire revenge. Most, though, were only too delighted and took full advantage of the situation. The few who had collaborated with the DeÁine, and had used the roles given to them to lord it over the others, now came to regret it. They were quickly pointed out, and Allainn had them put out on the road with food and what they could carry, for he feared that once violence between the townsfolk started, it might not be so easy to stop. He did not want to come back this way in a few weeks and find makeshift gibbets filled with the guilty and some innocent alongside them, and a town turning on itself. Kotor had suffered enough without that. In a similar spirit, he also offered the young men of the town the opportunity to fight with his men. Additional numbers might count if they were to go up against men hardly any better trained, but more importantly, it would remove those who could be inclined to take action out of youthful impetuosity.

He took two days to allow his sergeants to drill the youngsters and to sort out where they were best placed. Time he took to compose a message to go back to Eoghan, and to bundle up the most valuable of the papers to be taken to the safety of Wolfscar as fast as possible. Two lances made up of the lightly wounded set off north, as the rest headed south and heading into enemy territory in earnest. He took three days to march to Tisza, not because the terrain was particularly hard, but because he had scouts out all the way, since he did not want to go charging over a seemingly empty hill only to find himself right in the midst of a training camp. Their knowledge of these camps being so sketchy, nobody even knew whether the DeÁine trained with proper weapons. Recruits surprised could still be dangerous if holding real spears or swords in their hands. It also gave his own men time to do some of the basics with their own raw recruits, and with that being done with a lance to each new man, Allainn felt confident that what they lacked in time would be partly compensated for by the quality.

By the time they were within a mile of Tisza they had remained unnoticed, much to Allainn's amazement, and he deployed his men once more. Under cover of night they swept around until they had virtually encircled the camp which lay just out of sight of the town of the same name. A town which his scouts reported as being even more ground down and miserable than Kotor. At least the men of Kotor had been able to arm themselves from the smiths' forges which they worked at, and every man had a sword or spear of good quality. Ellis commented that he had no idea what they would arm anyone they got from Tisza with, probably wooden clubs and broom stales at a guess, and those likely to be half-rotten!

With the first glimmer of dawn on the horizon the Order's men crawled forward, keeping low in the stunted bushes and tatty grass tussocks. Any of the Kotor lads who thought they would be making a glorious charge into the camps were swiftly disabused of such notions. This was the kind of raiding tactic the Brychan sept were masters of and knew how to make the most of. So once right up to the palisade fence, men paused and listened.

However nobody of any consequence was up and about this early. There was the smell of a few fires being prodded into life which suggested that the camp cooks were already up, but that was it.

Silent and swift as rats boarding a ship, the battalion entered the compound, having cut their way through the scrub and stakes palisade fencing. Everyone knew they could not risk a pitched battle, and men tore into the dormitory wooden halls like the Dragon of Death the DeÁine swore on. It was slaughter pure and simple. The kind of callous butchery the Island men despised and deplored, but sometimes it was necessary and now was one of them. The stakes were too high, and any man who had come and made it this far was too committed to the DeÁine, or too indoctrinated, to risk leaving to have at their backs. Only in a few places was there anything like proper fighting to be done, and those were where the trainers were. Men who had served in the Jundises and been moved, for whatever reason, to bring on more men of their calibre.

It took one turn of the glass, that was all, and they were done.

"Burn it!" Allainn commanded. "Not a stick to be left standing!"

Oil from the kitchens was used to liberally souse the bodies and buildings and then torched. From a few flickers, the whole place suddenly became a roaring inferno, for the buildings had been close together with the training grounds located outside the palisade. Some of the young recruits had been horror-stricken to recognise lads they had grown up with amongst the dead, but the experienced men were quick to point out that those same men now would not have hesitated to kill their own mothers if their DeÁine masters had commanded it. So it was in sombre mood that Allainn's small army marched westwards, having eliminated over two thousand in something nobody would grace with the title of a battle. For all that it had been deceptively easy, it still left a nasty taste in everyone's mouth.

Allainn was now faced with a choice. He could go over what passed for high land in this part of the Islands, which were small ridges, and remain out of sight. On the other hand, he could use the road which ran from Tisza to Endrod. That was quicker by far, but had the disadvantage of passing through the town of Lovrin. Here the local lads proved their worth, for they were able to tell Allainn's men that the folk of Lovrin had become known as troublemakers. Sick of repeatedly being overrun by recruits from the camps on either side of them, the townsfolk had risen up, prodded out of their suppressed state by the extreme behaviour they had had forced upon them. Many of the Kotor men were insistent that these days Lovrin was a town of women and children, the men having been driven out, killed or forced into the camps themselves.

For his part, Allainn was sincerely hoping they had been driven out not killed. Men who had fought that long against the DeÁine would have valuable local knowledge, quite apart from the experience of living out of sight of their enemies. What he was not prepared for was the number of men who suddenly appeared out of the marshes alongside the road when they were within sight of the town. Home-made bows and arrows, of poor quality but likely to still be effective, were pointed at his men who all stood still and tried not to look too threatening – not an easy task for so many veterans. An afternoon of careful negotiations, and the Kotor men's witnessing of the end of the Tisza camp, finally brought about an acknowledgement that Allainn's men were really who they said they were. And with that Allainn found himself with several hundred new men all of a sudden.

He had not recruited at Tisza itself. The few young men they had left who had not been in the camp were needed far more there if the townsfolk were to hope to rebuild their lives. Now, though, he found that the women of Lovrin had been smuggling their sons out to join their fathers as soon as they were getting to an age where the DeÁine might take notice of them. And in the ten years since the last major rebellion, the numbers of the outlaws had swollen considerably.

Now they marched into Lovrin by Allainn's side, and in short order the DeÁine's leading men in the town were cut down. At a meeting in the town's main square that night, Allainn told the townsfolk what they were going to do and why, then left them to make their own decisions. This time he knew he did not have to labour the points. These people had paid the price of resistance, and if there was a way they could live without the DeÁine they would seize it with both hands. He was therefore not surprised to find that when they came to move on in the morning, that his army had grown again. So much so, that with the men from Kotor as well, he was up to nearly an additional six hundred men. The young boys were staying behind, much to their disgust, but that was one point where Allainn gained much approval from the Lovrins as his men firmly, but kindly, ejected the youngsters who had tried to creep in amongst the ranks unnoticed.

He also had to do a little reorganising. He divided the new men among two revised divisions of six-hundred Order men, each led by Ellis and Lackland, so that each newcomer had two Order men about him. The remaining eight hundred Order men, in their sixteen companies, he took under his own direct command. This way he could still afford to recruit more men and be able to fit them into his command structure. It was cumbersome but it took some of the strain off Ellis and Lackland, and so they marched on towards Endrod.

Here they all knew that the chances of another quick victory were slight. This was where the more advanced recruits to the DeÁine army lay, and nobody expected to be able to surprise them in their beds. Yet by the time they were a couple of miles short of Endrod, the scouts once again had made no contact with anyone.

"Where in the Underworld have they got to?" an astonished Lackland wondered. "Are they away somewhere?"

But the Lovrin men were quite clear that even if the DeÁine took their recruits out during the day, they did not risk staying out for the night with them until they were almost ready to be handed on to the highest bidder.

"Too risky," the one leader from amongst the Lovrins told them. "Too much chance they might slip away under the cover of darkness. Only when they are utterly bound to their squad, and all ties to family are forgotten in those dreadful places, are they even halfway trusted. And most go to the slave Seljuqs, even so. Only a few from any shipment of slaves will stay to be trained further."

Nor, apparently, did the DeÁine gather these promising men together into units any larger than a squad of around twenty. Progress in how to act in a larger battle would come once they had been assigned to whichever Jundis their group was purchased for. They trained as a squad and were purchased as such, the Lovrins said. Nobody bought a complete Jundis off the Souk'ir these days, although the Order men had heard of such things in the past. So no whole, united Jundis awaited within to match them man for man – Allainn's biggest fear over Endrod.

"So individually they'll be superb fighters, but as yet they won't be acting together," Ellis said cheerfully as he relayed the information to Allainn and Lackland. "It seems more likely we'll encounter pockets of real resistance in amongst a world of chaos, because those destined to be slave soldiers will wait to be told what to do."

Bizarrely, though, they once again got up to the walls of the camp under the cover of darkness without encountering a soul. Scouts reported that this time there were sentries, but it seemed as though these were men for whom it was still a training exercise. They certainly were not experienced in fending off an enemy, or expecting anything other than a feint of an attack by their trainers. Allainn's men slipping in and silently slitting their throats was achieved with unreal ease. So too was much of the take-over of the camp. There was some heavy fighting in patches, and they lost a couple of the new men in the process, but considering the numbers they had gone in against, it was achieved within a ridiculously short space of time and the kind of tiny casualty list the Order had not had in a very long time.

"I can't believe our luck!" Lackland gasped, as he stood with Allainn in the central parade ground and surveyed the scene. This camp was much larger in terms of the facilities within it than Tisza, and had clearly handled the recruits after Tisza had done the basics. In their search the men had found large quantities of uniforms and weapons waiting to be used for whichever family the next batch were to be assigned to. Something which had given Allainn ideas!

"To take this place *and* then have the means to disguise ourselves! We couldn't have asked for more!" Lackland added, as he shared a moment of keen anticipation with his leader, where the only thing in question was which way they went now.

# Chapter 7

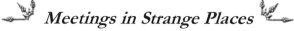 *Meetings in Strange Places*

### New Lochlainn: Beltane – Solstice

However, as they spent the next day getting men appropriately kitted out with their acquired new uniforms from Endrod, there was a further development. It was the last day of Beltane and they were being treated to a perfect Islands' summer day, with clear skies and sunshine in which they could see for miles. Their own sentries were much more alert than the DeÁine's had been, and first Lackland and then Allainn were summoned to the lone watch tower to have a pair of riders pointed out to them coming in at speed.

"Looks like it's urgent news, whatever it is," the sentry told his senior officers.

"Right, get someone into a spick-and-span uniform who can speak DeÁine," Allainn ordered. "Send him out with a couple of men to find out what this is all about. You never know, it might be about these anonymous newcomers. If they question what he's doing in uniform, get him to tell them that he and his mates were just waiting to be deployed. Get the whole story before killing them. We need that intelligence!"

With archers hiding in the shadows of the gates, ready to bring the messengers down if they turned tail and ran, the fake DeÁine marched out and began questioning the pair. They need not have worried about what the messengers would think of them, they were too busy rattling off their own news to take any notice of whom they were speaking to. It was presumably so inconceivable that the camp should be anything other than the way it had been for decades, that any changes were accepted as something ordered from on high and not to be questioned.

Allainn's fake guards persuaded the men off their horses, and were able to march them right into the camp and up to Allainn himself before they realised anything was amiss. As they fell gibbering to the ground, abasing themselves in panic, the leading sergeant could hardly wait to tell Allainn the news.

"There's an alien army just down road at Bocsa!"

"What?" Ellis exclaimed, coming up from behind. "Where in the Islands did that come from?"

"Don't tell me the DeÁine from over the seas have landed already!" Lackland gasped in despair.

But Allainn was less despondent. "No, it can't possibly be them if he's in this much of a froth," he declared, even as the local man who had done the talking confirmed it,

"No, he was most insistent! It's not DeÁine whoever it is. He said he was sent, because the town was alerted by seeing them marching over the hill towards them from Arad. That's the next town westwards. He says they have no uniforms but there's a big banner with a tree on it."

The three leaders exchanged glances of surprised. That sounded like one of their own. But nobody they knew of had come this far west. Who in the Islands was it?

"Only one thing for it, then?" Ellis received a nod from Allainn and turned to a captain behind him. "Tell the men to pack up! Quick March order! Be ready within the hour!"

When that hour came around, the men were lined up and waiting. They had kept the helms and tunics of the DeÁine they had salvaged, and many of the recruits now sported shiny new scimitar-shaped swords. But aside from that the army was taking nothing more to burden them. They left the camp at speed and carried on marching into the evening, blessing the lengthening days which helped them. Up at first light, they continued at the same punishing pace, only slowed down by the new men's inexperience at this kind of marching. It forced Allainn to order a longer break in the late morning, and again in the late afternoon, than he would have needed with just his own men, but having the locals was worth making the adjustments for. By midday the following day they were coming down into the river valley where Bocsa lay, and watching another army marching out on the southbound road towards where their local men said the town of Gaj lay.

"Who *are* they?" wondered Ellis, shading his eyes as he desperately tried to make out any kind of detail which would give them a clue. Whoever they were they were disciplined beyond the likes of the renegades from Lovrin. Someone had them marching properly, although it seemed as though some men were doing better than others. While most looked fairly professional, they spotted a bunch in the middle of the column who seemed to be struggling to maintain proper distances, and whose rhythm was more ragged.

"Hang on, who are *they*?" an archer said suddenly, and following his outstretched finger the officers saw figures they had not spotted before on the edge of the ragged section of the column. Then they realised why. As the section passed them the four men suddenly broke into double time and got to the head of the column, this time two of them going to the other side of it.

"Islanders?" someone gasped in astonishment. Nobody dared say what would be even more amazing, which was, what were men of the Order doing here?

Now everyone was staring intently at the column. A man rode at the head, but four others were also mounted, two going up and down the front third of the column, and two more doing the same at the rear third. They were not having to instruct the men they were marching as much as the central four on foot, but every so often a man was pulled out of the column and a pack rearranged, or the riders paused to speak to someone.

"Hounds of the Wild Hunt! Look at how they're riding!" a voice broke the silence with.

"They're *ours!*" someone else gasped.

"Right, let's get down there and find what in the Islands is going on," Allainn ordered, and the men set off down the hill in a new direction, bypassing the town and heading straight for the bridge which would lead them onto the southern road.

From the rear of the column they heard a warning shout go up and the whole column ground to a halt. The men turned to face them and appeared to be getting ready to fight.

"Get any DeÁine gear off!" Allainn bellowed as he ran. "Make it clear we're not their enemies!"

Down on the road Oliver could feel his heart pounding. Whoever these men were they looked desperately professional, and the number of them! There had to be over two thousand of them! He looked at their own troops. The two hundred he and the others had left with when they had separated from Will had been augmented substantially. Illia had been a poor recruiting place, and Palic not much better, but once they had got to the high grounds around Mol the locals were far less repressed. They had had plenty of volunteers from the mining town of Arad at the head of the Drina too. Men heartily sick of hauling coal out of the ground for masters who treated them worse than animals. So much so that, although it was a little out of their way, Labhran had decided that it was worth making the trip to Bocsa when they had been assured of another substantial recruitment.

Now that detoured looked like costing them dearly. The thick end of five hundred additional men were now on the road with them, but it was still a total of five hundred with very limited experience, and Oliver was not fooled by what sort of showing they might make against a force such as this, even if they had not been outnumbered four to one. They had hardly had chance to get them able to march properly much less give them fighting training.

*Hamelin, I might be joining you sooner than I expected*, he thought sadly. He missed his old friend desperately and was finding it increasingly hard to keep shouldering the burden of command, and he knew Friedl and Bertrand were struggling too. Only Lorcan was doing what Oliver thought of as really coping, and even then he was finding it hard going with so many men needing basic instruction. The four enlisted men had risen in Oliver's esteem day by day. Despite being a lot older than him they were indefatigable, constantly on the watch for who needed telling how to do something or making sure nobody got left behind on the road. Where they would have been without them Oliver could not bear thinking about, but a little voice in the back of his mind said that they would never have got this far. They would have been back at Choa at the original planned rendezvous waiting for Will and the others, he guessed, with just the handful of men they had got from Ilia and Palic.

He rubbed his eyes as if to clear them to see better, but also cuffed away the tears which crept up unbidden on him every time he thought of Hamelin. Then he saw it.

"Wait!" he yelled along the line, and heeled his horse in front of the waiting men to tear up to where Labhran had positioned himself in the centre. "Look at their feet!" he called before he even got up to them. Everyone squinted into the distance, but it was Lorcan who caught on to what Oliver had seen.

"They're wearing Order issue boots!" he called in confirmation.

"And they're marching double time!" Bertrand called from back where Oliver had been.

"I'm going to meet them," Oliver announced.

"No!" Labhran replied urgently. "We need you here! Send another!"

"No," Oliver called back over his shoulder, already heeling his horse away from the road and out into the countryside. "It has to be one of us from the Order!"

Friedl came and put a restraining hand on Labhran's arm. "He's already worked out we don't stand a chance if these men attack," he said very softly so nobody else would hear. "If Oliver is wrong and they are hostile, he'll just be the first to die, not the only one. We'll all be feeding the crows!"

Luckily Oliver's horse was a lot more rested after two days in Bocsa than its rider was, and the strong animal ate up the ground between the two forces without effort. In return several sharp-eyed men around Allainn had observed Oliver and come to the same conclusion, that he was definitely one of theirs. Nobody hindered him, but the men parted in such a way that he was steered towards Allainn. As the horse skidded to a halt mere yards from Allainn, the Ealdorman took in the battered and worn uniform and the deep, dark smudges under the young man's eyes.

"Who are you?" Oliver demanded of this unknown person before him.

"I think that should be, 'who are you, *sire*,'?" Allainn reproved with a twinkle in his eye and no reproof in his tone. "As it happens I am Ealdorman Allainn of Blass."

Oliver's jaw dropped and he nearly fell off his horse rather than dismounting. He took a step forward and staggered a little. "Ealdorman? Oh thank the Trees!" It was virtually a sob and someone came forward to loop a supporting arm under his before he fell over. "Oh Blessed Rowan, am I glad to see you!" His words could not have sounded more heartfelt.

"And who are you?" Allainn asked gently.

"Oliver of Prydein, sire. Sent by Master Brego with some of the men you see down there. We were supposed to be following one of the Abend, then it all got a bit messy and we got stuck in New Lochlainn."

"So I see. Are you in command?"

"No, sire." Oliver struggled to stand unaided, but his knees seemed to have suddenly lost their ability to hold him upright as the waves of relief washed over him. Here was a proper senior officer. Someone who would have the right kind of experience to be in command, not making it up as he went along, as he had felt he was doing. And Blass! That was one of the great fortresses on the Castle's Road. That meant that the men of Brychan were finally out from being trapped by the snow. He fought his wavering mind back into focus to answer the question.

"Our leader into New Lochlainn was a man called Labhran. That's him down there. He was one of the Covert Brethren before Gavra Pass. There's another of the Brethren with our other part – a man called Saul who got left behind. They've been guiding us as best they can." That raised some eyebrows, but Oliver thought it was more that they knew who Labhran was, rather than over what they were trying to do.

"So Labhran's here, is he," Allainn said, confirming Oliver's suspicions. "Well let's not keep the legendary man waiting!"

By nightfall the two forces had combined, and once Allainn had got the bones of their story out of the Islanders he insisted that they get some sleep. His men were nowhere near as weary, and even with their own recruits, they still had enough experienced men to be able to join every new man with a fully trained member of the Order. What had deprived Allainn of sleep was this talk of a new vast *army* of DeÁine – *that* he had not expected!

For the eight of the Order who had travelled through New Lochlainn together, though, the relief was beyond description and, past caring what anyone thought, they collapsed into their bedrolls the moment the food had been eaten and slept the sleep of the dead. By the time they were woken up the next day, the rest of the camp had been got going, and they only had time to eat some breakfast which had been saved for them before they were called to join Allainn, his officers, and Labhran, who had clearly found it much harder to relax and still looked dog-tired. Allainn had evidently got more out of him while the others slept, although Lorcan whispered to Oliver not to feel guilty over that.

"I suspect talking to him on his own has done more to sort things in both their minds than anything we've said," the Ergardian Knight concluded, and Allainn was certainly now very well-informed given the sudden change in his mood towards the sombre.

"We have some serious decisions to make now," he told them all. "I can't tell you how much your news of this new army complicates things for me. Our original intentions in coming south have become a small part of something far bigger. From what I've heard, this remarkable General Montrose will be meeting you at Cluj on the Janja?"

"Apparently," Lorcan confirmed. "He sent a message to our first intended meeting place outside of Choa. We'd sent a man back there too – to say we were heading for Arad right in the north of the Drina system – but Will had already realised we wouldn't be back at Choa for a while. He'd looked at a map and thought that he could get the ships he's got up the Janja River, but wouldn't be able to get far up the Drina, because he's now found out it's much the shallower of the two.

"That's why he suggested we march straight east to Arad and cross the river by bridge and on to Gaj – his message said there's no bridge there for us to cross by. Then, depending on how much resistance we'd already met, he suggested we go across country to Cluj, and once there, if all was well, recruit at Bors going by road. It wasn't ideal, though, because we've been resigned to missing places. It was only because we went to Mol that we heard about Arad being such a good prospect. Going on what we saw at Illia and Palic, we'd begun to think we were never going to get an army! The trouble is, we've no idea how many other towns are ready to rise up."

Allainn smiled, albeit with strained optimism. "Luckily we can now supply some of that information. We've been told to steer clear of Surcin, which is on the most easterly arm of the Janja, because that's where the Hunters train – and it's a big camp! Our locals also don't think there's much point in going to the eastern coast. They say Ada, Mako and Pahi will all have had the stuffing knocked out of them by the Tabor Souk'ir. But Selo is apparently a hotbed of discontent and so is Javor. I've therefore made the decision to send Commander Ellis that way with half a battalion of our experienced men plus those from Lovrin, who are the ones who can best keep up. He'll then go directly south to Cluj from Javor and ensure that the town is clear for when General Montrose comes."

"So what will we be doing," Labhran asked suspiciously, still too tired to be polite, and rather worried that everything had been taken out of his hands at a stroke. He was not sharing Oliver's sense of thankfulness just yet. Would this Ealdorman commit his men to going across to Rathlin to fight? Or would he be insistent on them defending the coast? That could destroy Will's plans to bring an army into the battle, and it startled Labhran to realise how much he had come to believe in what Will was trying to do. He cared deeply that it should have a chance to succeed and said so, bluntly.

However, Allainn did not take offence at the brusque tone. "I understand you concern. And never fear, we will fight! But we have to get there first! Now... To start off with we shall all march on Gaj. That makes sense, I hope you'll agree, since it's the one town in this area where none of us have been to yet. It's also the centre for the Chowlai family, so we should make sure we've sorted that nest of rats out before we turn our backs on them. If we do it when we have all our men together we'll be a formidable force. I really don't want any warnings getting out."

Labhran grudgingly nodded, noting that Bertrand and Lorcan, as the two truly experienced Knights, were displaying clear approval of this methodical approach. The way they had all been running on instinct since they had got to Mol had quietly been bothering him too, but with no means of doing anything different he had kept quiet. This was sounding more like something Maelbrigt would be saying, and that was assuaging his qualms by its familiarity. Maybe it was as Oliver and Hamelin had said, he saw the worst even when he did not need to and, from what Allainn was saying now, this ealdorman might be an unexpected bonus after all.

"After that, I propose that our other new recruits will go with Lackland along with enough of our men to begin training them – another half battalion should do it – and go down the road to Bors and on to Cluj. They can take their time and get some useful grounding on the way. If all you've said to me about this new DeÁine force comes to pass, then I totally agree with General Montrose – we have to get an army up from this side of the border if we can, and it will be all the more effective if none of the DeÁine have a clue that we've taken their men from them. Once we know we have Gaj secured and Lackland has led the recruits off, the rest will follow us under my command over the Drina and target the towns on the western bank. We'll be in the territory of the Indiera, who could be a real headache, and this is where I need your input. Did you see any sign of them when you passed through the north of their holdings to Arad?"

"Not a peep," Oliver answered. "Mind you, the area is less than picturesque what with all the mines. I suspect that the big men of the family wouldn't want to be lingering there unless it was to stamp on rebels."

"Do you think it likely, then, that they might be at Lupa?" Allainn asked, looking pointedly at Labhran. "You know more of the DeÁine mind than us. Is it in character to think that if the Chowlai are at Gaj then the Indiera might be directly over the river from them? The river is wide there, but Lupa and Gaj must be within sight of one another."

Labhran thought for a moment then replied. "I think it quite likely. The different military families liked to be apart and have their own lands to rule as they wished, but they were also terribly competitive. They liked to be able to show off to the others if they had something they thought the others didn't. The Souk'ir probably aren't that different to the Donns. Having a river between them would probably be enough of a barrier so that the territories didn't get blurred, and at the same time close enough to sneer at one another from time to time."

"So you think that we might begin fighting the Chowlai and then have the Inchoo wade in if we're not careful?" wondered Freidl.

Allainn nodded. "Which is why I wanted your opinion. If Lupa is just some scruffy old Attacotti town, then when we take Guj we can go in hard but without worrying about cover. But if there's another lot of DeÁine just sitting on the opposite bank, then we should go in more covertly so that they don't see what's happened until it's too late. If they're not in residence then we've lost nothing by being wary, and we'll just have to be cautious about going into Kovin and then Danj as potential Inchoo headquarters. But that caution is going to cost us in time, and that's something which I'm aware is now much more pressing. Do you have any knowledge of how things stand at Drinjaca at the mouth of the river?"

Labhran did not have to think about this one. "No, but I think by the time we get there, Will should have been there in front of us, even if you're thinking about marching your veterans hard and fast."

Allainn smiled at all of them. "Very well, gentlemen! Let's get this army on the road! Ellis, let your men eat, then get them on the road and let's see what men you can get from Selo and Javor! Lackland, pick the men you know who are best at training. You can make a move with them once we've taken Gaj. I want both you and Ellis to be at Cluj for the fourteenth, if at all possible. Everyone else will come with me to take Lupa, and then we shall do our recruiting down the Drina. We have two thousand of our own and over half a battalion of new men here. Let's see if we can make it a thousand recruits by the time we reach General Montrose!"

He would have been substantially more optimistic had he know of what was coming along in his wake. As promised, Eoghan set about watching the great DeÁine citadel of Bruighean, but was cunning enough to pull his men back out of sight. He hoped to lull those inside into a false sense of security, assuming that the Knights had taken one look at their might walls and, fearing the return of the Donns, had retreated. A siege served no purpose at all, for he knew that there must be stores and a source of fresh water within the vast complex, enabling the defenders to sit there for months if need be. His one hope was to let them come out to him.

However, he was totally unprepared for the surprise which greeted him two mornings after Allainn had gone. A man hurried into the makeshift shelter, which acted as their command centre in the same woods Labhran's group had hunted in, barely able to contain his excitement.

"Sire!" he gasped breathlessly, "You must come quickly! Come to the road!"

"Whatever is it?" demanded Eoghan.

"The army of the north, sire! It's there! Out there on the road!"

Eoghan felt his heart sink into his boots. He had not even known there was an army of the north within New Lochlainn. Granted he had had more than his hands full with the usual incursions through the Brychan Gap, but he should surely have heard something of it? Then he realised what the man was saying.

"Ealdorman Phineus is there with the men from Peruga, and so is Ealdorman Errol! They're waiting for you on the road to the south!"

Eoghan grabbed his sword and dashed out after the man, finding himself running down the slope to where the road ran away from Bruighean to the south. There, arrayed along the road and forming a huge semicircle of armed and very dangerous-looking men, were four battalions of the Order. As they saw him hurrying to them, three riders broke from the formation and cantered up to him.

"Fancy finding you enjoying the spring sunshine here!" quipped Phineus with a grin as he vaulted nimbly from his horse.

"How in the Islands did you come to be here?" Eoghan spluttered, torn between delight and disbelief.

"Ah, that's quite a tale!" Errol said, dismounting a little slower, but then turning to bring the third rider forward. "This is Sioncaet. He passed by us a couple of months ago with a general from Rheged. They were on the trail of Quintillean and two hostages he had with him. Since then he's been having an interesting time, to put it mildly! But the most important news he's brought back is that there's another DeÁine army on the way to the Islands. You have to hear this!"

And Errol and Phineus briefed Eoghan with speed on this new development.

However, Sioncaet was also far from silent in all of this. "When I left Will, his intention was to make for the south and raise an army," the former DeÁine minstrel told them firmly. "I rode with all speed eastwards, expecting to have to cross the border before I found anyone. I could hardly believe my luck when I met this lot six days ago out on the northern plains of New Lochlainn! We'd turned north in order to avoid this place, despite it being slower off the road, and I'd been pretty appalled at the height of the flooding in the one spot we passed where we could look across as far as the great river."

"Aye, it's a mess and a half!" Errol agreed. "We guessed long ago that the floods would be the worst in living memory after all that snow, so as soon as Phineus got to me and told me what Corin was doing in going in support of Berengar, we agreed we had to act fast. We'd scoured all the land from our border westwards and southwards to the first of the really big tributary rivers. Then when the melt started in earnest we had a stark choice to make. We could continue to watch the border, but that would mean we'd be prevented from moving any further for possibly months. We'd be confined to the north coast. Or we could trust that we'd done a good job of clearing the DeÁine from the north and risk moving.

"We chose to send a message by hawk to Esgair, telling them that as soon as they could start moving, they should check our backs. Then we crossed the River Vaii before we got trapped behind it – even then the bridge was only passable by rigging high walkways to it, it's probably underwater by now. We'd sorted out Turnu already, and Gura Vaii was no problem – thanks to Will Montrose alerting the townsfolk – so we were making a methodical sweep south. We thought you might be free of the snow sometime about now, and intended to get to this citadel and send you a hawk, if you weren't here already." He chuckled at the memory. "We thought if you'd been cut off you'd be champing at the bit to get into the fight just like we were!" Then he sobered. "Meeting Sioncaet put a whole different complexion on things, though."

"If we don't join the others, their odds against winning the coming battle will be even slimmer than they are now," confirmed Phineus. "Even if Berengar has a total victory over the DeÁine from this side of the mountain, he'll be fighting terrible odds against these newcomers."

"But we can't leave Bruighean undefeated and at our backs," fretted Eoghan. "If we're to be that outnumbered, it could be disastrous for them to come upon our rearguard just as we engage the new threat."

"No you can't," agreed Sioncaet. "Which is why I'm suggesting that you burn them out. You have enough archers with you now to pour a rain of flaming arrows into that miserable place. The stone keeps won't burn, but there are enough ordinary houses to well and truly catch light. Even before we saw you, we estimated that we had enough archers and men who could pull a bow to do the job with. Sooner or later someone is going to open the great gates in panic, and I also happen to know where the picket gate is!"

As dusk fell, Bruighean became completely encircled by the Order. The main clustering of archers was around the western semicircle, because that was where the ordinary houses lurked behind the great curtain wall. But there were still men around the back, on the eastern circuit, standing well back and ready to take aim at the spots where Sioncaet assured them there were gaps, windows, or vulnerable roofs. An uncanny hush lay over the countryside except for the soft crackling of the hundreds of small fires, lit and just waiting for the fire-arrows to be ignited from them.

On the still evening air a trumpet sounded, and suddenly there was furious activity. Archers plunged pitch-coated arrows into the fires and then fired at will. It was not the massed, co-ordinated volleys they used in battle, for the need to loose the arrows before they became too encased in flames was paramount. Yet flaming spike after flaming spike rose into the air and descended out of sight into Bruighean. At first there seemed to be no discernible effect, then there was a roar and a whoosh and a column of flame shot into the air. More followed it, to be rapidly followed in turn by heavy billowing clouds of smoke, until the air above Bruighean was all black and red.

"Come on!" Sioncaet heard Phineus mutter as they sat waiting beside one another on their horses. "Do you want to cook to death? To the Underworld with the highborn! Leave them to roast!"

Then they saw the first smoke-blackened figures start to stream out of the picket door. Only a moment later the main gates too were pulled open, and the poor and lowly of Bruighean spilled out in screaming terror. The army let them go. They posed no threat and none were armed. On into the night the Knights waited until long after the lesser folk of the citadel had run away or congregated in huddled fear like sheep at the rear of this terrifying foe. In the end, the ealdormen posted guards and let the men sleep. The citadel was still burning and far too hot for them to make their way inside yet, and clearly what troops there were were holed up in one or several of the great keeps.

With the morning light Bruighean was still wreathed in smoke, but not so dense that it would be dangerous to venture inside. Wrapping damp scarves over their mouths and noses, the Order men skirmished in, every room in every house being checked for lurking assassins. In little under an hour they had reached the half-moon sweep of buildings containing the temples, and encountered some bizarre but limited resistance. Priests flung themselves at the armed men with much fury but with no real fighting skill, forcing the men to fend off screaming, clawing, half-dressed priestesses in the strangest variant on combat they had yet experienced. In desperation they finally accepted that these maniacs were never going to be turned from their self-destructive path and cut down all but the youngest. It did not sit well with the men, but this was war, and if they did not subdue this fortress then there was no way they would be able to aid their friends and fellow countrymen.

Finally there was nothing left except the huge keeps. Here at least the DeÁine's arrogance helped them, for they had clearly never expected anyone to get beyond the great outer wall. The doors to the keeps were large, ornate and double – utterly useless for real defence purposes – and they gave in under the use of some battering rams enterprisingly created out of fallen oak beams from other buildings. Now there was hard fighting with the royal household guards. Bloody, close-quarter work and finally the Order men took real casualties. However, there was never any doubt about the real outcome due to the overwhelming number of Order troops.

As he walked back into the royal apartments for the first time in over nine years, Sioncaet shuddered. Too many memories flooded back, and he silently prayed that Labhran was still holding up under the assault from his own nightmares.

"Let's find the Power-room!" he called to the Foresters who had been detailed to accompany him, and together they set off up to the higher floors. He would have loved to have Maelbrigt with him – especially with some more Celidon Foresters. They were the men for this kind of enclosed work, and they were also more expert at this kind of tracking. The Brychan Foresters were more masterful at countering the big blasts of Power, and there had only been a handful of companies up in the north since most used their skills down in the Brychan Gap.

*Go upwards!* a quiet voice said inside his head, making him jump. Where had that come from? He felt a moment of blind panic. Surely after all these years of never feeling a thing on the Power he had not become sensitised? Could it have been going into the Power-room at Tokai? He shook himself and took a deep breath before hurrying onwards.

*No, go left!* the internal voice said again when he ascended a flight of stairs, and was about to go right on the landing at the top. Now he was really frightened! He had thought he might actually have been hearing a whisper from the strange disembodied ancients the first time, or at least that was what he had been trying to convince himself it had been. This was definitely right inside his head, though! *Oh sweet Rowan, don't let me be going mad now, not at this time of all,* he prayed silently. *Please don't let me have to fight one of the Abend in my head as well as with the army!*

Yet he turned a corner, opened a door and there was the now familiar pool in the centre of the room. *Destroy it!* the head-voice almost screamed.

"It has to come down!" Sioncaet ordered with all the authority he could summon in his frightened state. "Get any vessel capable of carrying water and empty it."

With so many willing hands, the destruction of the Power-room at Bruighean was accomplished in one night. It took another three days before the three ealdormen were happy to march away and leave the citadel, and in that time the place underwent a severe scouring. Anything which might vaguely constitute being used as a weapon was burned or broken. Everything, that was, except a large hoard of small devices which Sioncaet told the Knights were the lesser pieces of the Power. The vast majority were locked into a basement room of the central tower, which was where the wounded would remain to act as guards on the place – and the still catatonic Kenelm with them, since Sioncaet had found nowhere else to leave him. However, Sioncaet collected enough specific alien pieces to fit into a sack and slung them across his saddle, informing the others that these could be used for healing, and that Taise and Sithfrey at least would be able to use them. They might just save the life of someone vital, he added pointedly.

So on the fourteenth of Beltane, the long lines of Order men once again took to the road. By the last day of the month they were marching in to Kotor and were delighted to hear of Allainn's successes so far, having already passed Mereholt and seen some of his handiwork. Now though, they had to make a serious decision. Should they march on with all speed and catch up with Allainn? He could not be more than a couple of days ahead of them, and they knew from the folk of Kotor that he had been heading for Tisza. Some men hurried on ahead as messengers, but were waiting for the three leaders and Sioncaet when they got to Tisza. The smoking remains of Tisza camp spoke of Allainn's success, but the locals said that had been a week ago and that Allainn had headed west.

"We can't afford to go chasing all over the New Lochlainn countryside looking for him," Sioncaet said regretfully. "If he doesn't know of the fleet coming, then it's not surprising that he's not heading for the coast. But we need to get all of you to where we might meet Will Montrose."

The three ealdormen, and their commanders who were in the meeting with them, all agreed, but Phineus added a thought of his own.

"These folk say that Allainn was avoiding Surcin in the far south because it's where the Hunters train. That's sensible enough given that he thinks he's on his own. But with the numbers we have here, we could do some real damage to them. We might even be able to annihilate the whole camp, and that would really be something, would it not? To dispose of the worst fighters from this land forever!"

"How far?" Eoghan immediately asked, while Sioncaet felt a silent thrill that not one of the leaders had countered the idea, but were all looking intently at the makeshift map they had drawn in chalk on a kitchen table borrowed from a willing local.

*Yes! Take out the Hunters!* the voice in his head said, startling him all over again so that he nearly missed what the others said next. The voice had been gone ever since the Power-room came down, and he had been dismissing it as a temporary aberration brought on by the room.

"I reckon three days or four days to Backa and the same from there to Surcin," a keen young commander was saying.

"So we can be there by the twelfth?" another said.

"Let's do it!" Errol declared. "Wipe out the Hunters, then find some ships and find your friend Will, Sioncaet!"

# Chapter 8

## *In With a Chance*

### New Lochlainn: Solstice

As night's shadows spread across the River Drina, the small rebel army crept towards the DeÁine-held town of Gaj. Their approach was complicated by the fact that the land was all low-lying, and there was nowhere for Allainn and his men to get any elevation in order to observe the town. Even worse, they were informed, south of the town the countryside was a maze of reed-beds, which would not only be treacherous to traverse in terms of the soggy ground sucking men down, but with it being early summer they were now filled with nesting birds. Nobody had even considered going that way. One false move and they would have been given away by disturbed flocks of screeching water-birds defending their young, and with no possible way of quietening them down again. However, that meant either coming at the town from the north-east, which virtually forced them onto the broad and exposed road, or creeping along the river bank to come in fully from the north.

"How many guards do you think they might have posted about the place?" Allainn had asked the local men amongst his makeshift force. "Do the Chowlai Souk'ir consider an attack a possibility?"

The locals admitted that they thought the Chowlai family would have some sort of guards around them, but that they had no idea how many. Much, they confessed would depend on whether the family were in residence, or whether a substantial group were away trading. If at home, the family's Donns might well be pulling men out to the town just to give them more room in the barracks.

"And where are these barracks?" Bertrand asked suspiciously. "In the town itself?"

All the Islanders could see what he was getting at. If the soldiers were encamped within the town itself then the fight could get very bloody indeed, firstly, because there would be almost no way of surprising them. But secondly, because it would be all close-quarter work where the burden would fall heaviest on Allainn's experienced and highly trained battalion, and yet these were the very men they could least afford to suffer heavy casualties amongst. Luckily it was Saul who came up with the most useful thought.

"I honestly doubt that the Chowlai – or any other DeÁine highborn family – would be happy having the great unwashed any too close to them," he mused. "Let's face it, at Bruighean the army is kept outside the walls, and that's far closer to the border and potential attacks."

"That's true," Oliver agreed, desperately trying to keep up an outward show of optimism he did not feel inside. "I can't imagine any Island military leader leaving the bulk of his men in such an exposed encampment. I mean even in peaceful Prydein, as it once was, we had *walls* around the barracks at Freton. Not big castle walls, I'll grant you, but good stout palisades up on a bank and a ditch in front. And we were the *least* military Island! Rheged's coastal army camps that we saw on our way through were much more fortified. I think Saul might be right."

"Then where in the festering Underworld will they be?" muttered Lackland darkly. "Where in this sodden, stagnant landscape is there enough solid ground to build a camp on?"

In the end all they could do was expend valuable time scouting around and confirming that the fighting men were nowhere their side of the marshes. So with weapons muffled, they slunk across the tussock-ridged ground from the north in the dusk, and prayed that nobody was watching too hard. There was a heart-stopping moment when the leading men saw a man leap up from where he must have been sitting, point their way, and then sprint off to his left. A sharp-eyed archer brought him down with a single shot, and those beside him swiftly dealt with the other six men who tried to raise the alarm.

Everyone froze and listened intently. Had anyone within picked up on the dying screams? A moment later a figure appeared out of what appeared to be a picket gate in a wooden fence. They heard him call out to the dead men, but his voice sounded slightly drunk and hardly worried, and before he spotted the corpses he was one himself.

In a furious scramble the men skirmished forwards, low and fast, coming up against the fence. This close, they could see that it was a paltry affair, which had everyone perplexed until they slunk in through the gate and saw what lay beyond. The original town defences of Gaj lay further on inside – a high earth bank rising to the height of two men – and cutting the inner town off from the sprawl of humble cottages and downright decrepit hovels encircled by the fence.

Allainn signalled his men to spread out, and whispered orders to his captains to check whether these ordinary folk were all that lived in this outer semicircle. When a door was fearfully cracked open and a pale face peeked out, one of the resistance leaders from Lovrin slipped forwards and spoke softly with the occupant. He came back to Allainn grinning.

"I think you might recruit quite a lot from here if you can get rid of the DeÁine," he said with relish. "They're sick to death of being trampled underfoot, and the old man there says many of the young men had a bit of a go at them a few months back while the family and their guards were away. He says the young men of the town are under guard in the barracks, which are out on the road south towards Bors!"

"Great!" Allainn sighed with relief. "Then let's get on with taking this mud-bath of a town!"

Once inside the town's protective bank, the men were astonished by what they found. Whatever original Attacotti housing had once existed here had been flattened decades ago. Instead, around two dozen imposing and ornate great houses stood, each within their own ornamental gardens. The separation points were wide, flag-stoned roadways, but within each garden there were many paths as well. It was unlike any town the Islanders had ever seen, for even in the various capitals the need for space precluded such extravagant pleasure grounds – and these were purely for pleasure since there was not a vegetable patch to be seen. And even at this late hour, the men could see because light spilled out of so many windows, all filled with more of the expensive glass woven in webs of lead into large sheets, which Allainn's men had seen the last time they had taken a home of a Souk'ir.

What was encouraging was the fact that a good many windows near where they entered had wooden planks nailed over them. Clearly this was a result of the young men's insurrection which had yet to be fully repaired, but it served Allainn's force well too. Taking advantage of the pockets of darkness the boarded windows created, his men spread themselves out around the houses. With the number of men they had it was possible to send a good mixture of veterans and their new allies to each house, Allainn taking the farthest one from the gate with a mixed company so that he could give the signal to attack, knowing that all others would be in place.

Standing just out of sight from a pair of lead-paned coloured-glass doors, which gave out onto a paved area bedecked with fancy seats, Allainn took a deep breath. He paused and listened, confirmed that no sounds of alarm had begun yet, then took a firm grip on his sword and shouted with all his might,

"For the Islands and the Rowan! Attack!"

"For the Islands and the Rowan!" echoed back at him from all corners of the grounds, accompanied by the sound of dozens of glass windows being smashed in. Terrified screaming soon joined the soldiers' shouts, as the occupants were confronted by these dire apparitions who came in such numbers like demonic flood! Even without Ellis, who had left two days before, there were still three quarters of the original Order force going in, and the DeÁine were no match for such overwhelming odds even if the Hunters had still been there.

Oliver found himself attacking with a blind savagery he had never felt before. It was as though something which had been steadily boiling up inside him had reached bursting point. He would never have thought himself capable of hacking down a mere servant armed with nothing but a silver tray. Yet one look at the woman's alien features had been enough to brand her an enemy in the brief flash of thought before he was swinging his blade down in a welter of blood. It no doubt helped that before they had approached Gaj, the army had been sternly told by Allainn that anyone within a DeÁine house had to be so well trusted they must, by association, be considered an enemy.

The two Covert Brethren had confirmed this. With so many slaves around in a Souk'ir compound, only the most trusted would find their way into the houses, and the Covert Brethren had never been able to infiltrate the Souk'ir fully because they kept fewer close servants than the other nobles. The lesser slaves who did the real dirty work were frequently changed to avoid them becoming too familiar with the Souk'irs' routines, or establishing friendships and associations. So it was not until he came upon some cowering servants, haggard and in tattered rags for clothes, that he was jolted out of his slaughtering frenzy. Shaking in both body and mind, he dropped his blade down and leaned on it, panting.

A moment later another of his men almost bowled him over coming in through the door at speed.

"Not these!" Oliver commanded hoarsely, knocking the man's blade down even as he realised how much he must have been shouting in rage. "Take them outside. They're the Souk'ir's prisoners not ours."

By the time he got back outside, it was to see that many of the others of the Order had also refrained from killing the most lowly and downtrodden.

There were not many, and a substantial number of them spoke no language known to the Islanders apart from a few words in DeÁine. Certainly none of these would be able to fight with them. Instead they were herded off to one side, and some of the men were detailed off to go and fetch them food and drink. Going by the way they devoured what was brought to them, they must have been kept short for a very long time, and it was clear that none of them would present a security problem, for they were far too interested in getting the first decent meal in ages to take much notice of anything else.

As dawn came, Allainn drew his men back from the river bank, for the gardens of many of the largest houses had grassy swards leading right down to the river itself. They found the real inhabitants of Gaj more than willing to allow the men to retreat into the shanty town again, for they were treated as liberators, while across the wide water they could see the grand houses of Lupa. Now it was clear why there was so much space between these mansions. It allowed the DeÁine to pose to one another and still be seen, even here where the River Drina was wide. Across at Lupa, there were also mansions with gardens running down to the very banks, and Allainn spent some time with his senior men on the upper floors of the largest mansions, gazing through spyglasses at the lie of the land across the water.

Luckily for them, a heavy belt of rain had come in just before dawn, and so the only movement seen on the other side of the river was that of a few lonely gardeners, out tending the pampered plants. Some movement was visible in the great houses through the large windows. However, most of the occupants seemed to have succumbed to ennui and were hardly seen at all. This posed something of a problem for the liberators, since they guessed that they could hardly be seen to be actively moving about in Gaj without raising suspicions. Allainn wanted all the corpses out of the houses and put into pyres before things got unhealthy, but it meant an awful lot of scurrying out through back doors and taking circuitous routes through houses, to move in and out through doors which were not easily seen from the river. He also decided that Lackland should depart straight away. They had plenty of men to take Lupa, since the locals said that the Indiera also had their soldiers further out in a camp on the way to Kovin.

Therefore Lackland set off with his half battalion of five hundred Order men, the two hundred recruits aside from those from Lovrin whom Allainn had gained, and the near three hundred men Oliver and Labhran had recruited so far. It was therefore a mixed battalion, but a full one and with each new man partnered by one from the Order. He was heading south to deal with the Chowlai's army and then recruit at Bors before meeting Ellis at Cluj, and by leaving at midday it gave him chance to attack the army camp at dawn the next day.

For the remaining Order battalion staying with Allainn, there came a point when there was nothing left to do but get some sleep. When night fell, they would be hurrying down to the water to commandeer every boat they could get their hands on, but they could do nothing until the light went, and at this time of year it was a long wait. While Allainn and his captains naturally congregated together, Labhran found himself with Oliver, Friedl and Bertrand in what was apparently some kind of library. Somehow they could not face the bedrooms for reasons none of them could put a finger on, and for a while they all sat on some cushions on the floor in gloomy silence. When Lorcan appeared with Evans, Waza, Topher and Mitch, though, the atmosphere lightened, especially as the newcomers brought with them liberated food from the Chowlai's kitchens.

"One of the lads got the range going!" Topher declared cheerily as he handed out piping hot fresh bread rolls. "Some of the others got going on the dough, then decided that it would be quicker to bake rolls than loaves with so many to feed."

"So we took the liberty of getting some stew going in a big cauldron over the fire in one of the other rooms," Waza added with relish and holding up the steaming basin he was carrying. "This is our share!"

Topher was getting a fire going in the grate as they spoke and then put one of their camping kettles on it to boil. "Soon have a brew going!" he declared, and suddenly the others realised how cold and hungry they were.

As they tucked in, Evans quietly spoke to his mates as they made much of stoking the fire.

"What did I tell you? They're moping too much! It's all well and good that we found Ealdorman Allainn. And I'm not complaining that we've had the strain taken off us a bit. But just now these five haven't got much of anything to do."

"I know what you mean," Waza said with a sly glance over his shoulder to make sure they were not being overheard. "I'm getting right worried over Captain Oliver. He's a nice young chap but out of his depth here. Totally unprepared for all this! And since we lost his pal he's all at sea. I'll be glad to get back to General Montrose, 'cos he seems to have a knack of making them look for'ards, not back!"

Evans shook his head and sucked through his teeth. "Nah, I'm sorry, mate, I don't think we got time to wait for that. It's got to be the best part of two weeks before we can hope to meet the General again. We've got to come up with something ourselves and much quicker than that."

"What are you lot up to," Lorcan said, wandering up at that moment. "I know you all too well by now not to spot the signs."

"Shhhh!" Topher hissed softly at his Knight. "We were saying how poorly young Captain Oliver is looking now. We've got to do something, boss. The strain is off us now to find the extra recruits, and that's half the problem for them!"

Lorcan looked up and around the room, as if idly gazing about him, but also letting his glance rest upon the four huddled in the opposite corner.

"See what we mean?" Mitch said, under the cover of standing and handing over a battered campaign mug, filled with steaming herb tea of some blend his men concocted themselves. "We've got a good fire going now, and yet they haven't even moved to come closer, even though it's a bloody chilly day for this time of year. I know we're all tired, but it's something more than that."

Lorcan's nod was almost imperceptible, then he turned and wandered casually across the room.

"Come on," he said lightly. "The lads have got a brew going now. Don't sit over there in the draught! We'll all be cold enough later on!"

Bertrand was the first to look up. The oldest of the Knights who had set out from Prydein what seemed like an age ago blinked, then shook himself and gave a faint smile back. "A brew? Oh that's welcome!" he said gratefully and pulled the younger, lighter Friedl to his feet and chivvied him towards the fireplace.

Bertrand returned and caught Lorcan's gaze, then seemed to catch on to what the Knight was trying to do.

"He's right!" he said with what cheeriness he could muster. "Time enough to be cold later! Come on Labhran, up you get!" And putting a hand under the former-spy's arm, he helped him to his feet and then steered him towards where Friedl was coming out of his torpor as he ate the hot food.

"And you, Oliver," Lorcan added kindly. "Come on! Come and join us by the fire."

The young captain looked up at him blankly for a moment, clearly so lost in his own thoughts that he had forgotten where he was.

"How do you do it?" he asked forlornly. "How do you find the strength to keep going when the price is so high?"

The enlisted men quietly breathed a sigh of relief. If they could get him talking then they could support him.

"It is a high price," Mitch said, walking over with another of their battered pewter mugs and squatting down beside Oliver. "I won't insult you by saying it isn't. When the rest of my lance drowned in the wreck off Brychan on our way here, it was like someone ripped the guts out of me. We'd been together for years! The five of us were like brothers. Then suddenly there was just me. I mean, I knew Evans and Waza 'cos we used to be in the mess together. And Lantoney, my Knight, was mates with Lorcan here. But it wasn't the same as having the five of us together. And I felt so bloody guilty for being here when they were gone. Nothing prepares you for that feeling!"

"Absolutely!" Topher agreed, wandering over and helping Oliver to his feet, before grabbing the cushions to bring closer to the fire. "Like Mitch, I lost everyone else in the lance I'd fought in for nearly eight years. You bond a lot in that time when you're fighting! I sort of knew Teryl's Cody and Trip from a manoeuvre we went on a few years back. We fought side by side then. And I knew all the others by sight from around the mess, but we weren't in the same groups of mates who usually congregate together. That tends to be the men you trained with, or have fought with over the years – and as you've noticed, there's quite a range in age between us lot."

He took a deep breath and plunged in. "You aren't alone in your grief, Oliver. We understand how you feel because we've all lost people we were very close to as well. I've got a wife back in Ergardia, you know, but in some ways she'll never know me like my old mates did. There were things we went through together which bonded us closer – in a different sort of way – than having a family did with her. Her and the kids I love to bits, but they don't necessarily understand me the way my mates in the lance did."

"Dead right!" Evans said with feeling. "My missus is the apple of my eye, mind you, and I'd kill any man who laid a hand on her..."

"...Flaming Underworlds, Evans! No-one would *dare* lay a hand on your misses!" Waza snorted. "She's twice Evans' size!" he explained in an aside made with a wink to the Prydein Knights.

"Yeh, yeh! You can mock!" Evans retorted with the lack of rancour that came from familiarity. "But *if* someone laid a hand on my Bessie ...well I'd bloody kill them ...if she didn't get in first! But what I'm a'saying – you great daft turnip-muncher! – is that despite all that, she doesn't know me as well as you, you sorry old fart!"

"I don't fart like you!"

"Yeh, but Bessie don't know that! Not to hear her complain, anyhow!"

"Well I've known you longer," admitted Waza.

"And in all sort of situations," added Evans, with a knowing wag of a finger. "Who pulled you out of that brothel in Celidon before you ended up singing with the girls in the chapel choir?"

"Well how was I to know that 'she' was a 'he'?" spluttered Waza. "I was a nice well brought up lad! I had no idea things like that went on in the slave camps of the DeÁine, ...or that they'd carry on with such heathen practices when they got the chance not to!"

Evans winked at the others again. "Brought up in the sticks!" he said in mock confidentiality. "Only used to sheep as an alternative, you see!"

"Piss off!" Waza laughed, lobbing a crusty bit of bread at him.

"You see?" Lorcan said when they had all stopped laughing. "You'll never replace Hamelin, Oliver. No-one can take the place of him, because no-one else has those same memories of things you shared. But that's a way of making sure he lives on, too. Share those memories you have of him! Don't keep them squirreled away like some miser. He was a good man and he at least chose his way of leaving this life, and it was in order to do great good. Hold onto that at least!"

"And it don't mean that you won't have new good memories of a different kind, either," Evans added.

"That's what I think Sioncaet kept trying to tell you," Bertrand chipped in, but directed pointedly at Labhran. "You can't change the past, but that doesn't mean there can't be a future. It might not be the future you expected, but that doesn't mean it couldn't be good in its own, different, way."

"Then Sioncaet was right," Topher agreed. "I never expected this! But I'd like to think that if my mates are watching me from over in the Summerlands, that they approve. When we hauled Wistan and Kenelm out of that DeÁine infested palace, even while I was running for my life, I'd got these thoughts of how Harry, Dai and Eric would've been with us all the way on that mission. They bloody hated kids getting hurt! But those thoughts won't stop me from looking out for my new mates here, either."

"But how will I ever break the news to Alaiz?" Oliver sobbed as his grief at last broke through his restraints. "It isn't just me, is it? She'll be devastated!"

"I don't think you can predict how that will go," Topher said, dropping a sympathetic arm around the younger man's shoulders. "I've seen bad news broken to many women when we've come back into camp. Some whom you thought would fall to bits take it with surprising courage. Others, who you thought hated the sight of their husbands after years together, sometimes take it harder than you'd ever have thought. Sometimes it comes down to faith in the hereafter, but not always. You just can't predict it, so all you can do is mourn for him yourself, not for her too. She'll do it in her own way when the time comes, and maybe you'll be a part of that and maybe you won't. Don't beat yourself up over what might not happen."

For the rest of the afternoon the men let Oliver have the consolation of allowing his bottled up grief to flow, and certainly by the time Allainn sent word for everyone to congregate, he seemed calmer if not much happier.

With a black and rainy night in full spate, the force made their way across the river. Pleasure rafts and other strange vessels, all heavily laden and low in the water, were propelled by whatever means the men could come up with between more substantial and equally laden boats. By some miracle all the men crossed the wide river in two disaster-free journeys, and without casualties of any kind, leading many to believe that their venture was blessed in its aim. Blessings from the DeÁine gods, however, were certainly in short supply when they fell upon the unsuspecting Indiera Souk'ir and their household slaves, who died with the same speed that the Chowlai had. Boats were then sent back for the leading men of the Gaj township to come and inform their opposite numbers in Lupa of their sudden change in status, who arrived for all to see with the morning. Yet again the Order men were greeted with nothing but shocked joy and relief, and Bertrand, Friedl and Lorcan, at least, began to entertain the hope that they might yet have something approaching an army to fight the new DeÁine threat with.

By the time Allainn marched the men out of Lupa a day later, they had another seventy-five recruits, and after torching the Indiera's army camp, freeing some prisoners, and marching into Kovin town, they had another hundred. Seven days later they were marching into Danj with an army of over a thousand, and heard their first news of Will. News which managed to raise even Labhran out of his melancholy, for Will was clearly tackling his objective of raising an army with gusto and no small success.

On the third of Solstice, a day before Allainn's force had taken Gaj, Will had sailed into the coastal town of Sips. Whatever had happened there had to have been good, because on the sixth he had fought a sea battle at the port of Drinjaca and won. The jubilant occupants of Danj relayed news to the effect that there had been many slave ships in Drinjaca harbour, and that the men amongst them had joined with Will upon their liberation, on the promise of being given ships to return home with once the seas around the Islands were free once more of the DeÁine and their ships. And only the day before, if the weather and his luck held, Will had been due to sail into Janja – the home port of the Dracma!

"Blessed Rowan!" Labhran had muttered in amazement. "He's going to tackle one of the two strongest Souk'ir in their own den!"

"And with a good number of very angry and vengeful slaves at his heels," a substantially cheered Oliver added. "I wouldn't want to be in the Dracma's shoes when *they* catch hold of them!"

Will had indeed sailed into Janja. Sailed in and breathed a huge sigh of relief that his intelligence had been correct – the Dracma hierarchy had taken themselves and their army off to somewhere else. He was less happy once he discovered that they had gone in convoy with the Tabor Souk'ir and the two leading Abend towards Brychan, but there was nothing he could do about that yet. Right now he needed to see about getting even more men to his side.

He had recruited mainly sailors at Sips, and this had helped him immensely with his transportation problems. And it was not that he was ungrateful for the thick end of a thousand slaves whom he had picked up in Drinjaca. Any man was welcome at the moment! But there was a limit to how easily he could train the slaves, when many of them did not understand a word he said.

What he prayed for every night was more men who understood Islander, and had some fire in their bellies to make them want to fight to free their homelands. Apart from the one brief message over the change of rendezvous, he had had no word of how Labhran was doing, and deep in his heart of hearts he was worried that the former Covert Brethren and the traumatised Oliver might simply not have the energy or hope to convince the wavering. So far he had about a thousand slaves, plus roughly eight hundred recruited soldiers and five hundred willing sailors getting them there, but that was not enough. It was not anywhere near enough!

It was therefore a good thing, he decided, that the new fallback meeting he had relayed to Labhran was the town of Cluj. Originally they had all expected Will to have to avoid Janja, and so had decided on Cluj as somewhere they could all reach overland. Now, though, Will wanted to recruit as he went too. So first he sailed to into the eastern arm of the Janja river system, up the Sombre river to the town of the same name, and to his delight managed to get another two hundred and fifty willing men from the large market town. There was no point in going further up the Sombre, for there only lay the Hunters' lair of Surcin. He was therefore prepared to detour to the other Janja river system port of Suho, when a chance meeting with an excited captain of a large barge told him of an unexpected delight.

"There's an Order Commander up at Cluj!" the captain called across to him as he manoeuvred his flat barge, laden with swords and weapons from the forges of the northern towns alongside, and allowed these liberators to strip his cargo bare. "They told me to look out for men marching under that flag of yours. I never expected to see ships, though!"

"We got lucky!" Will called back.

"Well I think your friends did too!" the captain responded cheerfully. "Commander Lackland said to tell you help is at hand and to make all speed to the meeting. Oh and the word from another ship is that there are more men up at Surcin, and they aren't Hunters!"

"Lackland?" Will turned to Saul and Jacinto. "Who the fuck is Lackland? And who are these other men?"

Nobody knew the name, and so with great trepidation Will's fleet headed up river. When they came within view of Cluj as the river Janja narrowed, all in Will's party stood at the ships' rails staring in astonishment. As far as they could see in the confines of the narrow river banks, before the steep walls of the sunken fjord valley rose about them, there were men. Not just a few hundred – thousands!

"Sweet Rowan! Where did these all come from?" Kym breathed to Newt.

"Not a clue, boss," Newt gulped in awe, then mimed the question to Busby and Toby who were on the next ship and also looking to them as if to find an answer. But shaken heads all round only confirmed that this was a surprise to everyone. Any doubts Will might have had were quashed as his ship edged up to the end of the long quay, and saw Labhran and several strangers dressed in the Order's uniform. As soon as the gangplank could be run out, Will was on it and hurrying down to the quay.

"Gentlemen, may I introduce you?" Oliver asked with undisguised glee. "General, may I present Ealdorman Allainn of Blas Castle. Ealdorman, General William Montrose of Rheged."

"Ealdorman?" Will choked. "And Blas? Isn't that on the Castles' Road? How did you get here with all the floods?"

"Through the mountains," Allainn said with a satisfied smirk. "A trick the Foresters kept up their sleeves, and a rare treat it is too! But before we get into that, I think what might interest you more is that I brought my full two battalions from Blass."

Will nearly wept with joy. Two full battalions of men from an Order with real fighting experience was beyond anything he had dreamed possible. Yet the rest of the news was nothing but additional bounties.

"Your Captain Oliver and Labhran did rather well recruiting, but so did we once we heard what was needed," Allainn was continuing. "All told we have the same again in new men from this side of the border. We have a total of four thousand men, General, and also my two experienced commanders. I suggest you work with Commander Ellis and I keep Commander Lackland. That way we both have some support."

Will coughed to clear the choking in his throat. "Oh we've got a few more than that!" he managed to get out. "I too have a thousand Attacotti from this side of the border crammed into these ships. But on top of that we have over six hundred good seamen who are willing to transport us in these ships, and on top of *that*, we've freed around two thousand slaves. They won't be so easy to direct because half of them don't understand us, and we have to relay our requests through the ones who do understand. But they want to fight. By the Trees they so want to fight the DeÁine! But I have to ask you, have you heard of anyone going to Surcin? The river captain who told us about you said there was another force up there. Who can that be?"

"And they aren't DeÁine?" Labhran checked.

"Not according to our captain," Teryl confirmed. "He was positively full of the news. Way too happy for it to have been DeÁine – and I reckon he'd know the difference, if you know what I mean."

"Can you fit us all in to these ships?" Allainn asked next. "Would you think it a bad idea for any of our men to be in amongst the slaves in a ship, for instance? Would it be safe? Or are they not sure who's friend or foe?"

Will scrubbed his hands over his face, desperately trying to rearrange his thoughts with all these new developments. "Well I've put Jacinto in charge of one lot," he informed Allainn. "Those are the ones who I think are steady enough to fight well, and Jacinto deserves a chance. It took me a while to remember where I'd heard his name before, but then it came to me that he'd been mentioned when we were at Roselan. He was said to be trouble back then, but I think he's a very different man to that now after all he's been through, and he's certainly doing a bloody good job of settling the ...well, the *saner* slaves.

"There's another ship load who are sailing their own ship, and I wouldn't want to set foot on that one! It's the last one just pulling in. They're all baying for blood! Driven half mad by brutality, grief and homesickness. When we catch up with the DeÁine, I've told the few amongst them who understand us that they can be first to land, and I'm going to stand back and let them go, because they're such a manic force I certainly don't want them behind us and any of our lads getting in their way! There's no doubt they'll take horrific casualties, but I don't think there's a way to stop them, or of getting them to stand back and come to the fight with the rest of us.

"The rest of these ships have loads of room on board. I brought them along because the sailors were willing and I didn't want any returning DeÁine coming into port behind me, after we'd gone, and then having the use of them to pick up troops from elsewhere. So yes, there's plenty of room for you and your men."

Then he looked over Allainn's shoulder and his jaw dropped even further. "Are those *women* in fighting gear?"

"Oh ...yes! That's Captain Elen and her girls. Berengar seconded them to my force because they're Foresters and they were the ones who opened the way through the mountains for us. I've kept them with me because coming into New Lochlainn, I thought their know-how might come in handy!"

Will shook his head like a punch-drunk fighter. "Female Foresters? Flaming Underworlds!" Then he blinked and a grin began to spread across his face and he clapped Allainn on the shoulder. "By the Trees, you've just shift a big burden from off my shoulders! I've got your Berengar's two sisters here! They were taken prisoner by Masanae and we liberated them with our Wistan. I'd be delighted and relieved if your Captain Elen would take charge of them!"

"The Grand Master's sisters?" Now it was Allainn's turn to be aghast. "Cross of Swords! That's a complication I never thought to be dealing with!"

"Neither did I," Will shot back dryly, "and complication just about sums those two up! I'd defy any man to control them, which is why I'm going to wish them onto your lady Foresters. If anyone can do the job it's them!"

They spent the next day sorting out their forces, for with so many experienced troops now on hand the leaders were quick to spread the novices out amongst them. The intention was to board the ships the next day, but the first companies had barely made it on board, before the Order scouts Allainn had sent out came hammering back in on the hard-worked horses.

"Sire! Sire!" the leading rider called out, waving frantically at Ellis as the first senior man he could spot. "An army, sire! Ours! Coming over the ridge, sire!"

Ellis dropped what he was doing and ran, with two of his captains to meet the scouts, then ran at full pelt off up the hillside.

"What in the Flaming Underworlds has got into Ellis?" Lackland fretted, drawing Allainn and Will's attention to the running commander. "Where's he going and why hasn't he got any guards with him?"

Then the scouts were up to them and panting their news. In astonishment the leaders looked back to the ridge where Ellis had now disappeared from, then saw him coming back a few moments later gesturing furiously at them. Over the ridge they sudden saw the tip of a standard, and as the sea-breeze caught it and lifted it, Allainn laughed out loud.

"Sacred Root and Branch! It's Eoghan! The old bugger must have got into Bruighean quicker than expected!"

He, Will and Labhran hurried forwards, but in pushing through the crowds of their own men, they did not see more of the newcomers until they were almost upon a beaming Ellis and a very familiar figure.

"Sioncaet!" Labhran cried with delight, finding himself relieved beyond words to be reunited with the person he now recognised was his closest friend. It had taken the events of these last few months to force him to take a good look inside, but he had belatedly come to realise just how loyal both Sioncaet and Maelbrigt had been and appreciate it.

However Will was both happy and worried. "Did you send word to Brego?" he asked anxiously when he could get a word in. "Do they know about the fleet?"

Sioncaet gave an inscrutable smile. "Well I couldn't get back into Brychan because of the floods," he said, but to Will's puzzlement with remarkably little regret. Then could not bring himself to tease his new friend further. "But I did bring you an awful lot more men to take across with you!" And he gestured behind him to where, to the open-mouthed astonishment of Will and the others, two more standards were wheeling to the left and right of Eoghan's.

"That's Phineus and the men of Peruga!" Sioncaet said with a smug grin. "Seems he remembered you, for some reason! He and Ealdorman Errol were already sweeping west when I got to them."

"How many?" Will croaked, feeling his legs begin a dangerous tremor in his relief.

"Another six thousand!" Sioncaet said happily, coming to grasp the swaying Will warmly. "You did it Will! You've got an army!"

"By the Rowan and the Cross of Swords!" Labhran sobbed, unable to keep the tears from flowing in the emotional release as he came to embrace them both. "Nearly fourteen thousand! Fourteen thousand men between the Order, the recruits and the slaves. I never dreamed it would happen like this. And the DeÁine effectively already out of New Lochlainn already! I never thought to live to see the day!"

# Chapter 9

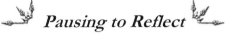

## *Pausing to Reflect*

### At sea: early Solstice

On a bright and breezy first of Solstice, Maelbrigt was leaning against the rail on a rolling merchant-ship feeling happier than he had done in a very long time. The only thing stopping him from being out and out joyful was the presence of Taise. Not that his feelings towards her had changed in the slightest – far from it. He could not have loved her more, and the troubles they had been through in the last few months had only strengthened their bond. It was rather that he would have felt a lot better if he had been able to leave her tucked up behind the safety of the impregnable walls of Lorne Castle. If his teachers amongst the Foresters had been anything like correct, Lorne would withstand an assault even by one of the Abend. Yet it was not just the physical danger which worried him. Taise, with her ability to use the Power, was awfully vulnerable to mind manipulation by the Abend. Here at sea it was unlikely to happen, especially given the Abend's antipathy to brine, but at some point Taise would have to disembark and that was when she would be most in danger.

"Stop brooding," a cheerful voice said at his shoulder, and he turned to meet the gaze of Sionnachan as the big ealdorman of the Ergardia Foresters came and leaned alongside him.

Maelbrigt immediately smiled. It was such a relief to have Sionnachan by his side in all of this. For a start they had known each other off and on for more years than either of them cared to recall, but it went beyond that. However much Maelbrigt enjoyed the company of men like Ruari MacBeth, it was not the same as being with someone like Sionnachan. Someone who was as immersed in Forester culture as he was.

The one person he had found something of an echo of these feelings with was Sioncaet. No matter how appreciative audiences were of Sioncaet's performances and artistic skills, it was not the same for him as talking to, or playing with, another musician. Maelbrigt was not a musician as such, but, because the Foresters higher incantations were sung rather than simply recited, singing was included in their training. Anyone who aspired to get beyond the basic entrance level in the Foresters had to be able to follow pitch and phrasing, and for the highest ranks it was almost essential to have perfect pitch because of the complexity of some of the incantations they were expected to know. Having had his abilities honed already, Maelbrigt had easily followed Sioncaet's intricate weavings of melodies and harmonies, and it had cemented their friendship in a way which belied the amount of time they had spent together.

A glue of a very similar kind bound Maelbrigt and Sionnachan. It allowed them to shortcut any lengthy explanations before they could begin discussing difficult problems, often carrying on in a strange kind of shorthand which left others baffled as to what in the Islands they were on about. Already they had had several in-depth conversations about what incantations to use where and when, talking about nuances so subtle it left Taise and Sithfrey stunned. Taise in particular was mortified at discovering the depths of Maelbrigt's knowledge, mentally cringing at the way she had talked so loftily about her own studies back when he had made her aware that he knew she was DeÁine. During the years they had lived so close to one another, if she had concealed her own intellect, then he had done the same and more. The two DeÁine scholars once again felt more than a little chastened over the way their own teachers had ridiculed and dismissed Island culture as backward, and having so little depth as to not be worth observing, let alone preserving.

Twice in as many days Maelbrigt and Sionnachan had asked them if they could try something out on them, with the result that both had felt something of the powers these extraordinary men could summon. It was not the kind of personal sucking up of the Power the talented amongst the DeÁine did. Rather it was as though they tapped into something much more fundamental, more naturally occurring, and utilised it without the kind of personal aggrandisement the former acolytes were accustomed to sensing.

On both occasions, Maelbrigt and Sionnachan had wanted to try different modulations of particular chants. The two senior Foresters had begun by singing something at them softly in one key, and had then moved up and down the tonal range bringing in upper or lower harmonies as they experimented. In one instance they had hit a particular sequence, having finely tuned it, and the next thing Sithfrey and Taise had known they were being brought round by a bunch of very contrite Foresters, who nonetheless could not quite disguise their excitement at their success. And as Maelbrigt had explained before they began, the whole reason they wanted to do this aboard ship was because Taise and Sithfrey's senses were already dulled by the sea around them. He had been most insistent with his fellow Foresters that he would in no way countenance such experiments once they were back on dry land – the potential for doing permanent damage was too great.

After that, Sithfrey and Taise had been issued with small wads of felt to stuff in their ears, and had been sent to sit right up at the bowsprit of the ship, while Sionnachan and Maelbrigt took all the Foresters off to the rear of the deck and rehearsed. Two hours later the leaders proclaimed themselves satisfied with the results and they stopped for the day. However, this morning the pair had begun drawing up what Taise could only assume would be an elite squad, and Raethun had come and kept them company but, she suspected, was also there to watch in case of any adverse reactions.

Raethun himself was not even in the running – and not just because he was one of Maelbrigt's trio of bodyguards. By his own admission he struggled to sing the basic Ergardian chants, and it had been partly this which had forced him to remain on Celidon. The Ergardian sept was so well-endowed with potential recruits they could afford to be fussy over whom they selected, with the result that all the Ergardian Foresters were what could only be described as at a minimum musical, if not downright gifted.

"I just wasn't up to scratch," the young Knight confessed to Taise and Sithfrey, as they sat watching sea birds wheeling overhead. "Despite all the training that Foresters like Bosel and Aldred gave me, it came down more to the way the two different septs operate. On Celidon we always anticipated fighting in small units. Even in a big battle we were the ones who'd be the skirmishers, and the best, like Maelbrigt, also become assassins bringing down individual threats. But the Ergardian sept has the potential to be used as one big unit, and when they use some of their chants it's the difference between one man singing and using a whole choir. The power they can generate is something quite amazing, according to Aldred anyway. I've never seen it myself, but I believe him. And the complex sounds they produce are quite amazing. So it's really important that you don't have a few warbling away off-key and spoiling the unified sound. That's why I would've had to go into the ordinary Knights if I'd gone to Ergardia, and it's why I stayed with Aldred and Bosel to train with the things Celidon sept does well instead."

"Are there things you do better?" Taise was curious. After all her beloved Maelbrigt was a Celidon man first and foremost, and a little bit of her did not want to think of him being secondary to Sionnachan. "I mean, the Celidon sept surely isn't second rate?"

"Oh no! Not second rate by any means, and yes, we most certainly do do some things better." Raethun was most emphatic. "That's why Maelbrigt and Sionnachan make such a good team. Sionnachan needs Maelbrigt's know-how, too. It's hard to explain the differences to you, especially when I daren't demonstrate anything. The best way I can think of is this. Master Sionnachan is like the man leading a whole choir — he chooses the pieces and sets the key they sing in. Whereas Maelbrigt is more like the gifted solo singer. The man who can hold a whole hall rapt with his lone voice. In contrast, the Foresters of the Brychan sept are expert at countering the physical threat from Power-wielding DeÁine. So they'll have ways of disrupting the flows of energy if the Abend and their acolytes tried to do something like conjure up figures out of soil or stones, for instance, because they're even more in tune with the Trees attributes than the rest of us."

In the long hours spent travelling to Belhaven to embark on the big ships, there had been plenty of time to talk, and amongst the tales Maelbrigt had retold had been Sioncaet's long-past experience of watching the Abend create huge figures out of sand to hunt and destroy escaping slaves in the last Land of Exile. Taise had not witnessed that long-ago event but Sithfrey had, and his voice had lent weight to Maelbrigt's telling for the younger members of their force who had yet to see the Abend's full might. That was why Raethun had picked that as his example, knowing that it would mean something to Taise and Sithfrey.

"The Brychan sept can hopefully do something about it if the war-mages start throwing balls of Power-fire at us, as well," he added. "The kind of thing Ivain described Calatin using when he led Duke Brion's army against them. It's kind of big-scale stuff, if you like. The things which can wipe out a whole company at a glance, but it's also quite distinctly tangible stuff. These are spells which cut and slice and hammer at men's bodies and kill that way. That's why they use the sacred woods so much. You'd never get a Brychan Forester without a full set of wands! And probably with a few spares tucked in his saddlebags for good measure!

"But they mostly fight company by company at a minimum, and sometimes as whole battalions. Big threats using big swathes of Power require a massed response, and the Brychan Foresters can be every bit as complex in their weavings as the Abend whose conjuring they're responding to. That said, those sort of threats don't happen that often, but you need to have just the right response when they do, so the Brychan Foresters do huge amounts of research – very much like the Ergardians do and for the same reasons, if not the end results.

"The Ergardian sept are good at countering attacks on the mind," he continued. "So if the Abend are trying to befuddle the opposition with glamours, for instance, then these are the lads you want in your army. That's why that awful storm at New Year did so little damage to southern Ergardia. It was partly to do with Ergardia itself repulsing the edge of the storm, of course, but it didn't hurt that all the southern preceptories felt the first twitches and started singing their hearts out, so that the glamour just dissolved instead of driving folks mad."

By now Matti, Kayna and Andra had come to sit with them and were listening enthralled.

"What about Rheged?" Andra asked. "Don't they have a specialism amongst their Foresters?"

Raethun scrunched his face up. "Yes and no. The Rheged sept was always more filled with ordinary men than Foresters. What they do is work within the army. I can't think of anything Aldred told me where the Rheged Foresters fought together as a large unit. What they do – or did when there were more of them – was defend the men around them from magically created threats, but ones which were individually distinctly physical. Things like spears with enchantments woven over them, which might threaten a small company, or Hunters with swords which had been somehow enhanced. Also, individual physical summonings like grollicans and baneasges. Stuff like that. Local problems, rather than big-scale threats. The Rowan only knows what will happen about them in the future. I suspect that will be for Master Ruari to decide."

"So do you do more small-scale stuff, then?" guessed Matti.

Raethun now grinned and rocked his hand. "Kind of. Like the Rheged men we're more concerned with individuals, but we've had far more Foresters than ever they've had, and we've been substantially more active. We, too, can do things to stop grollicans and baneasges, or for making a strike back at triads, but we're best at the stuff which strikes at men's hearts and tends to be individual and less visible. If you think about it, people's emotional responses will vary enormously to the same set of circumstances. What one man might shrug off as simply unfortunate could bring another to his knees, and if you didn't know them, you wouldn't be able to predict which way someone might respond."

146

"And you do?" Sithfrey sounded doubtful.

"Yes, in as much as it's no coincidence that it was Celidon's Foresters who worked most closely with the Covert Brethren, for instance. We're the ones who specialise in things like acting as bodyguards. Situations where the strike is likely to come at someone very specific; or where a small group of people need to infiltrate a dangerous area. We're trained to pick up on when people are being manipulated, too. It's no coincidence, Sithfrey, that Maelbrigt picked up so quickly on how you'd been used by the Abend to track Taise. It's very much his area of expertise. But he also caught on very quickly as to how you'd been manipulated before that. How the torture had been tailored in just the right way to make you malleable to the Abend's plans. Enough to break your will, but not enough to utterly destroy you.

"It's also no coincidence that you've found the will to resist the Abend since coming here and being with the Foresters. Much may have happened with you and Sionnachan, but I'd guarantee that Maelbrigt set your feet along a path which made it possible for you to find your way out of the fear and confusion. You weren't just weak, you know! You'd been actively attacked in such a way that you might never have found a way to be yourself again if you'd stayed in the west."

Sithfrey's appalled expression needed no explaining. The DeÁine scholar was clearly looking at his initial encounters with Maelbrigt in quite a different light, and also visualising what his life might currently have been like had his boat not been blown off course and brought him to Maelbrigt's attention.

"And you, Taise," Raethun continued. "Those incantations he kept up over you after you handled the warded parchment which made you so sick? They weren't just a random regurgitating of everything he'd learned in school. Even as worried sick as he was then, he was still taking in to account the person you are. So he wouldn't have used anything pertaining to someone who was weak-minded, or prone to act selfishly to the detriment of those around them. He knew you, and so he took into account the way the warding would have attacked *you*. Oh, that ward was designed to fend off all and sundry," he quickly added. "I'm not for a moment insinuating that it was sitting around waiting just for you alone. Of course it wasn't! But he did take into account that not only would it have been worse for you because you are DeÁine, but also that in another way it wouldn't have struck at you so hard as it might at some, because you did it out of a desire to help.

"Think of it like treating a dog bite. Although the actual wound was bad – like if someone's bite wound began to fester – you would be like a person who'd got in the way of a guard dog and understood that, and was therefore unlikely to suffer the mental trauma of someone who had randomly blundered into the guarded space, and was already scared stiff of dogs."

Understanding suddenly registered on Taise's face, for as a gifted healer this was something she understood. "Ah! Yes, someone like that might ultimately suffer even worse from the shock than from any puncture wound! I've even known people who died from extreme shock when they weren't physically hurt that badly." She stared off into space for a moment. "How fascinating!"

"And subtle!" Sithfrey added wryly. Then groaned and shook his head. "Sionnachan was right! We've been infected by these men, Taise! There's no place for us in DeÁine society now. Could you ever go back to living amongst people who look down on the Islanders for being ignorant savages when we've witnessed this degree of learning and subtly? I couldn't! And I don't want to!"

"So much to learn and unlearn at the same time," Taise agreed.

"If I get the chance I really want to go back and study with that ancient Master Forester, Arsaidh. Immaculate Temples, Taise! He made me feel like a junior novice starting all over again, but in some ways it was worse because the *breadth* of his knowledge was blindingly clear."

"Our training was so blinkered," Taise admitted, giving a watery smile. "And I wouldn't be so fast to think of learning just from the Master." She leaned over and patted Raethun's hand. "You, my dear, may have much you could teach us for all your youth!"

Raethun blushed scarlet at such praise from his leader's lady, but then quickly added, "Well the first bit of advice is to stay well behind the Foresters when it comes to any conflict! That's not cowardice in the case of you two."

"No indeed!" Kayna said with greater force. "You *must* stay behind them! Especially with you having that Gauntlet, Sithfrey! The last thing we want is for you to end up being hit by the incantations meant for the opposition – not least because, being closer to it, you'd get the brunt of the undiluted attack."

Matti's squint, Moss, had been listening intently to all of this and suddenly chirruped his agreement most forcefully, which raised an eyebrow with Sithfrey, who had been looking a bit sceptical at the advice until now.

"See?" Kayna chuckled. "Don't forget, I grew up in a Forester grange, Sithfrey. I might not have been taught in the way Raethun and the others have been, but an awful lot seeps in when you're exposed to it day in and day out."

"Is that why you insisted on being by Matti's side once we found out she was to use the Shield?" Andra suddenly exclaimed.

As Kayna turned a little pink at being read so accurately, Raethun began nodding. "That's not such a bad idea," he said encouragingly. "Trees forbid that Matti should get separated from the main force, but as a woman you can go to places with her where it might be difficult or inappropriate for us men to go. I know it's a weakness the more experienced Foresters were alert to. I remember Aldred saying to me that in the distant past it wasn't so much of a big thing, because most of the people the early Foresters guarded were men who were in positions of power. Positions that few women ever got to. But once we were making runs in and out of New Lochlainn to the Covert Brethren it became pretty clear that at some point we'd have to have women amongst the Brethren.

"And if we had female spies, then it would've been much better if we'd had women amongst us who could've gone in and out to meet them. Some meetings were covered up as romantic assignations, but those had their problems. Either the female contact had to seem like some man-mad slut who took an endless stream of strange men into her quarters, or one of our men had to make repeat runs in – and the risks attached to regular meetings quickly shoot up. It would've been so much better if we could've had two or three women whom our informant could've met during the course of her normal daily routines. Far less suspicious."

He nodded thoughtfully. "In fact, I think we should start polishing up your training and building on it straight away, Kayna." He got up and smoothed the creases out of his breeches. "I'll go and have a word with Maelbrigt while they've paused for a bit," and strolled across the deck to where Maelbrigt and Sionnachan were having a discussion to one side.

To Kayna's surprise, only moments later Sionnachan came over and took her by the arm with a stern expression but a twinkle in his eyes. "Come on, you!" he said warmly, and marched her off down below without giving her chance to protest.

In the meantime, Maelbrigt was coming their way having called five men to him who were now closely in his wake.

"What's happening?" Taise asked him worriedly. "Kayna's not in trouble, is she?"

"No more than usual!" Maelbrigt chuckled. "Although no doubt she'll be cursing me by the end of tonight! Again, as usual!"

"Sionnachan's taken her to Captain McKinley," Raethun explained as he jogged up joined by Ewan and Tobias, all of them grinning. "She's going to get properly trained so that she can work with us. As she already knows the basics, it shouldn't be too difficult for her. It's not like she's got to start from scratch."

Maelbrigt nodded. "Sionnachan and I agree that Raethun's idea is a very good one. Kayna can share a room or a tent with you, Matti, in a way that only Taise besides could do. We'd both feel much happier if you *both* have someone around you even in the most private of moments. As for the rest of the time, these are your new bodyguards," and he waved his hand at the five men standing behind him.

"My bodyguards?" Matti grimaced and took a deep breath.

"Is there a problem with that?" Maelbrigt queried, puzzled by her reticence.

Now it was Matti's turn to turn pink. "Oh, I'm sorry! ...No, it's just that my experience of bodyguards hasn't been exactly good. It usually meant that someone felt that I needed shepherding. That the dreadful wife of General Montrose wasn't behaving as a nice lady should!"

Maelbrigt's frown of worry dissolved into a grin. "Oh, that's all right, then! If it makes you feel any better think of the lads as the Shield's bodyguard, then, instead of yours. And believe me, what they're going to be showing you how to do would have those stuffy courtiers fainting just at the thought!"

In turn Matti relaxed and Maelbrigt turned to make the introductions. "You'll be keeping Sergeant Iago, of course. I don't think it would be possible to separate him from you without a fight after all you've been through together! He and Kayna will be there to watch your back and you alone. However, these lads have experience of fighting with a shield-wall, and they'll be able to help you a lot when it comes to confronting that DeÁine army we're heading towards. They're Sionnachan's men rather than mine, because we envisage you having to deal with large scale attacks, and Raethun says he's explained why the Ergardian lads are better at that than us.

"So ...this is Sergeant Tir and men-at-arms Cromm ...Briste ...Leag ...and Diogal." Each man came forward and solemnly shook her hand as he said their names. The sergeant was a grizzle-haired veteran who looked as though he was carved from rocks. An angular face seemed to be more craggy planes than flesh, and it topped off a square body almost as wide as he was high, making him look like a boulder in his mailed shirt. Even his eyes were an unrelenting grey and Matti felt her heart sink. It seemed unlikely that she would be forming any kind of bond with this man.

Mercifully Crom and Briste turned out to be brothers, and looked like a pair of ageless dwarves fresh from the mountains. Long grey-brown beards were neatly plaited to keep them tidy, and if they were every bit as stocky as Tir, they had sparking blue eyes the colour of a mountain lake and ready smiles which Matti found herself echoing. And Leag and Diogal were younger men, closer to Matti's own age and of altogether more human appearance.

"Sergeant Tir will be your liaison with the main army," Maelbrigt elaborated. "He'll keep you informed about what the tactics are, and how you can fit in without getting in the way and unwittingly ending up getting hurt. Thank you, Tir..." and the veteran gave them all a curt nod and walked away.

Without intending it to be quite as obvious as it became, Matti gave a sigh of relief, causing Diogal to chuckle.

"Yes, he's a bit dour, isn't he!"

Matti immediate felt rather ashamed. "Oh dear, was it that obvious?"

"Yes," teased Maelbrigt, "but I was rather hoping that you'd have a bit more faith in me than that!" As Matti turned even more scarlet he continued. "Tir's a very experienced man, but as Raethun and I found out the hard way, these weapons of the ancients don't conform to conventional ways of fighting. Just as Raethun came up with a way of me using the Sword without breaking my back into the bargain, I've picked these four for their original thinking more than anything else. Briste and Crom come from right in the heart of Ergardia, up in the mountains beyond Elphstone where the Bowl is, and they both have a real affinity with wood. They've produced some of the most amazing shields themselves – made them from scratch – and we think that they'll pick up on stresses and strains in the Shield for you when it gets used in battle."

As Matti and the others turned to look at the brothers again, they were astonished to find them sitting on a large coiled rope with a blissfully happy

Moss between them, who was having his ears silked by the pair – eyes half closed in pleasure, and the nearest thing a squint could manage to a smirk on his face. Clearly their affinity extended to ancient creatures as well as the venerated Trees.

"Do you think you'll be able to help me carry it, as well?" Matti asked them. "Only there's no way I can begin to lift it on my own."

"We'd thought of that," Doigal said from beside her. "We're going to make a carrying frame for it. If we have a good long pole – and the ship's captain is letting us commandeer a spare length of oak he carries in case of needing to splint the mast or the spars – then we can all carry it. We'll make an A-shaped piece for the middle so that the Shield stays upright too. That way we reckon we can even run with it. You'll be in the centre with Briste and Crom on either side of you. That means that in a very practical sense you'll also be protected by the Shield's bulk. Leag and I will be on the outer ends of the pole – still able to take some of the weight, but also prepared to let go and fight if we need to defend you both."

"Both?"

"Well you're going to have to take Moss into battle with you," Leag gently reminded her. Matti's horrified expression, which was mirrored by Taise, Andra and Sithfrey, confirmed to the Foresters that this aspect had been overlooked. "I'm sorry, but I don't think you can get away from that," he added regretfully. "I know it seems awful to have to take such a defenceless little creature into danger, and that's why we're glad that you'll have Iago and Kayna along as well. They can guard you while we look after Moss' safety."

This act of thoughtfulness did more than anything to endear her new companions to Matti, and she immediately nodded her assent to this tactic.

"I'll leave you lot to get acquainted," Maelbrigt said cheerfully, confident that Matti was in good hands and went to find Sionnachan once more. However, having found him Maelbrigt confessed his newest fear.

"May the Trees forgive me for not thinking of this, but it really hadn't occurred to me until Leag said it to Matti," he groaned. "How in the name of all that's sacred am I going to keep Squint safe, Sionnachan? In the heat of battle we've worked out nicely how to keep me from being filleted, or as near as you ever can. But Squint? How can I take him into that maelstrom? He's utterly defenceless! I just had this horrible vision of him trotting along right on my heels and being cut to ribbons! I can't do that! Sweet Rowan! I've lost Aldred and Bosel recently and they were two of the very few friends I have left living. It brought it all back. The reason why I happily stood down from active service. How the cost weighed so heavily on my conscience."

When Sionnachan had first heard that Maelbrigt had found a soul-mate, he had been surprised to find that he felt more than a little envious. Now, seeing the way it was tearing at his friend worrying about his lady's safety in this coming war, and the weight of that of Squint as well, Sionnachan was revising his view of such deep love. From where he was standing it seemed to be coming with an awfully high price. And now this matter of Squint being in close danger was twisting the knife in Maelbrigt's soul.

"Steady now!" Sionnachan growled with mock sternness, grasping Maelbrigt's shoulder and giving him a small shake, then patted him sympathetically. "Honestly, my friend! Did you think we'd expect you to think of everything all by yourself? Young Raethun has been proving himself quite the tactical thinker, even if he couldn't hold a tune in a bucket!"

"Raethun?"

"Oh yes! Must be Aldred's legacy after all that training he gave Raethun. So you see he might be gone, but he lives on in other ways! He's suggested that we give Squint his own bodyguard of shield-men. We had a look at several chaps while we were sorting out Matti's men for her because they'll need to have similar qualities – not swordsmen like your lads. Currently your master farrier is putting a short-listed eight through their paces. He's very fond of Squint, you know. He was most insistent that they be the right sort, to the point of near insubordination, so I told him his reprimand was to not stop until he'd got those right men! Somehow I don't think he looked on it as much of a chastisement." Sionnachan's wry grin told Maelbrigt that his friend had not been that put out by Farrier Armstrong's attitude either.

"So what are they going to do? Stay as close to me as possible while keeping Squint behind a shield-wall?"

"Pretty much. They'll have to work out the exact responses for moving about, of course, but Armstrong and Raethun seem to think it's workable."

"Thank the Maker for that!" Maelbrigt sighed in relief. "I've become terribly fond of the little soul." Then, his equilibrium restored, he grinned at Sionnachan. "And what about Arthur? Any thoughts on how we're going to keep him from being in the forefront of the battle?"

Now it was Sionnachan's turn to groan. Currently Arthur was having enormous fun swarming up and down the masts with the sailors, allowing

Sionnachan and Maelbrigt to get on with much needed preparations. However, neither was fooled into thinking that this would keep him out of their hair for much longer. The small boy had a knack of turning up at meetings when they least wanted him to – just when they were discussing some lethal tactic or ploy they might want to keep him well clear of.

"I'll keep him with me," Sionnachan said through gritted teeth. "You can't be expected to handle the Sword, keep Squint safe and watch Arthur too. He's a full-time job all by himself. And for that reason, although he gets on so well with Raethun, I don't want him near your bodyguards either. He could unwittingly distract them, and I don't want his young life further blighted by guilt over being the cause of you coming to harm. No, he'll have to be with me ...although I think I might need to chain him to my belt! I can't think of any other way to stop the scamp from getting in over his head!"

A day later, Aneirin suddenly appeared in their midst to tell Maelbrigt of Brego and Berengar's success at wiping out the DeÁine army, and the Donns in Brychan. He made little explanation of things and it was left to Matti's partner, Owein, to come along later and fill in the gaps. Matti had been wondering why he had been so absent while she had been at sea, and had thought the ancients might be as disturbed by the brine as the Abend were. When she realised how much of the co-ordinating he had been doing she was both relieved and cross.

"This isn't right," she said sternly to Maelbrigt, having cornered him out of earshot of Taise. She did not want her friend to hear her getting into an argument with her beloved, for Matti was determined that Maelbrigt should back her in this. "If we're all supposed to fight as one, then that has to be the ancients too. You can't be out there in the front of the army doing your stuff and thinking that we're behind you, only to find that Aneirin hasn't bothered to tell Owein or Urien what he's planned. I know Urien's an awkward sod! Poor Cwen's going to have her hands full with him. We can't have our two at odds with one another as well, or it'll just be chaos!"

However, Maelbrigt needed no prodding. "I know, I've been thinking the same thing," he pacified Matti by saying. "The only thing stopping me from saying anything to him until now has been the fact that we've not seen them in action. I had hoped that when push came to shove, all the posturing would disappear. Now, though, it seems to me that they weren't exactly united in helping Brego. I know we weren't there, but as the holder of the

Knife, and given that Brego has no ancient of his own, they should've behaved better. Peredur, Cynddylan and Owein seem to have been running themselves ragged while Vanadis, Aneirin and Urien swanned in and out when it suited them.

"That cannot happen again! It wasn't fair to Sooty either, and I certainly won't tolerate Squint and Moss being messed about like that, never knowing whether an ancient will come when they're needed. If the one allied to a particular squint can't come for whatever reason, then one of the others should step in, regardless of whose squint it is."

"How do we deal with this, then?" Matti asked. "I might have run a very big household for years, but I don't think treating the ancients like a sulky maidservant is likely to work."

Maelbrigt suddenly grinned. "Do you know, I think it might? If I have a go at them they keep hiding behind the excuse that I don't know what it's like to fight with the Treasures and the squints. If you take them to task they can't claim that a difference in experience is the cause of the trouble. Do you think you could do that?"

"Do I? You just watch me!" Matti said vehemently, which only broadened Maelbrigt's grin.

When Aneirin next appeared Maelbrigt studiously carried on with his conversation with Sionnachan and Matti's four Shield-bearers. Instead, Matti appeared at speed across the deck, and slid to a halt directly in front of the ancient's form.

"And where have you been?" she demanded in the tone of a mother chastising a very naughty child.

Aneirin blinked and then stared haughtily at her. "I have not come to speak with you," he replied dismissively. "Maelbrigt, I need to speak to you!"

"You'll speak to me!" Matti retorted forcefully. "Maelbrigt has other things to be doing than being at your beck and call all the time."

Aneirin made to protest but got no chance.

"You expect us to wait on you at every turn! You pop up out of nowhere, issue your demands and then disappear before we've had chance to ask you anything *we* might need to know. Well that has to stop! If we must be united, then we cannot have you picking and choosing which of us you deign to speak to at any given time. At the moment only half of you are working *with* us. Which means they are run ragged.

"…No, don't interrupt! …Owein hasn't had chance to do *any* work with me, because since I was chosen for the Shield he's also been trying to help Master Brego and the men of Brychan, too. And the same goes for Peredur and Cynddylan. *You* had the luxury of Maelbrigt being the first to receive his weapon, so you've already had plenty of chances to try things out. But also, *you* have a trained soldier to work with. Someone who knows how to handle weapons and use tactics. In that sense Maelbrigt needs you less than I need Owein, and Cwen will need Urien. But *we* can't get their help, because just to get everyone to a point where we can fight this battle with the ancient Island weapons, we've all needed some general help. And yet despite the fact that you have almost the least to do of any of you, *you* have failed to even begin to shoulder some of the burden!

"And you can pass this on to Vanadis, too! She needs to start getting her hands dirty instead of playing queen bee all the time! Master Brego doesn't have one of you, yet despite the fact that Master Hugh won't need her help for a good while yet, she too has made no effort at all to step in and fill the gap your insane fellow ancient left when he killed himself. Who precisely does she think is going to do the liaising with Master Brego when we get to fight the DeÁine? How will you feel if she sits back and waits at the Bowl, and expects *you* to help Maelbrigt *and* translate whatever Sooty needs to relay to Master Brego?"

Aneirin blinked at the furious figure confronting him, and Maelbrigt was secretly amused that the grumpy ancient was looking suitably chastened. That last comment seemed to have been the one to really hit home. He had no doubt that Aneirin could picture Vanadis remaining at arms' length. Now Matti was pointing the finger of blame at Aneirin and pressing home her point.

"Well you've done the same thing to poor Owein, Peredur and Cynddylan! Shame on you! It's not being clever. It's not being all-knowing. What it *is* is being plain petty! We've got a little boy of ten years old here with us who knows how to behave better than you! Arthur wouldn't be sitting on the sidelines letting others do all the hard work for him…"

"No I wouldn't!" the boy in question said firmly, sliding down one of the ropes from the rigging and doing his usual trick of appearing when least expected. He landed on the deck by Matti and squared up to the ancient, hands on hips and a very disapproving scowl on his small face. "You listen to her, mister! It's hurting the squints too! They're getting ever so wound up when they know their people are in danger, or need to know somefin', and you lot can't be bothered to turn up! You don't fink of no-one but yourselves – not even the others like you! I wouldn't have you lot in my gang! I'd kick you out straightaway!"

Aneirin had reeled back from Arthur, and the adults were perplexed at the way he seemed to be far more shaken by Arthur than by Matti. Whatever it was, it had Aneirin shaking his head and then for once politely excusing himself before disappearing.

"That was odd," Sionnachan murmured to Maelbrigt, as Matti congratulated Arthur on his timely intervention.

"Yes it was, wasn't it! I wonder if it's anything to do with this strange empathy Arthur has with the squints?"

The Foresters' Ealdorman quirked an eyebrow. "Hmmm, maybe. It's the only thing which makes any kind of sense. Why else would he go all wobbly when Arthur spoke."

"Ah, you noticed that too? I thought for a moment that it was my eyes, some trick from the reflections on the water, but he was definitely a little less solid wasn't he?"

Sionnachan sighed. "Why did this have to happen in such an almighty rush?" he complained. "Both of us could do with examining this talent of Arthur's much more closely."

"Never mind," Maelbrigt consoled his friend. "You can put him through as many tests as you like in a few months' time. Nobody's going to let him get into danger this time, so the only question is whether *we* survive the battle. After that, Arthur has years of growing up to do before he'll ever be in a situation even remotely like this. And I sincerely hope by then that his talents with the squints will be of purely academic interest, and the DeÁine will be gone for good."

However inside, Maelbrigt was quietly worried by this new turn of events. He had the awful feeling that if only he could stop for a moment and really think about it, without a hundred other things niggling at the back of his mind, then he would be able to work out the significance of it. And even as snowed under with other concerns as he was, he was sure that Arthur's seeming influence with the ancients was important.

Yet in the four more days they had at sea he still could not put his finger on why it troubled him so much, and as they came into view of Droman Point on Rathlin, the sight they saw pushed it further back. There before them were ships all over the bay leading back towards Kylesk. Merchant ships as big as their own were either anchoring further out, or were making their way into the bay. The lookout called down that they would be queuing to get to the quay at Droman, and by the time they had closed on the waiting ships, they could see men clustered in ranks on their decks.

"Prydein!" Matti gasped, pointing to the flags flying from the nearest masts. "It's Master Hugh's men! Ruari did it!"

"Somehow I doubt he did it alone," Kayna teased, although pleased at the sparkle which had come back in her friend's eyes. "I don't doubt Ruari's good, but I suspect Master Hugh might have had a hand in this too."

In far off Taineire there was also much discussion going on. For once, the remaining six leading ancients were assembled in the underground cavern which held the main controls to the system that supported what little life they had left.

"I felt it, I tell you," Aneirin insisted as Vanadis and Urien shook their heads in disbelief. "When that child appeared in front of me I felt something of one of us in him."

"But he's just a child," Owein protested. "According to Maelbrigt he's about ten years old. A street orphan of unknown parentage. He isn't even of old stock. How could he have any connection to us?"

Peredur held up a thoughtful finger to halt anyone else from speaking. "On the other hand, he's the one who has the uncanny affinity with the squints."

"Is he?" Vanadis immediately questioned.

"Yes he is!" Cynddylan retorted forcefully. "By God, Vanadis, it's no wonder the Islanders are running out of patience with you! I'm starting to do the same myself! If you'd done any work with them and the squints when they first got together, you couldn't have missed it."

"Agreed," Owein admitted. "I, for one, don't doubt the connection for a moment, or that there's something special about the boy. What I'm trying to reason out is *how* it could happen that Arthur has some connection to us. It's so long since any of our kind were around in a physical sense, surely it can't be inherited? Our ancient bloodlines must be so diluted as to be indistinguishable from any other."

"I see what you mean," Peredur agreed. "It can't be his physical heritage, which means it's something else. ...Tell us again, Aneirin. What was it like when Arthur spoke to you?"

The senior male ancient's shape quivered momentarily in disquiet. "It was in his voice. For a moment it was as though it wasn't a mere boy in front of me. It was as though someone else was speaking to me. There was something so familiar in it. Something older. Something going way back. ...Or maybe some*one*!"

# Rathlin showing troop movements

# Chapter 10

 *Reconciliation*

## Rathlin: Solstice

On the second of Solstice, Ruari was stood with Cwen, Ivain and Swein in the prow of the ship as it came into land at Kylesk. To his delight, the returning Prydein merchantmen had been accompanied by others from the north and west, some coming without being asked having tried to land and trade at Brychan, and getting a nasty shock as to the turn of events since they had last seen their home ports. Strangest of all were two huge seagoing vessels from the southern oceans, with their square towered, carved prows and their single huge, ribbed sail at each of their three masts. They had heard tales of the DeÁine fleet and had spread their sails to stay ahead of them. Now they were keen to aid in the overthrowing of the DeÁine tyrants in the hope that if the hold was broken in the Islands, then their homelands would stand a chance of gaining their freedom too. Ruari had not trusted them enough to put any of the key personnel on board, but carefully manoeuvred a company of the Prydein Order containing experienced sailors onto each – just in case it was a sham. However the foreign ships had been as good as their word and the journey uneventful.

What pleased Ruari greatly was that he was able to bring far more men than he had anticipated in this shipment. One more journey and the whole contingent from Prydein would be assembled on Rathlin, and that should hopefully happen around the tenth. For now, though, he was relieved to see Breca standing waiting to greet him, for although Cynddylan had reported back that the first landing had encountered no resistance from the Attacotti, Ruari was comforted to see it for himself. The three helpful ancients were so busy, an un-predicted fierce fight could have taken place before they had had chance to spot it.

"Welcome, Master Ruari!" Breca called, coming forward as soon as the ropes had been thrown to the quay and the ship bumped gently against the stone jetty. The ealdorman was obviously anxious to pass on some kind of news, and Ruari gestured to the three Treasure holders to take their time, while he used a rope to swing ashore without waiting for the gangplanks to be run out.

"News?" he asked the moment he was face to face with Breca.

"Yes, but first, you must keep Cwen and the Spear well away from Magnus! Without its presence he's become almost fully sane."

"Really? That's interesting."

"It's more than interesting, sire. He's been downright valuable in the time I've been here! We've had more than just co-operation too. He'd already done some scouting before we arrived, and since then we've sent out parties of equal numbers of our men and his. You see, he'd had a run in with one of the Abend around the seventh of Earrach – I suspect it might have been Helga. He and his men thought they were in for a fight and a half, but then suddenly she upped and returned to Brychan."

"That must have been to do with the impending return of Quintillean which Owein told us of," Ruari surmised.

"Possibly, but the two leading Abend didn't show their faces over here until something like the twentieth of Beltane, a good month and a half later, and they appear to have come from New Lochlainn not Brychan. I was here with Magnus when one of his relay riders came hammering in with the news that they'd landed. His men are dedicated, I'll tell you that. These men rode through the night over very tough terrain to bring the news, and I've had to rely on them. Without the ancients calling in, I had no way of being able to ask what's going on with the Abend. But I'm rather worried over what Berengar and Master Brego might be facing. You see Quintillean and Masanae have now gone to Brychan too. We've recently had a hawk in to that effect from one of my men who went out with Magnus' lads."

"Thankfully we've heard through the ancients that Brego and Berengar took Arlei on the twenty-seventh," Ruari added, "so you needn't worry on that account anymore. That was nearly a week ago, so if they'd had problems there I think we'd have heard by now. They had remarkably few casualties, but apparently the Abend weren't anywhere near Arlei then. They were all supposedly at Farsan according to our ancient spies. The last I heard, Master Brego and Master Berengar were in hot pursuit and aware of the Abend's presence. Brego's ploy is to have them think we're content with brandishing our weapons at the DeÁine along the Brychan coast, not to follow them immediately – especially since the Abend shouldn't be aware of us landing here."

"That's interesting," Breca mused. "As of the twenty-seventh we knew that all the Abend were back on Brychan soil, but let me tell you, the men they brought with them aren't! There have been a great many men disembarking from Souk'ir ships on the northern coast, and we believe them to be the Souk'irs' own Jundises. We've had a hectic time sending warnings out for all of Magnus' people to come here with all possible speed, because the early signs are that they want to wipe out every person on the island."

"What?" Cwen exclaimed, having come up behind them and heard the last bit. "But what of the folk we have around Loch Canisp?" She felt her heart sink that all their efforts to save them might yet come to nothing.

"Well this is what makes me sure Magnus is no longer any threat to us," Breca hastened to add. "Without any prompting from me he said that if his folk fled east then at least they wouldn't draw the Souk'ir's force down onto your people as well. He's fairly confident that his own clans will be capable of taking to the hills if they have to. Even the women and children apparently know of refuges they can get to. Places the Jundises won't follow them to or find. Many made a run for the coast and got picked up by galleys. We think they'll mostly be alright, and although Magnus is expecting a few casualties amongst the very old and the sick who can't flee, hopefully it won't be anything worse.

"In the mean time, I've used those men I dared hive off from my force here to scout southwards. I'll admit we haven't got very far, but the people they encountered who aren't allied to Magnus nonetheless said that they hadn't seen any sign of the new DeÁine yet. The ports of Lowes and Farr had already joined with the township of Kinloch, which lies inland from them, and had started to get a militia together after Cwen's warning." That brought a smile to her face, some good had come about at least. "I hope you don't object, but I sent a company down to join them. It seemed too good an opportunity to miss for us to get extra men. They'll do as much training as they can before we reach them, and of course they'll act as advance scouts too."

"And what of Alaiz?" Cwen demanded before Ruari could say anything, but she was echoed by Ivain and Talorcan who had barely been able to contain themselves while Breca spoke.

"She's alive," a familiar voice said from behind Breca and Eldaya emerged, smiling. "Do you want to come and see her?"

Ruari had a feeling that nothing he said would have stopped them, so together they trooped along the quay and past the decrepit buildings until they got to the one where Eldaya had set up her temporary refuge. Once through the door, though, the three streamed past everyone, Ivain and Talorcan taking the stairs two at a time and Cwen not far behind. The rest of Talorcan's lance were barely a few paces behind them, and in turn followed by Scully and his men.

"Hey! Steady on!" Eldaya called urgently. "She's very weak! Don't all pounce on her at once!"

Her words remained unheard and she hurried with Ruari to join them. Inside the room, though, there was a hush which Ruari found worrying. No happy chatter. No choruses of welcome. As he got through the door, the other men flattened themselves against the walls so that he could make his way to the end of the bed, where Talorcan sat on the one side, and Ivain on the other, holding the hand of a desperately pale young woman. Cwen was leaning over Ivain and gently stroking the girl's hair. For a moment Ruari did not even recognise her as the shy but vibrant young girl he had met way back on Rheged at Gerard's home. The determined girl he had chased around Gerard's courtyard with a wooden sword had become a frail figure, seeming to be almost consumed by the lives growing within her. Alaiz was awake, but her eyes had lost their sparkle and she seemed very distant, smiling faintly at both Ivain and Talorcan as they spoke in turn in very gentle tones.

Ruari halted and turned to Eldaya. "I'm no midwife, but she doesn't look well at all," he said very softly, feeling that he had hopefully understated what he felt. To him it looked more like Alaiz was dying, although that was a word he did not want to use around Ivain or Talorcan.

Eldaya tugged at his sleeve and drew him back to just outside the room. "No, she's not well. I've done all I can for her. But the simple truth is that she should've been in bed weeks before she was brought here. No-one's to blame. Master Brego certainly didn't know she was pregnant when he sent her, because Alaiz didn't even realise it herself. Since then, from what she's told me, your men did all they could to make things easier for her. It might have been enough, too, if she'd just been having a normal pregnancy. But twins are desperately risky at the best of times. We lost her mother-in-law in labour a little over a month ago, which didn't help. Gillies might have been a nightmare to be around since she became addicted to the narcotics some of the Attacotti use, but she was the nearest thing to a mother Alaiz knew, and she's mourned the loss of her deeply. It was one thing to be at loggerheads with her while she lived, but once she'd died, Alaiz could remember again the person who'd been so good to the orphaned little girl who came to court. That and the constant worry over her friends has taken its toll on her too. I'll not deceive you, I'm deeply worried about her."

164

Ruari looked back into the room and saw that Ivain's head was now bowed and was clearly crying – he must have just got the news of his mother's death. Swein had come to bend over him and was comforting him, yet an even clearer sign of Ivain's grief appeared. The three squints came up the stairs as fast as their furry feet would carry them having been left behind in the rush, all whistling distraughtly and making a beeline for the bed, their bodyguards hurrying in their wake until they saw Ruari and Breca. Daisy, Eric and Dylan surrounded Ivain, all keening at his feelings of loss. As Cwen and Swein tried to calm them, it was Tamàs who understood them first.

"Too close to their own loss," the elderly archer said perceptively. "They've lost the all Guardians they had contact with, and they came perilous close to losing one another. No wonder they'm so upset."

Alaiz must have managed to say something, because Ivain picked Eric up and sat him on the bed beside Alaiz, the high tester-bed being too tall for the squint to get up on his own. His ears were semaphoring furiously as he gently leaned forwards until his nose touched Alaiz's, then he suddenly seemed to become aware of her belly. His ears shot straight up and he peered intently at her considerable bump, then whistled with such excitement that the other two pushed forwards and put their noses right on the sheets covering Alaiz. The whole thing was so comical it broke the tension, and even Ivain could not refrain from smiling. The three squints then began a whole series of clicks and chirps as if they were trying to communicate with the babies.

Talorcan stood up and turned to Ruari, raising his hands in bemusement. Clearly nobody else was going to get a chance to speak to Alaiz until the squints' curiosity was satisfied. So slowly everyone filed past the bed, just saying a word or two to Alaiz until all but Ivain and the squints were left in the room. Talorcan closed the door firmly behind him as the last one out and said to Ruari,

"I think those two have a lot to say to one another. It might be the first time they've really had chance to know one another without some courtier or other interfering."

Ruari took the hint and summoned all those involved to the hall downstairs, where someone had already brought in light refreshments for them. They were deep in discussion with Magnus – who seemed less susceptible to the Spear now that the squints were here – as to deployments and tactics when Ivain finally emerged, pale and looking more worried than Breca had ever seen.

"She's sleeping," he said shakily, then clamped his hand across his mouth and tried to stifle the sobs welling up inside. "Oh Blessed Martyrs, don't let me lose her too!" he choked before being enveloped by Talorcan's hug. The Knight held him tight as he finally lost his restraint, and the rest of Talorcan's lance gathered round them and took them from the room with Pauli bringing up the rear. Swein looked from Ivain to Cwen and back, torn as to whether he should go to his friend.

"It's alright," Cwen assured him, coming to wrap her arms around him in an effort to halt the tears which she could feel welling up too. "Pauli and Talorcan will take care of him."

Swein nodded and hugged her back, realising that Cwen in part was blaming herself for not having been even more insistent that Alaiz stop with her and rest. It was something Cwen gave voice to when he took her out of the press of the company that evening, for a little fresh air in the overgrown garden at the back of the house. In its way the garden had a considerable charm even if it was now far from its original glory, for the roses had sprawled in a tangle across walls and up trees and were just coming into bloom, filling the air with their scent. From beyond its walls they could still hear the sound of boats casting off or coming in, and the rhythmic footsteps of the men who came off marching towards whichever billet they had been assigned to. Yet inside the garden there was a small oasis of calm away from the coming battle. Cwen sank gratefully onto a stone bench and sat breathing in the air while Swein held her hand.

"Poor Alaiz," she whispered. "All she wanted was a house with a little garden like this and to be with Hamelin. Now she might never see him again."

"But he might survive," Swein said encouragingly. "After all, he's off with Labhran somewhere. He won't be in this big battle." Then he took in the way Cwen was shaking her head as tears finally broke loose and streamed down her face. "Oh no! You weren't talking about Hamelin dying, were you?"

Cwen shook her head, then had to blow her nose before she could speak. "No, not him. ...She's so pale, Swein, and Eldaya says she keeps bleeding badly. That's partly why she's so white. She could expect to lose blood when she gives birth anyway. That would be bad enough if she was well and only going to have one baby. But she's going to have to give birth twice. That's such a hard thing for a woman to do even when she's been looked after all the way through her confinement." She gave a sob which seemed to have been torn from her heart. "I don't think she's going to live through it, Swein!" and she dissolved into uncontrollable sobbing.

It was so uncharacteristic for Cwen to be so pessimistic that Swein was shaken to the core. "Do you think she knows it herself?" he struggled to ask after the first wave of Cwen's crying had eased. Cwen's tearstained face looked up and she nodded. "Oh Trees," he sighed, and wished heartily that Berengar and Esclados were with them. They were so reassuring, he now realised. The world could seem like it was coming to an end and they would still make you feel as if there would still be something good coming out of it. He had not realised he had spoken it aloud, though, until Cwen said,

"Me too. Just now I'd give anything to see them both. Isn't it odd? I loved Richert desperately, and losing him was such a dreadful blow. But I miss Berengar and Esclados more than him these days, because we've been through so much together. My days with Richert, by and large, were easy. There was never anything to worry us beyond the slim chance of his wife coming to Amroth. If there was any supporting to be done, I've come to realise that it was me providing a refuge for him to escape the plotting and backbiting at court. I never had to rely on him in a crisis, because the only true crisis we ever suffered was the last one when he was murdered.

"But it's been Berengar who actually did the things I wondered if Richert would ever do. Who's protected me in times of trouble and stood by me. Him and Esclados, who's like the uncle I didn't have. I didn't realise how much they meant until the squints told us they were both well a few days ago. I hadn't realised they'd been constantly in the back of my mind. Now I'm worried sick for Berengar if he has to use this DeÁine Gorget."

Swein hugged her. "Don't you worry about that! If he does then Talorcan will almost certainly be doing it with him, and that's a comforting thought, isn't it? I can't imagine the two of them succumbing to much!"

Cwen managed a watery smile and by the morning had cheered up again, or at least was keeping her fears and doubts well hidden once more.

Meanwhile, although Ruari eagerly sent Breca out scouting with a substantial number of men, he kept the Island Treasures and all concerned with them tucked up in the house. Magnus had had a long conversation with Ruari, and to everyone's relief had understood the peril of remaining too close to the Spear even despite Daisy's presence, declaring he would take himself off with Breca, and then check on the retreat of his people from the north. However, he was still in the town when Peredur appeared to tell them of Brego's victory over the Donns. The celebrations were heartfelt but short-lived, for everyone knew it was far from being decisive, although it did feel good to know that the first of their objectives had been achieved. What marred it more than anything was Peredur's news that all the Abend were back on Rathlin as of two days ago, news which worried Magnus greatly and not surprisingly so. It was his people who stood to suffer most and soonest, and it leant an urgency to his mission.

For herself, Cwen was glad that Ivain had the sympathetic Peredur to work with. The ancient had apologised for not coming sooner when he had been made aware of Ivain's grief by Eric, an apology which was hardly needed given what had happened. It was the thought which counted, though, and Cwen resolved that if her having the grumpiest of the ancients saved Ivain from that kind of extra burden, then she would bear the trial of Urien more willingly. What intrigued her more was the way Ivain's relationship was developing with Talorcan. She was as sure as she could be that they had spent the night together. Something which was confirmed by the way the lance acted in the morning, behaving on the one hand as though it was the most normal thing in the world for the two of them to come in to breakfast together, and at the same time managing to challenge anyone to dare say anything about it.

A quiet word with Swein over lunch confirmed she had not been imagining things, yet increased her concern for Ivain. After a lifetime of being pulled left, right and centre to the extent where he had not even realised how he felt about his relationships, it was not a good basis for expecting him to cope with his grief well. Anyone might deeply mourn the passing of a loved mother, but most people did it with the support of other loved ones around them. Ivain, she realised, had nobody other than those like herself, whom he had hardly got to know that well, and she gave herself a little shake mentally. She and Swein would have to be strong for him in the coming days. Hopefully Alaiz would still be here when they got back from the fighting, and if not then she would bury her grief for this girl whom she felt so responsible for until there was space for her to mourn. Ivain would have to come first, not least because she had a sneaking suspicion that his feelings had already been in turmoil before finding Alaiz in such a state.

Cwen was also finding her respect for Ruari growing. He made a point of saying that the Treasure holders could have a few days respite, without doing any work on how they would use their powerful gifts. The excuse he gave out loud to the assembled company was that the ancients had told him the fleet with the Ergardian Foresters was not far away, and that as they were bringing Matti and the Shield, it was worth waiting for them. He also made much of Cwen finding a coterie of men she could work with, and declared that since this had already been done for Ivain and Swein, there was little they could do until all the Island weapons had been brought together. Many people studiously avoided looking at Ivain at this point, and Cwen could see that everyone was aware of what had gone unsaid – that Ivain needed some time to deal with his personal grief if he was ever to help them. It was tactfully done, though, and Ivain seemed happily unaware of Ruari's careful manoeuvring around him, and it was this for which Cwen was particularly grateful.

She was therefore feeling better all round when she came to review the men she had not seen before with Daisy. The white squint sat by her side on a balcony of one of the dilapidated mansion houses, while Ruari had the Order's captains files their men past them. It was a lot easier than when they had tried to do this on the road on Kittermere, not least because they were not looking at men who were so fixedly archers. As a result, Daisy was way more positive when she spotted someone, happily chirping and pointing with her paw without any of the doubts she had shown previously. The upshot of which was that Cwen found herself with a substantial number of men by the end of two days. This time it was almost exclusively the men-at-arms whom Daisy had selected, which could have caused problems by dividing up the lances to which they were attached.

However, Ruari swiftly decided that he would turn things to their advantage. Some of the chosen men were currently in newly formed lances, which was a normal process within the Order as men retired and adjustments had to be made. Where this had happened, the new lances were broken up again to fill the gaps in established lances made in the selection process. There were not too many of them, and so with the aid of a couple of experienced commanders, Ruari soon had them set up in lances where both men-at-arms could work with Cwen. These he rearranged into companies until Cwen was confronted with a whole half-battalion who would operate with and around her. The archers in these lances would provide protection for her and Daisy and the Spear, and so were not without their uses. He also declared to those who had not been chosen, or who came into a second rank of men who might do as reserves, that they had yet to find a similar group to work with the Shield. Nobody, he emphasised, should feel left out. There was much they yet had to sort out, and all would play a part in some way.

Cwen therefore felt much more confident when Urien finally returned, appearing as Ruari had the men make a first try of throwing ordinary spears while Cwen and Daisy held the Treasure. The ancient had evidently felt them connecting to it, yet his attitude was less aggressive than it had been before. His shimmering form stood to one side as the spears all took flight and thudded into the ground with professional precision. This time, though, there was none of the tingle of energy which had accompanied Swein and Ivain's work with the archers. Nothing like the charged and unified flight of arrows which had so nearly impaled Talorcan.

"Your heart isn't in it," he said to Cwen, although with nothing of his former asperity. "You have to *want* the Spear to engage."

Cwen sighed. "I'm beginning to understand that. The trouble is that there's nobody here I feel that angry about."

"Except maybe you," Ruari said curtly to Urien, having come up to join them. "And I don't think the Spear would let her aim it at you."

Urien blinked, somewhat startled by the bluntness. "Errr ...No, the Spear wouldn't let you do that. And regarding that, we need to talk."

Now it was Cwen's turn to look askance. Was this some kind of peace offer after all this time?

"Well this was a first experiment," Ruari said calmly. "I'll dismiss the men and we can go into the courtyard to talk in private." He did not want Cwen to be undermined in front of her new command if Urien's pleasantness was only a front.

He led them around the side of the nearest house, and into what had once been an elegant courtyard with a central pool. Gesturing Cwen and Daisy to sit on the stone edge of the pool, comfortably warmed by the late afternoon sun, Ruari stood with one long leg propped up on the rim and asked brusquely, "Well?"

To their surprise Urien almost appeared shamefaced as he began.

"We've been talking – the rest of us you call ancients. Aneirin has had a couple of ...errr ...strongly worded ..*errhem* 'conversations' from others amongst you."

"Really?" Ruari's voice carried a hint of sarcasm, although Cwen could see the twitch of a suppressed smile on his face. So the other Islanders had begun to lose patience too!

170

Instead of biting at the remark, Urien only looked more apologetic. "First it was your Master Brego. He was quite angry with Aneirin and Vanadis. And then Aneirin was confronted by the Shield-holder while Maelbrigt stood by and made no attempt to contradict her."

Cwen felt a little skip of amusement inside. So Matti was a woman with some brains and spirit! This was good news. She had quietly been praying that she would not be another Alaiz – a good person to the core of her soul, but hardly strong enough to cope with standing side by side with you when the world was coming to an end around you.

"Did she really?" Ruari was saying with strained innocence.

"Indeed. So much so that Aneirin came back and called us all to confer. Peredur, Owein and Cynddylan were most vocal in backing up what they said too."

By now Ruari had begun to scrutinise the cracks in the courtyard's pavers, ducking his head down in order to hide the growing smirk.

"The Shiel..., Matti... She and a small boy who travels with them said that if you all had to be united in intent then we had to be the same. We had thought it would sufficient for us to direct you. Had we been able to take a tangible form, of course, as we originally anticipated, we would have actively helped more. But it hadn't occurred to us that since we are so disembodied now that our intent might carry so much weight. Vanadis is now going to try to discuss a workable arrangement in which she can support both Master Hugh and Master Brego. I've been told by Owein that I need to develop the kind of relationship he has with Matti through Moss, with you and Daisy. Just as Peredur and Cynddylan assure me they have with Ivain and Eric, and Swein and ...err... Dylan."

Urien was clearly struggling with the allocation of proper names to the squints, and to calling the Treasure wielders by their personal names. Quite clearly such one-to-one relationships were not what they had ever expected. It made sense to Cwen, though. If she had grasped anything it was that they would be having to make split second decisions, and that would not be helped if they were hesitating at every turn over what the ancients were saying.

"Owein and I have now talked about how to use the Shield and the Spear together. This was not what I was expecting either."

*No, I bet you weren't!* Ruari thought, unable to feel any great sympathy for the struggling ancient.

"We thought we would be using them as we did before. But now Owein, Peredur and Cynddylan are telling us that you all have real experience and expertise at using these particular weapons in their original forms. You see, those amongst us who created the pieces you're now using, took their designs from weapons whose purpose they felt might remain recognised after our civilisation fell. They looked at designs for weapons from our own ancient past and did what they could with them. All they could do was hope that the shape would be familiar to whoever was forced to use them, because they were fairly simple and self-explanatory. I've been told to tell you that some among us have gone through our archives, and say that the Treasures were infused with Power thinking that that would be their only attribute.

"Your approach is one nobody ever considered, even back then. Owein says that your men who are travelling with Matti are adamant that they use spears as a defensive weapon as often as an offensive one. That spears are not usually used singly, but in groups to push forwards or hold a position. Yet I believed, from what was written down, that she would be alone while the rest of you fought, and that she would only need to focus the Power it draws. Owein says this isn't making the best use of it. Is this what you meant when you said that Cwen would hardly be needing to calculate things?"

This final climb-down, asking for advice, forced Ruari to relent. "Yes it is. The men you just saw us working with all have a good deal of experience of using spears in real combat situations. The commander I've assigned to work with Cwen, is actually a former man-at-arms who's risen through the ranks, and who fought in a spear and shield formation at Moytirra – the last time we fought a big set battle against the DeÁine along with the Abend plus many acolytes. He's gone away to consult with some of the other veterans to come up with some exercises we can try out with Cwen, to see if they fit her and the Spear's needs. What we really need you to do is to translate for Daisy. She's trying to tell Cwen how to link herself with the Spear, but it's very difficult for Daisy to convey complicated messages when she can't even speak proper words. We can supply the tactics, it's the intangibles we can't do."

Urien's ghostly head nodded solemnly. "Ah, I begin to see now what Aneirin meant when he said the others felt we were letting the squints down." He gave a sigh which hinted at just how hard he was finding all this. "Very well," and he stared at Daisy, who could apparently hear some

172

inaudible communication from him because she let loose a whole stream of her chirping noises, barely stopping to draw breath. Whatever she was saying to him, his level of surprise seemed to rise and rise. When she finally ran out of steam and sat panting gently he took a moment before he could speak.

"Oh dear! This is all quite perplexing! According to Daisy you are already tapping into the power of the Treasures in a way we had never anticipated, but which the squints say is infinitely more manageable than our approach. She wants me to show you how to widen and also narrow that power so that you can control it further. Unfortunately I shall have to go away and do more research on how you'll be able to do that, as it's something I've never even thought of, let alone done."

"It's a good job you don't need any sleep, then, isn't it?" Cwen said sweetly, causing Ruari to cover his snort of amusement with a bout of coughing.

As Urien gave a weak nod, a brave attempt at a smile, and disappeared, they became aware of Daisy making a very odd noise. Both Ruari and Cwen spun to look at the white squint, who was making a wheezing, asthmatic noise, then realised that it was the nearest thing the squints could do in the way of laughing. As Cwen and Daisy hugged, both giggling in their own way, Ruari stretched to ease his tense shoulders and felt some measure of relief. At least Cwen's initial nerves had gone and she was well on the way to being as relaxed as anyone could expect her to be in the circumstances. And that meant one less worry for Ruari.

Quite how he was going to help Ivain was another matter. Thank the Trees Swein was turning out to be a real asset in that way. If Ivain was a fast learner in some things, then Swein was outstripping him in others. The former courtier was very good at empathising with others and coming up with solutions which genuinely helped. Ruari was already thinking that if Berengar did not offer Swein a place in the Brychan sept he would gladly have him amongst his men in Rheged, if they all survived.

At least they managed to get through the remaining days until the Ergardian Foresters arrived without incident. Ivain's grief had calmed if not diminished, and Eldaya reported that Alaiz was saying that she felt so much better having had the chance to talk to Ivain again. She was not telling anyone, not even Eldaya, what had been said between the two of them, but it had brought about a reconciliation that both were very comfortable with, for which everyone was grateful. Both Alaiz and Ivain had been so dreadfully manipulated, everyone felt it would have been tragic if they had been unable to find a way back to being at least friends now that they had the freedom to act as they wished.

When the Ergardian fleet began coming in to the docks, Ruari was on hand to greet Maelbrigt as he disembarked. The two shook hands formally in front of the assembled welcoming group, but the smiles and words spoken were of real friendship. The welcome Matti received from the three other holders was equally as warm, and she felt for the first time that this might not be beyond her. That Matti had Kayna and Taise with her was something Cwen had not anticipated, but within minutes had decided that she could get on with all three of them. To finally have other women she could talk to again was a relief she had not thought to find in the midst of an army camp. What was blissful was to have Taise notice her concerned glances to Ivain. The DeÁine lady was tall enough to tower over her and yet there was no haughtiness, merely kindness and concern as she bent down to ask Cwen very softly if there was something amiss with Ivain. Drawing them slightly to one side, Cwen rapidly told them the whole tangled mess, their responses only serving to confirm her impression that these were women she could make good friends of.

That impression was strengthened when Taise's first request to Ruari was that she be allowed to see Alaiz, taking the time to explain to Ivain that she had been acting as a healer in Celidon for many years now. She also endeared herself to him by telling him how fond she had become of Alaiz in their time together at Lorne. She was careful not to raise his hopes that she could make Alaiz better, but her willingness to try broke the ice better than anything else she could have done. Sithfrey also declared his willingness to see if there was anything he could think of to help his young friend, and as Squint and Moss were also showing their trust of the two DeÁine, nobody objected.

All five squints trotted beside the women, Sithfrey, and Ivain with his permanent accompaniment of Swein, Pauli and Talorcan as they made their way to the house where Alaiz lay. The squints' reunion had been touching to watch and everyone assumed they did not want to be parted. What Cwen had not expected was for Maelbrigt and the big Forester Sionnachan to hurry off to retrieve something from the ship, and then come trotting in their wake. Sionnachan was explaining something to Ruari as they came jogging up to the others just as they reached the front door, but then would not say more, although Cwen had spotted him making a pointed glance towards Ivain. However if that was the Forester not wanting to give Ivain false hope, then she was willing to contain her curiosity for now.

At Alaiz's bedside Taise displayed a professional attitude, gently questioning Alaiz as her long fingers delicately felt and probed. Eldaya's scowl at her territory being invaded by one of the enemy was something Cwen quickly tackled. If Taise had more healer's knowledge and it could help Alaiz, she pointed out firmly, then what she was was of secondary importance. However there was no mistaking the way Taise's buoyant good humour seeped away. She was too good at tending the sick to allow her concerns to show openly, but to those who had seen her not an hour earlier it was clear she though Alaiz's situation grave.

"What do the squints think?" Sionnachan asked Swein, clearly not wanting to ask Ivain to have to give voice to his worries in front of Alaiz. "Is there anything they can do to help?"

Swein shook his head. "They're very curious about the babies, but all I get from Dylan when he touches Alaiz is a sense of confusion. I don't think they quite grasp what it is to be a physical being yet, if that makes sense. They're still very tied into that feeling of existing beyond the world. Not surprising really given how long they were in that space between realities or worlds, or whatever it was. So they can't seem to see how there can be lives growing inside another one."

"No sense then that they could use one of the Treasures to heal?"

Both Swein and Cwen shook their heads, although Swein added, "Maybe if we had more time we might find a way, but we're still getting to grips with using them to sort out the weapons at the moment. That's hard enough because it's so unfamiliar. Other uses could be staring us in the face but we just don't have the experience to spot them."

"That's fair enough," Sionnachan said soothingly. "Don't worry about it. It's just that we've had a bit of a breakthrough with the Gauntlet. If Sithfrey hadn't had the experience of using other DeÁine pieces I doubt it would've ever happened."

He would not say more, but when two Foresters brought a heavy box in and sat it in the corner of the room the squints promptly moved to the other side of the bed. Their askance glances at the box told everyone what it was even before Maelbrigt spoke.

"Don't worry. It is the DeÁine Gauntlet, but Sithfrey's been able to change it." Then he became aware of Sithfrey's expression. "Sithfrey? Is there something wrong?"

The angular DeÁine scholar looked up from his scrutiny of Alaiz. "It's just that I've never even been a bystander in a situation as complex as this. Three lives within one? This is no simple healing we're talking about here. For situations like this a DeÁine family would call upon the very best healers from the Houses of the Holy, not some scholarly acolyte! And to the best of my knowledge twins have never even been *conceived* by a DeÁine, let alone brought to term. So even if I had trained for this it would still be new ground."

Maelbrigt sighed and wrapped a reassuring arm around Taise's shoulders, signalling both support and understanding even as Sionnachan patted Sithfrey consolingly on the back and said,

"Don't beat yourself up over this. It's enough that you were willing to even consider trying to help. Sometimes all you can do is accept your limitations and accept that, with the best will in the world, you can't always make things turn out for the best." He turned to Ivain to explain. "Sithfrey has used the Gauntlet once to heal a seriously wounded Forester. However, McKinley was in robust health to start off with and there were no complications. It was a simple stab wound. A single cut with an entry point whose passage it was easy to define."

Ivain nodded, not needing further details. "And you hoped it might be possible to do it again? Only this is so different he might end up doing more harm than good?"

Sithfrey breathed a sigh of relief, having been dreading the possibility that Ivain would bombard him with accusations for not trying. "Yes, that's exactly it! I can only focus a device – *any* device – on one person. The danger is that in saving one, I might harm the other two as they get caught in the backwash of Power."

"I agree," Taise said softly. "While there's still hope that Alaiz might deliver the babies naturally this shouldn't be considered, and if that doesn't happen then I would still back Sithfrey's caution."

On that solemn note they left Alaiz to try and get more sleep and trooped down to the hall, the house having become the billet for all the Treasure holders for Ivain's sake. The rest of the day was one in which Cwen got to know her newest fellow Treasure wielders and their friends, although Maelbrigt was more often than not in deep consultation with Ruari and Sionnachan. By the evening they announced that they would be searching for men who aligned with the Shield first thing in the morning, while Maelbrigt declared that he and Sionnachan would be taking the

Foresters off into the hills to practice something they were reticent to talk about.

"We'll probably hear something like a distant choir practice," Matti said knowingly, but Kayna shook her head.

"No, we won't hear a thing. Maelbrigt won't risk Taise or Sithfrey getting knocked about by whatever they're cooking up. It's interesting that Maelbrigt isn't going to be recruiting a cadre of his own to go with the Sword, though, isn't it! I suspect he's going to use the Foresters for that."

"Can he do that?" Taise wondered. "All of them, I mean. That's an awful lot of men for one person to control."

Raethun came and plonked himself down on the end of their table, bringing with him slices of a rich dried fruit loaf for them all. "Ah, but he won't control them all, Taise. That's why he and Sionnachan have been so deep in tactics while we've been at sea. I suspect he'll have maybe ten companies – that's a hundred lances which translates as five hundred men. What he's probably worked out with Sionnachan is what chants or incantations they'll use in response to any given threat. That way if one hears the other start up they'll know what to do. I'd also bet that when the Celidon Foresters get here that they'll go with Maelbrigt too. Don't worry, Taise, they've done this before!"

It was not quite the consolation Raethun had intended it to be, for Taise had visions of the massed DeÁine army she had seen back in New Lochlainn, and part of her still feared that these men were overly optimistic. However, she could do little but watch Maelbrigt march out in the morning and then focus on her own day.

After checking on Alaiz, she went to sit with Matti and Kayna as they continued the search for more men, finding that Ivain and Swein had also joined them, plus their inevitable accompanying men. Yet it made for an unexpectedly jolly party, all seated on the balcony once more. Talorcan's men made quiet, ribald remarks about some of the men which soon had them smothering laughter, and by the time they broke for lunch and to give Matti's Moss a rest, it was hard to feel too despondent.

Unfortunately the mood was shattered sooner than they anticipated. As they tried not to laugh too hard at Barcwith's comment on the selection of a squint-eyed veteran who looked as though he must surely see everything double, a messenger ran up to call them to the house. Alaiz had gone into labour.

All thoughts of selecting men gone, they ran back together and hurried up to the second floor chamber where Alaiz lay. Taise swept in and picked up a bag which she had left on a chest in the corner, pulling out a snowy white over-mantle which she pulled on over her other clothes.

"Everyone out!" she said sternly. "Even you Ivain. Eldaya and I need room to work. The only ones who can stay are the squints and Sithfrey." As Talorcan made to object on Ivain's behalf, Taise halted him. "This is going to get messy and the last thing Alaiz needs is someone getting distraught at what they're seeing. If you want to help, go and get me some *very* sharp knives and plunge them into boiling water when you've done. Then bring them to me in the water. Our old texts assure us this is a way of preventing any cuts becoming septic, and I've used it to good effect. Please go!"

With everyone out of the room, Taise turned to Eldaya, who had to admire Taise's authority at getting the men out of the room. "Now then, tell me what's happened so far..."

Outside the room, Talorcan deputised the job with the knives to Barcwith, and drew Ivain into the small chamber next door to Alaiz's. With Pauli and Swein he sat with Ivain, few words being spoken but doing their best to support him by their presence. Matti, Kayna and Cwen sat on the stairs.

"Do either of you have any experience of complicated deliveries?" Cwen asked hopefully.

Kayna shook her head. "Not a clue! I was always more occupied learning with the men in the camps. Give me a sword cut or an arrow wound and I can do a good patching-up job – not a proper healer's work, you understand, but good enough to keep someone alive until they can be properly treated. But this is something I've no experience of."

"Me neither," Matti added sadly, "although for Alaiz' sake I wish I did! At Montrose Castle we always had several women who knew what they were doing, plus their daughters or others whom they were training. There was never any need for me as the lady of the house to get involved directly as a midwife. What about you, Cwen?"

"Oh I've helped out at a few births, but nothing where it's been anything but straight forward. I'm so glad Taise is here to help Eldaya. I was dreading her asking me to assist her for fear of doing the wrong thing when she was busy doing something else." Barcwith came up the stairs carefully bearing the bowl of hot water with the knives in, wrapped in a thick cloth. "I think I'll take that in and just ask if they need me, though." She took the bowl from Barcwith and slid inside the room as Matti held the door open for her.

The rest of the lance came and joined Matti and Kayna on the stairs.

"Why did she say the squints could stay?" wondered Ad.

"I think they can sense the babies," Matti answered. "I can only assume she'll want them to tell her if they feel anything going wrong inside of Alaiz."

Mentally, though, all assumed that Taise would have no need of translating if that happened. They sat in silence for what felt like hours yet was not even one, everyone listening for the slightest clue as to how things were progressing.

"It's awfully quiet in there," Galey said nervously when the silence became so strained it was almost tangible.

"Aye, that don't bode well," Tamàs agreed sagely. "Should be far more crying out if she was doing a normal job of it."

In the room where Ivain was, they could hear someone pacing nervously now, which then got joined by a second pair of feet until Talorcan emerged onto the landing and began prowling there. Everyone was still listening so hard nobody said a word to him.

Suddenly Cwen appeared at the door, white-faced and looking very shaky.

"Would someone please bring Ivain in," she said huskily and disappeared again.

Within moments Ivain had dashed in with Swein, leaving the door open behind them. From the doorway the others saw a grim sight. It was not that bloody and Alaiz was draped decorously with a clean sheet, although all the other bedclothes had gone. Rather it was her stillness and the terrible quiet which unnerved them. Taise was speaking softly to Ivain, and one look at his face confirmed the worst. Alaiz was dying.

"I have to do it," Taise said gently in answer to an unheard question from Ivain. "The babies aren't in the right position, as I said. That means the cords are tangled around their necks and will kill them. And no, I'm so sorry, leaving it isn't an option. If we don't do this then both Alaiz *and* the babies will die for certain. This way we might at least save her or the babies."

"Save her," Ivain choked. "She's too precious to lose!"

"I make no guarantee," Taise warned him. "I said 'chance' and I meant it. I'll do everything I can for her, but we could still lose them all. But if the worst happens and we do, at least we can say we tried everything." She had just turned to Eldaya when Tamàs' voice broke the silence.

"If you'm going to cut her, then I can help."

"You've done it before?" Taise was astonished. He was a rough soldier, how could he have done?

Yet Tamàs nodded. "Aye. Only the once, but I did. I was a shepherd, see? I'd done it with sheep many times. Then there was this lass in a village we passed through. The old midwife hadn't the strength to make the cut, so she asked me to do it for her."

"And they lived?" Ivain asked anxiously.

Tamàs turned to him gravely. "I'll not make any rash promises, young sire. All I'll say is that the lass lived when we left a day later. But she were a robust lass. A farmer's girl, and healthy with it."

"And Alaiz is so frail," Ivain finished for him with tears falling already. "Very well. I understand. ...Do what you have to."

He stepped back and was immediately gripped firmly by Pauli and Talorcan, both to support him as he swayed slightly, and also in case he tried to rush in.

Taise leaned in over Alaiz and brushed her hair back with a soothing hand. "Alaiz? ...Alaiz, my lovely? ...Listen to me. We have to cut you open to get the babies out. If not you'll all die."

Alaiz's voice was too weak to be heard but those in sight of her saw her say,

"Save my children!"

"We'll do our best, but we should be able to save you," Taise said with a practised calm that Cwen envied and admired. She could not have held her tone that steady at the moment even with someone whom she was not fond of. Yet Alaiz found the strength from somewhere to protest.

"No save the babies first!" they saw her insist. "Give Hamelin his children!"

Taise raised her brows as she turned away signalling her doubts of that happening, then looked even more surprised as Tamàs called his fellow soldiers forward.

"Hold her steady," he said with battlefield calm. "If she don't move, we've got more control." He gestured Talorcan to the head of the bed and Kayna to the other side. "You two hold her shoulders still. Be firm!"

He had no need to tell Barcwith and Galey what to do. The two muscular men had already moved to where they could hold Alaiz's legs still without getting in the way of the healers. The squints also wriggled in so that they could touch Alaiz, bowing their heads and beginning to make a strange humming noise. What they were doing was beyond the Islanders, and if Taise knew she did not have the time to explain. A very pale Ad came forward with the bowl, tears running down his face but determinedly holding the bowl steady enough that the boiled water did not slop about.

Tamàs looked at Taise across the bed.

"Do you want to make the cut? Or do you trust me to do it so as you can do the complicated bit as soon as we're in?"

Taise glanced over her shoulder to where Eldaya was standing, deathly white and visibly trembling, then back at the old archer with his steady hands and gave a watery smile. "You do it. I trust you." And she did. She had seen how these men cared for Alaiz, and had heard enough of how they had tried to help her, to know that he was doing it out of love. For herself having the life of a friend in her hands was a new and unexpected trial, and she feared that for the first time her hands might not be steady enough.

His gnarled fingers gently probed the hugely stretched skin low down on Alaiz's abdomen.

"Ready?" he said without looking up.

"Yes," she replied, then was astonished at the speed with which he moved. The men must have honed the knives to a sharpness Taise had rarely seen, for no sooner had Tamàs plunged the point in then, with the strength of his bow arm, he had made the slicing cut. He had finished before Alaiz had even cried out. Taise gulped, then focused on extracting first one child and then another, handing the first back to a waiting Eldaya almost without looking. Eldaya might not have been the one to assist with the surgery, but she knew what needed doing with a new-born without having to be told.

"A boy and alive!" Taise said to no-one and everyone as she pulled him out and Tamàs cut the cord. She handed the slippery mite to Eldaya, who immediately took him to one side and began chaffing him into life. He had not made a sound yet, and she was quick to bundle him into well-washed soft towels and blankets to try and warm him through. However, Taise and Tamàs were already preoccupied with extracting the second child, a girl, and Kayna hurried forward with more towels and blankets since Eldaya was still busy with the boy. She could only copy what Eldaya was doing and hope that it would be enough, for Matti was in no position to help and neither was Cwen.

Throughout the process Alaiz had not made a sound, the squints, however, were now mewing softly as if in great pain.

"Oh Trees it hurts!" Swein gasped, and swiftly glances revealed Matti and Cwen grimacing in pain too and clutching at their stomachs. Ivain looked agonised, but from what cause it was impossible to tell.

"They're taking the pain for her," Pauli gasped in amazement."The squints are taking the pain!" Everyone was shocked and it only made them want to hurry the process even more. If the squints had made such a sacrifice to save Alaiz the pain, then they wanted to make their ordeal as brief as possible. She had mouthed asking to see the babies, and her frail hands flickered at her sides as she tried desperately to reach out to touch them, but too weak to do even that she could only follow them with desperate eyes.

As Taise removed the afterbirths, Tamàs gave a soft whistle and Decke came in with a small spirit lamp and a knife he had been holding in the flame. With great care Tamàs touched the red hot blade to the severed blood vessels he could get to, but a hand on his shoulder stopped him.

"Now I'll try," Sithfrey said with more assurance than he felt. They turned to see that he was slipping on the DeÁine Gauntlet.

"Take the babies outside!" Taise commanded, halting with a needle and thread in hand, and Eldaya scurried out with them, one in each arm, to the willing hands of the local wise women who had come to offer what help they could and were congregated outside. "I'm sorry Alaiz, my love, but they're just about breathing! We daren't risk them being harmed by any unseen forces the Gauntlet might throw out. Once you're well, we'll bring them back in again."

Kayna, Barcwith and Galey moved back, as did Tamàs, as the Gauntlet began to glow. The squints now quickly loosed their grip on Alaiz and backed away to behind the people. The air became charged, sending tingles across everyone's skin as Sithfrey drew in the Power. Then he spread his fingers and placed his hand over where the cut gaped raw and bloody. The pale glow spread into Alaiz and in front of their eyes the wound began to close. Yet Sithfrey suddenly began to waver.

"Oh no!" came his strangled gasp. "This isn't right!"

It did not seem to be going wrong, for Alaiz now blinked and opened her eyes, then appeared to focus on something in the haze of light now surrounding her. A smile of pure joy lit her face then faded as fast.

"Hamelin!" The cry was torn from her. "Nooo!" Then she raised her hands, and Matti and Cwen in a brief moment of hope dared to believe she might hold her children at least once. But far from reaching out to cradle a child, she plunged her grasping hands into the light right beneath Sithfrey's hand as he lifted the Gauntlet higher. He seemed to be desperately trying to disengage it or at least move it away but he never got chance. A flared burst of light from the Gauntlet all but blinded everyone with its intensity as Alaiz seemed to close her hands around something within the Power.

"Aaaaagh!" Sithfrey howled, trying to hold the Gauntleted arm steady with his other, yet swaying in apparent pain of his own. Talorcan pounced. He grabbed hold of Sithfrey's arm just above the edge of the Gauntlet, and as he clamped both hands down the light died with it.

"Alaiz!" Ivain sobbed, lurching forward with Pauli and Swein in tow, but Alaiz lay back on the bed, her eyes unfocused and no signs of life at all. "You said you'd *heal* her!" he screamed at Sithfrey. "You've killed her, you bastard!"

Yet Sithfrey had an unexpected champion. Eric scuttled forward and twittered urgently to Ivain, shaking his head at the same time. Perhaps because of the bond between them Ivain registered his presence when he would not have one of the men. Looking down at his squint, he watched as Eric stroked first his own hand with the soft pad of his forepaw, then went and very gently stroked Sithfrey's arm which still had the Gauntlet on.

"I think he's trying to tell you that whatever happened wasn't Sithfrey's fault," Pauli told Ivain sympathetically as Taise hurried around the bed to where Sithfrey was half slumped in Talorcan's arms.

"Take it off, Sithfrey," she commanded urgently.

"I can't," he sobbed.

"It's welded itself to his arm," Talorcan told her, for once sounding shaken to his core. "I felt it, Taise! He was being sucked into it!"

"It shouldn't have done that!" Taise was aghast. "None of the pieces of Power should! Not even the great ones!"

Talorcan shook his head. "I think it was Alaiz herself who changed it. Maybe because of being in the midst of childbirth? ...You tell me? ...What I do know is that I felt someone on the other side of whatever, or *where* ever, that Power is. He – and I think it was a he – was reaching for Alaiz, and she wanted to go to him."

"Did you feel anything else?" Taise questioned him, even as her sensitive fingers were probing all round Sithfrey's seared skin and the Gauntlet.

"Yes," Talorcan replied with an unaccustomed shake in his voice.

"What?"

"I think he was already dead. ...I felt something I can only describe as profound grief ...and something else. ...I think it was love."

# Chapter 11

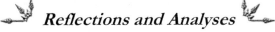

## *Reflections and Analyses*

### Rathlin: Solstice

When Maelbrigt and Sionnachan got back, everyone was still in shock. Having taken Squint with them, and with Maelbrigt's own sensations of pain, the two Foresters had been alerted to the fact that all was not well back at the house, and had cut short their practice, riding back at speed. Now they walked in to find everyone looking pale and badly shaken. Mercifully Eldaya had had the foresight to arrange for wet-nurses in advance, guessing that even with the best of outcomes, Alaiz would be unlikely to be sufficiently well to feed her babies herself. These women were in the house already, and the two tiny infants were swiftly handed into their care – something everyone was grateful for, since nobody felt that caring for the new-borns was something they could've coped with just yet. The two were still alive but it was still early days yet, and no-one was daring to predict whether they would survive the next week or so.

Ruari had appeared swiftly when summoned from the practice grounds, and now arranged for Alaiz's body to be tended to, then ushered the others downstairs. However, with the Power at the heart of what had happened, he was glad to step back and let the Foresters take over. With typical decisiveness, Sionnachan set the Foresters to chanting wards around the house while planting wands, and to making calming teas of some blend of herbs he chose not to reveal to anyone, but which Ruari guessed had been subject to incantations too. Once Sionnachan was satisfied that they were sufficiently protected from any Power-based summoning, he came to where Maelbrigt knelt in front of a seated Sithfrey, examining the Gauntlet.

"Will it come off?" he asked, deferring to Maelbrigt's expertise in this matter.

Maelbrigt grimaced. "I don't think so. Every chant I've tried only gives Sithfrey more pain."

Squint let loose another stream of agitated chirps and whistles, something he had been doing ever since they'd got back, and Aneirin appeared.

"He was asking you to come, wasn't he?" Maelbrigt said with a steely glint in his eye. "Next time make it a bit quicker! He wouldn't ask you to come somewhere where there was danger to you."

"But the Gauntlet!" protested Aneirin.

Sionnachan, still standing, moved to look Aneirin right in the eye. "Remember what we said before? About supporting the squints? Try *harder*!" There was a tone in his voice which brooked no argument and Aneirin took a ghostly deep breath. It was a tough learning process for him, and the Foresters were making it clear that he and the others were the ones who needed to adapt. Ruari, too, stood with arms folded and a very disapproving glare fixed on the ancient, making Aneirin think that he and the others had not quite anticipated *this* kind of unity when they had created the Treasures.

"Now then," Sionnachan prodded. "*What* is Squint trying to tell us?"

Aneirin listened as Squint rattled off a string of clicks and chirps. "Oh," the ancient for once looked chastened. "He says that the other squints are well. They haven't been harmed by what happened. They're just sad."

"Understandably," Ruari said with some asperity. "They must have felt Alaiz die!" Despite all the men he had seen dying in battle, Ruari was not so hardened that he could not be deeply moved at the loss of someone whom he had seen as an innocent caught up in this war. He might not have been so close to her as veterans like Talorcan had become, but his grief made him angry that these seemingly all-knowing ancients had not appeared to try to offer advice which might have helped save her.

"Yes, they did," Aneirin said, humbled. "Squint says that they also say that someone Alaiz loved very much had already died."

"So it *was* Hamelin she saw?" Cwen asked through her tears.

Squint's chirp to the affirmative was expanded.

"He says that this person – Hamelin? – died in a way which was connected to the Power." Aneirin looked perplexed. "He's implying a sacrifice. ...I don't quite understand what he means. He says Hamelin wasn't killed purposely in some ritual, but there seems to be a ritual in there somewhere."

A clearly exasperated Squint began trying to tell Aneirin over again when Ruari interrupted. "Of course! Hamelin's a Knight, or was! Did he sacrifice himself to save someone else?"

Squint let out a long whistle of relief, then gave Ruari what could only be described as a look of gratitude, compelling Ruari to guess again.

"So was there a ritual going on and Hamelin interrupted it in some way?"

Squint became positively excited.

"Because of that did something of Hamelin go into the Power?" Sionnachan wondered and got another excited chirp of confirmation, making the Forester catch Ruari's eye and then roll his eyes in exasperation in the direction of Aneirin. The ancients could be desperately slow to catch on sometimes.

Maelbrigt stood up and joined in. "Ah, that starts to make sense! Talorcan says he could feel the Power running through the Gauntlet. Like it was using Sithfrey – rather than the other way round – as a channel to move through, then it was like a flood and nearly drowned him."

Talorcan himself, seated with an arm around Ivain, shot a worried glance across to the two Foresters and Aneirin. "Very like! I felt like I was the only one who could reach into the flood to catch Sithfrey. It was sucking him in too! Thank the Trees I'm of mixed blood. I suspect it was that which enabled me to stay grounded. The pull was incredibly strong."

Aneirin now began to comprehend what had happened too. "Oh! ...Squint says that it only worked because both of them, Alaiz on your side and Hamelin on the other, desperately wanted to connect with one another. They were apparently actively reaching for one another. ...Ah, yes! He says it's very unlikely to happen again because it took a very strong bond to make the link in the first place. He also wants to reassure you that there's no danger to anyone here of the Gauntlet reactivating itself in this way. It won't start up alone."

"Thank the Trees for that!" Maelbrigt breathed in relief, then hardened his tone. "You could have come sooner and saved us a lot of anxiety over that!" he chastised Aneirin. "The squints picked up on it and have been wearing themselves out trying to tell us. Give them a little more consideration in future!"

Ivain was trying to stifle his body-shaking sobs without success, and even the normally cynical Kayna was red-eyed as she said, "So they're together now. I'm so glad. She was totally besotted with him."

Pauli glared at her, not happy that from his perspective she was rubbing salt into Ivain's wounds. However Kayna was not deterred. She went and crouched in front of Ivain and pulled his hands away from his face so that she could look at him eye to eye. "You said just now that what made all this worse was that she never had a chance to be happy. Well I think that's part of what your Eric, Squint and the others are trying to tell you." Eric came and pressed his long thin nose against Ivain's, so that they were forehead to forehead. "There you are! I'm right aren't I, Eric? When she was with Hamelin, Alaiz was *very* happy."

Eric's whistle of agreement startled Ivain so much it cut through the tears and he looked up properly.

"Really? She was truly happy?"

Kayna looked to Matti and Taise to help her as she said,

"When we were at Lorne Castle she was never far from him. Even Master Brego couldn't keep them apart."

"That's right," Matti added. "And Hamelin's friend Oliver told us that he'd never seen Hamelin so smitten either. So you need never think that it was one-sided, it wasn't. She was loved back."

Taise nodded from where she stood just behind Maelbrigt, not wanting to get in his way but not wanting to be too far from him just now. "Be glad she had her time with Hamelin, Ivain. And think of it this way. If she loved him so much, how would she ever have coped if she'd lived and then found out a different way, maybe much later on, that he'd died? Wouldn't it have been crueller for her to then have to live having lost him forever after it had taken her so long to find what she really wanted in her life?" Kayna and Matti had a sneaking suspicion that came from her own heart, and hoped Maelbrigt would not be taken from Taise. "She loved you too, you know. She often told me so. It just wasn't that kind of love."

Ivain hiccupped, then managed to blow his nose and straighten up, his grief not assuaged but the first terrible wave of anguish had past. "I know. At least we had that. We had time to tell one another what we felt. I should be grateful I had the chance to tell her how sorry I was for all that she had to go through in my name."

"And there's something else," Cwen added, having had Daisy desperately trying to mime something to her to tell her without words and unable to attract Aneirin's attention. "There are the two children." Daisy whistled emphatically. "I think another part of what's upset the squints who were here so much, was that Alaiz was torn between the love of her tiny children and her love of Hamelin. What made the difference," and she stopped to check with Daisy that she was getting this right, "was that she knew *you* were here. Right *here* at the time. She knew you would look after the children and not let the same happen to them." That last bit was something of a guess, especially as she had not known Alaiz all that well, but the squints were all vigorously chirping their agreement. "She didn't even have to worry that any message might not find you. She'd spoken to you and she knew you two still had a strong bond after all. She knew she could trust you implicitly. That you would love these children for her sake, leaving her free to be with Hamelin again and not alone. Can you use that thought to ease your pain?"

Ivain's expression was enough for them to see that it was. Ruari came over and gave Cwen a hug. His respect for her intelligence and kindness was growing daily.

Swein was also lifted out of his torment and able to smile at her too. The sight of Tamàs slicing into Alaiz had very nearly torn him apart, even though it was to help her. It was a ghastly reminder of the event which had set him on this path in the first place – the witnessing of King Edward's dreadful murder of the man he now knew had been Berengar's half-brother. So much blood, even if this time two lives had emerged out of it to balance the great loss. He knew he would be back to eating just vegetables again for many days to come after this. It also made him remember once more how much he owed to Cwen, and now that Ivain had ceased his convulsive sobbing, Swein left him to Talorcan and went to hug Cwen in Ruari's place. It was half for her comfort and half for his, and by the way she hung on tight to him he guessed she felt the same. This had been a stark illustration of a price they might all have to pay in some form in the coming weeks.

"But what of Sithfrey?" Maelbrigt asked the ancient, his hand on the DeÁine's shoulder. "He's in a lot of pain. Can we get the Gauntlet off?"

But Aneirin shook his head. "No. And that's partly what Squint wanted to tell you so urgently. He says you *must* stop using the chants on the Gauntlet. Without them Sithfrey's arm will heal. You're not helping him, only making him feel worse."

"But he can't take it off," Sionnachan fretted. "How can he heal with that thing on him?"

Swein's Dylan, the least upset of the squints who had been in the house that day – perhaps because Swein had the least personal bond with Alaiz – moved from Swein's side and came to put his nose close to the Gauntlet. He appeared to sniff at it then chirruped at Aneirin. The ancient did not question what he heard but translated,

"Apparently the Gauntlet always had a healing component in it. Dylan says that they couldn't feel it before because of the taint the Gauntlet still carried from the DeÁine. When Alaiz died it cleaned the Gauntlet for good.

It's become neutral – not DeÁine or Islander. He thinks it would now heal anyone as long as Sithfrey wills it. Dylan says he won't have to try so hard to do that either."

"When his arm and hand are healed, will the Gauntlet come off of its own accord?" Maelbrigt asked Squint.

However none of the squints seemed able to answer that.

"Well we'll have to leave it for now," Sionnachan said reluctantly. "I'm so sorry, Sithfrey. Can you cope with it until we can get you back to Ergardia? When we have the time, I promise you I'll find a way to get that cursed thing off you, believe me, I will!"

"I believe you," Sithfrey said weakly, "but for now could someone find me a cushion I can rest my arm on so that I can get some sleep with it on me? It's quite a weight now I've had it on for hours."

It was a sombre evening, and a night when most of them slept through simple emotional exhaustion. The next day Maelbrigt and Sionnachan went off to continue their experiments in the arcane, but none of the others did much and Ruari did not press the matter. He was now severely worried about Ivain, and took Pauli on one side that evening after a day of observing the young king.

"How much more of this do you think he can stand?" Ruari asked worriedly. "I'm not being critical. I think he's done amazingly well to have got this far. It's phenomenally bad luck that since landing here he should have lost both his mother and the girl he loved as a sister, if not as a wife. Is he cracking under this strain? Because if so, I have to think about whether he should have the burden of the Bow to carry as well. I cannot, in any conscience, ask him to continue preparing to take it into battle if he's falling to bits. What we need from him would be a tall order from a hardened veteran, which he's certainly not. I won't humiliate him, have no fear. But I'd rather move him to a place in command of the archers with one of my most experienced men to aid him, and let Tamàs take over the Bow with Swein, if continuing is going to break him."

Pauli scratched his chin and stared out of the window for a moment. They were looking out over the garden, and down below Ivain was walking the paths with Talorcan, his hands fluttering in gestures to accompany whatever it was he was saying. Talorcan was keeping pace with him silently, allowing Ivain to give vent to whatever the subject was that he was so passionately expounding upon.

"I think he's going to mend," the older Knight said thoughtfully. "What he said about making his peace with Alaiz? That's a big part of it! If he'd not had that I think it would be so much worse – then you might well have been right to think of changing his role. As it is, they understood one another at the end. There was no blame on either side. ...They could see how they'd been controlled. ...Had been manipulated and unable to help one another. ...And I think Talorcan and Swein have helped him enormously."

"I'm glad to hear that, but how? I mean apart from the obvious! I'm not so blind that I can't see that he and Talorcan have gone from hating one another's guts to something quite the opposite!"

Pauli smiled. "Yes, quite a turn up for the books, is that! But you see, when I first met Ivain there was no hint of him showing those kinds of feelings. Instead the poor lad just felt so bloody guilty that he wasn't able to make what he thought were the proper responses to the women the court threw at him at every turn."

"Flaming Trees!" Ruari gasped. "You mean he didn't even know himself?"

"No! And that's what's been so good about him finding Swein and Talorcan. Swein spotted it straight away, and I think since then he's been doing all he can to make Ivain feel more ...comfortable inside his own skin, is the only way I can put it. Simply as a friend. There's nothing beyond a standard friendship there, but it's the understanding which counts for so much. Of course there's definitely more than that between him and Talorcan! But it helps so much that Talorcan thought the world of Alaiz too. There's no jealousy over Ivain's grieving for her, and if it's a bit more muted – because Talorcan isn't one to be emotional in front of others – he's also mourning for Alaiz. I think Talorcan's channelling Ivain's grief in the way that he's learned to use his own. Building on his own experiences, and showing Ivain ways for it to make him stronger when we face the DeÁine, not weaker."

Ruari accepted Pauli's assessment for that night, but was further assured when the next morning Ivain said that he would like to start working with the Treasures again. That seemed a little too fast for Ruari, even though he understood that Ivain felt the need for distraction from his loss. So he had Ivain and Swein talked through some of the Order's massed archers' tactics instead, under the caring tutelage of Tamàs, Brock and Rollo. It was enough to keep them busy without taking any chances, besides which, Ruari wanted to give the squints a further day to recover. He was alert to the fact that this was probably the first time any of them had experienced death as people knew it, and did not want them underestimating how deeply they had felt what had happened – in all senses given that the Power had been so strong in the room.

When Magnus returned the next day with Breca the whole thing had to be gone over again, the Attacotti leader expressing a deep and genuine sorrow. Nothing would do but he insisted that Alaiz be laid to rest in a grave in the rose garden for now, and set his men to the task, with strict instructions not to damage the plants she had loved so much.

"If we live through what's coming," he said, both hands braced on Ivain's shoulders and looking him straight in the eye, "I promise you a fleet of my galleys will bring her in state to wherever you want to lay her to rest permanently, whether it's on Kittermere or Prydein. She may have first come here dressed like a serving wench, but she'll leave as befits a gallant queen. In the meantime we shall fight side by side to avenge her. Will you do that? Will you fight with me, King Ivain?"

Ruari, Maelbrigt and Sionnachan all tensed. The wrong word now and who knew how Magnus might react? He was sane for now, but none of them were all that sure how strong a hold he had on things. They need not have worried. Ivain squared his shoulders and clasped Magnus back.

"I'll fight with you, Morair of the Attacotti! The DeÁine won't disturb Alaiz's rest or threaten her children while I have breath in my body."

"Nice use of Magnus' title," Sionnachan observed to Maelbrigt softly. "Sounded like he was treating him as an equal. I see what Ruari means. He's got the makings of being a great king if we can keep him alive that long!"

"For Prydein's sake we'd better!" Maelbrigt murmured back. "Celidon survived losing its leaders because the Order was always strong there. But Master Hugh's had to fight tooth and nail to maintain his influence on Prydein, yet even he can't live forever. When that time comes the Island will need a strong king, and it would be even better if he was there before that to help rebuild it after the current devastation. Prydein left to its bickering nobles could descend into the ruined state we're seeing here on Rathlin. You'd never know, except for the crumbling manor houses and merchants' mansions, that Rathlin was once as vibrant as Prydein. And the rest of the Islands would also suffer if Prydein fell into decay and nobody watched the southern sea lanes. Having seen how Ivain's archers look up to him already, I think it would be a good idea if I arrange for some of my Foresters to act as his personal guard, when they get here. Men who, if it all goes badly wrong, will get him off the battlefield at all costs. He's the one of all us

Treasure wielders who carries the additional burden of a whole Island looking to him."

Sionnachan nodded, but privately thought that Maelbrigt had missed something there. If Ivain's archers looked to him, then the Celidon Foresters looked to Maelbrigt, too, in their own way. Catching the eye of Maelbrigt's old friend and sergeant, Eadgar, and of the young Forester Raethun, he signalled them to meet him outside. He was gratified to find that Raethun had swiftly included Ewan and Tobias in the summons, so that he was talking to all of Maelbrigt's close coterie. In stark terms Sionnachan outlined what his fears for the outcome might be.

"Celidon has suffered enough already," he concluded. "Along with Ergardia, of all the Islands it's best suited to retreat to should the DeÁine win. A place we can launch some kind of resistance from. Trees forefend it should come to that! But if it does, we shall need Maelbrigt for all that he symbolises to the folk of Celidon. I charge you now, with my full authority, that if we get to a point where we cannot possibly save the Islands, you must remove Maelbrigt from the battlefield. You'll probably have to knock him out to do it! But if you have to hog-tie and gag him to get him away, then that's what you must do."

Once the tall Forester had gone, though, Raethun held the others back and drew them off into the stables.

"I don't know about you," Raethun said carefully, "but I find it rather worrying that even Sionnachan is talking about defeat. How many times since we've got here have you heard someone say, 'if we survive'? It's like we've half given up the fight before we've started."

His friend Ewan had already been nodding his agreement before Raethun finished speaking. Now the less extrovert Tobias was tentatively nodding, while Eadgar wore an expression of startled concern.

"Lost Souls, Raethun! No, I hadn't noticed it until you've just said it, but now I come to think of it, you're right!"

"Where do you think it's coming from?" Tobias wondered. "I believe you've hit on a very real danger. I have no doubt of that. Master Sionnachan is anything but the morose type normally and neither is Maelbrigt. Therefore this reeks of outside influence."

Ewan sniffed. "Yes, but whose?"

Eadgar blinked in surprise. "What in the Islands do you mean?"

"Well think about it," Ewan expanded. "We've got the Maker only knows how many Foresters here, all with their whiskers twitching like so many cats for the slightest whiff of anything the DeÁine might have thrown at us. Is it likely that they'd all miss something so big it can affect so wide a range of people? So it's not very likely it's the DeÁine. ...But what if it's the ancients?"

"The ancients?" Eadgar gasped, but Tobias was quick to see the implications.

"Oh yes, it could be them! We've not questioned them in so many areas because we haven't had the time – and going on what we've seen with Urien and Anerien, they might not know, anyway! And they are more than a little dotty, aren't they! Such advanced age can bring on gloominess in people, so why not in them? And if they're linked to key people, then maybe some of it is seeping back along that connection."

"Flaming Root and Branch!" Eadgar swore. "So what can we do?"

"Watch them very hard when we go out on exercise tomorrow," Raethun said decisively. "If it *is* that, then when Maelbrigt in particular gets away from the other Treasure holders, he should perk up a bit. Be more his normal cheery old self. And Sionnachan. We must watch him too."

Yet as they got back into the hall, and the assembled captains and leaders took their places at the long tables for a meal, Magnus provided another possible answer to their question.

"May I address your men?" he asked Ruari and Sionnachan respectfully. Breca was furtively signalling to them that this was important, and so both nodded despite their private misgivings.

"Gentlemen! A moment's quiet, if you please," Ruari called out, and the room's hum of conversations faded.

"Thank you," Magnus said, rising to his feet. "I sharn't keep you from your food, gentlemen — and ladies, too! But you should all hear this. My men have scouted alongside your Commander Breca, here, and what we've seen affects us all. Without knowing it we've been very lucky! We'd had messages that the Abend had landed back on this island, may the Goddess curse their rotten souls! What we didn't know at that point was which way they intended to move. I know you hoped, as I did, that they would be trying to get around the floods in Brychan to get back to New Lochlainn before the new DeÁine arrived. Maybe to get more troops, or just to reinforce their holding on what they had.

"Sadly, we were wrong! They came south!" Inadvertently many gasped. "We've all had a narrow escape," Magnus continued. "They were only the other side of the highlands, on the eastern shore of Loch Canisp, a couple of days before those of you from Ergardia landed."

Ruari sat bolt upright. "You mean my men and I might have had to fight the Abend alone?"

"It came close to it," Magnus agreed, "although at that point they were still smarting from the blow your men on Brychan dealt them. And also, they only had the men they brought in ships, not any of their old army. Breca tells me the Abend aren't known for their personal bravery! ...Anyway, luckily they had no reason to look this way.

"Four days later it was a very different story! Breca and I were watching them by then from the cover of the highlands. We've discussed it, and we agree that it must have been at the time when dear Alaiz died that we witnessed something very odd. We'd had them in our sights for the best part of day ourselves, and my scouts who'd caught up with us had been shadowing them since they marched out of Temair. Until then they'd shown every sign of heading purposefully south, to meet with the ships from across the sea we presume. The few of my folk who got in their way were massacred."

At this point Magnus' eyes flashed with anger. "They shall pay for that!" he swore. "But by and large my folk eluded them. This surely angered the Abend, for many of my people whom the scouts passed spoke of feelings of despair and of loss of hope. This is not like them! Breca tells me he thinks the Abend may have loosed another of their glamours."

"Indeed," Breca interposed. "Thinking of the dreadful events of last New Year, it occurred to me that this sounded worryingly similar. We talked it over and I believe that what saved Magnus' people from worse, and therefore unwittingly ourselves, has been the Abend's desire to keep any hint of chaos hidden from their approaching fellow DeÁine. Ealdorman Hereman and I spoke some time ago about these new DeÁine, and of our worry that there might be acolytes amongst them even if there were none of the strength of the Abend. Yet if there are acolytes amongst them, then surely would be aware of any surge of use in the Power?"

"They would," Taise's gentle voice carried across the room in the hush, earning her a respectful nod of thanks from Breca before he continued.

"This made me think that they would therefore moderate their actions. We all know that the DeÁine frequently take a hammer to crack a nut. So normally they would've been blasting at us with the Power, and been going all out to eradicate those who got in their way. They don't bother to make subtle approaches in such things. So what's saved us is their own desire for preserving themselves, for saving face with the others. But there's more..." He gestured to Magnus to carry on.

"Four days ago the Abend halted in their tracks. The men with them carried on marching until they were almost past them. We watched them. Something had the Abend all of a lather, by the Goddess it did!" Magnus grinned wolfishly. "We had to lay low in the heather, for even the likes of us could feel the waves of their sendings washing over us in waves, looking for something. Trying to find something. It crept over your skin! Like a dog sniffing at you and passing on. Whatever it was they were looking for, we reasoned, it must be so specific that we as soldiers didn't register with it. Oh they were looking for *something*! They were looking so hard even *we* could sense the worry in the touches of Power! We just couldn't think what, or why it should be right there and then.

"Now, though, we know! It was the changes in the Gauntlet they felt! And I think they felt it was near. For a whole day they stayed put and their men with them. After that they stopped questing on the Power, and we could risk moving to come back here. But make no mistake, gentlemen. If they get so much as another sniff of the Gauntlet, then they'll move and move fast. Breca and his men think what saved us is that the Gauntlet is so changed that it must have felt more distant, ...or diluted, ...with it being less DeÁine now. So far they've crawled through this land, presumably wanting to make sure that there were none to oppose them – or so they think! If they have the need, though, they could be here, or within striking distance with those cursed balls of fire, in little over four days. They don't know the ways through the highlands like me and my men, so they'd have to go around, but there's a river valley which would aid them once they got beyond the first day."

"They have the best part of six thousand men with them too," Breca added solemnly. "Four Jundises and two Seljuqs."

"Where in the confounded Underworlds did they get them from?" fumed McKinley, looking to Sionnachan in frustration. "I thought the ancients said that Master Brego wiped out the Donns' force?"

"These were Souk'ir," Breca supplied, and got a groan of disbelief from many men. It was rare that the trading families stirred themselves, and it had been all too easy to think that they would remain in New Lochlainn, sitting there in luxury until the Islanders could deal with them as part of the mopping up operation after the main battles had been won.

"Bastard Hounds of the Wild Hunt!" Sionnachan swore. "The bloody Souk'ir to boot!"

"There's another aspect," Raethun said nervously, standing up and hoping this would not be his first and last speech to an assembled force. "May I speak, sires?"

With Sionnachan and Maelbrigt both gesturing him to continue, Raethun told the gathering of his observations. By the time he had finished men were looking worriedly from one to another. "We feared it might be the ancients, you see," he concluded, "because we hadn't bargained on the Abend being subtle."

As he sat down Sionnachan stood up. "Foresters! Tomorrow at dawn you will assemble outside of the town. With me you shall deal with this glamour!"

"And what of the Gauntlet?" Everyone stopped as Talorcan's voice cut sharply through the buzz of enthusiasm from the Foresters. "We have a terrible problem here, in case you didn't spot it. Sithfrey *can't* take it off! So what do we do? Keep him holed up and insulated from the world until the Abend are long past us, and hope that nothing touches his heart? That nothing makes him have the faintest desire to help or heal? If he could remove it, we could put it back in its lead-lined box and be fairly sure that it would remain inert, but we can't."

Sithfrey looked gaunt as he leaned forward in his seat. "I should take it out of the camp," he said with as much firmness as he could muster. He looked hopefully to Andra, sat at his right side and was thankful to see the former monk's smile of reassurance. Andra would come with him, at least, and that gave him the strength to say what he feared most. "I should ride as fast as I can away from you all and then draw some Power into it. That way the Abend will turn and come chasing after me. They want the Gauntlet very badly, they won't be able to resist its pull." He swallowed as the few mouthfuls of dinner he had had so far rose back in his throat at the next thought. "If the squints are right and the Gauntlet has been changed permanently, then even if the Abend take it off me by force, it might rebound on them dreadfully."

He had no illusions about how the Abend would remove it. Dead or alive they would hack it off him! They would not wait to find a different way. He swallowed hard again. Somehow, in all of his imagined endings, he had never dreamed that his death would be in an act of self-sacrifice to save all these others. *No true, full-bloodied DeÁine would do such a thing*, he thought. *It seems I shall pay a high price for becoming one of the Islanders and having my eyes opened to higher ideals.* He closed his eyes and took a deep breath to fight down the panic which was rising within him. He would not show it outwardly. He would not flinch from this necessary duty when nobody else could do it – although he knew now that any number of the Foresters would have willingly taken the burden from him if they could. Yet before he could open his eyes again, alongside Taise's protest he heard Sionnachan and McKinley's too.

"Oh no you bloody well don't, Sithfrey!" McKinley said forcefully. "At least not without me and my men, anyway! You're one of us now, come what may!"

Meanwhile Sionnachan first addressed Raethun. "Now I see how right you were! ...Sithfrey, all is not lost! This gloom, ...this miasma, ...has infected us all! ...I believe that Sithfrey is correct in saying that we should move the Gauntlet, not least because Master Ruari has to wait here for the last men from Brychan. But we must shake off these thoughts of defeat before we've started! Maelbrigt and I have already discussed how we might split our force in the light of him using the Sword. So we shall just do it a little earlier than planned!"

He scanned the assembled men and found the commander he was looking for. "You and your men will stay with Maelbrigt for now until the Celidon Foresters get here. The remaining battalions will follow me once we've collectively dealt with the glamour first thing – so make sure you have all you need packed and with you tomorrow! We shall be marching fast!" He smiled at Sithfrey as he continued. "I believe Sithfrey has the right idea. Move well away and then make the Abend sit up and take notice. However, we shall then keep moving! We'll make as if we're trying to get ahead of the Abend and aiming for the south coast. A second brief burst should do that. That should worry the living daylights out of them! One of the Treasures going by an unknown means directly towards these other DeÁine? Oh that's going to have them in a flap! And if they start panicking then they're more likely to make mistakes. So after that, Sithfrey, we'll find some way of keeping you calm, and at the same time watch for where the Abend go tearing off to. That will give us the added bonus of warning us where the fleet intends to land."

"If you're going south," Magnus' distinctive lilting voice chimed in, "then I know just the place! Breca told me the Abend don't like sea water? Well the loch beyond Kinloch township is brackish on account of it being so low lying. Once upon a time it had a broad outlet to the sea, but it silted up over the years and now it's mostly a boggy river down to the sea. But the winter and spring high tides wash enough salt water back up its course to keep the loch from becoming truly fresh water. The whole thing is brackish, and now we're in summer and the water level is lower, it's more salty as the water dries and leaves the salt behind. There's an island in the middle, too! Just right for Sithfrey to hide out on!"

"Then we shall regroup at Kinloch," Maelbrigt declared. "Hopefully by then we shall have a better idea of where the Abend are heading to, and we shall be able to consider where we shall bring them to battle."

"Do you think you can choose where you fight them?" an astonished Andra asked, before he recalled who he was questioning and in front of their men.

"Oh yes!" Maelbrigt said adamantly. Taise suddenly saw what Raethun had meant. This was the old Maelbrigt. Decisive and determined, not the man beset by doubts of late, yet something bothered her and she decided she would speak to Raethun again later. She also noticed that she could hear a low humming going on. Maybe that was what had caused the change? Looking about the room she was fairly sure that it was Sionnachan's Foresters who were taking it in turns to provide this background modulating note. In the meantime Maelbrigt was answering Andra's question.

"The new DeÁine will have to land on the shore, but we don't have to fight them there and then. In fact it would be better if they come inland a little, because we don't want them jumping back on their ships and retreating to live to fight another day. We want rid of them once and for all. All of them! So we shall allow them to begin to march inland. If they don't do it of their own accord then we shall have to lure them somehow, and that's when we shall know how to proceed once we know where they'll be starting from. We can do much to redress their advantage of superior numbers if we can fight them in the hills and moors, not on the flat plains where they can overwhelm us."

Everyone gradually settled back down to eat, but after the meal was done and Maelbrigt and Sionnachan had disappeared with Ruari to confer, Taise managed to catch Raethun. He readily agreed to meet her somewhere quiet, and so once again the little group found themselves in the stables.

"What's worrying you, Taise?" Raethun asked kindly.

Outwardly the tall DeÁine lady was the image of calm, but now that

Raethun was getting to know her he could see that she was fretting over something.

"It's this business of the Abend sending another glamour," she said tersely. "I don't doubt Magnus for a moment with regard to what his folk have felt. It's a typical Abend thing to do. And I'm sure he's right to think that it's been projected this way as well. But now that you've made me think about this, I'm sure Maelbrigt and Sionnachan were becoming more gloomy even back when we were on the ship. That can't have been the Abend! Not while we were on the ocean! They wouldn't be able to have such fine control in those circumstances."

"You're worried that it might be the ancients after all?" wondered Ewan.

"I am. It's the only thing which fits. And it worries me because Master Brego has another of the more pessimistic ancients working with him in the form of Vanadis. Look at Ivain and Swein. They're very downcast at the moment, but for understandable reasons. And their ancients aren't half as bad. In fact from the little I've seen I would almost guess that we're infecting those two with our optimism. Yet how will that help? If the ancients need to be unified in their intent, then it could prove as dangerously divisive if three are raring to go, and the other three are anticipating defeat before the first blow gets struck."

Maelbrigt's coterie all looked grave. Taise had made a vital point and not one of them doubted her reasoning.

"Is there anything we can do?" Taise added plaintively, worried for how this would affect Maelbrigt above all else.

"We tell him straight out," Eadgar said firmly. "I've known Maelbrigt a long time, Taise, and in desperate situations. He won't just dismiss us, and he'll see the reasoning – he's not that much under Aneirin's sway."

"Yes," Raethun agreed. "And once Sionnachan's gone, he'll be staying here for a few days at least, so now's the time to tackle this while we have this respite. Let's go and talk to him now."

"But they're planning," the more conventional Tobias pointed out, used to not disturbing senior officers unless commanded to.

"Then we'll be saving him the trouble of repeating it to Sionnachan," Raethun replied breezily, and set off with Taise, Eadgar, Ewan and Tobias hurrying in his wake, his confidence fuelled by the way he had come to know the Forester leader in the last few months.

In the early hours of dawn all nine thousand of the Ergardian Foresters marched out of Kylesk, radiating out like spokes from a wheel rather than in one long line. By the time the first rays of sun were creeping over the eastern horizon, the Foresters had formed a huge arc from shore to shore around the Attacotti town, but facing outwards. Taise stood with Raethun, who had insisted that she come to witness this along with Sithfrey, who was standing holding a horse, his arm in a sling, and looking nervous, even though Andra was chatting to him in an effort to calm his nerves. Sionnachan took a deep breath and sung a low note. The men next to him took it up and it radiated out away from him along the line. He must have been counting to himself because he suddenly changed note and began singing, the men swiftly synchronising their timing to match his. The first notes were wordless, then as the sound began to build in complexity the Foresters began to use words. At first only one or two, used individually, which then were expanded on, until there was a chant going on beyond anything Taise or Sithfrey had ever heard. The language was one neither the Islanders nor the DeÁine knew, but Magnus, who had come too, thought there were bits he could pick up – it was the ancient, potent tongue of the Islands! Now he sidled up to Taise.

"By the Goddess that's something to hear!" he breathed softly. "Did you know they could do this?"

Taise shook her head. "Never even suspected it."

Her flesh was a mass of goose-bumps and prickles that had nothing to do with the slight early morning chill. This chant was pulling at something primeval, something raw and untamed and yet heartening not threatening – at least not to those of them behind it. And because it was in an archaic language, she had no clue what the words actually meant. They could have been chanting a death wish on all DeÁine for all she knew. Taise felt a deep shiver run down her spine at the thought of how it might feel on the other end of it. She could feel a vibration building, and she suspected it would be rattling her teeth loose if she was foolish enough to get in its way.

Sionnachan bent and plunged a sharpened wand into the ground with the other Foresters in complete synchronisation with him. The singing only dipped fractionally before the Foresters stepped forward as one and continued singing, accompanied by a low rumble in the earth.

"The oak," Raethun said quietly to Taise and Magnus. "Protection. It always comes first unless there's a very good reason why it should be one of the others."

The next cycle of chanting was shorter before they bent and plunged another wand into the ground.

"The Yew. Another protective tree," Raethun told them.

Now Taise noticed the notes rising a little, but also spotted that Maelbrigt, who had been standing directly behind Sionnachan, had not moved but was singing something different. Raethun tapped her on the arm and pointed off to the left where they could see McKinley also stood still.

"They're anchoring the spell," Raethun explained. "There'll be an anchorman about every fifty men. They're the strongest solo singers – the Celidon sept. Men who can hold a sequence even when all around them are singing something totally different. If they wanted the glamour-breaker to spread outwards and keep going then they wouldn't use them. This time, though, they want to create a refuge, so they're anchoring it very strongly to this area."

Another wand went in, the Ash, and now Taise could feel something through the soles of her feet, a vibration which seemed to be pulsing in strange waves. It was nothing compared to what happened when the Foresters sank the Birch wands in, though. At that point the ground was visibly rippling, with bushes shaking and the few trees there were shook as though a strong wind was passing through them. Taise looked worriedly to Raethun but he was just grinning at her, not remotely concerned by this upheaval. He placed a hand on her arm as if to brace her, which perplexed her since she was in no danger of falling despite the rumbling earth. Not wishing to offend him she did not brush it off, then was suddenly glad he was holding onto her. As the Rowan went in the growling ground fell abruptly still and silent, but there was a rushing of air from behind her which took her by surprise. The air rushed by her and out beyond the ring of wands and seemed to dissipate into nothingness. Immediately she felt her heart become lighter than it had been for many days.

"The Birch drives away malignancy," Raethun explained as he helped Magnus to his feet once more, the hefty Attacotti having been taken unawares and bowled over by the gust. "The Rowan is what finally broke, then repelled, the enchantment."

Taise looked to Sithfrey. His expression told her that he was as impressed by this as she was. He also looked almost hopeful, and Taise did not need any magic to know that he was thinking that if the Foresters could do this, then maybe Sionnachan was not being unduly optimistic when he said he would free Sithfrey from the Gauntlet. It made their goodbyes a good deal less fraught, and Taise was cheered to hear Sithfrey asking Sionnachan if they would be doing anything as bad as the mountain climbing they had done before, then the shared smile as Sionnachan had vehemently shaken his head. It pleased her that Sithfrey, who had once been such a haunted and prickly soul, had at last managed to find the simple pleasure in his life of friendship with Andra, McKinley and Sionnachan. Watching the eight battalions of Ergardian Foresters marching out behind him, Taise was also comforted to know that he was as safe as it was possible to be when the Abend were on the same island.

A greater surprise came as they were walking back into the town. Swein and Ivain came jogging up to meet them with expressions veering between amusement and confusion.

"What did the Foresters do?" Swein asked as they drew level.

"What we intended to do," Maelbrigt answered evenly. "Drove out the negatives and fears eating at peoples' souls."

"Woops," Ivain responded with something almost approaching a sense of fun. He was still prone to bouts of crippling grief, but was improving by the day.

"Why 'woops'?" Maelbrigt asked guardedly.

"Because you seem to have driven Aneirin out too," Ivain replied, his eyes shining with amusement. "Peredur and Cynddylan have had no trouble coming to Swein and me, and Owein can get to Matti too. But they tell us that Urien can't seem to get past an invisible barrier to come to Cwen, and Peredur says that Aneirin is going nuts on the other side of your barrier, or whatever it is. He wanted to tell you to stop but you couldn't hear him. The funny thing is that the squints seem to have been perked up no end by it."

Maelbrigt gave a throaty laugh, making Taise realise how long it had been since she had seen him do that. Once upon a time that warm chuckle had been the cause of her not taking him seriously, for she could not imagine how he could have maintained his cheerful demeanour if he had led a dangerous life. Now she knew better, but it pulled at her heart to be so reminded of the peaceful times they had had together. Maelbrigt, though, was anything but downcast. With their guarding battalion of Foresters already back in camp, he hurried them back to the town, then got Cwen to mount up and together they rode to the ring of wands once more. He had asked Ivain, Swein and Matti to stay behind to emphasise his message, but allowed Taise to observe, along with his band of four – who had charge of Squint and Daisy in their litters – and Ruari.

At the edge of the Foresters ring of wands he asked Squint to call to the ancients, and in an instant a very irate Aneirin and Urien appeared beyond it.

"Remove this at once!" Aneirin demanded.

"No," Maelbrigt answered bluntly. "Now you both listen to me and think on this! We did this to repel the DeÁine – specifically the Abend. You were not the target of this, and that's proven by the fact that Owein, Peredur and Cynddylan can all come to their respective holders without any problems. So the problem is with you two, and I suspect Vanadis too! You three are infecting anyone connected to you with your pessimism and negativity. I know because I can feel it! And more than that, Taise has made an important point. If we need to be united in our *desires*, then so do you! It's no good to us having three of you optimistic and wholeheartedly behind us, and the other three going through the motions but not believing any good will come of it. You tie our hands in that way just as much as by not helping the squints, or not turning up when we need you to enlighten us on some detail.

He sat up straight in his saddle and looked sternly at the two ancients. "So this warding-wall stays! It's to keep us hidden from the Abend, and for that reason alone it must not be removed. We set it up to also deflect the Abend's glamour which was inciting Magnus' people to give up, and it's done that very well. Noboy was more surprised than us that you three should be caught up in it too. So for you two and Vanadis, you'll soon know when you've overcome your own fears and doubts, because at that time this will cease to be a barrier to you. And if you need a further incentive, neither Cwen nor I will be coming out for several days, and neither will the squints. Owein has just told us that the first wave of Brego's men from Brychan will land at Temair tomorrow, but we'll have to wait for them to march down to us. You should also think on the fact that these coming men are *my* Foresters and those from Brychan under Ealdorman Warwick. If we have to, we can therefore do what we've done here every night we make camp!"

Maelbrigt turned his horse and winked at Ruari, who had a look of wry amusement on his face. As a parting shot over his shoulder as he turned and led the riders away Maelbrigt added,

"We shall be spending the time preparing. I suggest you do the same!"

# Chapter 12

## *Dangling Temptations*

### Brychan & Rathlin: Solstice

Outside of Eynon, Warwick stared sadly at the line of Foresters' graves on the slope above the sea. That deadly searing sheet of Power had taken them all by surprise – if this was what they could expect when coming up against the Helm, then it did not bode well for the future. Although the regular Order men had also taken serious casualties from the fighting, this almost felt worse for the reason that they had been caught so utterly off guard.

"Stop beating yourself up," Berengar said softly, appearing by his side. "You couldn't possibly have known! Even at Moytirra the DeÁine didn't have the Treasures with them, did they? The last time any Islanders fought against those fell creations was five centuries ago! In that time we managed to forget how to use our own Treasures, so it's certainly not down to you that we're unprepared for the ways these cursed Abend weapons might manifest themselves. If there was complacency over the danger, then it took its toll long before any of us were born."

"Indeed," Brego agreed, joining them. "It's what Sioncaet said back at Lorne. It's the difference between us seeing those days as in the far past of our ancestors, yet for Quintillean it was in the days of his youth. There never was any doubt in my mind that when it came to playing this particular game of catch-up that the Abend would win hands down. The big question was only when and where this blow would fall, and for my part I'm very glad that it happened when the Abend were so far away and the strength diluted. You may have lost two companies worth, and have equivalent to another two who now won't come with us to Rathlin, but it could have been worse. Much, much worse!

"What if we'd discovered what the Helm could do in the first charge against the new DeÁine? What carnage might have ensued then with their superior numbers? So spend your time instead thinking about ways to reflect that thing, or something to deflect it from us for when we encounter it again. I'm not asking for the impossible, because I know that you can't counter that kind of strength and simply blast it back at them. Just try to find some way to send it flying off into the skies, or down into the earth."

Warwick nodded weakly, then took a deep breath and straightened his shoulders. "Sorry. ...I always knew we might pay a high price for ridding ourselves of the DeÁine. I suppose I'd allowed myself to think that it wouldn't be just yet – not in this fight – once we knew the Abend weren't with the Donns."

"We all did," Berengar said regretfully, and looked beyond to where the graves lay of some seven hundred of his men. It was too many when viewed as men he had come to recognise individually, whatever his mind said to the contrary and given that they had annihilated the ten thousand facing them. Double the number of dead were wounded, and while a good two thirds of them would survive with proper care and rest, they were nonetheless men Berengar could not hope to march to Rathlin and then on down through the island. He looked at the camp where the wounded lay and then at Esclados.

"Don't even think of asking me!" the old Knight warned his friend and commander. "I'll do most things for you, Berengar, but I won't stay behind! Not even for the sake of the wounded. Not even if you order me to – I'll risk a reprimand of insubordination on my record for that! For a start, I want to see Cwen and Swein as much as you do!"

Berengar smiled ruefully. Esclados knew him too well! Yet he still wished his oldest friend was not going to risk his life in the coming fight. It was utterly illogical, for Berengar was fully aware that if they did not succeed, there would be few refuges in the Islands which would stand against the DeÁine's wrath. *Just one*, he found himself praying at nights, *please save just one of my friends, don't let them all die with me. If even one survives to live free then I won't complain.*

For now, though, they had to move on. The pyres heaped with the DeÁine dead had burned for days, wafting a dreadful stench of burning flesh across their camp no matter where they seemed to move themselves to. To be rid of that at least was a welcome thought, and if nothing else, Berengar was looking forward to smelling clean sea air.

Down in the bay between Farsan and Eynon, a whole flotilla of ships lay. Some were coming in, and others spreading their sails to leave, as they engaged in an intricate dance to get to the quays and let the men embark. The Celidon Foresters were already aboard on the first ships to dock. Berengar had a feeling that now they knew they were only that short voyage from being on the same island as Maelbrigt again, even Brego could not have held them back. In the light of that, Brego had insisted that Warwick's

Foresters go with them too. The ancients had assured them that the DeÁine had only halted for a few hours then had continued on south, so there was no danger for those remaining on Brychan if they were minus Foresters.

Instead, Brego wanted them at the forefront of this army's advance, checking for any traps the Abend might have set, and double checking the information the ancients were feeding them. It was not that Brego lacked trust in their spirit-like allies to keep faith with the Islanders, simply that he did not trust them to see the obvious when it was in front of them. He would take the observations of a few keen-eyed soldiers any day over those of something he could not help think of as a ghost.

At the quay Berengar said farewell temporarily to Brego too. The Grand Master had insisted that Berengar's men embark before his own, and it was not out of courtesy. Berengar's men had fought hard at Arlei, then had had to march hard, then fight again, so Brego wanted them to begin a leisurely march down through Rathlin to regain their strength. If there was any blisteringly fast marching to be done he wanted it to be done by his Ergardians, who had so far been kept back from the worst of the fighting. Anyway, with the big transport vessels and trading ships of the deep oceans, the trip across to Rathlin would only take a bit over a day and a half. This time his men would not be all strung out, days away from one another, as they had been coming to Brychan.

When they landed at Temair, Berengar and Warwick were astonished to find not only Owein from the ancients waiting for them, but a band of Attacotti too.

"Maelbrigt and Sionnachan asked me if I would deliver this message to you," Owein said politely. "They said that you should follow these men. They'll show you the quickest way to get to Kylesk where Maelbrigt is waiting for you. While you were on the water there's been something of a development," and with that Owein told them of how the Forester's chant had unwittingly affected the trio of ancients. "I'm afraid Aneirin can't reach Maelbrigt at the moment," Owein said with more than a hint of glee in his ghostly face, "so if you want to send a message back I'll take it with me now, if you don't mind."

Berengar was a touch surprised, but hurriedly conferred with Warwick and Esclados, then turned back to Owein. "Can you tell Maelbrigt that Warwick and all the Foresters we have here will march to join with him as requested. However, my men can't manage such a fierce pace just yet. We shall commence marching down the interior of the island so that we're well on the way south by the time Master Brego lands."

"Then I shall come with you," a brawny Attacotti said, trotting his shaggy pony forwards. "I'm Colm Ap'brien, one of Magnus' clan chiefs and these are my men. ...Tom, you'll lead the Foresters to Kylesk – Archie, Col, Lindsay and Dougie, go with him. Jamie, Mungo and Gordie, you're with me." He turned again to Berengar. "I have much to tell you on the road, but for now we shall take to the less well-travelled tracks to avoid following in the Abend's footsteps. Your ghostly friends have brought warnings from the others that they fear the Abend may have placed traps for anyone following them once they felt the scale of your defeat of the Donns."

Berengar refrained from saying what was on his mind, which was surprise at so few Attacotti being about the place. From all he had heard, they had given the Knights of Prydein a real headache with their raids. Yet so far he had hardly seen enough men to launch a decent raid, let alone cause trained Knights any problems. It gave him a moment of quiet worry over what kind of troops would be coming to join them from Prydein. Had Master Hugh been too out of touch while Amalric had acted as Master? Were his men only a shadow of their former competency? That could prove lethal against the coming huge DeÁine army if true!

Instead he was glad he had said nothing when they stopped for the night. There, nestled deep in a long glen in the highlands of northern Rathlin, was a huge township. Not a proper town as any of the rest of the Islands would know it. It was far too haphazard for that. But it did contain several hundred people scattered in reed-thatched, turf-walled long-houses up and along both slopes. People who readily came to them with food, and whose women willingly changed bandages on those who had only light wounds, and who had determinedly come along.

"How many men do you have here?" Esclados asked casually, looking about him.

"Oh, I'm only one of the minor clan leaders," Colm explained. "I can field about fifty men at a push, not counting boys. The first time the Abend landed they took us by surprise and I only had a hunting party with me – too many young lads to fight properly."

The Knights scrutinised the township more closely but could not see any sign of these men, something which Colm guessed they were doing.

"Oh you won't see them here at the moment," he said blithely. "They're off with Magnus' chief war-leader in this area."

"Doing what?" Berengar asked cagily.

"Tracking the DeÁine," was the airy answer. "They won't even know they're there!"

"Isn't fifty a bit of a risk against the six thousand we're told the DeÁine have with them?" wondered Esclados. "I mean, if they get spotted and have to fight their way out. The Abend don't have to look with just their eyes, if you get my meaning!"

"True," Colm agreed, "but we don't intend to go blundering in like a boar in a field of bullocks. ...Anyway," and he grinned with ferocious pride, "there's a few more than fifty! When I said I'm a small chieftain, I meant it! My warriors are with Greum Caimbeul. He's the big man in these parts, and he has three hundred of his own men with him. And I mean the veterans! You might never have thought the day would come when you'd be thankful for our skirmishes with Prydein, eh? But all have fought against your own!"

"Caimbeul's sent the young lads with his cousin to meet with Magnus. Didn't want any youthful hotheads taking it into their woolly pates to go plunging down the hill to have a scrap and giving the game away in the process! And that's not counting the men from the other small clans near Loch Canisp. Caimbeul commands a force of around five hundred all told. Not enough to tackle the thousands with the Abend, but plenty to get them away if they get spotted!"

Berengar blinked in a desperate attempt not to show his surprise. He dared not meet the eye of Esclados or Warwick, although he was sure they would be thinking the same as him. How many men *could* the Attacotti bring to the field? For this was something they had not even considered to date.

Late that night, in the sanctity of a shared end-room in the long-house of the chieftain, when all around were hopefully asleep, Berengar did broach the subject.

"Were you two as surprised as me at the number of fighters these clan leaders have?" he whispered softly.

In the pitch black, he heard rather than saw Warwick turn over on the other bed so that he was facing him. "Yes, although more at the number this Caimbeul has under his command. I sort of expected that a decent clan might have fifty men. It's the kind of number you need to make sure that you can fend off the attentions of raiders, or acquisitive neighbours, in order to survive. I wasn't expecting that to be the case for someone who professes himself to be a very *minor* chief, though. And I certainly didn't realise that the big chiefs amongst the Rathliners had five or six times that number."

Esclados muffled a cough with his hand then said,

"But did you notice he said it was in this part of the island? I'm lying here wondering how many major chiefs Magnus has under his sway, because the way Colm was talking, this Caimbeul is far from being the only one."

There was a moment's silence before Warwick said, "I've been doing a bit of calculating, and I'm now thinking that maybe Magnus could bring as many as another thousand to our side."

"That would be a blessing," Berengar breathed, "because I've been doing some calculating too! Brego brought sixteen thousand with him, and they're pretty much all still with us. His men only took a handful of casualties at Arlei, and none at Eynon. He says that Master Ruari, as we should properly call him now, will lead around nine thousand from Master Hugh's Prydein sept, if the Prydein militia of archers are going to stay with the Treasure holders."

"Is that for certain?" Esclados wondered.

"I think so," Berengar answered cautiously. "Of course both Master Brego and Master Hugh can only rely on what these ancients are telling them. So we must hope and pray they aren't pulling the wool over our eyes for some inscrutable reason known only to them. However, I can see the reasoning for having three thousand of the finest archers in the Islands protecting our only defence against the DeÁine Treasures, can't you?"

"Oh Spirits, yes!" agreed Esclados heartily and heard Warwick's grunt of agreement too. Then the Forester spoke again,

"So given that you have roughly a company short of eight and a half thousand still, that means of the assembled regular Order we have something just under thirty-five thousand. I've got as near to sixteen hundred Foresters, give or take, which with Maelbrigt's three and a half thousand from Celidon and Sionnachan's nine thousand – if he's managed a full muster – then we've got a whisker over fourteen thousand Foresters. That gives us..."

"Too bloody few!" Esclados snorted. "Barely scrapping fifty thousand all told, and the cursed DeÁine are bringing double that!"

"And that's not counting the Souk'ir the Abend have with them," Berengar added, unable to keep the worry out of his voice. "If we were evenly matched, then an extra six thousand wouldn't be too much of a problem."

"But not when we're two to one against already," Warwick sighed. "Lost Souls! We need the bloody Attacotti , don't we!"

"Every last one," Berengar reluctantly admitted. "If they do nothing more than take out a Seljuq or two of slave fighters, they'll be doing us a big favour."

"We'd better pray that Magnus' sanity holds on, then," Esclados said with more hope than he felt.

Come the morning, Warwick and the Foresters headed over the hills with their guides, plus some men who had been out hunting when the call to arms had come, and were now heading for Magnus too. Berengar and Esclados followed Colm, as he took the rest of them at a more sedate pace higher into the hills.

"We'll stick to some high valleys for now," he told them. "Then there should be a day when we can march down on the lower lands before we get to where the Abend stopped. After that I'll send you on with Jamie, Mungo and Gordie. I shall go back and make sure the rest of those coming get brought this way."

In reality it was only another day before Owein again appeared and requested that Colm return to guide the next shipment, who would be landing in three days' time. Yet by then Berengar had managed, with Esclados' help, to ascertain roughly the number of Attacotti fighters. It was a cheering thought to know that it might be nearer to two thousand, but that was not the only thing lifting their spirits. When they had arisen in Colm's township, they had all been aware that they felt as though a gloomy cloud had lifted from over them. Warwick had sniffed the air before he departed and proclaimed that it felt suspiciously akin to Forester work, and since then Berengar and Esclados had found it notably easier not to dwell on the gloomier aspects of their situation.

Warwick himself made good time with the Foresters, and five days after parting from Berengar and Esclados he found himself meeting an old friend he had thought he might never lay eyes on again.

"Maelbrigt! By the Trees! It's good to see you again!" he exclaimed happily, taking both of the proffered hands and gripping them warmly.

"It's good to see you too, Warwick," Maelbrigt agreed.

"And it seems you've been busy! Was that your work I felt in the morning about five days ago?"

Maelbrigt gave a broad grin. "Ah! I'm glad you noticed it! I was hoping it would spread, but we haven't got the manpower to be sending out Foresters to check." He told Warwick of the ring of wands he had laid down with Sionnachan. "After that, when Sionnachan and most of the Foresters had gone, I got to wondering. I think Magnus has got pretty acute feelings for when the DeÁine are brewing up trouble, given his close contact with the Spear for so long. So I was inclined to listen to his story of what he'd felt back when stalking the Abend. ...You see, while we've been waiting, I've also been assessing how many men he has,..."

"...So have we," Warwick interrupted. "It's far more than we'd thought!"

"...Yes it is! So one way of making them look kindly upon us seemed to be to remove the last of the Abend's miasma which was giving them unfounded doubts. I took Sionnachan's remaining battalion out beyond the ring and we did another incantation, but left it unanchored." He looked at Warwick's quirked eyebrow and smile and grinned more broadly. "Well alright, then, we gave it a bit of a push in the right direction, too! Paid off, though, didn't it?" And both he and Warwick laughed.

After that, however, Maelbrigt was busy welcoming his old comrades from Celidon. It took the rest of the day to get everyone settled and sorted, but come the evening meal, Maelbrigt had the chance to introduce Warwick properly to Taise and the other Treasure wielders. It was a lively meal, filled with good humour, and Warwick was pleased to also get to know Ruari better. Magnus was also something of a surprise, for the Attacotti leader was far from being the repellent thug of repute. Warwick could not quite work out whether he had never been quite that bad, or whether the return to sanity had also seen him becoming more the man he must once have been before the Spear rocked his mind out of kilter. He was not going to argue, though. Magnus on their side was a whole heap better than Magnus against them!

"What's the plan now?" he asked when the three leaders congregated, before retiring, in what had temporarily become the Islanders' strategy planning room.

Ruari and Maelbrigt shared a conspiratorial grin. "Well what we didn't want to make too much of in front of our newest ally is what Sionnachan's been up to," Ruari informed him, and between them they brought him up to date. By the time he had got to, "and we're marching out at dawn the day after next," Warwick was agog, and yet at the same time more fired with optimism than he had felt in weeks.

What Sionnachan had been up to was quite a lot! Four days out of Kylesk he decided that they were far enough from the Island Treasures to risk taunting the Abend. He arrayed his Foresters to either side of where he and McKinley's lance remained with Sithfrey. The spot could not have been better, having ancient woodland climbing from the valley floor on either side, under whose canopy the Foresters were camouflaged. Sionnachan wanted them on hand in case the Abend summoned something dreadful, like several grollicans, to seize the moment and try to take the Gauntlet, but at the same time he did not want to alert the Abend to just how many men he had if they should use the Power to spy on them.

"Take your time," he said to Sithfrey now. "Reach into it and feel for the Power. Get comfortable with what you can hold before you try and direct it anywhere."

The DeÁine scholar gave him one of his baleful glances, although Sionnachan was sure he was not imagining that those looks were more habitual now, rather than expressing any real doubt as to what the Foresters were telling him. Andra was stood right by Sithfrey, supporting him by his presence even though there was little else the monk could do yet. They had promised Sithfrey that they would sedate him with speed if he was in the slightest danger of being overcome by one of the Abend, and Andra held a blanket for under his head and was standing close enough to help Sionnachan catch him. Sithfrey began breathing deeply and steadily to calm himself, then opened himself up to the Gauntlet. The wash of Power took his breath away.

"Sithfrey? Sithfrey? Are you all right?" he heard Andra asking, urgently as he swayed alarmingly. Andra was refraining from touching him for fear of disrupting the Power, and the unknown consequences that might bring, but only just.

He managed a tight nod, but could not speak since he had his teeth gritted so hard it was making his jaw ache. The Gauntlet settled to a steady vibration, and now that Sithfrey had got over the initial shock of the volume of Power, he found he could sense a way he might use it. Controlling it, though, would be beyond him.

"Is it worse now than when you first used it?" Sionnachan asked, bothered by the grimace on Sithfrey's face and the way he was starting to sweat profusely.

"M'hmph," Sithfrey grunted in confirmation.

"Could it be due to the Abend being nearer and having two of the other Treasures?"

"M'hmph!"

"Then just push towards them," Sionnachan instructed him. "Don't try to be clever with it, or too refined. Use a simple command with the Gauntlet, 'find the others' would do, and then let the Power go."

The words were hardly out of his mouth before the eruption of Power shot out of Sithfrey and headed south-west as straight as an arrow. They could not see it. This was no sheet of coloured light, visible to the eye. But they could trace its passage by the flattened grass and shattered bushes and saplings, while some of the larger old trees were uprooted and fell to the ground, all pointing the same way. Sithfrey staggered and was just gulping in huge breaths of air when he reeled backwards.

"*Who are you who dares to use one of Volla's own?*" a voice seared into his head. "*Bring it to us immediately!*"

"Quintil..." Sithfrey managed to whimper, and in a trice Sionnachan was at his side and clamping a pungent cloth over his nose and mouth. As he sucked in the heady and incantation-infused concoction, the world went black and he keeled over into Andra and Sionnachan's arms.

Instantly the Foresters saw the Gauntlet go from glowing back to its normal dull metal.

"Will he be alright?" Andra fretted, even though Sionnachan had warned him of what he was going to do.

The Foresters' commander smiled. "Oh yes, he'll come to no harm. That was the whole point of it. He'll wake up in an hour or so, and it's only going to take that long because of the large amount I used. I wanted him to go straight out, before they had any chance to worm their way into him, and I infused the sedative with every DeÁine repellent I could think of to make sure they didn't linger! He's the connection, and without him the Gauntlet couldn't continue the link to the Abend."

"Poor Sithfrey!" McKinley sympathised. "The one Abend he was most terrified of was the very one he hooked. He's being extraordinarily brave!"

In the Abend's army, four days beyond them, pandemonium had broken out. The Abend had screamed for their individual litters to halt, and had then piled out with an uncharacteristic disregard for ceremony. They were just beyond the western end of a stretch of water which the maps they had appropriated at Temair told them was called Kinloch.

"Who in Volla's name was that?" Barrax yelled at all but Laufrey. "I thought you all said that only one of us could use the great Volla's armour?"

"What haven't you told us?" Laufrey demanded suspiciously.

However the established Abend members were in no mood to be quizzed. Quintillean was rubbing his temples from the backwash of Power which had come with the abrupt termination of contact. Something in the way the connection had snapped had ricocheted the Power like a mirror reflecting a needle of searing light back into his head. He was getting very sick of these contacts with inferior beings who knew nothing of how to ride the Power, and yet cause all manner of pain and problems for the chosen ones by their erratic contacts. He was going to do something truly exquisitely painful to this one when he got his hands on him, whoever he was!

For now he snapped at the others, "He wasn't controlling it!"

"Ah! So maybe a renegade acolyte?" Magda guessed. "That would explain why he had the strength to blend with it, especially if he's used some of the minor pieces in the past. That has to be someone who's had some measure of training, you know. It couldn't be anyone *less*. No half-breed or turned Hunter." Personally she thought it less likely that a Hunter would turn than one of the self-serving acolytes whom Helga and Geitla had brought along in recent decades. The selection of those two really had not been the Abend's finest hours! A thought occurred to her, could it be the lost acolyte Taise? She had the capability to use one of the great pieces but might lack the practice to be controlled. "Are you sure it was male?"

"Definitely!" Quintillean growled, not liking being questioned.

He was saved further affronts to his fragile status by the appearance of Dagmar dragging their twisted acolyte, Fenja, along by the chain which went to the collar, welded by Power around her neck.

Dagmar went straight to Helga and announced, "She knows who it is!"

"Do you, now?" Magda purred, managing to make those three words sinister and threatening to Fenja if she proved to be wrong.

Dagmar thrust her forwards, Fenja going down on one knee and bowing her head, eyes averted as she declared, "It's Sithfrey, oh Great Ones!"

"Ah! One of Taise's little friends!" Anarawd recalled instantly. Sithfrey had made little impact on him for his own sake, but he had made it his business to know everything about anything which related to the woman he had once hoped to control the Treasures through.

The other Abend had been looking blank at the name until Anarawd spoke, but now they were suddenly alert.

"What's he doing with the Gauntlet?" Tancostyl fumed.

"He was sent after Taise, wasn't he?" Eliavres said slyly, noting that Anarawd was startled by this, but that Masanae and Helga expressions of strained innocence and unknowing were not convincing. So he had been right about that too! The two schemers had not wanted Anarawd to have control over such a powerful woman, although what Anarawd had wanted with her he could not determine. "Maybe instead of him finding Taise, someone else found *him*?"

"He was always weak-willed, oh Great Ones," Fenja supplied, still kneeling in the dirt. "You tortured and tormented him at Bruighean befor..."

"...The royals!" Masanae immediately leapt to the conclusion at the mention of the royal stronghold. "They're trying to beat us to the coast! They're thinking they can make a pact with the Sinuti!"

"I briefly sensed many men around them," Quintillean added thoughtfully. "It cannot be those irritating Islanders who fought the Donns. They haven't had the time to get this far!"

"No," agreed Barrax, applying more thought to the situation. "There were no ships on the horizon when we journeyed across, and we checked several times for signs of pursuit. Also, given that they were behind us then, they would have to have overtaken us, and we couldn't fail to have seen them doing that. Therefore I agree. It cannot be that army from Brychan."

"Although where that army came from is a mystery!" Helga snorted irritably. "The cursed Knights don't have that many castles in that part of the Island! What did they do? Grow webbed feet overnight and swim the floods?"

Barrax looked disdainfully at her and caught Laufrey doing the same. Give them time and this one would have to go! She was too much of a liability.

"From the north, of course!" he chided her with scant patience. "It's the only place those Islanders could have come from. It explains why they took so long to challenge us, too, if they had to march all the way down the island."

"But the Donns said..."

"The Donns were fooled!" Barrax cut her off. "They should not have underestimated the Knights!"

"Do you imply that mere slave fodder could match a DeÁine?" Masanae demanded with icy effrontery. "That such base creatures could come up with..."

"...Low, base cunning?" Barrax interrupted again. "Of course I do! Great Dragon of Death! Wake up all of you! All they had to do was forge some messages to give the Donns what they *wanted* to hear! I'm not suggesting the impossible, as if they found their way into the Houses of the Holy or entered Bruighean! We're talking simple forgery of a few letters here! And only good enough to fool a bunch of men who regularly pound one another's heads with their duels and mock battles, at that. Great Lotus, they wouldn't have to be subtle!"

The rest of the Abend simmered angrily in their respective styles for a few moments, but then sullenly agreed that Barrax had to be right. All except Eliavres. He was not going to say a word while they were all spitting at one another like so many cats on heat, but he was not so sure that it *would* be impossible to find the Knights in New Lochlainn by now. They had been gone an awful long time – even Anarawd as the last of them to come east – and even the Knights might think to take advantage of their absence. They had certainly had time to come out of the north on the DeÁine's side of the Brychan mountains too, and what would they have known when so many of the nine had been on the sea? He would worry about that later, though. First, they needed to make sure they greeted the Sinuti in style, and this bickering over past events was getting them nowhere fast.

"Then we should meet them," he declared with resolute calm. "Never mind where this Sithfrey got his hands on the Gauntlet, or how he got here. We must wait and greet him and his new 'friends'! Barrax is right! We need to act, not sit around fretting over things which can't be altered. Later on we can analyse this to make sure the same thing never happens again. But not now! Let's get close to this turncoat acolyte, because then we can take the Gauntlet off him with ease. And it will show the royals, or whoever it is with him, that only the Abend can truly control the Great Volla's gifts!"

Eliavres was not too convinced that it was the royals either. It was the kind of silly mistake the likes of Masanae and Quintillean made time and again because they never bothered to get to know the other highborn DeÁine. He, on the other hand, knew Queen Eriu very well, and he therefore knew that neither she nor her closest allies were so inept at political survival as to come to the Sinuti as a divided force. The queen he had been cultivating for so long would grit her teeth and back the Abend in the face of the Sinuti, even if she was gagging on her own bile to do so. No, this stank much more of Islander, but when he tried to suggest that he was very swiftly cut short.

"Oh don't be ridiculous!" Quintillean snorted. "They have their own quaint charms and spells, but really... to suggest that they might have even the faintest idea of what to do with the Great Volla's armour they captured? *Phaa*! Of course not! If they had, they would surely have done *something* with them in the long years they've had them."

*Very well*, Eliavres thought, *on your heads be it! But I think you'll get a shock when you meet this force*! And at the same time he marked that down as yet another reason why Quintillean would be the one going back to Lochlainn to face the Emperor's wrath. *You're talking your way out of leadership of the Abend every time you open your mouth, and you haven't even the wit to see it!*

He was further shocked by the leaders' naivety when Masanae sent a flash of a message towards the Gauntlet.

"*Come to us*!" she commanded. "*We shall wait by this water the slave nation call Kinloch. Then you may join with us in greeting the Sinuti.*"

She did not bother waiting for a reply, expecting Sithfrey's training to kick in and for him to defer to her, which was just as well. Poor Sithfrey had only just woken up when the message seared into his head.

"Ouch!" he whimpered. "Oh Blessed Lotus! That was Masanae! She say's we're to join her by Kinloch to go and meet the new DeÁine, the Sinuti."

"Flaming Trees!" Sionnachan gasped. "Does she think you're with other DeÁine, then?"

"Seems so," McKinley agreed, as he helped Sithfrey take a third swig of mead which had another of Sionnachan's special potions in it, this time to restore him to his normal self.

"I didn't get much," Sithfrey gulped. "It was too fast. Too short, for anything more. But I got a hint of disdain, of looking down on us. I think she either thinks we're the dregs of the army which failed them in Brychan. Or, she thinks we're with another force – maybe from Bruighean?"

Sionnachan looked at McKinley who grinned wolfishly back.

"Then I think it's time we earned our keep!" the captain said with relish.

"Eight thousand of us here. Six with the Abend! Sounds like it's time we took advantage of having superior numbers to even the odds for later on."

"Just what I was thinking," Sionnachan said enthusiastically. "We can't engage with the Abend, even with those odds, but we can do some serious damage to that escort of theirs."

Fired with their leader's eagerness, the Foresters regrouped and hurried onwards. Sithfrey and Andra were on horses so that they could cope with the Foresters' pace, and as McKinley jogged alongside them, he explained.

"The Abend will be expecting us to drag our feet if anything. To be arguing the toss between ourselves as to what to do for the best. So we can surprise them by getting to them a good day earlier than they expect, maybe more."

Sithfrey and Andra did not press him further for he needed his breath to keep jogging, but both worried that these Foresters were not taking the Abend seriously enough. After all, there were now a full four war-mages there, and they already had the Helm and the Scabbard – and Sithfrey, even with the Gauntlet, was no match for that!

A little under three days later they were still worried, and all the more so for lying prone in the heather beside Sionnachan and McKinley on one side, and their old friend Captain Ulfhart on the other, looking from a short ridge down onto the army surrounding the Abend. Sithfrey could not see what the Foresters were so happy about until Ulfhart leaned in and explained.

"They've pitched camp in clusters, but that makes it all the easier for us to pick out the prime targets. If we create a sense of panic, there's no clear route in or out of that camp. Men will be falling over one another, and they've got to get clear of the tents before they can think of getting into some kind of battle formation."

Sionnachan wriggled back down the slope until he was off the horizon, then stood up and gestured his leaders to him. The eight commanders and several of their captains huddled together around Sionnachan, so that the two outsiders had no clue as to what was going on. Then suddenly everyone was running back to their men.

"Keep an eye on these two," Sionnachan said with a wink at Ulfhart as he hurried past with McKinley on his heels, for the experienced captain was acting as Sionnachan's aide now.

Ulfhart drew them off through a stand of rather stunted hawthorns, then led them at a crawl up another spur of the ridge.

"The trees are in the way here for the others to use this patch," he said confidently. "We'll be out of the way, but you'll be able to see."

For a while nothing seemed to happen, and Sithfrey and Andra found themselves drowsing off in the warm afternoon sun after the past several hectic days. Suddenly Andra was wide awake,

"I can smell smoke!" he hissed urgently to Anson, the archer, who was closer to him than Ulfhart. His fear was of some arcane fire sent by the Abend which made Anson's answering grin somewhat perplexing. Then he followed to where the archer was pointing for him. All along the ridge archers knelt just out of sight from the other side, and every so often there was a small pile of twigs and dried leaves – the kind of things which would catch fire easily. Anson then tapped his arm and pointed further back from the ridge. A tiny number of proper fires had been started, none of which were smoking badly, and men stood close by, poised with bundles in their hands which Andra presumed would take the fire to the archers' waiting tinder.

"Won't the DeÁine smell it?" he whispered worriedly to Anson.

The archer shook his head. "We didn't strike our flints until they started lighting their own cooking fires. If they smell smoke they won't think anything of it. All we have to do is make sure they don't *see* smoke coming from where it shouldn't."

"But what are you going to do?" Sithfrey was still half asleep and confused.

Anson and Ulfhart with the rest of their lance gestured for them to look at the enemy's camp once more in answer.

"We're going to set fire to the camp," Mace said with vulpine anticipation. "A surprise attack a full day ahead of when they're even remotely expecting someone. And a night attack – or nearly!"

Andra was thinking furiously. He could remember Ruari saying something about night attacks, and then it came back to him.

"But doesn't this mean that you won't be able to launch a night attack on the main army?" he asked tentatively. "I think Ruari told me that it's a trick you can only pull off once in any engagement, because after that your enemy is prepared for you to do something like that and you lose the element of surprise." He was rather worried that Sionnachan might, in his enthusiasm, be limiting Ruari and Brego's options for later on.

Ulfhart smiled at him. "For a monk who knew nothing of war a year ago, you're certainly learning fast! And what Ruari said was right, especially

220

when you're talking about the kind of war Ruari and his men were fighting in the east. But the army which is coming will be too big for that kind of tactic anyway. A hundred thousand is a vast number of men by day, let alone by night. By the time we'd waded through those ranks we could get at first, the ones behind them would have plenty of warning of what we were about. What might happen then is that the fighting would get very bloody, and in the dark we'd risk leaving wounded behind – and you don't do that with the DeÁine!"

"So this won't alter our chance for later on?" Andra checked.

"Not at all," reassured Anson. "If anything it will help if we can get rid of these Souk'ir troops."

Off to their right, the sun was making its last showing between a few scattered clouds and Rathlin's western hills. As it disappeared, and the landscape was instantly transformed into a muted tapestry of greys, blues and purples, they heard first one owl call, then many. A low humming then caught their ears and out of the dusk flew thousands of flaming arrows. Most arced gracefully through the air and landed in the camp, catching tents and men alike. Some, though, flew with uncanny precision to the tents in the middle of the camp, all of which were larger and grander than those around them. Their exotic silks caught fire even faster than the fabric of the soldiers' tents, and in a heartbeat the tongues of flame had shot up the sheeted fabric and turned the tents into torches.

"That should give the Abend something to keep them occupied," Ulfhart said cheerfully.

The DeÁine camp was now chaotic, filled with screams and shouts, while dark smelly smoke began to swirl about the place from the burning cloth, causing even more confusion. Andra tore his gaze away from the Abend's flaming tents, realising that the archers had next targeted the men on the edge of the camp, and were now hurrying down to catch up with the rest of their lances. The men-at-arms were working with frightening precision on the perimeter, cutting down all who got in their way. At the camp's edge these were the Seljuqs, and as Andra's eyes became accustomed to the half light he could see that these men had never had any tents in the first place. Where Sionnachan's tactics were working well was in depriving the slaves of those to whom they looked to tell them what to do. The Jundises were stumbling around in the fiery confusion, and without them the Seljuqs were easy prey for the superior number of Foresters.

Suddenly from the heart of the camp there was a whoosh of air, and the tents of the Abend were blasted out of existence, flames and all. In the open space left, they could see certain figures standing still and an eerie glow forming about them. Before the balls of Power-fire even got loosed from the Abend's fingers, horns had been sounded and the Foresters were pulling back. Sithfrey felt a ripple of panic run up his spine. Now they would see what the Abend could do, and he curled up, wrapping himself around his Gauntleted hand as much from primal instinct as from any belief that it would shield him from their view.

As the pulsating globes of Power rocketed outwards towards them, Sithfrey let out a whimper and '*Noooo!*', only to find himself being flipped onto his back as the Gauntlet also flamed into life. Instead of forming Power-fire of its own, though, it created a fan-shaped shield in the air, radiating several feet off the ground and spreading quickly, against which the Power-fire exploded. He had not quite managed to totally quench the bolts, but they were shattered into lesser bolts whose Power leaked away even as they continued to fall, most being easily dodged by the Foresters and impacting with hardly a sound on the soft ground. Fountains of earth was all the Foresters had to contend with.

Another volley from the Abend came sailing over the ridge, and a startled but a hopeful Sithfrey now extended his arm, pointing upwards and willing the Gauntlet with all his might to protect all those beneath its shield. The blaze of light as the two Power-based forces came into contact was blinding, and another volley was coming towards them before the others had barely hit. Acolytes must have been joined to the Abend because there were far more than just nine in each blasting, and the second was greater than the first. This time some of the Power-fire balls got through, but Sithfrey's shield had still somehow deprived them of much of their force. The glowing orbs ploughed deep furrows in the earth as the Foresters scattered out of their way, then fizzled away into nothing. It was a good thing, too, because Sithfrey was shaking like a leaf and just about holding his Gauntlet-arm up with the aid of the other and Andra supporting both.

"No more!" he pleaded with a whimper. "Sweet Mother Ama don't let them send any more! I can't do it again!" But he was saved that trial.

"*Traitor!*" The word blasted through the air on a sending all could hear. "*You shall live to regret this day!*"

However, Sionnachan's men were hardly hanging about to bandy words with the Abend. They were running for all they were worth, Sithfrey and

Andra shoved up onto horses again to keep up, and heading for the loch. As they ran, the men took it in turns to stop and shove wands into the ground and say a few words, before sprinting like hares to get back amongst the fleeing company. Sithfrey was slumped in his saddle, only held up by Mace and Anson running on either side and holding him on. Andra, however, was alert enough to notice that there was no sign of pursuit, not even from any sendings of the Abend. He half expected the baneasge summoning he had been told the Abend could use, to be inhabiting the waters of the marshes they ran through as they neared the loch, but all was quiet. All he heard was the splashing of men's feet.

Magnus had been truthful in his description of the Loch of Kin. It was a brooding salt marsh at the outlet end, and brackish all the way to its inlet, and the Foresters plunged in. Most then paused in the shallows, and luckily for them the shallows were extensive. This was not a deep loch. Ulfhart, however, kept going leading Sithfrey's horse, with Anson, Mace and Andra in his wake, until they came to a small island in the middle. Then they allowed the two civilians to dismount and announced that they would be spending the night here. Both Andra and Sithfrey thought they would be too scared of the next Abend assault to sleep, but as the darkness settled deeper and nothing happened they both gave in to their weariness.

In the morning, after an Abend-free night, they woke to find Sionnachan sat close by with McKinley and his men, making breakfast over a goodly cooking fire.

"Come and have some griddle cakes before Sionnachan scoffs the lot!" McKinley called cheerily.

Sithfrey was suddenly aware that he was ravenously hungry. Hungrier than he could ever remember being, come to that. He walked stiffly to the fire, but after that found himself eating round after round of the sweetened flat breads that Mace was doing a first class job of turning out. As he realised how much he had eaten he faltered, rather embarrassed at what the Foresters might see as greediness.

"No, no, you carry on!" Sionnachan insisted. "After what you did last night you must build your strength back up again."

"Where are the Abend?" Andra asked, almost not wanting to know the answer but feeling he had to ask.

"Packed up and headed south," McKinley told him with a grin. "We think it was when they realised how many men they'd lost..."

"...Or rather how few they had left!" Anson corrected him as he scooted two more cakes Andra's way along with a pewter mug of scalding caff. "Charming lot, your Abend! They just disregarded the wounded. They must think they're worth nothing now that they can't fight. Left them behind and just marched off with those who were able to."

"We'll go into the camp today," Sionnachan said calmly, as though he was planning a mere training manoeuvre. "I wouldn't risk any man in there in the dark – too much potential for hidden traps – but today we'll sort out the living from the dead. We might get some resistance from the old Jundis men. No doubt some would carry on fighting with only one arm, one eye and a leg. But without the Abend there we can sort them out easily."

"Did we lose many men?" Andra asked, dreading that they might only have half the number they had set out with. Sithfrey had done wonders, but those Power-fire balls had scared him rigid!

"Ten!" Sionnachan said triumphantly. "Of course, no man's loss should be taken lightly, and we've a good deal more than that with cuts and bruises, but none of them who won't live to fight another day. Not bad for a night's work, eh?"

Therefore the trip back to the camp was cheerful right up until they crossed the ridge. Below them the field was flattened. Not a tent pole stood up. Not a soul moved. There were no wounded, only dead.

"Great Ash, who links this world and the next. Make a bridge of your mighty arms for those who fall to the Summerlands. Protect their souls on their journey beneath the shade of your leaves," Sionnachan intoned. "Great Ash in you we trust," to be responded to by all the men around him with,

"In you we trust."

And all along the ranks Sithfrey and Andra could hear the same prayer.

"They didn't deserve this," Sionnachan growled, his voice tight with fury. "No matter who they were fighting for. To lose some men in battle can't be avoided, but to slaughter your wounded is unforgivable!"

"Maybe they still thought you were a DeÁine force," Andra said, thinking aloud. "Given that Sithfrey used a DeÁine weapon to defend us."

Sionnachan whirled round and gave Andra a piercing glance. "Go on!"

"Well, if they're *really* worried about these new DeÁine, they wouldn't want to meet them with a big chunk of their army bleeding and burnt, would they? It hardly gives the impression they're in control!"

"They'll try and pass it off that they only ever came with a small troop," Sithfrey added with certainty. He could see it now that Andra had put his finger on it. "Their pride will never let them tell the truth – that they were beaten by surprise tactics and the folly of their own men in making a camp nobody could get out of."

Sionnachan's scowl lifted. "Do you know, we'll make military men of both of you yet!" he complimented them.

In the DeÁine army things were nothing like so cheerful. Maj'ore Tabor was in a towering rage at the casual waste of his men. Yet he alone could do nothing against the Abend for his fellow Maj'or, of the Dracma had died in the night, incinerated in his tent before anyone could save him. So too had so many of their leading men. What men there were, he now pulled back around him, men of both Souk'ir families preferring one another's company to that of the treacherous Abend's escort. And the gap between the two groups widened as the day went on, for nobody wanted to be close to the Abend.

The nine were in a fury of apocalyptic size. Even the acolytes were walking with heads cast down, too scared to even look towards the litters which the tuatera lizards were bearing. There was an almost visible haze of Power swirling about the swaying howdahs as the Abend argued and gnawed at this latest problem. Blame and accusations flew back and forth until Eliavres thought he could knock all their heads together – even Barrax and Laufrey, who in this respect seemed no better than their elders.

"Shut up!" he finally bellowed verbally, as the only way to get heard over the Power-shared arguments. "Phol's bollocks! Do you *want* the Sinuti to know we fucked up?"

The swirling Power suddenly dropped to a trickle as his words sunk in. In the stillness they all became aware of it. That sense of something very close and listening carefully. Eliavres had to admire the amount of control Masanae swiftly acquired as she sent out a needle-thin questing.

"Great Lotus shrivel their souls and Mother Seagang rot their bones!" he heard her swear across the narrow divide between howdahs.

Clearly his warning had proved more accurate than expected. A heartbeat later Masanae's drapery was flung back and the senior witch glared out at the others. Eliavres managed to conceal his smile at the sight of them all peering out like so many petulant children, although the worst by far were Quintillean, Helga and Anarawd. Magda was less than happy, that was clear, but he caught her eye and received a nod of support from her. Clearly she was looking to him for his assessment, which pleased him greatly deep down inside. It signalled that finally they had moved beyond teacher and student. Now, though, was not the time for thinking out the implications of that power shift.

"They were listening, weren't they," he stated flatly. "Well that shoots down any chance we have of pretending that nothing is amiss." He paused, waiting for anyone to dare start squabbling again. Nobody did. *Thank Esras for that!* he thought with relief. *Maybe at last they're truly understanding the depth of the shit Quintillean has dropped us in!*

"Do you have a plan, poppet?" Magda asked in studied casual tones, although her eye contact with him alone was almost pleading.

He winked covertly at her and saw her recover some inner composure. So she trusted him that much? That was flattering and unexpected! He cleared his throat and called for his drivers to stop, gesturing the others to get down. When they were all stood together, isolated in a circle of the tuateras, he spoke.

"This must be presented to the Sinuti as the actions of a renegade faction within the acolytes and minor families," he said firmly. Helga made to argue but for once he was beaten to silencing her by Laufrey, who simply elbowed Helga hard in the gut. As Helga made gurgling noises and looked daggers at her fellow witch, Eliavres continued.

"Think! If they think we've been beaten by a bunch of savages we'll look utterly incompetent! However, they've all played the games for long enough to know about power-wresting. Someone from within taking a stab at grabbing power is familiar, at least. It's less than ideal, but they will accept it and we save *some* face."

"And Maj'ore Tabor will keep quiet?" Anarawd snorted.

"Of course he won't, you fool!" Magda snapped. "That's why he can't be allowed to live."

"But not yet!" Eliavres added forcefully. "It must be done subtly! Later! With the finest needle of Power and carefully timed so that to the Sinuti he will not appear to have been got out of the way. He must get us to the coast and act as our guard until then. Even with his men dragging their feet as they are, they still discourage any from coming upon our rear."

"The Gauntlet is not behind us anymore," Masanae said with icy dignity. "I have checked," and her tone dared any to argue with her assessment.

Eliavres was not going to be drawn into more bickering. "Well that's to the good," he said smoothly. "We can greet the Sinuti, show them the Helm

226

and the Scabbard and then tell them that the Gauntlet is on this very island and ripe for them to take."

"You can't do that!" Quintillean exploded. "Give one of Great Volla's..."

"...Phol's cock! Did your exploits in the islands addle your brains!" Eliavres' temper was finally stretched beyond bearing. "Did you hear nothing? Learn *nothing*? This Sithfrey has no *control*! He's barely managing the simplest of drawings! Do you think any of the Sinut acolytes will do better? So let them do the dirty work with *whoever* it is who's with Sithfrey, pulling his chains – because by the state you've said he was in, it isn't his plan. *He's* no match for an Abend without his protectors!"

Quintillean's intended riposte was timely halted by Masanae kicking his shin, but it was enough to let Eliavres' words to sink in. Of course! Once the Sinuti had it, it would be so much easier to channel Power into it. They could be half a camp away. That wouldn't matter. If he got a clear shot at the Gauntlet he could take it off any of them through sheer strength in the Power. His lips curled in a feral smile. Then he would be leader once more!

Eliavres saw the smile and smiled back. *Immaculate Temples, your wits are gone, Quintillean, just like your predecessor! Well if you've taken that simple bait, then you can get on with it. Snatch the Gauntlet and get on that ship back to Lochlainn. And while you're flat on your back over the ocean, the Sinuti will have the Gauntlet back off you in a trice. Then the only things which will keep you alive will be an express order from the Emperor himself to leave the torturing of you to him. Without that they'll flay you alive at the very least. You rubbed their noses in the dirt for too long, and with too little justification, for them to forgive you in the next thousand years.*

Eliavres turned to get back into the howdah and caught Magda's eye again. He did not need the mind contact of the Power to know that she was thinking the same. Let these dead weights sink in the mire of their own making. Let the Sinuti sail for Lochlainn. And then they could begin making their own Empire somewhere nice and warm, and leave these festering wet rocks in the northern oceans to Helga – if she survived.

# Chapter 13

## Differing Viewpoints

### Rathlin: Solstice – Grian-Mhor

Spirits were high as the long line of men marched out of Kylesk. In the vanguard were the Celidon men with Maelbrigt. Following them came Ruari at the head of a long column of men which included the Treasures, the squints and their attached people. Behind then came the Attacotti with Magnus proudly leading them, and if their marching was a more ragged affair than the Order men's, then nobody was going to comment on it. Warwick brought up the rear with his Foresters, having lost the argument that his men were the least connected to the Treasures, and should therefore take the risks associated with being in the lead.

"Of anyone, I'll be able to feel the Abend coming," Maelbrigt had said firmly. "If Ruari and Taise will keep Squint by them they'll have plenty of advanced warning of trouble coming."

That was one argument he lost, though. Squint was having none of it! The little creature could be remarkably stubborn when he wanted to be, yet that wasn't all. When he set up an ear-piercing whistling at being separated from Maelbrigt all the others did the same in support of him. And since this was tooth-wrenchingly piercing to human ears, Maelbrigt had not even got to the ring of wands before Ruari was galloping up to him with the reins of Squint's litter horses in his hand.

"For pity's sake have him!" the big Knight said forcefully, "before we all go deaf!" and thrust the reins into Maelbrigt's hand. "Now will you be quiet?" he demanded of Squint, who looked up at him with mournful, liquid brown eyes and tweeted apologetically, then looked at Maelbrigt as if to say 'it's all his fault'. Both men could not help but laugh, Maelbrigt sighing and shrugging at Ruari, who turned and heeled his horse back to the now quiet ranks behind.

Squint was not the only one not happy about being separated from Maelbrigt, and after the first day Taise was allowed to ride beside him, although this had less to do with her protests than Maelbrigt's conviction that all was safe, once the ancients had brought word from Sionnachan of their second encounter with the Abend's force. Maelbrigt, Ruari and Warwick all sent their endorsement of Sionnachan's actions via Owein when he went back again. They all had no doubts that Sionnachan had done the right thing in attacking the Souk'ir – anything which reduced the numbers they would face in the major battle was a good thing, they felt.

His caution in not following was also endorsed. There was nothing to be gained from provoking the Abend further into trying their strength with those Treasures they had. Moreover, despite the fact that the collected Islanders would be outnumbered two to one, everyone agreed that they would rather fight the massed DeÁine now. Having the newcomers forewarned sufficiently for them to stand off in their ships, then maybe flee only to remain an unseen danger in years to come, was not something they wished to incite – although they acknowledged that it might happen despite their best efforts. Yet for now they were in relative safety riding to join with Sionnachan, and so Taise got her wish and rode beside Maelbrigt.

Indeed these were a glorious few days. The weather blessed them with a fresh wind coming up off the sea to keep men and horses cool enough to march in comfort, despite the almost cloudless sky. Like Sionnachan before them, they avoided the humble coast road, instead making a straight course south-by-south-west over the moorland. It allowed more men to march abreast and kept the whole company closer together, however Ruari had to make adjustments several times. Out of the hills came more and more men to join Magnus' men. Ragged men by their clothing, but armed with weapons which looked well used, their experience was emphasised by the number who sported visible scars and battle-gained deformities.

Magnus had marched out of Kylesk with his own clansmen and those of Colm Ap'brien – a thousand tough, scruffy fighters at Magnus' back. Yet a day later the rest of the column saw plaid-clad men come streaming over a ridge to their right. Ruari kept his own men marching and signalled to Warwick to do the same thinking Magnus could deal with these at first, then was startled to see the age of some of the newcomers. With speed he galloped his horse back to Magnus, silently thanking the Trees, the Blessed Martyrs (so beloved of Andra), and any other deity who might be listening in, that Magnus had had some decent horses in his stables. Of course, the chances were that these beasts were originally the Order's anyway, but this was no time to quibble. He would have been quite literally run ragged if he had had to go up and down this long line on foot.

"Children?" he demanded of Magnus as he drew level with the Attacotti warlord. "For pity's sake, Magnus, who will found the next generations of your people if all your sons get killed?"

Magnus turned his odd-coloured eyes to Ruari, then gestured to the lad he had been welcoming. "Tell him, boy," he commanded.

The lad, who could not have been above thirteen, looked up at Ruari on his horse towering over him without any sign of fear. "Me mam sent me," he said simply. "She said don't come back until they'm all dead."

"Your *mother*?" Ruari was aghast. "Where's your father?" He looked around at Magnus' men in the hope that an irate parent was already ploughing his way towards them to clip the lad's ear and send him back, preferably with the promise of strong words with the mother when he got back too!

"Dada got killed in the end raid last year," the lad said. "He was the last of ours. Mam says that unless we kill the DeÁine, we'll all be dead next year anyway 'cos we need help to plough the fields, and we can't do that if the men are away fighting."

Ruari's askance glance at Magnus only confirmed that the lad spoke the truth.

"My people were on the verge of starving before this," Magnus said gruffly. "We have nothing left to lose."

"Sweet Rowan save me!" Ruari breathed. He had had no idea that things were this bad, then he looked hard at the food bags the men carried. His own men had come well laden, prepared to march through a countryside already stripped and held against them, where any re-provisioning which was not done by hunting or gathering would have to be done at sword point. They had saved their supplies while in Kylesk too, but now Ruari saw in a blinding flash of insight that they might well have consumed everything which would feed these folk over the coming year, except for the crops yet to be harvested. He rode up to a man and seized the bag from off his shoulder. The man growled and made to protest but saw Magnus' warning frown. Ruari undid the string top and plunged his hand inside. All that was there was hard baked bread, and little of that too.

He handed the man his sack back and turned again to Magnus who just shrugged.

"By all that's holy, man, why did you say nothing?" Ruari demanded, appalled. "You didn't need to feed us if you had so little!"

"We have our pride," the Attacotti warlord said. "It's the only thing we *have* got left! Anyway, if we hadn't been hospitable, wouldn't you have been suspicious of us? We're not so stupid as to think that you wouldn't know the Attacotti are honour bound to offer food and shelter to travellers who are friends or allies. Better to tighten our belts and let you choose to help us, than have you think us enemies you dare'd not have at your backs and slaughter us.

"We know the consequences of not supporting you! The start of all our troubles was when you all censored us for not fighting the DeÁine with you. We've had Moytirra thrown in our faces by merchants and nobles enough! No-one ever bothered to ask why. That we'd already fought alongside our cousins in western Brychan, and seen that disappear under the DeÁine, leaving us with almost no men to defend ourselves. We were on our knees and all your fine nobles did was spit in our eyes – I'll not risk that again! This time we'll fight with you and hope that you don't go back on your promises of help later. At least that way there's a faint hope you'll stop hunting us like animals. That's not a remote possibility of that with the DeÁine, so you're the lesser of the two demons who plague us."

Ruari shook his head in despair. He had heard from Eldaya what Alaiz and she had thought. That Hugh had been too busy dealing with the threat to see the damage that the Island traders had done, and the desperation that lay behind the Attacotti attacks. Now he was hearing and seeing the truth of it. It also appalled him that nobody had ever asked *why* the Attacotti had begun an armed rebellion. His father and the other leaders should have had the wits to recall that west of the Brychan mountains was Attacotti homelands. Or had some highborn fools thought that it mattered less that it was the Attacotti who were overrun than Islanders?

He pulled his horse off a little way and began counting. By the time Magnus brought another wild and ferocious clan leader named Tormod Ap'caoig to meet him, he was fairly certain there was the thick end of another thousand in Magnus' ranks. Some must have been boys from the homes of those already marching with them, for they melted into the ranks, and Ruari saw more than one man drop an arm around the shoulders of what he guessed must be a son or nephew. Others formed whole new companies, often calling to the men in the column and getting ribald remarks back. A certain amount of rivalry clearly existed between these clans, although Ruari did not expect it to lead to any trouble in the current circumstances.

That night he called all the captains to him, including Maelbrigt's and Warwick's, and collectively he briefed them as to the state of the Attacotti.

"Flaming Underworlds!" Warwick swore. "They're fighting on worse than our barest field rations!"

"Which is why I want you to all go back to your men and work out how you can divide up the rations we have," Ruari instructed, and nobody argued. "We shall be with the Ergardians in around nine days, and that will allow us to re-balance the supplies a second time, but for now we move to foraging order! I want men to be gathering anything edible as they go. All food is to be shared!"

"How many more do you expect?" Yaroman asked from his position beside Maelbrigt.

"I think we could have almost the same again as we've had today," Ruari told them. "Magnus tells me that when Raghnall Friseal gets here, he'll bring an even bigger group from around the shores of Loch Canisp."

"Let us help," Swein spoke up. "Cwen and I did a lot of food distribution when we were evacuating southern Brychan. We know what to do."

"So do I," Ivain said with a smile to Swein at finding yet another point on which they thought the same.

"I think we should do it," Cwen agreed. "If it comes through us, it'll look less like you're giving Magnus' men handouts. It's not much, but it'll be a small salve to their pride – especially if they think of the Order as part of the cause of their misery. If your men can make up the food into bundles, then we'll hand them out."

Matti stepped forwards. "I'll come with you, too. I ran the castle for most of the years while Will was away. This is something I know as well."

Ruari looked at them, then at a startled Warwick and at Maelbrigt, who was smiling and nodding as if he expected no less from his fellow Treasure wielders. "Very well. I think you've made a good point, and at least you four are all mounted, so you can catch up easily when you've done. Men, have the food ready for the morning."

He had a small moment of pleasure in the morning watching Magnus' face when he led his clansmen up to the point where the Treasure holders waited. As Cwen and Matti stepped forwards on one side, and Kayna and Swein on the other, and handed men parcels, Magnus was caught so off-guard that his jaw dropped. Clearly the four could not do it all alone and so Scully's men had joined them along with Talorcan's lance. What surprised even Ruari, though, was the sight of Ivain coming on foot leading the Prydein archers over to line up along the road and start handing out food. Talorcan handed out a couple, then walked over to Ruari, who had just finished explaining to the stunned Magnus that he had no intention of leading famished men into a fight for all of their lives.

"Well?" the rather harried Ruari asked, thinking that if being Master of the Rheged sept was going to be much more of this, then he was going to be asking Brego for lessons in diplomacy in order to cope.

Talorcan gave his usual sardonic smile, although Ruari noticed it had somehow lost some of the bitter edge of late. "Ivain had a chat with Cwen, Matti and Swein last night, and they decided that they'd need a good many more hands if this wasn't going to take all day. He said the Prydein archers should do it because they aren't regular soldiers. A good many of them have Attacotti blood in their families too."

Ruari turned and looked to where the archers' long lines were bordering the stream of Rathliners. There were some striking resemblances amongst them now he came to look at them, and apparently it was not lost on the Rathliners either. The atmosphere was becoming far more relaxed.

"Ivain thought it would cause less offence coming from men who were the nearest thing Magnus' people have to clans-folk," Talorcan added. "He *asked* his archers – he didn't need to order them – and they didn't need any encouragement, they followed him without question."

"And he was right," Ruari breathed softly, then shook his head at a new thought. "If Amalric de Loges wasn't already a gibbering idiot, I'd turn him into one for what he did in holding Ivain back. What a waste of a talented leader, and for what? To massage the egos of a few petty lordlings! Hugh should never have stood down, and certainly not for Amalric!"

Talorcan sniffed. "I don't care if he's a vegetable! If I get within reach of de Loges, he'll have a pillow over his head and I'll put him out of his misery! Pathetic little turd! I'll not have him lurking in the background when Ivain starts rebuilding Prydein."

That sounded very much as though Talorcan intended to stay at Ivain's side, Ruari thought, but tactfully refrained from saying anything. It occurred to him that this might be the saving of Talorcan. Something which rekindled the human spark inside which had been buried for so long. It would make Talorcan all the better a leader too. However both he and Talorcan were distracted by another sight. They expected Maelbrigt to be up at the head of the column, and so they were surprised to see him scouring the lines of Magnus' men.

"What's up?" Ruari asked, leaving Talorcan and riding to join the Forester.

Maelbrigt grimaced. "I've lost Arthur again!"

Ruari rolled his eyes in despair. Only three days out of Kylesk and they were already having trouble keeping track of Arthur. Then he heard Maelbrigt's sigh of relief.

"There's the little bugger!"

"I thought you said he was like you at that age," Ruari teased.

"Then this is a bloody penance for all the grief I must have given my mentors," Maelbrigt muttered darkly, as he heeled his horse forward. "Arthur? What in the Islands are you *doing*?"

The small figure, who was standing in front of a semicircle of around thirty boys of mixed ages, turned with an expression of innocence. "These lads ain't got no men in the army to go wiv'," he explained as if it was the most ordinary situation. "So I told 'em we got to be a gang together. Like we was back in Trevelga. That nasty wizard come there and we gave him what for. I told these lads that."

Ruari heard Maelbrigt's stifled groan as he dismounted.

"Arthur," Maelbrigt said with more patience than Ruari would have used, and bending before his small ward looked him in the eye. "Back then that war-mage was busy trying to control a lot more other men. You and your friends weren't the sole target of his interest, and he was also trying not to be noticed for what he was. This time it won't be so simple. We wouldn't have all these men here if it was."

"I know that," Arthur replied, his small face a picture of adult gravity. "But they ain't got no-one to watch out for 'em. They come'd 'cos they was the only ones left in their families to come an' fight. They sez it was their family obliga... oblig..ashun."

Maelbrigt bowed his head and Ruari felt his frustration. How his friend was going to make any sense of this was beyond him. Arthur was not at fault, and he had a fair point – nobody was specifically going to look out for these boys when the real battle got going. Ruari wished he could parcel the whole lot of them back to where they came from. A bunch of young lads barely big enough to wield a spear or handle a bow were not going to make the slightest difference to the outcome of a battle as big as the one they were anticipating. Without Magnus' backing he had no chance of making that happen, though, and he wondered whether if Magnus did back him and sent these boys home, that the Attacotti war-chief would lose some credibility with his men.

Drawing in a deep breath, Maelbrigt straightened again. "Very well, Arthur. You have until noon to gather up any other boys who have no-one – and I do mean *no-one* – to be with. I'm holding you *responsible* for this. If they have an uncle or an older brother, or even a cousin, amongst these men, then that's where they must stay." Ruari watched as Arthur became fully focused on Maelbrigt. Personally Ruari would never have thought of making Arthur responsible, but clearly Maelbrigt had far more of a gift with rebellious children, or at least with Arthur.

"When you have all the *true* orphans, you will bring them to me. Do you understand? To me! We cannot have you wandering between the groups, because if you do, nobody will know if you come to any harm or are in danger – which is what you've said you want to prevent."

"What are we going to be doing?" Arthur asked cagily. "Taise said I should be scrubbing myself more often."

Maelbrigt had to turn away to smother the grin which broke out, and Ruari also had to hide his amusement. Clearly Arthur feared that Taise would be put in charge of them and subjecting them to endless baths – apparently a fate far worse to a small boy than fighting the DeÁine!

"Are you alright?" Arthur asked solicitously at Maelbrigt's fake coughing which covered the laugh he needed to release.

"Yes, I'm fine," Maelbrigt answered turning back to Arthur with his composure just about restored. "What you'll be doing is forming a bodyguard for the squints. But I'll be putting Farrier Armstrong in charge, so mind you do as he says!"

"Yes, sire!" Arthur beamed enthusiastically, pulling himself straight and giving Maelbrigt a good attempt at a proper salute, before turning on his heels and calling the other boys to follow him.

"Is that wise?" Ruari asked. "Giving him ideas that he's going to be fighting?"

Maelbrigt smiled. "Ruari, he's going to fight anyway, unless we bind and gag him and stick him up a tree! And even then I wouldn't be certain the scamp wouldn't wriggle his way free! So the only way we're going to have any chance of preventing that is if he thinks he's part of the plan anyway. Now we've all agreed that the squints are our most precious resource, and they'll be protected by my men. So where safer to put a bunch of children than right next to the squints? At least there he'll be defending, not in the thick of the advance! ...And if they do have to fight, then we'll be in a terrible state anyway, and be unlikely to be around to worry about it!"

Ruari would have loved to see the expression on Farrier Armstrong's face when Maelbrigt broke the news to him, but he was too busy to indulge such whims. Ivain came jogging back up to join him, along with the archers, the food parcels having been distributed, and confirmed that they had plenty to spare for any newcomers who might be in similarly straightened circumstances. That was just as well, since they were about to stop for the night when the promised Raghnall Friseal appeared with his men. It was evident from the start that relations between Friseal and Magnus were not as cordial as with the other clan chiefs, resulting in a long and wearing evening for Ruari. Friseal was disdainful of Magnus taking food from men whom he clearly thought as being only the lesser enemy rather than allies. No matter how carefully Ruari explained it, he found Friseal refusing.

"Bloody pigheaded, stubborn Attacotti!" Ruari fumed, as he took a break from negotiating to eat his own meal.

"I think you'll also have to keep him well away from Taise and Sithfrey," Kayna observed. "At least Magnus had reason when he was being difficult."

"Has he made any attempt to get near to the Spear?" Ruari asked Cwen around a mouthful of hot stew.

"None at all," she replied. "In fact I'm pleasantly surprised at that. I was expecting to keep turning around and finding him lurking behind me."

"I suspect it's got a lot to do with Daisy," Swein said thoughtfully. "Having her here, and fully bonded with the Spear and Cwen, means that the Spear isn't radiating its energy about the place. So Magnus doesn't feel any kind of pull now that it's found its proper user."

Ruari offered up more heartfelt silent prayers of thanks as he continued to eat, accepting Swein's assessment. But Swein had not done.

"I wonder if this clan chief would be more impressed with us if we showed him something of what the Treasures can do in the right hands," Swein mused.

"We're not shooting at Talorcan again!" Ivain said firmly.

"I wasn't thinking of that," Swein hurried assured him. "It was more along the lines of asking some of the archers to fire a volley normally, then do the same with us included. It won't be quite as spectacular, but surely it would make him think twice?"

"I doubt it," Ruari sighed, "although it was a worthy thought, Swein. This man's so suspicious he'd probably think we were trying to intimidate him, or were warning him what we'll do to the Attacotti once we've dealt with the DeÁine."

Any further speculation was halted by a man coming running to find Ruari.

"That Friseal has challenged Magnus to a fight to decide who leads the Attacotti," the man gasped.

"Oh, you are joking!" Ruari groaned. "A leadership fight! What an *excellent* time to choose to challenge Magnus!"

He ran and vaulted onto his horse, regardless of saddle or bridle, and with just its halter turned it and heeled it towards the Attacotti. There was no missing the right spot, for between two large cooking fires, everyone had cleared back and were standing in a large circle. Greum Caimbeul was standing in the middle, a hand on Friseal's chest and talking urgently to him while Magnus stood impassively, with folded arms, several paces behind Caimbeul.

"Don't be such a fool," Ruari heard Caimbeul saying urgently, as he used his horse to force his way into the ring. "This is all wrong, Friseal!"

"Yes it is!" Ruari declared loudly so that all could hear him. "We face the worst enemy of many generations among any of our people and you want to fight one of your own?"

"The Attacotti should be led by the strongest man, then," Friseal announced, "not some old leader who hides behind his women!"

Magnus stepped forwards. "Is that what this is about? The women? You're pissed because I listened to Eldaya instead of giving her to you as a bed slave?"

"It was my men who brought them back to Kylesk! I should have had the pick of the reward! I wanted her! If you were determined to preserve them, then you still had the pregnant, scraggy redhead. Not such a stunner as Gillies, but once you'd drowned her pups she would have kept an old man like you happy."

Even as Magnus squared up to him to declare, "We were born in the same year, you and I! So if I'm an old man, so are you!" another voice cut through the evening twilight.

"Drowned her pups?" it said with dangerous calm. "My, you're the big man, aren't you!" and Talorcan walked into the ring.

Ivain, Pauli, Swein and the rest of the lance were right behind him, but they spread out around the ring, facing the Attacotti.

"You want to fight?" Talorcan sneered, prowling with feral grace towards Ruari and handing him his sword. In a light linen shirt, and with just a knife in his hand, the unwary might have thought Talorcan was biting off more than he could chew – until he reached over, grasped his collar and pulled the shirt over his head to throw it to Ad, who caught it deftly. In the flickering light of the cooking fires, it was still possible to see the multiple scars on his muscled upper body.

"You want to fight?" Talorcan repeated. "Then fight me!"

"I've no fight to pick with you, Knight," sneered Friseal.

"Well I've one to pick with you!" Talorcan snorted, gently swaying like a bull about to charge. "That scraggy redhead you wanted used as a whore was my friend! She was my other friend's *wife*, too. I've no fight with Magnus because he treated her with respect. He behaved like a leader should. You? You're not fit to lead! ...And if you want any other reason, I'm half DeÁine!"

Friseal growled and Caimbeul stepped smartly back, retreating with Ruari to the perimeter of the ring. The pair circled one another like dogs, each watching the other for an opening. As one they lunged at one another, knife blades flickered in the flame-light, and there were grunts and scuffles before they parted again. Talorcan had got two nasty cuts in on Friseal and had only received a minor scratch himself. They circled again, Friseal making a couple of slashes with his knife but never coming close enough to make contact with Talorcan.

Suddenly Talorcan pounced, throwing his knife into the dirt and using both hands to assault his opponent with. He landed several hard punches on Friseal, stunning him and knocking him to the ground. Talorcan leapt on him like a dog on a bone, pinning him to the ground and giving him another punch on the jaw for good measure.

"Go on then! Kill me!" gurgled the trapped war-chief, but getting a knee in the balls instead from the crouched Knight above him.

"Oh, he's not going to kill you," Ivain said calmly, walking over to where Friseal was pinned with Talorcan's arm across his throat, but writhing with the pain from his groin. "*I* am King Ivain of Prydein, and for your foolish endangerment of what is already a desperate mission, I have something quite different in mind for you! ...You will swear Clan Friseal's loyalty to me *personally*."

There were gasps all round as Ivain's words filled the expectant silence. "Never!" Friseal managed to choke out.

"Oh you will! If we have to take all night at this, you will!" Ivain declared, looking around to the encircling Attacotti, some of whom were muttering darkly to one another at this new turn.

"When the DeÁine have gone," Ivain announced loudly to the whole assembly, "I intend to give this island to the Attacotti as their own homeland. It will be *yours*! Not held only by force. Held by *right*! And what's more, I shall insist that the Prydein merchants reopen the old trading routes. And they *will* trade fairly with you, because the Knights of the Order will monitor them, and woe betide any merchant caught fixing prices or trade routes! For I have a duty to you as I do to all the rest of my people. You might not care to acknowledge it, but that makes it no less binding for me.

"So in all conscience I cannot do any of this if the first thing that will happen will be for it to plunge Rathlin into civil war. You need one leader who can sign the treaties and agreements for you. Together we can put sheep back on these hills to give you money, and trade to put food in the bellies of your families. Magnus has already agreed that this *needs* to happen. That Rathlin should no longer stand alone."

He turned his gaze back down to Friseal but continued speaking to the crowd. "So you, Raghnall Friseal, are the fly in the ointment which will help your people heal. Therefore, if you will not work with Magnus, you and yours must remain under my jurisdiction. And therefore, like all my subjects, you *will swear fealty* to me! ...I have no intention of punishing the ordinary people of Clan Friseal. They will enjoy the benefits along with the other clans. And in your stead I shall oversee their well-being. But *you* will not have your freedom from Prydein's rule until you can show me that you understand the obligations that come with that freedom. ...You ...*will* ...yield!"

Breca and Hereman, who had hurried across with Haply and Grimston from another part of the camp, looked to one another.

"No mistaking whose grandson he is now!" Hereman said, with an amused twinkle in his eye.

"Spirits, no!" Breca agreed. "That was a masterly move. He's very much *King* Ivain now, isn't he!"

The Attacotti were all a-buzz at this surprise. Only Magnus wore a small smile, making Ruari and the others think that he must have been talking to Ivain about this already. Slowly men began to trickle away, talking in groups, any thought of a leadership fight forgotten. Only Friseal remained on the ground, still pinned beneath Talorcan who still wore a ferocious snarl.

"If you don't want to lose your clan as well," Talorcan hissed in his ear, "then I would think about making that oath if I were you! I'm sure there's another member of your close family who could step up as leader if you got a knife in the back in the coming battle!"

Friseal glowered furiously at his captor, and at the tall, dark and handsome royal who stood watching him with an inscrutable expression. "I swear," he ground out through clenched teeth, "but I also swear that if I should catch up with you when your guard dog here is gone, then you'll pay for this humiliation!"

Talorcan's smile was fierce and humourless. "Might have a long wait, then! Trees willing, I'm staying with Ivain for a very long time!" He eased his weight off Friseal but gave his head a sharp smack back against the ground as the clan-chief began to rise. "That's so *you* don't forget! You're King Ivain's man now, and if you break that oath I shall personally take your head off!"

He nimbly sprang back out of range of Friseal, and took several steps backwards before averting his gaze from the swearing Attacotti chief. He took his shirt back off Ad and stood very close to Ivain, who was smiling with real affection at him.

"Blessed Martyrs and Lost Souls!" Haply breathed to Grimston. "I hope I live to see the day when the court gets to see Ivain standing with Talorcan at his side in the great throne room!"

Grimston chuckled. "Flaming Trees, that will put the cat amongst the pigeons, won't it! No queen, but a big brute of a Knight who'll take on anyone who gives hard looks to his beloved! And what in the Islands will his title be?"

"Well whatever it is, nobody will be making snide comments about *him* being a girl!" Haply agreed as they watched Ivain and Talorcan walk away with arms around one another, then stop to kiss with obvious passion.

"Best start saying prayers that Talorcan survives, then," Breca said quietly, having come up to join them. "Having lost his mother and Queen Alaiz, it would be too cruel if Ivain lost the true love of his life."

That was a very sobering thought, for none of them doubted that someone like Talorcan would be in the thick of the fighting. A similar though occurred to Ruari as he walked away with Hereman, although he was too realistic to think that anything he did could possibly ensure

Talorcan or Ivain's safety – and he had no doubt that Ivain had got under Talorcan's guard to a similar extent and potentially would be equally mourned by the taciturn Knight. Talorcan might struggle every bit as much to cope if it was Ivain who was lost, for Ruari believed that if Talorcan shut out all feelings again, it would be beyond anyone's power to make him trust enough to care about anything, or anyone, ever again.

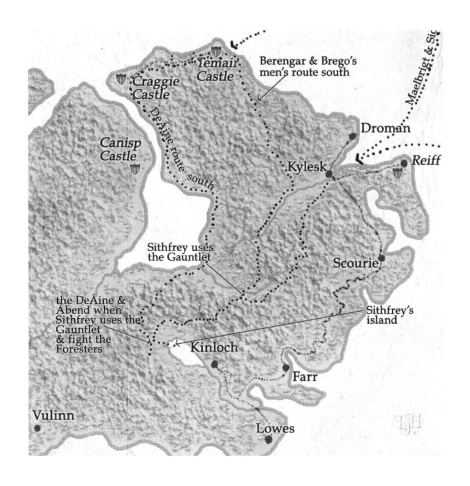

In the map:

Maelbrigt & Si[c]

Temair Castle

Berengar & Brego's men's route south

Craggie Castle

Droman

Canisp Castle

DeAine route south

Kylesk

Reiff

Sithfrey uses the Gauntlet

Scourie

the DeAine & Abend when Sithfrey uses the Gauntlet & fight the Foresters

Sithfrey's island

Kinloch

Farr

Vulinn

Lowes

# Chapter 14

## *Strained Relationships*

### Rathlin: late Solstice – early Grian-Mhor

Berengar stood in his stirrups to look back along the line of men following him. The march down through Rathlin had been less of a trial than he had expected. Much of that was due to the guides Magnus had provided, for they had taken the battle-weary Brychan men by easy trails over the moorlands and through the hills, thus cutting off many miles. It had also saved them encountering any traps left by the Abend. Their enemies had followed the coast around to where the land sloped down towards the opening to Loch Canisp, and had then headed inland along the lowlands beside the water. So the only point where Berengar's men had had to tread carefully had been when they finally had to come down to river running into the end of Loch Canisp. There they had had to rely on the good offices of the ancients to inspect the land for them, although Berengar would have been much happier if it had been Warwick and his Foresters doing the sweeping.

However, the ancients had not led them astray, and soon the army was dealing with the much more tangible challenge of getting across a major river. Luckily, with Rathlin having had less than its normal quota of rain and snow, and having reached high summer, the river was running low. There was also a very broad natural ford, where great pavers of rock provided firm footing for a crossing. Berengar was grateful for that seam of hard rock in the soft, peaty land for it saved him the time-wasting job of building a bridge. Much of the slopes around the great loch were heavily wooded, so there would have been no lack of material, it was simply that it would have been physically wearing when there were more urgent calls on the men's strength. As it was his men were picking up nicely. They had been in good shape before they had started out, and those who had sported minor wounds after Eynon were recovering well. Even the weather had been kind to them, and despite his common sense telling him off for such fancies, Berengar could not help but see it as a good omen.

As they had come up from the river valley, and headed for the last few rolling hills before their arranged meeting place with Sionnachan and Maelbrigt, Berengar had looked back and seen men on the horizon. A flag had been waved at them, and he realised that Brego was barely a day behind them now, hence his rear inspection for the third time that day. The remainder of his men – the fittest companies – were with Brego, and Berengar would be glad to get his force all back together again.

"Should be with the others by tomorrow night," Esclados said softly, but with an encouraging smile. "Then you'll be able to see her again."

Berengar could not refrain from smiling in response, even though there was a part of him which wished her far, far away and safe instead. Then when they got to within sight of the camp at the edge of the Loch of Kin, it was to see another long column of men coming in from the east, too. Maelbrigt had arrived with Warwick and the Foresters, and with a tall blonde man of substantial presence.

"Berengar! It's good to see you again!" Ruari greeted him, as they both entered a central circle of shelters which Sionnachan's men had made out of boughs and branches.

"It's good to see you too!" Berengar agreed heartily. "I have to admit to feeling greatly relieved at finding that I knew at least one other Master." He saw Ruari blink. "I know, it takes some getting used to, doesn't it! I think I'm just about over looking behind me when someone walks up to me and says 'Master'. But I still feel like I'm wearing someone else's boots, and that I'll wake up and find they've come to reclaim them."

Ruari gave a wry chuckle. "I sincerely hope your Master Rainer *doesn't* appear from his grave. He wasn't a great man out in the field even in what passes for peacetime in Brychan! At least I can count my predecessor as a friend and a worthy man to have to live up to, although that does bring its own weight to the situation!" He inclined his head back to where Warwick was speaking to Esclados. "Your head Forester seems to have great faith that you'll hold up under the strain, which is not to be dismissed lightly." Then he grinned broadly. "But enough of this! We can catch up later. There's someone with me who wants to see you very much, and I gather you might be wanting to see her."

Berengar blushed but had no time to protest as Cwen appeared behind Ruari running towards them.

"Oh Berengar! I'm so glad to see you!" Cwen cried from the heart, as he swept her off her feet and hugged her tight. "I've missed you so much! And you, Esclados," she added, as she saw the elderly Knight from over Berengar's shoulder.

"We've missed you too," Esclados rumbled affectionately, reaching over and squeezing her hand which stretched out to him. "And I have news for you! We've seen your father and your family are all well."

"Oh thank the Trees!" Cwen gulped, another major worry lifted. She knew she could have asked one of the ancients to check for her. Urien would have been the obvious one to ask, but since he was still less than helpful it was far an easy request to make. And she had felt awkward about putting another burden on the others, especially since it was for her benefit alone and not as part of the war plan.

Now, though, she became aware of Berengar still holding her tight and saying ever so softly, "dearest Cwen" in a tone which made his feelings clear. Her heart gave a small lurch. She had not expected that! And yet ...now that she came to face the matter she had to admit that her feelings towards him had become much more complex. Even as she had grieved for Richert, Berengar had been making a space of his own in her heart.

Back then she had seen it as friendship, and him being a person she could rely upon in a desperately needed situation. Nor could she put her finger on when precisely things had changed for her. Esclados was still the comfortable uncle-type figure, but Berengar's continued tight hug was doing other things to her body as well, making her wish for a little more privacy than was to be had in the middle of an army. She did not dare turn her face to him and kiss him for fear of where it might lead!

Luckily Taise caught her eye, and inclined her head towards the more enclosed shelter which she and Maelbrigt had been allocated by the tactful Sionnachan.

"Come with me," she breathed into Berengar's ear, then wriggled free of his grasp but taking hold of his hand once her feet were back on the ground.

Berengar seemed to wake from a dream and looked to Ruari, but the Rheged Master was assiduously avoiding looking back at him, instead drawing Esclados in the direction of Swein. So he responded to Cwen's tug at his hand, and once behind the draped blankets which shut the shelter off from public view, Berengar swept her into his arms and kissed her passionately. What took him by surprise was her response, for she not only kissed him back with an equal desire, her hands were also investigating the lacing on his breeches. It took him a second to recall that this was no fragile virgin, for it was so easy to think of Cwen as unsullied. Of course, he mentally kicked himself, she had had a healthy relationship with a man for several years. She was no stranger to the physical side of romantic contacts, but at that point he stopped thinking as Cwen demonstrated just how familiar she was with the male body.

Outside, Taise did not know whether to laugh or despair. For all her attempts to give Cwen and her lover some privacy, she was being thwarted by Daisy of all people. The white squint was standing rock still a few feet from the draped blankets, ears twitching wildly and head cocking from side to side as if she could see through the blankets. Maelbrigt was currently trying to persuade her to come away with Squint and himself, but that only resulted in excited tweets and whistles between the two squints.

"I think they find our affections fascinating," Maelbrigt finally admitted in defeat to Taise and to Matti, who had come in the wake of a curious Moss.

"I think the only thing stopping all five squints sitting out here is the reunion going on with Swein and Esclados," Matti told them. "Esclados is hugging Swein like he was his own lost son."

That was a pretty good description of how Esclados felt. "I'm so proud of you, laddie," he declared, hugging Swein so hard the young former courtier thought his ribs might struggle to get back to normal breathing afterwards. Esclados then held Swein out at arm's length as he looked him up and down, allowing him to draw a much needed breath. "You're looking well! Very well!" The old Knight shook his head in wonderment as he glanced down at Dylan, who was standing very close. "So *you* now have the Island Arrow. That's no mean achievement! Despite so many men of the Order about the place, you've become the one – which just shows what you might be capable of. I always hoped you'd find your inner potential. I just didn't expect it to happen so fast. Nobody can ever say you're nobody after this! This wee chap chose you above them all!"

"Well not quite Dylan on his own," Swein corrected him, blushing furiously. "The Guardians had a say in the matter too. I think if they'd had any real reservations, it would've been Dylan who would've had to think again."

"They clearly saw nothing wrong with you, though, did they?" Esclados insisted. "And I hear from MacBeth that you've been a great help to the others who've been chosen."

"That he has," Ivain said warmly, and getting introduced as a result.

Even Talorcan found himself feeling pleased at Swein's reunion. The lack of parents at critical moments in their lives had been a topic he, Ivain and Swein had talked about as they had ridden together. It had been the first time he had let his guard down so much, but it had been so natural when for the first time he was conversing with men whose childhoods had also been little short of disastrous. As a result of the others' equally honest responses, it meant that he knew how deeply Swein's family's rejection of him had hurt. He had almost felt glad then that he had no memory of the father who had been gone before he was even born, and that he could lay his natural mother's appalling behaviour down to her being highborn DeÁine. It was certainly better than trying to sort out why your parents, who had presumably married for love, should hate their own child so. He turned to watch Ivain, recalling that the one man Ivain thought of as a father was Master Hugh, currently far away in Ergardia and too far from Ivain to turn to for support. He half expected to see Ivain saddened and

246

withdrawing into himself at yet another painful memory. Instead he found Ivain watching him back already, an inscrutable expression on his face. He quirked an eyebrow in silent question at Ivain, but the young king simply smiled and shook his head.

However, Ivain made a point of getting Berengar alone later on that evening as the three contingents congregated to familiarise themselves with one another, or refresh old friendships, depending on their situations. After answering some of Ivain's probing questions, Berengar was beginning to get rather worried, although Cwen kept making positive responses, until she suddenly gasped and clapped her hands to her mouth.

"Alright, that's enough," Berengar said firmly. "What's going on here?"

"I never saw it," Cwen gasped in disbelief. "I knew Esclados' story and something of Talorcan's, but I never thought them connected."

"Well look at them," Ivain said with a smile, gesturing to where the press of bodies had shifted so that they could see Esclados standing talking to Swein with Talorcan.

Berengar felt a cold shiver run down his back as the realisation sunk in of the resemblance between the old Knight and the younger one. "Sacred Root and Branch!" He shook his head in amazement. "...Sweet Rowan, you can see it! ...Esclados lost a son by a DeÁine lover. And now you're telling me that Talorcan was punished by his DeÁine mother for being the son of a Knight. ...Can they be father and son?"

"Yes, I think they are," Ivain said with great conviction. "The question is, do we tell them? If we were in a quiet place with no threat, there wouldn't be any doubt that we should. But now? Will it hamper them to know? Is it too sore a point to open as a wound? You know Esclados. Is he likely to come undone at the discovery?

"I think I know Talorcan well enough by now to think that he'll never guess, unless we make it obvious to him. He's never looked for his father, so it's hardly at the fore of his mind in the current situation. But Esclados? You say his lost child has never been far from his mind. Might he guess anyway, and would that hurt him?"

Berengar regarded his oldest friend affectionately. "I think we're unsure enough of how many of us will survive as it is. Esclados has hunted for his child since the time he knew of its existence. It would be truly tragic if he was to die and never have known that he took his son by the hand. And anyway, two men fighting below their peak will make little difference in a conflict the size of which we're facing. No, we must tell them!"

And with that he led Ivain and Cwen towards the other trio, Daisy and Eric scurrying in their wake, ears twitching in excitement. No doubt it was that which alerted the others, for Berengar had barely reached the three before Maelbrigt and Squint hurried up with Taise, Kayna, and Sionnachan, while from another area Ruari appeared being guided by Matti who was in the wake of Moss. The Prydein men, who were sitting or standing around the fire, looked up in surprise, alerting the three targets.

"Is something wrong?" Talorcan asked sharply seeing the perplexed expressions on a lot of the faces.

"Not *wrong*," Berengar said very carefully. He took Esclados by the arm as Ivain did the same for Talorcan, smiling encouragingly. "There's something you both need to know." He turned to Esclados. "Prepare yourself for a shock, my friend," he said gently. "You two will have to compare the details very carefully and decide for yourselves whether this is true, but we think you and Talorcan are related."

"What?" Talorcan spluttered, totally taken aback. Ivain gripped his arm a little tighter and whispered,

"Just listen."

Berengar took a deep breath and transferred his hand so that he had an arm securely around his friend's shoulder, just in case the shock was too much for Esclados. "Talorcan was born to a DeÁine mother. I don't know all of his story, but Ivain tells me that he suffered terribly for being brought into New Lochlainn as the son of a Knight."

Esclados gave a cry and went white, Cwen hurrying to his other side to hug him tight.

"Spirits!" Swein gasped. "And you, Esclados, lost a baby when your DeÁine lover disappeared into New Lochlainn. Talorcan's your son!" He looked from one to the other and back again. "Blessed Martyrs! You two even look alike! How did I not see it?"

"Ivain did," Cwen said quickly, making Talorcan whip round to look at his lover in shock.

"You are alike," Ivain said with gentle affection. Talorcan, however, was shaking his head in denial, too shocked to speak. Esclados, though, now found his voice.

"My son!" he gasped with joy, and before anyone could stop him he had shaken off Berengar and Cwen and pulled Talorcan into one of his bear-hugs. "My son! ...I've searched for you for years! ...I thought I'd never find you! ...All the times I looked for you in New Lochlainn and you were here in the Order after all!" He sank to his knees and clasped his hands in prayer. "Thank the Trees! Thank you! Great Rowan be blessed for this. After all the time I spent praying, to have my prayers answered!"

Yet if Esclados was the more emotional of the two, it was Talorcan who was the most shaken. He had always thought that if he met his father, it would be him confronting a man in denial. A man for whom this was an unwelcome, and shocking, consequence from one of many casual couplings. It was not that which had bothered Talorcan. He had spent enough time with soldiers to know that men deprived of a home, and the physical relationships which went with it, would have casual liaisons. He was not the first or the last child with a missing soldier for a father, and he had served with many of them too. What had angered him was why an Order soldier would think it acceptable to rut with a DeÁine? It had never in his wildest dreams entered his head that his father might have wanted him.

"Did you love her?" he managed to croak out. "Or was she some stranger? A chance to vent your feelings on one of the enemy?" He could just about understand that, even though he was repelled by the idea of raping anyone. "Was it only later that you thought of me as some unexpected consequence? Did I come from one night?"

Esclados struggled to his feet. "Great Maker, lad, no! I've never taken *any* woman unwillingly! ...Your mother told me she was exiled from the rest of the DeÁine. I lived with her for four months, and I believed that when I was moved north and eastwards, that she would follow me with the other wives and women. Sacred Trees, I was planning to *marry* her! It was only when we got back from patrol to the castle where I'd been re-stationed, that I heard via the other women that she'd refused to come. That when they'd had to make a run for it from a DeÁine raiding party, that she'd gone *to* them instead.

"The women said she went saying it would save them. They didn't know what to think, but they got away and so assumed that maybe she *had* deflected the raiding party away from them. It was only years later in my search that I came across a soldier who said that they'd been in time to chase the raiding party. He said that a pregnant woman had seemed to be *in charge*! They were coming from the right place. It had to be her! It had to be my Erin."

"Erin. ...Eriu." Talorcan snorted. "She chose an Islander name very like her own." He was still watching Esclados cagily. "And you say you searched for me? ...Why?"

"Why?" Esclados gasped, dumbfounded. "Because you're my *child*! I didn't know if you were a boy or a girl, but I prayed in the chapel every night for you to be spared."

"He did," Berengar confirmed. "I've known Esclados for over twenty years, and in that time he's never stopped looking and praying you were safe."

Talorcan's guard seemed to melt a little. "So you didn't deliberately leave me behind because I was half DeÁine? ...You didn't even know I was a boy? ...That must have made me harder to find," he conceded grudgingly.

"It did," Berengar answered for an Esclados stunned by the thought that Talorcan might think he was that unwanted. "All he could do was try to trace the movements from where he'd last known she was. When he finally had to give up on that, he went through all the records of children brought into Brychan who might be of mixed blood."

Cwen patted Esclados' hand comfortingly. "But you didn't find him because he wasn't on Brychan. He wasn't even in the care of the Brychan Order then."

Esclados' eyes brightened with understanding as he took in the Ergardian insignia on Talorcan's uniform. "You were on Ergardia!"

"Not all the time," admitted Talorcan. "I was rescued by the Covert Brethren. Your lover was no mere DeÁine girl. She's Eriu, mother to the DeÁine king Ruadan – or so she says! He's supposedly my younger half-brother. They certainly have an odd relationship if they are mother and son, ...but then she was always a warped, vicious bitch!"

"Great Rowan save me!" Esclados gulped. "I thought her far lower than that! Was it for an heir she used me? Berengar and I have talked over this so many times. The only sense we could make of it was that she had a husband who couldn't give her a child, and she thought to deceive him. We couldn't work out how, though."

Talorcan snorted derisively. "Well if it was, she certainly didn't want *me*! But then who really understands the warped twisting of the DeÁine's minds?" He shivered in revulsion, even as he was thinking that Esclados' reasoning might make the nearest thing to any sense of the situation. It was something he himself had never considered.

"If there was a DeÁine husband I never heard of it. ...But then she can't have said more than a few words to me in my whole life, so I'm not the one who'd know! ...Once she'd caught the eye of King Nuadu, I was a nasty reminder of her past she didn't want – whatever that past was! If the Covert

Brethren hadn't found me and got me out I doubt I would have survived much longer.

"They thought I needed to be well away from the frontier, so I was sent to Ergardia. The trouble was, having potent DeÁine blood in me, I didn't exactly thrive on Ergardia. It's easier now that I'm older, and although I wear the Ergardian uniform, technically I suppose I'm still part of the Celidon sept. But despite being officially quartered on Ergardia, I have to take time away from the Island regularly. As a lad, Ergardia's potency had me dizzy and nauseous after a month or so. So six months later I was taken permanently to Celidon and put into one of the granges there."

"And a regular pain in the arse he was too!" Maelbrigt teased, lightening the atmosphere when everyone laughed.

"But he made Knight!" Esclados said with great pride. "I feel like someone answered all my hopes tonight! Not only is Swein free from his demons and looking set to be a fine member of the Order ...but I find I now have a son who's a *captain*! And we're all together, too!"

Talorcan looked at Esclados' beaming smile and felt rotten. He could not manage even a glimmer of the same feelings of joy. "Look I'm sorry," he managed to get out. "...I really need to think about this. ...And whatever kind of son you thought I might be ...I'm probably not that person, alright?"

Now Esclados managed to rein in his jubilation and see Talorcan's side of this. The empathy he had used to such great effect on others in times of crisis, now gave him a fund of experience to draw on to see the other side of this coin. A child who thought he had been deliberately abandoned would hardly have been longing for the day when his father reappeared. And another thought crept up from the depths of his mind. Swein had been telling him only tonight that he and Talorcan had been helping Ivain come to terms with his sexuality. Therefore Talorcan was surely the same as Swein. Yet, even in an army which was as understanding of difference as the Order was, there were still those who made their dislike of such men very clear. Ultimately you could not force people to tolerance, just hope to inform them and let them come the understanding themselves. Maybe some such encounters also made Talorcan wary of engaging with others.

"You need to let it sink in," he said kindly, "I know I do! Come! Let me embrace you one more time, and then I'll leave you to catch your breath!" He went and wrapped his arms around Talorcan and held him tight, but felt the younger man tense. "You're my *son*!" Esclados said softly, looking into his eyes. "Whatever you might think, that makes you precious to me."

251

"I might not be quite the son you think I am," Talorcan repeated dryly, wishing the old Knight would take the hint and save him from being hurtfully blunt.

Esclados released him although kept one hand on his shoulder briefly. "You're *exactly* the son I would have wished for!" he said reassuringly. "You're a Knight, and all that goes with it!"

"But not all Knights are quite the same!"

"No they're not, but 'different' isn't the same as 'bad'. I know some of what you are, Talorcan, and it doesn't change how I feel about you. ...Ask Swein!" And with that Esclados patted Talorcan on the shoulder and turned into the embrace of Cwen and Berengar.

Talorcan staggered away from the fire, his lance, Swein and Ivain surrounding him.

"What did he mean, 'ask Swein'?" he demanded hoarsely, after Barcwith had thrust a flask of uisge into his hand and he had swallowed deeply to numb his shattered nerves.

"I think it's that I thought, when we first met, that he would hate me for how I am," Swein explained. "He was the first person after Cwen who didn't make me feel dirty and perverted for having been one of King Edward's lovers. He's saying he knows how you are – what you are with Ivain – and that he doesn't censor you for that." Then Swein could not resist teasing him. "Of course, when he finds out how awful you are at following orders, that might make him wince a bit!"

The rest of the lance guffawed at that, which even raised a glimmer of a smile on Talorcan's lips. Then it pounded in on him again. A father! And there had been him thanking the Trees that he had no a family! He looked to Ivain who was laughing and saying something he could not quite hear to Barcwith and Galey, but which had them in gales of laughter. Suddenly, between Ivain and Esclados he found he had a whole lot more to lose in this coming fight. He had been approaching it with the same dispassion as any other encounter with the DeÁine – it was a job which needed doing and the sooner the better. If one of his lance, or more, got killed, then he would mourn their loss. But they were different. He knew they were with him for their own reasons and of their own accord. Ivain was a different matter. He was here by fate not inclination, and now the old Knight who claimed he was his father seemed to have been drawn here too. It was a long time since Talorcan had felt so confused, and yet he could not seem to manage to dismiss Esclados from his mind either.

Unable to sit still a moment longer, Talorcan sprang to his feet and ran to the horses.

"Let him be," Barcwith said, putting a restraining hand on Ivain's arm as he made to follow. "He's better left alone when he's like this. He can't cope with people fussing over him. He'll be alright. Come the morning he'll be in his bedroll and acting like nothing happened."

"Yes, but something did happen," Ivain cautioned, "He's found his father!"

They both turned out to be right. In the morning Ivain awoke to find that for once Talorcan had beaten his men to getting the campfire blazing again, and there was already a large can of caff brewed and ready to drink. One look at Talorcan's face, though, revealed that the Knight had found little peace or comfort in his late night solitude. Once everyone was tucking in to the breakfast griddle cakes and porridge, Ivain drew Talorcan aside a little so that he could speak without an audience.

"Look, I know this is terribly disorientating for you," he began in consolation, "but will you just think on this, please? You and/or your father might not survive the coming weeks any more than any of the rest of us. That means you don't have the luxury of taking your time to sort out your feelings. That's bloody harsh and it's unfair, but it's the way things are at the moment, and just as I've not had chance to properly mourn my mother and Alaiz, you have to deal with this now. Just as you said I should try to deal with my grief in bite sized pieces, maybe you need to think about coping with this in bits instead of all at once? Esclados seems a decent man. Swein can't speak highly enough of him – and that alone should tell you something of what he's like! If not for your sake, then for his, can you spend some time talking to him? He's getting on in age, Talorcan. That might mean his reactions aren't as fast as they once were..."

"...And he might well be one of the ones killed," Talorcan finished for him.

"Yes he might! So, given that he cared enough to spend all those years searching, despite having so little to go on, he deserves a little comfort. I'm not asking you to embrace him totally as your father, of course I'm not. That would be too much. But can you approach this another way? Can you think of it in a more detached way? As if you maybe *aren't* his son, but make an effort to go through the motions to provide him with the completion he so desperately wants?"

Talorcan took a deep breath and rubbed his face, thinking. "I see what you're saying. Take a step back and treat him as if he was Barcwith or Tamàs needing to be told stuff about me. Man to man, not father to son."

"Exactly! Take the pressure off yourself! Stop worrying about whether you can be the *son* he wants." Ivain paused then added, "I'm also thinking of you and how you might feel if something does happen to him, and then you find out that he was your father beyond any doubt. If you've done what's possible at a time like this, you'll feel a lot better than if you then have to carry on knowing that you rejected him. It would be a bitter pill to swallow if you had to live with the knowledge that you never even tried to talk to him, let alone anything else."

Talorcan nodded and took a long drink of his caff before answering. "Thank you. ...If I stop thinking of myself as *having* to be his son it ...well, it gets a bit easier."

The first time the two met again was later that morning, when all the Treasure holders were called together in the inner circle of shelters. Sionnachan and Maelbrigt were taking them through some of the potential situations they might encounter in the battle, and with Ruari, Berengar and Warwick adding to the information. As Swein's main supporters, Talorcan's lance were included alongside Raethun and Scully's men, but Talorcan himself was less involved, since he would have to stand back when the Island Treasures became truly active. He found himself standing at the back and only a few feet away from Esclados, and so, bracing himself, he moved closer.

The older Knight glanced sideways at him and smiled, but his first words were reassuringly away from their own relationship. "Will Cwen cope, do you think?" he asked. "She's a wonderful girl, but it's a lot to ask of her – taking a full battalion of a spear wall into battle."

Talorcan's mouth was as dry as ashes, but he managed to respond. "I know what you mean. I worry for both her and Matti. We can do this over and over again, talking them through it, but facing a real enemy is such a different thing."

He gulped in more breaths to calm his racing pulse in order to continue. "As I see it, Maelbrigt is fine. He's seen more action than most of the men here, and he'll be fighting with his old companies. There are few unknowns for him. For Spirit's sake, the man has even gone up against the Abend back at Gavra Pass! I know. I was there! The highborn DeÁine froze my blood, even standing back and taunting them from up on my horse, where I could turn tail and ride like the Wild Hunt back to safety. But he was up on the valley wall, straight up above the Abend's acolytes! And when they started blasting him, he and his men only gave up the ground they wanted to to seal the pass. That was some courageous stand!"

Esclados suddenly realised in a totally different sense who he was talking to. At the time of Gavra Pass, even in the mad scramble to get to the north and aid the Celidon men, he had known that there was a Knight of mixed blood who had been used to taunt the royal DeÁine. It made his head reel to realise that that had been his son! He could well have lost him right there and then! Courageous did not even begin to describe such an act, and his sudden rush of pride almost overwhelmed him. But Talorcan was continuing.

"In a funny sort of way, I think Ivain will be alright too. He's going to be fighting with the Prydein archers, and he's known so many of them through all of the ups and downs of his life. They've been one of his few constants, along with Master Hugh. So he knows they'll stand or fall together. There's familiarity and trust aplenty, and that's a huge advantage."

"And what about Swein? Have you seen the scars he carries? I tell you, the first time I dragged him off to the baths to clean him up, back when we first met, they shook me rigid. I've never seen scars like them! Even the worst battle scars don't overlap like them. That sight haunted me for weeks, and the Rowan knows I've seen enough grim sights in my time!"

Talorcan grimaced. "Yes, they're pretty appalling aren't they! It's one of the things which broke the ice between us when we got together in Prydein. He's the only person I've ever met who could look at my scars, and instantly pick out the ones done when I was a boy in New Lochlainn."

Talorcan had actually forgotten who he was talking to at that point, and Esclados, conscious of the way his son was speaking freely, had to bite his lips to keep from crying out in his horror at this admission. His child had suffered for his Islander birthright, and therefore because of himself. It was not a comfortable revelation to have to hear. Luckily Talorcan's gaze was fixed on Swein, and he continued without any sign of having heard Esclados' strangled gasp.

"Mind you, my scars are nothing in comparison. I don't have the burn marks, for a start." Esclados heaved a muffled sigh of relief. Thank the Trees for that! "But do you know what I think is making all the difference to him? It's the fact that he's not alone in this! For all that he was at the centre of the royal court in Brychan, when things went massively wrong he was so very alone. This time he's got true friends with him, and beyond that a huge number of men who will support him. And he now knows that to the core of his being. He hasn't any doubts because he knows only too well what the other feels like. What it is to be alone."

"That's reassuring," Esclados said with feeling. "I'm very glad he feels like that, because the boy I first saw wouldn't have trusted anyone. I expect we have Cwen to thank for that!"

"And you!" Talorcan quickly added, trying to ignore the way his feelings were skittering about all over the place as he spoke. "He's very quick to credit you and Master Berengar for showing him that he could be different." Then mentally squirmed uncomfortably at the sensation of unexpected pleasure that this man was also now connected to him in a not dissimilar way. Curses! He thought he had just got the hang of how to talk to this parental apparition! Then got another shiver of something which felt suspiciously like pride at Esclados' surprise and modesty as he said,

"Really? Berengar and me? But we did nothing. We just treated him as we would anyone!"

Talorcan could not find the right words to respond to that with, or at least nothing which would not lead him into the quagmire of talking about feelings at a level he had never had to before. That he could not cope with just yet! Instead he braced himself and returned to the Treasure wielders.

"Ermm... Well Ivain and Swein get on really well too, so that helps. And they've had longer than the others to work things out about how these Treasures work when you put them together. And that's part of what worries me about Cwen and Matti. They're both amazing people, brave and intelligent. But they hardly know one another. Add to that the fact that they've never fought in any sort of battle, and I think that tactically they're the weak point."

"Scully's a good man," Esclados said encouragingly. "He and Cwen have been through enough together that she trusts him. With his lance at her back she'll allow herself to be guided by their experience, I'm sure of that."

Talorcan nodded thoughtfully. "There is that. ...And along that vein, Matti has the same kind of faith in Sgt. Iago. If he works well with the men Maelbrigt picked out to work with her, Matti might fall back on them. But I think that Kayna might turn out to be the biggest asset there. Maelbrigt virtually taught her to be a squire. If they'd had a female force in the Celidon Foresters she'd have been a Knight, no doubt about it. She's got a real talent for tactics and she's a formidable swords-woman. It's a pity that Matti's been chosen for the Shield, because it's not Kayna's weapon of choice."

"Ah, so that's why Kayna is sat beside her," Esclados observed. "...So where will you be come the battle? I heard what happened when you got in the wrong place with the Bow and Arrow! I'm guessing you won't be amongst the ranks around the Treasure wielders?"

Talorcan snorted ruefully. "No, it probably wouldn't be a good idea! Actually I have no idea where I'll be."

Esclados, though, had had an unsettling thought. The recollection of another time he had heard Talorcan's name recently had his stomach lurching sickeningly at what it entailed, but he braced himself and spoke up anyway. "I understand that one of the Guardians told you that you could use ...or rather you could at least handle one of the DeÁine Treasures?"

"Hmm... Maybe!"

"Did you know that Berengar briefly used the Gorget to taunt the Abend?"

Talorcan whipped round and looked sharply at Esclados, who then outlined what exactly had happened at Arlei. By the time he had finished, he was fairly sure that Talorcan had taken the bait, for he had suggested that Talorcan and Berengar together might be able to wrest enough control of the Gorget to make it a disruptive force for the Abend. He was hardly wildly keen on the idea of either his oldest friend or his newly acquired son even being in this battle, but if they had to be there, then having them both together where he could watch their backs was about as good as it was going to get.

He found an unexpected ally later in the day when Brego rode in at the head of another long column of men. The Grand Master of all the Order listened carefully as he was briefed about plans already made and approved them all, then heard of Esclados' idea, which had already been put to Berengar.

"I think that's an excellent idea," Brego declared. "While I was quite prepared for Berengar to have another shot at using the Gorget if necessary, I wouldn't underestimate its strength. I think having both of you using it will give you double the control – especially since Talorcan has felt what that kind of power can be like after his experience with Sithfrey. But more than that, if the Abend strike back through the Power at you, I don't think they'll expect to find two of you. They themselves would never entertain the idea of sharing the Power. I know we felt that odd blast through the Helm, but I'm betting that that won't happen again. Whoever this new member of the Abend is, he'll find himself coming up against the internal politics of the Abend if he tries it again – not least, I would think, of Quintillean insisting that if Tancostyl is going to share, then he should have first use. And if that happens, then from all we know of them, Tancostyl won't share at all. He won't risk Quintillean overwhelming him and taking the Helm for himself."

However Berengar was now looking to Talorcan. "How do you feel about using this thing?" he asked guardedly. By now he had been around the camp enough to know that Talorcan was hardly the passive sort, and what he did not want was to be tied to a man who might rashly want to go about trying to use the Gorget in order to provoke the Abend. Thankfully Talorcan's response was swift and without any sign that he had to think twice about it.

"I'd rather never use it at all, if I'm honest. That horrible sucking sensation I felt when Sithfrey was connected was fearsomely strong." He shuddered at the memory. "I've felt some stuff the Abend have thrown about over the years, but nothing like that! In truth, I don't think we stand a chance of doing any real damage to one of the Abend wielding one of the other Treasures. They'll be way stronger, and more practised, than us. If you and I have to use that thing, I think it will be under similar circumstances to when Sithfrey protected Sionnachan's men – purely defensive and when there's no other option."

Berengar felt a relief he managed not to show. Some of Esclados' natural common sense had obviously been passed on to his son after all. Yet Brego did not let it stop there.

"Your caution is well founded," he agreed, "but that doesn't mean you can't spend some time while we march south talking about what you think you *might* be able to do. Please think very hard about how you might do something like fragment their sendings – rather than stop them altogether. How you could maybe use the fact that there's two of you against their one. It doesn't have to be all about strength, remember. Use your tactical skills to think of ways in the same way that you would use a small force to harry a large one. Because every instinct of mine says that the Abend won't share, and that's a very small but significant advantage. My nightmare ever since this whole thing began has been that this new Abend, with its fresh members now, might just join together and channel their united Power through the Helm."

He was not the only one shuddering at the thought of that! Yet relief came not from Brego but from Taise.

"But Master Brego's right," she said with confidence. "That will only happen in the very worst scenario for the Abend, not us. Only nearly obliteration would make them consent to do that, and in those circumstances, I'm sure that more than one of the nine would already have to be dead for them to see it as their only way out. I truly don't believe we will ever face a united nine with the Helm, and in any possible linking, I think you can absolutely discount Quintillean or Masanae being involved. Those two are far too conscious of their standing within the nine to ever stoop to liaise with the newer members. They'd probably rather die first!

"Leaders of the Abend don't just step down, and never have. They either die as heads, or they have something happen which so weakens them that they're not quite themselves anymore. Even after his exploits on Ergardia, I don't think Quintillean is quite that low yet. He'll be trying to assert his authority just now, not allowing anyone to question it or erode his standing by accepting any kind of joint role."

In this Brego and Taise were uncannily correct. As the Abend argued their way southwards towards the coast, Quintillean was making just such a point. He had been aggrieved at the way that Tancostyl had allowed Barrax to join in using the Helm. He was the senior war-mage, and to his mind the Helm should have been handed to him anyway. Tancostyl's refusal to do that irritated and angered him all by itself. To then find himself in second place to the newest male of the Abend was almost unbearable. At every opportunity he chipped away at their alliance until Tancostyl finally exploded, and in a flash of temper informed Quintillean that if he was going to sabotage his and Barrax's experiments, then there would be no sharing at all. And with that he had retired to his howdah in a huff and refused to speak to anyone.

When Quintillean then began to nag at Anarawd to hand over the Scabbard things went from bad to worse. Even Eliavres was enough of a true Abend to take offence at that. He had been the one who had made the retaking of the Scabbard possible, and if anyone was going to be the next in line to use it it was him! Both he and Anarawd were furious by the time they had spent several days fending Quintillean off and in a blazing row, which was only verbal out of a sense of self preservation regarding the Sinuti, the five male Abend ended up retreating to their individual howdahs and not speaking to anyone for the rest of the journey to the coast. However this forced the four witches, congregating around a fire built less for warmth than for the light it shed, into an agreement of sorts amongst themselves.

"He has to go," Magda said to Masanae. "Surely you can see that now. We wouldn't even be here if it wasn't for Quintillean's rash move in inviting the Sinuti."

Helga was already nodding before Magda finished speaking. "Just think of what a mess we'd be in if we still had Calatin instead of Barrax! At least Barrax is still with us. Calatin would have turned his howdah around and gone off into one of his wanderings regardless of the consequences!"

"Sweet Lotus, that's a grim thought!" Laufrey muttered, for as a senior acolyte she had known Calatin, if not from physical proximity.

"And for similar reasons I'm glad we have you, poppet," Magda added. "Dear Geitla could be most unpredictable at times."

"Any progress there?" Masanae asked tersely. She was far from happy about being forced into agreements by things out of her control, although most of her ire was turning on Quintillean these days, rather than the rebellious three sitting with her.

"Nicos says that Geitla's spirit is all but gone now," Laufrey answered. "Two days ago he said he could hardly feel any trace of her at all. There's certainly nothing left which he can interact with."

"And are we sure it's Othinn who's taken her over?" Masanae was trying to pretend that she was still leading this meeting, even though in her darkest, unacknowledged recesses she knew she was only one of four equals amongst the witches now.

Laufrey nodded. "Nicos certainly thinks so and he's all we have to go on."

"And will he fight with us in some way?"

"Maybe, ...but how that will manifest itself I pure guesswork."

*On no it isn't*, Magda thought gleefully. *My darling boy will follow my lead! He'll use what he's learned from being Jolnir all this time. He's harvested the dead, now he'll use them!*

# Chapter 15

## *Preparing for War*

### Rathlin: Grian-Mhor

On the fifth of the new month the entire Islander army was finally assembled around the Loch of Kin and in the tiny town of Kinloch itself. With the coming of Brego's well-supplied troops two days before, it had been possible to redistribute supplies so that Magnus' ravenous men had been given both food to march with, and double rations at meal times to get them back to their full strength. The militia from the southern fishing ports of Rathlin had also been accommodated into the army, although well away from Magnus' men. Brego had no desire for further divisive arguments to break out, having heard from Cwen how little regard the hardworking townsfolk had for Magnus' raiders. And Brego very much wanted to remain on the right side of the townsfolk. They had willingly told him that they had plentiful supplies of dried fish at the coast, and Brego reckoned those might be needed to supplement his supplies when it came to getting his men back home, for he very much hoped he would be leading a considerable number back. He was refusing to let himself even think about the details of leading a defeated army back through these hills.

At the same time there was another surprise. Aneirin appeared in their midst, almost as if he had been pushed through some invisible barrier. The ancient's form wobbled and flickered for a moment before he regained control.

"Ah! You made it!" Maelbrigt said with a wry smile. He had insisted that the Treasure holders remained surrounded by the Foresters' weavings, pointing out that the ancients had to overcome their attitudes as fast as possible and that this might just be the incentive.

Aneirin grimaced, then managed a watery smile before becoming solemn again. "I have urgent news!" he declared, making all the leaders look up. "The DeÁine fleet is in a place you call Vulinn Bay on the south coast, although many of their ships are east of that and landing troops at whatever bays they can."

"How many?" Maelbrigt asked urgently. "Was our intelligence correct?"

Aneirin's expression was confirmation all by itself. "I'm afraid so. The estimate of one hundred thousand looks all too true. Peredur and Cynddylan are watching them as we speak and trying to count them for you. However, Urien investigated those landing in the bay further on, and begged me to tell you that the DeÁine didn't just bring troops. They have some of their fighting beast with them!"

A collective groan went up from all who heard that.

"What sort?" Esclados called out.

Before Aneirin could answer Urien himself blinked into existence, making Maelbrigt and Cwen exchange surprised glances. Maybe this new threat had had a strange positive consequence if it was enough to bring the three reticent ancients to them willingly at last. The normally tetchy ancient was displaying none of his normal condescension and his voice lacked its former snide tones.

"They're unloading a ship's worth of cages as we speak," he told them, "and I think there's at least another of the great transports waiting to pull up to the particular place where they seem to think they can bring the cages ashore easily. The upper layers of cages coming out of the holds have so far been filled with jaculi."

"Good job we brought the hawks!" Esclados muttered darkly. "There'll be work for Sybil to do!"

"Can your hawks deal with them?" Aneirin asked in surprise.

"Have you not been watching over the years?" Berengar was equally surprised that these strange allies had not observed even if they could do very little.

Aneirin had the grace to look faintly embarrassed. "Owein said you'd cope with these. I just didn't know how that could be. Now I realise he must have watched you do it before."

"Good for Owein!" Matti said with relish, glad that her partner at least believed in them.

Aneirin visibly winced. "Er'hem... Yes, well he did, and he said to tell you that although they have brought rather a lot with them, he doesn't think it beyond your numbers to cope with."

"That's helpful," Brego said gratefully. "What of the other beasts, though?"

Urien sighed. "Well I don't know what you're going to make of this. The slaves have plenty of their slave-masters with them. More than we think they've had in New Lochlainn for many years. So you have the edentulous and the rhynunguli to contend with there."

"The what?" several people asked.

"Which ones are the edentulous?" Berengar persisted. "We've not heard that name."

"Really? ...Oh!" Urien's surprise then seemed to evaporate. "No, ...no, I suppose you wouldn't. We know them as such because we know where they came from. The animals whose forms were changed and rearranged to make these beasts." He paused, sighed, then went on. "Well the edentulous are the ones with the long snouts. Big bodies with curved backs so they look hill-shaped from the side, and the head held low. Their natural protection runs in overlapping ribs along them. They're not particularly aggressive in their original form, and even now they're the easier to train of the two types, so that's why they're still in use, despite the fact that they panic more than the others. Unfortunately, as they are now, they have tusks on either side of the snout and very corrosive spittle, and are likely to stamp on anyone who gets in their path."

"Ah, those...!"

"Oh, *them* we've met...!"

"Bloody snouters...!" he heard various people muttering around him.

"It's not just the spit," a veteran commander added clearly above the rest. "If you haven't come up against them before, watch out! They snort snot at you more than spit, but it still burns! And by the time they've been ridden hard into battle, the spit's all over those short tusky teeth. So although they can't toss and gore you like the others, if they start shaking their heads about and catch you from the side, the wound infects and just keeps eating away at your flesh."

"Oh joy! Acid snot!" a young captain murmured into the momentary silence.

"And they still aren't as bad as the horny bastards," another veteran commented. "The snouters don't attack you of their own accord. The horny bastards do!"

Urien nodded. "The 'horny bastards', as you so quaintly call them, are the rhynunguli, and you're right, they can be easily provoked and once angered they're a law unto themselves. They can charge at much greater speeds than the edentulous, and they not only have teeth, those two razor-sharp horns along their noses can impale you even through armour. The slave-masters have pretty much even numbers of each of those, but you'll only encounter them when you engage with the Seljuqs. Rather worse, I'm afraid is that they've brought kokatrises and gryphes."

"Those names we know already, thanks to the Covert Brethren," Brego declared. "We'd also heard by the same route about which the rhynunguli are. You don't have to tell us how dangerous all these are!"

"Aye, the gryphes are bad enough," third veteran called out darkly. "Warped, Underworld-spawned felines! Worse than bloody alley cats for pissing their stink on everyone while they're ripping you to shreds!"

"But I'd rather them than the kokatrises," Esclados agreed. "I *really* hate the kokatrises! It's the cursed scales which make them so hard to bring down. And the fact that most of the time you're poking up at them in the air with your sword or spear! They don't go high enough off the ground for the hawks to be able to help us much, but still high enough to be able to land on your shoulders and rip you to shreds with those claws!" and he shuddered at the memory, as did several others nearby.

Urien looked to Aneirin. They had not expected that the Islanders would have such hands on experience of the DeÁine and how they fought. This battle at Moytirra (which the ancients had ignored since it was beyond the Brychan Gap, and their limit to observe with any certainty while the ice entombed them) had evidently been more significant than they had thought. The Islanders had clearly come up against a formidable force and learned much from it without any assistance from the ancients. Perhaps that accounted for the Islanders' impatience with them? They expected so much more from those who, from their perspective, were higher beings. However that seemed to be far from the Islanders' minds at the moment.

"All this means is that we must be more careful with our choice of battlefield," Brego said, even as Maelbrigt was echoing him with words of his own. The Grand Master nodded his acknowledgement of the Celidon Forester and Maelbrigt took over.

"More than ever, we cannot allow ourselves to be drawn into a fight on an open plain. If we do, we're allowing the kokatrises, in particular, the room they need to move. We must draw the DeÁine to a fight in the hills!"

"Surely that's easier said than done?" Urien said in disbelief, and as a consequence wobbling in and out of focus. "How can you hope to influence where such a huge force chooses to engage you? So why bother?"

"That's where you're mistaken!" Kayna corrected him, stepping forward to where the ancients could see her. "Even I know that you don't let yourself be manipulated into fighting a defensive fight unless there's absolutely *no* other choice. Maelbrigt's right. What we have to do decide when we dangle the bait, and what bait they're most likely to take. They're still DeÁine after all! They'll be vain and arrogant and after a quick victory."

"Yes they will!" Sionnachan agreed. "And for that reason, I think we should engage them as a split force. That way we can offer them what they'll think will be a simple victory over a force they desperately outnumber..."

"...But they *do* outnumber you!" Aneirin spluttered, now flickering rapidly too.

"Only by two to one," Brego remonstrated. "It's not good by any means, but it's not impossible either, and we beat them with those kinds of odds at Moytirra! They won't have forgotten that! Despite it being twenty-seven years ago, we have men here with us who fought as young squires and pages then. So we should expect *someone* with the DeÁine to remember it!"

"But you weren't fighting *these* DeÁine then!" objected Urien, his image now flickering wildly as his naturally doubting nature made him see the negative in the situation. "These were back in Sinut and might hardly have cast a glance your way!"

"No we weren't," Maelbrigt agreed, "and so we can't count on them remembering. But then that might also mean that they make the same mistakes the others did, and the Abend *were* there. Do you really think they'll just sit there and keep quiet? Don't forget, they have to give these new others some reason why they got such a hammering then, if for no other reason than to account for the fact that they've never been able to come east of the mountains with anything but lightning raids. And don't think the Donns who come with this new force won't ask! If they've *any* military experience, they'll want to know what to expect here. Now the Abend can verbally run us down and make us out to be a bunch of savages. But if they do that they risk seeming like incompetent fools. Do you think the Abend will chance that? I don't. I suspect that they'll try to make out that we have some kind of arcane power. They'll tell the Donns not to take us at face value. So I think we have to present them with a potential victory over a force about a quarter of their size. Even the Abend and any with them who remember Moytirra will think those are good odds."

"So how will you draw them?" Aneirin's figure had begun to seriously fragment as he had expressed his doubts and the Foresters' ward took effect. Now he forgot to be doubtful and his shape became more solid again.

"Firstly we have to wait for them to get everyone ashore," Brego said decisively. "They have to be committed to taking Rathlin first. And that plays into our hands, because once they start looking about them, it'll soon be clear that there's not much here for them. Rathlin has no riches, no fine houses for the elite to stay in. Nothing to recompense them for the expense of coming here. At that point, I don't think it's unreasonable to think that they'll take up an offer the Abend are bound to make, for them to move north towards New Lochlainn – and I don't think the Abend will demur if it's the newcomers' who make the move, because they can't afford to lose face by suggesting New Lochlainn isn't secure. We don't need them to do much. Just move away from the flat lands around the coast."

"What we want is hills," Maelbrigt said with a far-off look in his eyes.

"Yes, hills!" Sionnachan agreed with a wicked smirk on his face.

"Oh you've got hills!" Magnus joined in for the first time. "In fact you've got two choices. You can lure them eastwards, coming towards here and Lowes on the coast. There are good rolling uplands between there and here. Plenty of land for you to hide men in!"

"Ideally more than upland. We want proper hills," Maelbrigt immediately said, not wanting to say that he also thought they might have a riot on their hands if the militia from Lowes got wind of them drawing the DeÁine force down on their homes and families.

"Then you need to swing west more," Magnus said. "If you march due west from here the land starts to rise almost immediately. About four days march away the land is high enough for two rivers to rise on the far side to drain into Loch Canisp. There's a bowl of land to the west and inland of Vulinn where it looks like you can march up a wide valley between the hills and get north easily. You can't, it's a dead end, but you can't see that until you're trapped!"

"Perfect!" Maelbrigt and Sionnachan said in unison, and Brego was nodding along with Ruari and Berengar.

"So who dangles the bait?" Ruari asked.

"I do!" Brego immediately answered. "We'll get close enough to the coast for them to spot us then pull back a way. Those beast-battalions might serve our purpose more than theirs if we play this right! I'll be in the centre with my men. We're the biggest force, and in a place where they can't see us clearly laid out we can make it seem like we're a bigger force than we are. Berengar, you and your men will be hidden on my immediate right. Ruari, you'll be the same on my left. That way, if they don't nibble at the bait, I can signal you to come and close on me to make a larger target.

"...Sionnachan ...Hugh and I discussed this before we left Lorne. I want you and your Foresters on the far right, ready to come out of the hills and attack their flank. I don't want any Foresters in the main force. We have to assume the Abend, at least, know the Forester uniforms. If they do, they might think twice about taking us on and might dissuade the new Donns too. They might not, of course, but it's a chance I don't want to take. We can't afford to linger for long because our supplies will start to run out. If that becomes a necessity, we'll just have to fall back fast to Lowes and think again!

"...Maelbrigt, you'll be with all the other Island Treasure holders on my far left with Warwick and his Foresters and your own Celidon men. Sionnachan, I want Sithfrey with you. That way both the Gauntlet and the Gorget – with Berengar – are on the same side of our force and opposite the Island Treasures and, if there are any sparks flying when those start to work, the DeÁine force will be a barrier between you. Hopefully they'll catch the worst of any Power surges!"

The ancients did not quite believe this was going to work but left the army to do its plotting anyway, although not before having another run in with Arthur. As the Islander commanders began talking details, the two ancients were left slightly to one side. Just as they were about to leave, a small voice came from behind them.

"So you got yourselves sorted?" This time, although the voice was still a child's, it had lost all of Arthur's normal intonations and patterns. "Trust them! I have for all these years."

"Who are you?" Urien asked hoarsely. There was something so very, very familiar about this person if he could only get beyond seeing a child before him. He closed his eyes to listen better as young Arthur spoke again.

"I thought I'd gone. I thought I was dead! But somehow I managed to create a link with one of the Islanders. Since then I've come down the years as a passenger in many of their short lives. As each one dies, I find another host. This time, though, I deliberately chose to move on. It was a cruel choice, for in leaving her I killed my host. But in the part of me which is now in the Power, in the same way that you are, I felt things coming to a head. I also knew that if the Islanders have a fault it's compassion."

"You think *that's* their great fault?" an astonished Aneirin gasped. "I could think of a few more appropriate ones than that! Wilfulness, for a start!"

"Ah, but you haven't lived with and within them like I have," the voice replied through Arthur. "Oh I know your feelings are hurt, Aneirin. You expected them to be falling over themselves in gratitude at your help. But then you always were a bit too full of your own importance!" and the voice chuckled.

That did it for Urien. Suddenly he knew who it was he was hearing and it shook him to his core. "Artoris?" he gulped, eyes flying wide open. "God Almighty! Is that you?"

"Yes, what's left of me."

"But we thought you died!"

"Well I very nearly did. I suppose in some people's eyes I am dead, because I don't have anything physical left of me. Not even the entombed bodies you and the others have. And to be frank, after all this time it will be a relief to fully pass over. I've felt these changes coming from afar, and by now I knew I didn't have the strength left to make the hops between bodies on a battlefield. So I decided that I had to have one body and make it count for much more than its simple value. I shall be very sad to use this boy so cruelly, but he and I have a task to do. We must incite the Islanders to commit their forces without reservation or any kind of unwillingness to eradicate this enemy."

"They seem pretty committed to me," Aneirin said glumly. "They've been giving us a right time of it! And Vanadis is going to have kittens when she hears you're still here. I don't think you'll get much understanding for only being partly alive. She'll be mad that you still didn't make yourself known."

"Ah well, Vanadis will have to accept this. I don't have the time to argue with her. As for the Islanders, I think you've not realised that they will still be compassionate to any fallen. It's not in their ethos to slaughter wounded men, or to massacre men who surrender."

"And you want them to?" Urien was perplexed. "I know you always hated the DeÁine for what they did with our forefathers' discoveries, Artoris, but isn't that going a bit far?"

"This isn't for *me*," the voice said with some of Arthur's natural exasperation creeping in. "It's for the Islands! Don't you see? They have to defeat the DeÁine so decisively that they'll never, ever come back again! Half a millennium ago we gave them a bloody nose and sent them packing, but it wasn't enough. They crawled away and licked their wounds, then came back for revenge. But if they do that again, we aren't likely to be here to help them, and the weapons we left the first time might not survive either. It was touch and go whether they all survived this long! So this time there can be no survivors amongst the DeÁine. None who can run back and tell others that there are DeÁine weapons surviving in the Islanders.

"Indeed there can be no surviving weapons of the DeÁine's either! That's what brought them back, you know. We should have destroyed the damned things when we had the chance! The Islanders didn't know how to, but you could have – even from your tombs in the north! Back then you had the ability to reach out in a physical way. It could have been done. But we thought the Islanders' possession of them would act as a deterrent. Now we know otherwise. So this victory has to be complete. This invading army has to vanish from the face of the earth as if a mighty hand swept them away. Even long ago we couldn't save the lands to the east from this plague, but we can make sure that all around here in the distant west stay free from slavery to the DeÁine's poison. Now go and tell the others, including Vanadis, that I expect you all to be behind the Islanders every step of the way!"

With that the small figure yawned mightily and staggered off to a shelter where he curled up on a bedroll and went to sleep.

The two ancients looked about them, but none of the Islanders seemed to have noticed. Everyone was now clustered around a patch of earth which had been swept clear and had diagrams being drawn into it as the Knights planned. With no little trepidation the two ancients took a deep breath and returned to Taineire to break the news.

The ancients then converged on the Bowl and Vanadis. For the moment, Hugh and Arsaidh were seated in comfort under a large canvas canopy in the shade, with Fin between them. The squint was now looking much healthier, although he was still heavily scarred and had not grown any fur back. He did not like the ancients being around him, though, always shrinking close to Hugh whenever Vanadis or one of the others appeared, making it very clear that the squints had been all too aware of who had put them into the void between time in the first place. This made things difficult at times, but for now the ancients were glad of some separation from the Islanders' scrutiny.

"What do you mean, he's Artoris?" Vanadis demanded of Urien and Aneirin.

"Not him as we knew him," Urien said hurriedly. "He's half with us at best, but he occupies the small boy called Arthur."

"I believe he's buried what remains of himself deep in Arthur's mind," Aneirin added pensively. "He can direct Arthur from within. But communicating with us takes a huge amount of effort."

Neither wanted to say that Artoris had seemed a good deal less distraught at not being in contact with Vanadis, than she had been over losing him. Far better to imply that Artoris had not been in communication because it was not possible, rather than had not been inclined to. Inability must surely have played a fair part in his long silence, but both knew Vanadis well enough to know that she would not accept any half measures. If he could have raised even so much as a squeak, she would be demanding to know why he had not used it to contact her. This was proven by her next words.

"I'm going to see this Arthur right now!" she declared.

"No!" Aneirin exclaimed. "No, not like that!"

Vanadis gave him her frostiest stare. "Since when have you told me what to do?"

"For God's sake!" Urien snapped. "He's not trying to boss you about! Just listen, will you? Artoris has been watching the Islanders all these long years in a way that we haven't. So even I have to concede that he's spotted something we missed. The DeÁine can't be scared off! That's become blindingly clear from the fact that they're back here in similar numbers to when we fought them off. Artoris believes that if the Islanders don't annihilate them this time, they'll fall the next time the DeÁine return, because by then we really will be gone, and they'll have no protection against the Abend and their twisted creations. Can you argue with that?

"...No! So he has some idea of how to get them to commit acts which are repugnant to them – the wholesale slaughter of the DeÁine. But it has something to do with the boy he inhabits. I don't know whether he's going to use the squints in some way the Islanders won't like or what. Given how passionate they are about the creatures' well-being, and the bond he has with them, that would be my guess. But we therefore can't tip his hand to them by suddenly swarming all over this boy all of a sudden! Now do you understand?"

Vanadis pulled a face, then declared, "Very well! But I shall insist that we speak to him tonight when the men are all asleep."

As soon as the army camp went quiet and the darkness disguised movements, Owein went into the camp and persuaded Arthur to follow him quietly to a spot behind where some large gorse bushes grew tall enough to hide the ancients' apparitions. All of them congregated there.

"Artoris?" Vanadis said softly yet with intense yearning.

"Eh? Who do you fink...?" Arthur's perplexed frown relaxed in a heartbeat into blankness as his voice also changed. "Hello Vanadis! Didn't think it would be long before you got here!" It was not just the words but Artoris' typically dry delivery which was so uncanny. "Sorry I couldn't contact you earlier. It's taken many years of staying put behind other peoples' lives to regenerate me to this state. Now listen, I don't have long! When the battle engages I shall need you to keep the Islanders from spotting when I make my move. Stay close to your weapons! Vanadis, you in particular may need to ask one of these people to do as Galad did."

The ancients all looked from one to another in surprise. What did Artoris know that they didn't? "Don't ask me why!" he added brusquely. "I don't have the time or strength to explain! Now... here, tonight, you must go west and find Myrddin."

All of the others gasped and spluttered almost forgetting where they were until a sleepy voice called out, "Who's there?"

They all went silent until they were sure the unknown soldier was not coming to check on what he thought he had heard.

"I've felt Myrddin!" Artoris declared softly yet triumphantly. "He too is within someone! But he's west of here. It's only been the last few days that I've felt him, but it can't be anyone else. You must search for him *now*! We shall need him, if I'm not mistaken."

"You're sure? It couldn't be some trick of the Abend's?" Peredur wanted to believe Artoris, but could not quite believe that both of their best leaders had returned so fortuitously.

"It's him, no mistaking!" Artoris confirmed. "And it can't be any Abend, because he's getting stronger despite being on a ship coming this way! The sea is no problem."

"You've spoken with him?" an astonished Cynddylan gasped.

"Not in words. It's more that I felt this... 'itching' ...and reached out. I felt something reaching back to me. Not specific words but intentions. Intentions based on memories, and those memories can only be Myrddin's! Now I must go. I shall see you at the battle. They'll engage the DeÁine within days. Tell Myrddin we are of the same mind!"

The sleepy figure of Arthur turned and tottered back to his bedroll, leaving the ancients in confusion.

Cynddylan groaned. "Oh well, at least we don't need sleep anymore. Come on! We'd better go hunting while our Islander friends get their rest, and won't start asking questions about why we aren't here with them."

"West and over the sea," his brother Peredur said contemplatively, as they faded out together and projected their awareness in a different direction.

"Wait for me!" Owein called to them, and sped in their wake to quest across the sea. To their consternation the first thing they spotted was a flotilla of ships bearing the marks of the Souk'ir. Surely that was not what Artoris had meant? Yet they braced themselves and went closer to investigate. If this was some new threat then the Islanders still needed to know about it.

Oblivious to this, the next day the huge army broke camp and began the march westwards. The final group of Ergardians had caught up with them, and they had all the men they could hope to get now. If it was not big enough, then it would not be for want of trying! Sionnachan, as the man whose force had the farthest to go, led with some of Magnus' men acting as guides. Behind him came Berengar, with the militia men from Rathlin carefully amalgamated into his force, spreading their lack of experience out amongst men who did know what they were facing. In the centre came Brego, followed by Ruari and the Prydein men, and finally Maelbrigt with the other assorted companies, including Magnus' men and the Treasure wielders' own battalions.

Magnus' men had been allotted a task of their own, and one they were well qualified to do. Someone, Brego had decided, had to take the DeÁine ships. There could be no chance of the captains standing offshore when battle commenced, and then racing for safety when they saw the others falling. Everyone agreed that there could be no second fight of this kind if more came from over the sea – and Brego and Maelbrigt both confirmed that there must be others in a second and more distant place of exile, going on intelligence from the late Covert Brethren. And if the Islanders took heavy casualties of their own, then all feared it would be generations before they could amass this number of men again. The ships had to be taken, and Magnus' initial reluctance to be denied a place in the greater battle was swiftly placated when Brego told him that this task needed seamen, and the Attacotti were all they had. He and his leaders were further won over when told that they could keep the ships, and use them to trade between the Islands once the fight for their survival was past.

However, there was one point on which nobody argued. McKinley led out a fast group of scouts made up of Foresters and Attacotti under Colm Ap'brien. Everyone agreed that they would feel a lot better for an assessment of the threat from their own men, and Magnus volunteered his sturdy mountain ponies for their use to allow them greater speed. They returned six days later, as the Island army camped in the last mountain fastness before the land lowered towards the sea.

"Well?" Sionnachan asked, as he ran to take the bridle of McKinley's spare pony.

"Bloody good job we went!" McKinley said, looking both irate and worried. "Are the flaming ancients getting senile or something? Because they can't bloody count, that's for sure!"

Sionnachan hurried with him to the centre of the long encampment to where Brego waited with the other leaders, who had hastened to his side at the sight of the scouts return.

"Your thoughts?" Magnus prompted Colm.

"The Foresters and us are of one mind," the clan chief said solemnly, and respectfully deferred to McKinley, who rubbed his tired eyes and took a deep breath.

"I think where the ancients got into a muddle was in being able to estimate how many men any one of those big ships could carry," he began.

Ruari snorted in exasperation. "Oh we'd gathered that! In the last couple of days their estimates have gone up and down like a whore's skirt!"

Magnus quirked an amused eyebrow at Matti and Taise's askance glances, and Kayna's chuckle at Andra's instinctive blink of surprise. He was becoming more reassured by the day that these Knights, despite their fancy uniforms and flags, nonetheless knew how to fight, illustrated in part by the way nobody was worried about politeness anymore.

"How far adrift were they?" Ruari asked the scouts collectively.

McKinley grimaced. "Well we'd say that as far as the number of expected veterans goes, it's not that different. We already estimated that we'd be lucky to get away with thirty thousand of them, and in fact I'd say the reality is about at the top of our original estimate at something like thirty five thousand."

"But that's not the problem?" Sionnachan prompted.

"No, sire, not the worst of it. I think we can shed a bit of light on why they seemed to halt on their journey now. You see, when the captain Miss Cwen spoke to saw them he was right. *That* fleet did contain about a hundred thousand, because that's what's disembarking now, and there are about another seventy thousand in Seljuqs there. But the reason they're only just finishing landing is because of what's already clustered all around the army. They've brought *all* the beast battalions they must have had at this other place!"

"Cross of Swords!"

"Flaming Underworlds!"

"Oak protect us!"

The oaths of surprise and dismay radiated out as the news spread out.

"It's going to worse than Moytirra!" someone said, giving voice to the veterans' fears.

"How many beast-battalions?" Brego asked solemnly.

Anson winced. "Well there's definitely about three just with the jaculi, so thank the Trees we've got plenty of hawks from all the septs! We're going to need them!"

Mace nodded. "But rather worse news is that there must be a minimum of two each with the gryphes and the kokatrices, but more likely three. And every one of those battalions seems to have two Seljuqs with it. We could easily be looking at another ten thousand, and those with the added nightmare of the fighting beasts."

"May Jolnir the Soul Reaper take their rotten spirits to the Underworld!" Brego swore. "That old tactic! I prayed I would never live to see that one again! ...I must tell Hugh of this! ...Sooty? Would you tell Fin and ask him to get Vanadis to translate, please?"

Sooty stared into the distance and twittered, then excitedly thrust the Knife into Brego's hands. Holding the Knife with Brego, he then trilled something at great speed and a small cloud appeared, which then opened out like a smoke ring to display Hugh's figure with Fin beside him.

"Brego!" Hugh called cheerfully. "By the Trees! It worked!"

"That was a bit fast for Vanadis," Brego said in surprise.

"Oh she hasn't appeared yet!" a quavering voice said, and Arsaidh tottered into view with several Foresters at his back. "But we've not been idle while we've waited! I thought this might work, and very gratifying it is too to be proven right!"

"Now why doesn't that surprise me!" Sionnachan's amused voice cut through the silence of surprise on Rathlin.

"Well this is wonderful!" the stunned Brego gasped. "Now we can confer properly! ...Did you hear our news?"

"No, but Fin was so agitated and thrusting the chalice into my hands we guessed it was urgent. So we told him what we were going to do and he's done his best to put us right on the bits we weren't sure of. ...So what's happened? You clearly aren't about to fight today?"

In terse sentences Brego told Hugh of the newest arrivals.

"Hounds of the Wild Hunt!" Hugh groaned. "Beasts of battle! Just what we needed!"

"I know!" Brego agreed. "So the question is ...what do we do to lure them out? What did the old Masters do when you fought the beasts of battle in the Brychan Mere years ago? How did you get rid of the worst of them before the main battle at Moytirra? I wasn't there facing them at the time but with the main muster, so I have to rely on your memory for this."

Hugh grimaced and thought for a moment. "Well I'd expect the Donns to surge forwards with the slaves first. It's the scent of blood from the dead slaves which winds the beasts into a killing frenzy. They're halfway controllable until they pick up that. They'll march the slaves in to try to induce you into fighting, let them take terrible casualties while keeping the Jundises behind the beasts until they're in a right frenzy. Then they'll let them go and the veterans will follow hot on their tails to slaughter in their wake.

"So the trick we used is lure the slaves deeper and deeper into your trap before you shed a drop of their blood. Don't let them commit the slaves while the beasts and the Jundises have room to swing around or manoeuvre. Get them all into a place where there's little room to move and you can attack the Jundises and beasts with archers too, because if you can start to maim the beasts, their screams of pain will unnerve the rest of them and they won't fight so well.

"You also want them well forwards of the Abend. That way, when the jaculi and kokatrices get up into the air, they're in the way of the Abend throwing Power-fire at you at the same time. Alternatively, try to get the whole lot on the move, and then see if and how they're feeding the beasts. They must have had flesh of some sort on board the ships to get them this far, but they could be short by now. So if they think there's a quick meal to be had for the beasts, to keep them going before they have to fight in earnest, you might just lure the cursed creatures away from the main force and give yourselves time to deal with them first."

Brego turned to Magnus. "How far now to this big wide valley?"

"One day's march, no more," Magnus answered with confidence. Then seemed to be wrestling with an inner dilemma for a moment before he spoke, addressing both the men around him and Hugh. "Do you think it would work if me and my men tried to draw the beasties? Would they see us as less of a threat – more of a meal – and so let a few of these beast-battalions go after us when they might not risk it against the Order?"

Ivain came and put a restraining hand on Magnus' arm. "Are you sure of that, Magnus? It's a noble offer, but one which places your folk in great danger. More so than the rest of us, since fewer of your men have any kind of armour." He also hoped that the distant Hugh would see him acting in apparent alliance with Magnus and not dismiss the Attacotti leader. Magnus had come so far in such a short time, but Hugh had not witnessed the change and might react on the basis of past experience, and Ivain did not want to lose the truce they had.

However it was Maelbrigt who saved the day before Hugh even had time to object.

"That's an excellent idea!" he declared enthusiastically. "If we make the first few lines up out of your men, especially with some of the older lads at the front – although not your lads!" he immediately warned Arthur, whose eyes had lit up like candles at the prospect of fighting wild and exotic beasts. "If we put Foresters behind them with their plaids turned so that there's no insignia, we might well get away with it! Our plaids aren't that different from yours in colours, at least, and once we're a few ranks back, nobody will be looking at the detail.

"The Abend might even tell the Donns it's safe, given their brief run in with Magnus' men in the north – they'll underestimate their strength of numbers! Then once we've got them on the move and away from the rest of the camp, we can filter your men, and especially the young lads, back deeper into our ranks. If they then want to fight they can, although I'd rather leave the Foresters and archers to deal with these horrors. Your men are far more valuable to us if they can seize the ships."

Ivain was making encouraging noises for this plan, as were others. It offered Magnus an active part but with due recognition of how highly they valued him too, yet stopped well short of allowing the Attacotti to go on one of their wildly courageous, but often ill-fated, attacks. To everyone's relief he and his men agreed. However, getting the DeÁine into position was somewhat harder. Scouts went out thrice daily once the Islanders were just short of their objective, but reported that for the first day or so the whole lot just sat there at the coast.

Luckily, after that they seemed to react in a way which suggested that the Islanders had guessed right. These new highborn DeÁine were used to a much higher level of luxury – apparent by the huge, fluttering tents which sprang up like exotic flowers all over the encampment – and they clearly were not that impressed with Rathlin's beautiful but empty coast and mountains.

Two days later the whole lot finally packed up, and with much blaring of horns and banging of drums, the vast sea of slaves, soldiers and beasts crawled into action. Even then, Hugh appeared to them and told them to let the DeÁine army march for a full two days. The whole was so enormous that the rear ranks had barely moved from the coast on the first day, and there was no space for Magnus' men to slip behind and get to the ships. Therefore they all sat and fought their rising nerves until the rear ranks of DeÁine were out of immediate sight of the coast – it would appear again as the Seljuqs and Jundises climbed going inland, but not with sufficient clarity to endanger the Attacotti from an early a warning and a retreat to save the ships.

On the evening of the fourteenth of Grian-mhor Brego and Hugh conferred and then Brego issued the order – they would fight the next day! So after the evening meal campfires were doused, and the men marched under cover of darkness to just behind the ridges of the valley where they would fight. Then everyone rolled themselves into plaids and cloaks and tried, mostly unsuccessfully, to get some sleep. It was also when the leaders called the ancients to them and made a request for a widespread early summer's morning haze.

"Something nice and natural looking," Ruari said firmly to their spectral helpers. "It's already warming up nicely, and today's been positively hot, so tomorrow a nice haze as the morning dew steams off would be perfect. Nothing too thick! We don't want the Abend thinking it's feeding time for the farliath! We might want that later, anyway – the fog, that is, not the farliath!"

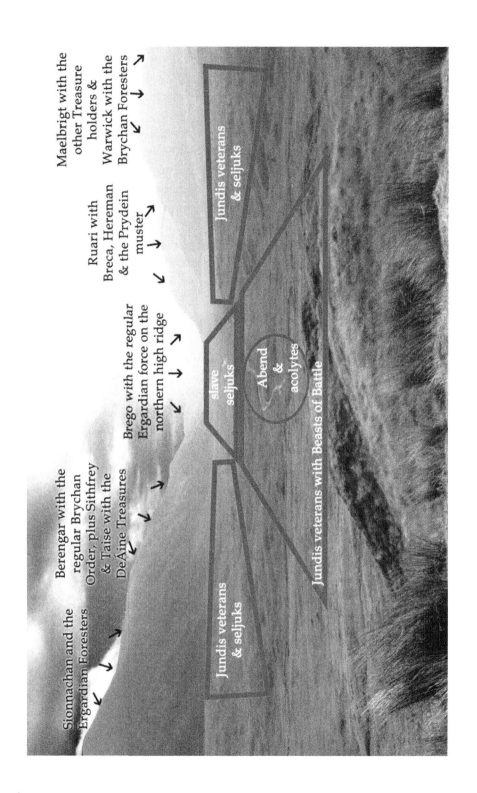

Sionnachan and the Ergardian Foresters

Berengar with the regular Brychan Order, plus Sithfrey & Taise with the DeÁine Treasures

Brego with the regular Ergardian force on the northern high ridge

Ruari with Breca, Hereman & the Prydein muster

Maelbrigt with the other Treasure holders & Warwick with the Brychan Foresters

Jundis veterans & seljuks

slave seljuks

Abend & acolytes

Jundis veterans & seljuks

Jundis veterans with Beasts of Battle

# Chapter 16

 *Three Fights and a Battle*

### Rathlin: Grian-mhor

With the first rays of midsummer dawn brushing the tops of the ridges, Magnus led his men down the long valley. The younger lads had been thrilled to be put in the lead – so much so that the only thing stopping the Knights from pulling them straight back into their ranks, and the safety from youthful folly, was the certain belief that as soon as they saw the fell beasts they would be running back of their own accords.

The five chosen companies of Sionnachan's Foresters marched hard on their heels. They had rearranged their plaids so that it would be so much harder to spot their allegiance behind the similar muted browns and greens of the front Attacotti men. Magnus' men marched with an arrogant swagger through the swirling mist of the rising dew, while high above them, those Foresters not within their ranks shadowed them up on the valley sides, crouching low so that if in danger of being spotted they could dive for cover behind the tall fronds of the plentiful bracken which smothered the slopes.

At the rear, Ruari was watching their advance with Brego and Berengar from the vantage point of a rocky knoll.

"Flaming Trees! Are all the bloody Donns asleep or something? Are their forward sentries blind?" he muttered in frustration, as the bait moved further and further down the valley without any sign of it being taken. His dread was that they would get so far from the main force, that if things went horribly wrong, they would be too far away for a rescue sally and a safe retreat. The huge opposing army was a long smear in the misty distance, with tentacles splayed forwards and deceptively placid for now.

Then suddenly it did go wrong! Ruari had had serious doubts about allowing Raghnall Friseal to take part in this foray, but had deferred to Magnus' wish for a united Attacotti action, and now he was proven right. He knew Friseal was over on Magnus' right and to his horror a scuffle of some sort broke out at the point where he guessed Friseal and Magnus' men were shoulder to shoulder. Then amongst a dozen or so it became a fist fight.

"Oh shit!" Berengar growled, "that's all we need! The scent of blood on the air!"

It did not take long either. Suddenly out of the mist they saw a whole flock of jaculi on the wing, heading straight for the band of men on the valley floor.

"Release the hawks!" Brego turned and bellowed, and the order was heard radiating out through the ranks. A soft rustling grew into a sound like thousands of hearts racing as flight upon flight of hawks beat their wings to rise into the air. They climbed higher and higher to gain the thermals which would aid their attack flights. Meanwhile beside the three leaders, an archer dipped an arrow into a small portable brazier and then, as it caught light and burned with a phosphorous glow, fired it straight up into the air. Taise had lent her expertise to that of the Foresters to ensure it would burn bright enough to be seen across the whole valley. It was the signal to the Order's archers to fire at will at any enemy.

They had hoped to wait until much later to use this, for half of the archers – and the half who had farthest to go and were therefore needed to cover Magnus' men – were still on the move just over the ridge on either side of the valley, trying to keep up while remaining stealthy, as the Attacotti moved further south than anticipated. As it was, the watchers saw men starting to appear on the skylines as the archers hurried up to get to a good shooting position in order to compensate for being too far back. No-one was loosing just yet but it would not be long, for the jaculi were coming at an incredible speed. Dropping towards the bait, they suddenly swept into swirling masses in preparation for diving down onto the terrified men below.

Already some of the young lads were running for all they were worth back along the valley. Yet this was now the worst thing for them to do, for the jaculi saw them as prey to be played with, not just food, and many began to single these boys out for attacks. The archers let fly as soon as they could, but the boys' best chance of survival lay with the hawks, summoned to attack by the Knights' bone whistles.

Like small thunderbolts they dropped down from way on high, plummeting almost vertically with wings folded back and talons stretching out at the last minute to strike at the jaculi's leathery skin. Those who pursued the boys now died in a flurry of hawks, ripped to shreds by beaks and talons, but their blood only added to the scent of an impending feast and drew the others onwards. Soon the air over the valley reverberated to a constant and ear-jarring cacophony of screeching, and was dark with the jaculi's dark, green-skinned wings. They flew lower than the hawks, unable to beat their leathery wings sufficiently hard to gain any real height, which in one way made them a good target for the hawks, but also masked much of the hawks' effectiveness from the observers. More visible was the progress of the archers, since they were firing from below. For although everyone would have been happier if the jaculi had been fewer, such a dense mass made the archers' job easier, for it would have been hard not to hit something in such a dense flock.

Small bodies began dropping like flies in a first frost, splattering themselves onto the ground and hampering the men's retreat, not only because the running men tripped on them, but because the acid mucus from the beaks of the falling jaculi still burned them even if the jaculi were dead. And any man putting his hands down to try and save himself when he fell, was likely to put them into something which raised great painful blisters, even in tiny amounts.

Someone in the DeÁine camp must have finally woken up to the fact that their pets had not just woken up to a sumptuous banquet of rabbits, yet still managed to misinterpret things. Other noises now joined in the endless screeching going on as keepers thought food was on hand for all of the beasts. In the distance, those of the Order high enough to have a view down towards the lowlands near the sea saw another mass heading their way, and signalled the information back along the ranks.

"Festering Underworld! Here come the gryphes and kokatrises!" Dana groaned, and Berengar and Ruari hurried away to join their own troops. This was something they could not just leave to the archers to deal with. Yet a different horror presented itself long before the beasts of battle arrived. The natural Island dawn mist had already almost disappeared even allowing for the ancients' intervention, but down on the valley floor another, thicker fog began to appear along the course of the small river which divided it into two.

"Oh bugger!" Piran swore as he ran beside Ruari. "Bloody Abend summoning stuff! What do *they* think is here? Are they intending to feed the acolytes on Magnus' men's spirits, too? That's all we need! Great Maker, this is all going base upwards in a hurry!"

Ruari glanced down at the river and swore too. "Merciful Rowan! We weren't expecting to fight the Abend themselves quite so early on," he fumed. "Jolnir's balls! This isn't going to plan at all!" Not that he expected battles to be neat and tidy, he was far too much of a veteran for that. But if there was ever a point when he could hope to have some control over how

281

things were going to play out, it should have been at this stage, before everyone was fully engaged. For it to have gone so wrong so early was not an auspicious sign!

Up on the valley walls, way ahead on both sides, Maelbrigt and Warwick on the left and Sionnachan on the right, were having much the same thoughts.

"We're going to have to engage!" Warwick said grimly. "If the Abend are going to add their tricks into the fray, then we have to be there too."

"I daren't lead yet!" Maelbrigt fretted. "We have to keep the Treasures in reserve for just a bit longer yet. If we don't," he grimaced, "we've played all our cards and given the Abend time to think of ways to counter them."

"I know," Warwick consoled him. "Look! Sionnachan's started moving his men too. Keep the Treasures' coteries here! I'll take just the Foresters with me." And with that he turned and sent signals along their line.

The Abend's fog was rising and spreading fast, and before Warwick's men had gone a few yards, the other side of the valley became obscured from them in white. Nobody could see a thing. However, Sionnachan had other ideas. If they could not see one another then they could still hear, and on the morning air came a brief wheezing noise, and then a droning, before a new sound took over from the last of the jaculi's cries. The lone piper who stood close to Sionnachan played a short phrase. Lonely, eerie and plaintive, it echoed around the valley walls. To the untutored it sounded like a jumble of notes. To the pipers it was instantly recognisable as the refrain from one of the fundamental pieces every Ergardian piper learned to play for use against summonings. As the lone piper reached the end of the phrase, he paused for one single breath.

When he blew the next note, every Forester piper along the hillside was with him and the effect was awesome. Obscured in origin to all immersed in the white damp wreaths, the long single notes seemed to be rising from the very hillside as the sound stretched out along the whole Foresters' fighting front, and for the non-Foresters it was the kind of sound which sent shivers down the spine. Drummer boys came in on the next note, and a wall of musical notes rippled out from the Foresters and floated down into the valley, sinking with the mist. As the pipers began to march forwards, the rest of the Foresters' force stood up and began marching with them. There was now no need to remain hidden since the Abend's mist was doing that job for them. And so the skirling of the pipes and the rhythms of the drums were swiftly accompanied by another, harder to place, noise. The Foresters marched quietly, but their kilts and plaids brushed the heather and bracken, so that a soft swishing, leaf-like rustling underlay the music, and only added to its unearthly quality.

The pipers of the Ergardian Order were in fine tune, and it only took Warwick's men a few phrases to realise what those opposite were playing. With the Ergardians' fine skills in such matters making them the acknowledged leaders, it only took a few notes more before the pipers with Warwick's force had blown air into their pipes' bags, and with the next phrase they joined in. It was a complex piece with many grace notes over an already elaborate base tune. The Brychan pipers made no attempt to follow the intricate, technical shifts at the top, but played the underlying tune with all the breath they had. However, some of the Celidon expert pipers on their side of the valley had clearly heard this before, and were following the pibroch laid over the top of the base tune with equal competence and – as far as anyone could tell given the echoes in the valley – in almost perfect time.

As they descended into the now coagulated fog, everyone's skin began to crawl and the Foresters began their chant, which would have been reminiscent of monastic plain chants except that it was not in any language the Islands' monks knew. Sionnachan had his sword drawn and a rowan-handled long knife in his other hand, as did every other man, and as the chant came round to start again he sang, "annad sinne earb a,"[1] with them. As he walked forwards into the thick, unnatural fog his pace slowed, not only because he could not see what he was stepping on and did not want to go sprawling, but also because he had every sense stretched to the limit.

Something flitted past his awareness to his left. Moments later he heard scuffling, and his men chanting in three-part harmony as they freed someone caught in the farliath's tendrils and dispatched it to the Underworld. Other rising chants made him aware of other assaults which must be taking place, and from across the river he heard a voice which sounded very like Warwick's rising briefly above the others to call in warning, "Thoiribh an aire! Farliath!"[2] Then calling again shortly after for a change in chants, from warding to attack, as they engaged several of the spectres hunting on their side of the river too.

Yet Sionnachan himself encountered nothing until he found his feet

---

[1] "In you we trust"
[2] "Take care! Farliath!"

starting to sink into wet ground. By now he had to be very close to the little river, which looped closer to the right-hand valley wall at this point, even if he could not see it. He took another step forwards and his boot splashed into water, not deep but over his ankles, but at that point something slithered past his foot. He froze.

"Baneasge!" he hurriedly called in warning to his men, then very carefully lowered his sword and probed the water in front of him. As he raised the point up again, something shot out and grabbed him hard about the ankle and tugged. Luckily, with him being such a big man, he must have been weightier than the baneasge expected, and although he was thrown off balance he was not fully jerked off his feet.

"Darach dionaibh mi! ...Beithe leighisibh mi!"[3] he declaimed, stabbing at the water around his ankle as he went down on the other knee despite his best efforts to stay afoot. Then he plunged his sword into the ground to anchor himself. Using his sword as a support to at least stay upright as he knelt with his trapped leg extended, he grabbed his long knife from its holster.

"Uinnsean treoraichibh mi!" he panted, stabbing down again. "Iubhar nuadhaichibh mi!" as he finally felt his rowan-handled knife connect with something. "Caorann leam comhraigibh!" The vicelike tendril at his ankle definitely flinched as he sank the knife fully into it. "Caorann leam comhraigibh!" he snarled once more, stabbing at it hard again.

"Naomh Freumh gabhaibh sibhse a Ifhrinn!"[4] he all but screamed in his fury, now plunging his sword into the tendril before it escaped, as he stumbled forwards on his knees, and then repeatedly laid into it with the knife until it lay totally unmoving.

As he stood up, panting and pulling his blades free, he realised that other voices were gradually falling silent. One last "Bocan bi dhfhalbh!" sounded somewhere off to his right as a final farliath was despatched, and then the fog began to blow away on the sea breeze coming inland. Unlike any natural fog this lifted in a mass from the ground upwards, and so before he could see his fellow Foresters he could see the nasty mess of the remains of the baneasge. It had no real form but showed as a long gelatinous white smear draped over the reeds, which slowly became transparent and then

---

[3]The shortened Forester battle version: Oak protect me! Birch heal me! Ash guide me! Yew renew me! Rowan fight with me!
[4]Sacred Roots take you to (the) Underworld!

disappeared into the water.

As soon as he could see about him he called for reports.

"How many farliath?" he called to his men. "How many baneasge?"

In short order they established that there must have been a great many of both, confirming in his mind that the Abend had been trying to feed their acolytes as much as themselves.

"How many bloody acolytes have you got with you?" he growled rhetorically, as he squelched his way forward to where Warwick stood waiting for him on the opposite bank of the small river. With the aid of a few good sized boulders midstream, Sionnachan managed to leap across without getting soaked and greeted Warwick, who agreed with his assessment of the situation.

"Definitely trying to fill the acolytes with stolen Power from our life forces," Warwick concurred. "The only bright side is that our taking on those summonings has made them think twice about letting the gryphes and kokatrises loose just yet." And he nodded off to his left, to where Sionnachan realised that the vast flocks had been halted as their slaves were herded in front of them as protection now. "I think we've made them think twice about us being easy pickings if nothing else."

In the opposition's camp there were plenty of questions flying. The Veroon and Komanchii Donns from Sinut were in a blind fury. The leading Veroon was nose to nose with Helga, apoplectic with rage as his favourite acolyte sat on the floor clutching her head in her hands in the after-effect of her connection to the farliath being so abruptly severed.

"Who are these aberrations?" he screamed at her. "What kind of place is this that they would dare to raise their hands to us?"

"One which we have been fighting to subdue for the last forty years," Helga responded with icy calm. "Immaculate Temples! You didn't think we'd just been sitting on our hands, did you?" She gave him no time to say that was just what the Sinuti did think! Instead, in a voice which could have been carved from the glaciers of Taineire, she snapped, "You should recall your history lessons, Donn Veroon! *These* islands are the place where the great Volla's armour was lost – not just by *our* predecessors, but yours as well! We might outlive these horrid lowlifes many times over, but that doesn't mean that they can't be an incredible thorn in our sides. And before you start throwing accusations at any Abend, you might want to ask yourselves where the Monreux, Corraine and Telesco are?"

"The Monreux were not of our stature," Donn Veroon snorted loftily. "If they have fallen it is their failing. *We* are not so easily quashed!"

"Oh? So you've just spent the last thousand years sullying your hands with underlings, have you?" Helga riposted snidely. "So you know how that feels then, Donn Veroon!" She knew he was caught with that one. For all that the Veroon's egos might want to think themselves superior to the Monreux, the truth was that they were equals in every way anyone other than themselves could see, and if anything the Monreux had often appeared to have the edge on the opposing Veroon in the long running vendetta.

As he was about to explode into another tirade, after puffing like a human volcano for several breaths, Helga wove a bond of Power about him, tying his hands tightly to his sides and lifting him off his feet. His face was a picture! *Yes,* Helga thought, *you've forgotten what it is to have the Abend about, not just acolytes whom you can cow and use as little more than slaves.* She gave him a shake as he dangled before her. "We are losing patience with you!" she snapped. "This is no simple bunch of sheep herders, waiting to be driven into compounds and used as slaves! If you want to help get the remaining pieces of Volla's armour back and go home in style, then you're going to have to *fight* for them. Really fight! ...If you can remember how to do that, that is? ...Or have you become soft living in your vills in the sun?" She gave him another shake at which he spluttered,

"Us? Soft? Never!"

"Good! Then you *will* think before you act again, and when you've proven that you can behave like one of the superior race, *then* we shall share our intelligence with you!"

And with that she dropped him, and turned on her heels to march into the circle of howdahs which the Abend had made into their private compound.

"Nicely done!" Laufrey said softly, falling into step with her as soon as she was within the circle, and its screening shield of Power which rendered them inaudible to any outside. "But what will you do when they find there is no intelligence?"

Helga made a rude noise. "Intelligence? They're the ones without any intelligence! What in Ama's name were they thinking letting the jaculi off like that? Did they think we'd just lined up the local rabbit population for their pets' consumption, like we'd had nothing better to do?"

Laufrey sniggered. "I see what you mean. And they have bred an awful lot of them, haven't they!"

Helga rolled her eyes in exasperation. "It defies the imagination as to why it's become the Sinuti fashion to wander around with a jaculus on your wrist for a pet! Who in their right mind would want that? The Lotus-forsaken beasts make a mess of everything they come into contact with, and they're of limited use as beasts of battle! Why in Volla's name did they not breed more tuatera if the conditions were right for lizards? If need be we could then at least have put some more slave drivers onto them!"

As the Abend were despairing over the logic of the Sinuti, the new arrivals were also fulminating over what they had found since landing.

"It's barely warm enough now!" a minor member of the Soullis fumed as he stroked a shivering jaculus perched on a gauntlet on his arm. "And this is their summer! Why would anyone want to live in a place like this? Remind me again why we came here?"

"Because the Abend have some of the missing pieces of the Great Volla's armour!" his father said waspishly. "Were you not listening? We get the other pieces too, get them back on board our ships and then, when we're in the deep ocean and the Abend and the acolytes are weak as kittens and lying in their own mess, we seize them! Then, my son, we can go back to Lochlainn with the Emperor's blessing and live in luxury, the kind of which even you cannot imagine!"

"Oh I don't know," he pouted, "I can imagine quite a lot!"

"Then you'd better put that lizard spawn of Esras down and start doing something about it!" his father commanded, and the young would-be Donn reluctantly put his pet into its basket of warmed sand and went to find his armour.

Within the Abend's camp Tancostyl was building into a fine rage very closely followed by Quintillean, Barrax and Eliavres. Nothing enraged a war-mage quicker than incompetence in their underlings, and the war-mages definitely regarded these Donns as that!

"We go in and we crush these accursed Islanders once and for all!" he fumed. "Send the beasts of battle in first! That should soften them up a bit! Then we end this once and for all!"

And for once all the other war-mages were in total agreement. So as the sun rose towards midmorning, the Donns were given their orders and the baffled DeÁine army actually obeyed.

Deep within the valley, the Island leaders had temporarily pulled their men once more back beyond the ridges once the beasts had also retreated. However, the respite had given them time to finish their manoeuvres, and the men were now deployed as per the original battle plan. It was just a matter now of waiting for the DeÁine to walk into the bottleneck.

"Here they come!" a keen-eyed scout with Maelbrigt and Warwick's force suddenly called. Everyone strained their eyes towards where he was pointing and saw that the grey mass in the distance was once more moving towards them. The signal was passed, and then they all hunkered down beneath their camouflage of leaves and bracken fronds to wait for the enemy's leaders to get beyond them. Brego had sent word that he wanted to see who they sent in first before he gave any order to engage. If the beasts of battle were at the fore, then he wanted the archers back at the head of the valley with all speed, for he would allow the beasts and their slaves to get almost to the point of spotting the dead-end. Then they could be shot down before they could do the defenders any damage. That, though, was their best option and the one all the leaders were praying for – to have the dreaded beasts at the front and the Abend at the back, so that they could deal with just the men in the middle before facing any arcane weapon the Abend might throw at them. It was not to be, for the Abend had changed their plans after the Sinut acolytes had started crying in pain at the destruction of the farliath.

"Soul Reaper take them!" Sionnachan cursed in concert with McKinley and those around him as the first figures became distinguishable. The DeÁine had sent in a whole wave of Seljuqs first, clearly expecting the Islanders to be daft enough to deploy their whole force to deal with them. Those Seljuqs would have to be dealt with, but they were not the priorities. Unfortunately those priorities were clustered together in the centre, for the marching acolytes were surrounded by the beasts of battle, and right at the heart of this force were figures who could only be the Abend. "Wait, men! Let the bastards go by! Wait until the Abend are beyond us! We'll come on them from behind if we can."

All the Islanders lay low and watched as the vast and exotic army tramped into the blind valley, discordant horns blaring and riders on tuatera banging pairs of great drums in unison to keep time. The Seljuqs were accompanied by far more of the slave masters than the younger knights and men had seen before. The Sinuti had had no battles or raids to deplete their stocks of the more trusted slaves. Nor were they short of the two kinds of beasts they rode upon. The gryphes must have been making the edentulous nervous, for they were making a strange wailing noise nobody had heard before, while within the ranks of the beast of battle, every now and then a kokatris or a gryph would rise into the air briefly. The scent of blood, albeit of the jaculi, was winding the animals up almost more than the men.

"Wait for it, wait for it!" Berengar echoed Sionnachan's order for his own men further along on the western slope. Esclados and a very taut Talorcan stood behind him. With Ivain on the opposite valley wall with Maelbrigt and the other Island Treasure wielders, Talorcan was experiencing pre-battle nerves of a kind totally new to him. He would have given anything to be over there with him, and yet he knew that with his DeÁine blood, he could prove more of a distraction there than a help.

Instead, he had given Tamàs strict instruction to watch Ivain's back, while he was helping stand guard over the box containing the Gorget and poor Sithfrey, who could do nothing to disguise the dreadful Gauntlet welded to his hand. Andra had his arm around his friend's shoulder as Sithfrey sat on the ground, his head resting on his arms which hugged his knees, so that he could not watch. If he could have he would have covered his ears too, but the weight of the Gauntlet made that too uncomfortable for anything but a few moments.

It was a desperate attempt on his behalf to try to avoid being tempted into using the Gauntlet, even though it would be for good rather than to aid the DeÁine. At some point he knew he would have to join in this fight, but not yet, he prayed, not yet. Any flow of Power was likely to bring one or more of the Abend tearing their way in a hurry, and if that happened Berengar was insistent that it would happen at their convenience, not the Abend's!

"Hold on, Sithfrey," Andra whispered encouragingly. "They're just marching at the moment, nothing more."

The earth was trembling under the hammering of so many nail-shod shoes as thousands of slaves tramped past them, and the noise of that alone muffled ordinary sounds more than either Sithfrey or Andra would have believed. Taise found it so jarring she stuffed her fingers in her ears, and crouched shivering beside Sithfrey in the hope that it would all end swiftly. Yet the Islanders' patience paid off, for nobody spotted those men already on the same side of the ridges as the slave Seljuqs.

At the far end of the valley, Brego saw the leading slaves come into view and signalled his archers into readiness, it would not be long now! And this time the plan was working! The Abend had passed Sionnachan and Maelbrigt's positions unheeded, and were pulling level with Berengar and Ruari, when finally orders began to be shouted from the DeÁine centre and they all began looking about them at the hillsides.

As soon as that happened, the archers from all the defenders began firing volleys, company by company, at any target they could see. The leaders had presumed that they would not have long to use this advantage before either the Donns broke up their forces, or the Abend used the acolytes to create some kind of defence, and were determined to make the best of it while they could. So waiting to make one unified volley was not an option, and the Attacotti, with their short hunting bows, were targeting the Seljuq outsiders, while the Order's longbows made use of their greater range and shot long barbed arrows deep into the Jundises ranks.

The heavy bows of the Prydein archers were enjoying particular success under Ivain and Swein's direction. These two were the only pair of Island Treasures operating at the moment, but Brego had his hand on Sooty just waiting for the Abend to come into the game. At that point he would link with Hugh, who was standing by with Fin and Vanadis back in Ergardia, and Hugh would begin scrying for them, maintaining the valuable overview of the battlefield which might just prove decisive.

However, the Abend almost immediately joined in in the most unexpected way. As the four war-mages focused on the greater force before them, it was Anarawd who sensed the Gauntlet and Sithfrey. Without waiting to consult any of the others, he seized the fourteen acolytes he was working with in a Power-link and dragged them with him into the surrounding Seljuqs and Jundises.

"It's up there!" he shrieked. "Get me to it!"

Yet he was wrong. Completely and utterly wrong! Sithfrey had unwittingly done something none of the Abend themselves could have achieved. His desire was so intense to direct the Abend away, so that his friends would not be in danger when he used the Gauntlet, that its defensive projection was manifesting on the opposite, eastern, side of the valley from where he and the Treasure lay. It was therefore towards an astonished Ruari that the Abend mage and his acolytes came storming.

"Flaming Trees! Who in the Underworld is this?" Commander Breca demanded of no-one in particular, as he directed his archers towards them. Like the other Abend down on the valley floor, by now Anarawd had a shield up covering his people from arrows, but its shimmering presence also made it hard for the defenders to see beyond it. However, Breca's question was answered as Anarawd raised his hand and directed a blast towards them. It struck their centre and blew Ealdorman Hereman apart, along with several of the lances surrounding him. Bloody fragments were all that was left of them, and with a savage roar the Islanders tore down the slope to engage them, rage and a desperate thirst for revenge powering them on.

It was the first engagement, and it brought more responses on its heels, not least the release of the gryphes and kokatrises. But for those on the Islander's left, the arrival of one of the Abend, and in such violent fashion, was the overriding concern. Their force immediately broke up, men scattering within moments in an ordered fashion to present smaller targets as they descended on the acolytes.

Yet from within the DeÁine force they also now drew a Jundis under the command of one of the Veroon. He had been furious to discover that the newest war-mage descended from his family's age old adversaries, the Monreux, and he had vowed to keep all the Abend under close scrutiny. So when he saw Anarawd heading off on his own he guessed, rightly, that there must be something of value to be gained.

In this Anarawd was both unfortunate and lucky. He was not anticipating one of the Donns to be on his heels quite so quickly – the Donns in Bruighean had become so used to both Anarawd and Calatin disappearing off on all sorts of weird missions that they would have ignored him. This was a complication which took him unawares, yet he was soon glad they were there, for he certainly had not realised quite how many of the cursed Knights were lurking in the undergrowth, and the Veroon Jundis was then a blessing for keeping so many of them occupied and away from him.

He pounded up the hillside, his whole being focused on the signals of the fabled Gauntlet – something he was sure he recognised now that he had had chance to use the Scabbard, and had become aware of the distinctive Power signals they created. Yet when he got to the spot he found nothing! Nothing except a big blonde Knight waiting with a crude sword, and it was pointing towards him!

For Ruari had spotted where Anarawd was heading and had signalled his men to sweep around the lone Abend and take out the Veroon Jundis. So as the majority of the Islanders plunged into their opponents, Ruari and a small group had shifted across until they were in line with Anarawd. The Knights and their men now rose out of the bracken and pounced on the acolytes, but Ruari swung his sword to flex his wrist and went on-guard face to face with Anarawd.

The Abend mage took one look at him and then laughed and drew in Power to blast this ridiculous man with. Yet Ruari knew instinctively from years of close quarter fighting what Anarawd had not worked out – they were now too close for Anarawd to use the Power, or at least the kind of blast he was preparing. The Abend of old always fought from a distance and inside the protecting ranks of acolytes, never one to one, and Anarawd completely misjudged the situation in his ignorance. Before Anarawd could even let fly, Ruari lunged in, feinted high at Anarawd's arm and then hit low in a compound attack. Ironically, it was the Scabbard which saved the mage, for it was strapped to his side, not quite as low as if it was being used to carry a sword in, but still low enough for the bottom of it to deflect Ruari's cut.

Ruari felt his sword bounce off it, and the strange currents which swirled around him in the air in the seconds afterwards. He knew that sensation! Those horrendous days he had spent carrying the Gorget to safety from Brychan to Ergardia came back to him in a flash, and he knew what he was facing. Which was rather more than Anarawd did. The DeÁine mage blinked as his Power-fire ball materialised three feet out from his hand, shot off into the distance and exploded in the air without doing anything any harm, then he shrugged.

No matter, he had once been the acknowledged duelling champion amongst those of the same generation as himself, back in the days before his Power had manifested and he had been taken into the acolytes. He therefore had no doubt that he could deal with this inferior swordsman. Immaculate Temples! Just look at the man! That was no way to come on-guard! And he drew his sword and dropped into the classic opening pose, from where he made the three preliminary grace-cuts, fluid sweeps of the blade the timing of which soon let any sort of dueller know what kind of blade-master you were facing.

Just beyond his blade, Ruari watched the fancy twirling begin in disbelief. What in the Islands was that all about? But if the idiot was going to leave him an opening like that he was not going to wait for him to finish before he took advantage. As Anarawd made the mistake of dropping his sword's point as he went into 'heron on the steps' – where he swung the blade down in an arc as he high-stepped forwards, then swept the blade back over in another arc to face forwards just as his front foot landed –

Ruari struck. He hacked at Anarawd's exposed free arm with a controlled sideways cut, then redoubled into a lunge, where his point took the mage under the ribs without ever making contact with the opposing blade. Leaping backwards, he still had time to parry the continuing clumsy cut Anarawd made, as the Abend's body's pain forced him to recognise the assault. The high step had turned into a tottering stumble and he gasped at the effrontery of this peasant. To attack while he was still in the opening moves! And it was not a mistake either, because the savage, shaggy dog was snarling at him and already coming back in on the attack again.

To his horror, Anarawd found all his duelling skills little better than worthless in the face of Ruari's years of experience of fighting in every kind of rough skirmish, and in battles large and small. The Knight gave no ground, signalling an attack one way and then cutting or impaling with another, or bludgeoning his way under Anarawd's guard on those times when feints did not work. The DeÁine had the advantage of height and strength, and a few times he managed to get in a few attacks of his own. However, all he managed were a few cuts, and nothing which caused real damage to this horrendous opponent who would not leave him be or cede an inch of ground, but kept up the assault.

And Anarawd was also no Hunter. No cocktail of drugs numbed his senses to the pain of the multiple cuts and stabs Ruari was inflicting on him, some mortally deep, and he lacked the war-mage's ability to fall into a red mist of rage where all became oblivion except for the burning need to fight. The loss of blood was taking its toll on him too, with his robes now becoming soaked in his own precious life-force, and in a blinding flash of memory he recalled that the last time he had been like this had been on the surgeon's tables in the Houses of the Holy. Then, the strange machines had saved him by pumping blood back into him, but they were far, far away, and it belatedly occurred to him, as Ruari lunged in and plunged his sword once more into Anarawd's guts, that he was dying.

Something skittering on the edge of his consciousness was whispering to him to embrace the Power. A half-heard promise of immortality in a voice which sounded faintly reminiscent of Othinn, and yet not at the same time. But the waves of pain which were making him shudder made him incapable of sufficiently clear thoughts to even begin to reach out, let alone embrace, anything so intangible. And when Ruari stepped in to administer the killing blow, all Anarawd could do was kneel on the Island dirt and watch that crude, oversized butcher's knife of a blade come at his chest. As

Ruari shoved his sword in up to the hilt, Anarawd's dying thought was a wish that the blow could at least have been made by a finely decorated rapier and somewhere warmer.

He keeled over, folding up so that he dropped to his knees with his head then dropping to the earth, so that he almost looked like he was praying. For an instant there was stillness, then a breeze seemed to break loose from within the folded corpse and lifted up to dissipate on the stronger gusts rolling in from the sea. From down in the Abend camp, even over the incredible din of battle, Ruari heard several eldritch howls go up, and guessed that the other Abend had felt their companion die.

"Pay the price! Feel the fear!" he snarled with savage glee, hacking the Scabbard off Anarawd and looping it loosely onto his own sword-belt. Then wrapping a kerchief tight around a cut on his leg, he wiped his sword on the dead Abend's back and went to find others to wreak havoc upon.

Amongst the Abend, Quintillean had felt Anarawd's departure rather than saw it, for at the time he was too busy picking out targets for his own lightning bolts of Power. The trouble was that it was so cursed hard to see where the Temples-forsaken Islanders were! Just when he was sure he had spotted a clump of them, he would blast that section of hillside and find that all he had vaporised was a mere one or two and a lot of dead plants! He knew when he had hit a good number because of the way their essence ricocheted back along the Power and fed him. It was the way a good war-mage kept going in battle, using the essences from the fallen to replace what had been expended. Now, though, he knew he was not doing as well as he should, because he was using more than he was gaining. In blind rage, he threw a blast randomly higher up the high valley wall and got a most unexpected reward. As his bolt almost connected, an opposing summoning of Power appeared out of nowhere and formed a shield into which his bolt exploded and shattered, without harvesting so much as a mouse's soul. It was the Gauntlet!

With a roar of Power-enhanced fury, he turned and stormed through the DeÁine ranks by virtue of sucking dry anyone who got in his way. Slave after slave turned to dust in an escalated version of the life draining normally done, until he was on the edge of their army. A Donn of the Komanchii spotted him, and wheeled his Jundis to follow in the war-mage's wake as he stormed onwards and headed up hill. Here it showed that the Islanders knew their terrain. As the men-at-arms and Knights deployed at the sight of the coming Jundis, now with another already on their heels and driving several Seljuqs ahead of them, the slope proved a sore trial for the attackers. The verdant hillside, lush with new grass, gave little purchase underfoot to those scrambling upwards, while those of the Order coming down needed to do little more than slide, and at speed, into them.

This engagement was closer to Sionnachan's men than the centre of Berengar's line, but the new Brychan Grand Master guessed what this war-mage was after.

"Jonas, with me!" he bellowed. "Stefan! Hold the line for me!"

Then ran with all his might south along the ridge towards where he knew Sithfrey, Taise and the DeÁine Treasures were. Jonas' men pounded into the DeÁine Seljuqs and tore them to shreds, battering their way deeper and deeper into the enemy line, even as they fought to ensure they did not slip lower down the slope. Suddenly he saw a flash of bright blue-white light, and a ball of Power-fire took out a cluster of Jundis veterans not far ahead of him. He glance up to his right and saw Taise standing close to Sithfrey with her hand outstretched, even as Talorcan and three of his lance hacked down any of the DeÁine who got close to them. The elegant lady looked like she might be sick over what she had just done, but Berengar prayed she could repeat that performance.

Chopping at the neck of a flat-faced veteran in a kokatris-shaped helmet, Berengar shouldered him aside and headed for them. He had just gutted another from the same DeÁine troop to emerge into the circle of dead which surrounded Talorcan's lance, when another figure burst out of the seething mass of fighting. In a blaze of burnished red armour, the head of the Abend emerged, and gave a vulpine lick of his lips as he took two strides towards where Sithfrey stood, hand up displaying the Gauntlet. The DeÁine scholar tried to form a defensive shield, but at this close range he was no match for Quintillean, whose counterblow bowled Sithfrey off his feet, and threw him back several yards to lie winded amongst the heather. Yet it was a mistake, for Sithfrey was now that much further away and another figure suddenly hammered into Quintillean, knocking him sideways.

Berengar saw Sithfrey go flying and Talorcan diving in to tackle Quintillean. He got to the tangled pair before Barcwith did, gesturing him back to Taise and Sithfrey, and then drew his long knife to join them. Quintillean's massive DeÁine strength was a huge advantage over the two Knights. Every blow he landed was far greater than any a normal man could have delivered, and Berengar arrived just in time as Talorcan's knife clattered useless from his hand as a punch from Quintillean's mailed fist numbed the whole of his arm. Berengar drove his knife into the folds of Quintillean's cloak in the hope of hitting a vital organ. Instead, the knife slithered harmlessly along the polished armour without finding a single chink to exploit, and Berengar only succeeded in throwing Quintillean off-balance, as he too tried to recover to a fighting position.

The big Abend leader swung his arm backwards with a snarl, and now it was Berengar's turn to feel the power of that fist as he received a winding punch in the gut. His breastplate should have stopped it altogether, but the DeÁine put a dent in the plate and shoved the whole thing back into Berengar's middle. As he gasped frantically for breath, Talorcan rose from the ground and resumed his attack.

Like a pair of terriers baiting a bull, the two Knights hung onto Quintillean and tried like mad to inflict some kind of fatal wound on him. By now they were oblivious to what was going on around them. Their worlds had condensed to a few square feet of rapidly churning earth which they slithered and grunted across. For the war-mage it was infuriating beyond words. He had rarely had to fight one to one with anyone, and as such his technique was hopelessly outmanoeuvred by the Knights' time and again. They were too close for him to use the Power on, and only his physical strength was keeping them at bay.

Yet there was the great Lord Volla's Gauntlet in clear sight! One of the Lotus-forsaken pieces he had endured the last five hundred years paying for the loss of! His fury lent him strength and he shook off both the Knights in a superhuman burst, then swept forwards with the Power to connect with the Gauntlet. At that moment he instantly knew that the Gorget was there too! Both of them! There and waiting for him to claim them! His objectives had finally come within his grasp! Both hands came up and he stretched out one to each of the Treasures, and screamed in triumph as he connected with both.

Berengar and Talorcan staggered to their feet in time to see Sithfrey wrenched off his feet as if a huge invisible hand had him by his Gauntleted arm, and the box containing the Gorget explode into fragments. Their eyes met and together they leapt forwards to break the two streams of Power. If ever their DeÁine blood was to count for anything it was now!

Berengar found himself struggling to breathe as the force hit him mid-chest, yet it also held him there. If he had had any more breath to lose, the realisation that the Power stream running through him meant that he could see deep into Quintillean would have taken it. The malice and evil which roiled around inside the ancient Abend was of a magnitude beyond anything he could have found words for. But Berengar also saw the weakness there. An absolute selfishness which would never see any advantage in acting with or for someone else, and he made a gamble.

"You can't have both!" he wheezed. "What will the other Abend say?"

It was not much but it did make the Power waver just a little. Enough for Berengar to shift himself sideways a bit, and then suddenly he was able to move again as he felt Sithfrey join him along the Power, shoving back at Quintillean with all his might. Yet instead of saving himself, which was what Quintillean would have expected, Berengar went on the attack again, grabbing a dropped knife from off the ground and making a series of blindingly fast cuts at Quintillean's exposed face. The war-mage broke all contact, as Berengar then jammed the knife upwards under a joint at the shoulder of the red armour, Berengar and Sithfrey both finding themselves being hurled backwards with the force of the Powered repulsion.

Talorcan had fared less well. He had no Sithfrey holding the Gorget into whose line of Power he had leapt. Instead he felt raw, unrefined Power tearing through his heart. Baring his teeth in a rictus grin he began hauling himself along the Power towards Quintillean like a man impaled on a long spear – knowing it would cost his life, but fuelled by courage to make it count. As soon as Berengar distracted the war-mage with the blade swipes at his face, Talorcan hauled himself faster down the invisible line, and raised the long knife he had retrieved as he lunged to stab at Quintillean's neck.

The point slipped, twisted, then sank into a different joint in the plating to the one he had been aiming for. No matter! All he cared about at this moment was taking down this bastard Abend for good. He used all his strength to twist the knife and felt the Power suddenly cut off, as Quintillean seized him by the throat and lifted him off the ground.

As if the world's time had suddenly slowed, he saw the next moments as if at half their natural speed. Berengar was struggling to his feet but too far away to aid him. As Quintillean held him aloft with his left hand he created a blade of sheer Power in his right, and turned to face Talorcan with a manic ferocity. An arrow thudded into the war-mage and then another, and Talorcan recognised Decke's distinctive fletchings on them, even if he could not turn his head to see who of his lance was firing. Quintillean's blade arm came back and then drove towards Talorcan's side. The young

Knight blinked, and then unexpectedly found himself falling as he heard more than saw someone else.

"You shall not have my *son*!" an older, deeper voice bellowed, even as a great spray of blood flew into Talorcan's eyes, blinding him.

Quintillean felt the Power rip back into him in agonising fragments. There it was again! That dreadful strange element which had destroyed their ritual in Kuzmin! There was blood. It should have fed him! It did not! Why? He reeled backwards as more of the arrows embedded themselves in his armour, none sinking very deeply, but every one of the sharp iron heads cutting into his flesh. Like a huge and angry hedgehog, he shook himself free of the dreadful person causing him so much pain and turned, only to lose his footing and go tumbling down the hill through a gap left as the rest of the fighting moved onwards.

"Esclados!" Berengar howled, as he saw the Abend's power-blade take off his friend's arm and slice deeply into his side.

The old Knight sank to the ground bathed in his own blood, at which point they all saw that the Power-knife had sliced open part of his gut too. Talorcan gave a sob of rage and despair. This was not right! Never, ever had he dreamt that his father would be willing to lay down his life for him, and now the one thing he wished was that he could go back and change the short time they had had together. In a frantic scramble he made it to Esclados' side and grabbed his remaining hand.

"So proud of you, my boy! Even though I have no right to be," Esclados whispered softly.

"You have *every* right!" Talorcan choked back.

"So glad I found you at the last!" It was almost inaudible and then Esclados' eyes closed.

"*Noooo*!" screamed Talorcan, as Berengar joined him to cradle Esclados' head. And the shadows of the others joining them formed a circle around a small patch of sunlight illuminating the spreading, liquid red covering the old Knight.

Across the valley, Ivain and Swein saw the skirmish around the spot where they knew Sithfrey and Taise were, and when Talorcan was impaled upon Quintillean's sending of Power, Eric and Dylan became frantic. There was no way that Ivain could miss that something had happened to Talorcan – Eric's feelings and sensations were being fed back right into his soul!

"Quintillean has Talorcan and Berengar!" he yelled to Maelbrigt, who was standing off to one side and a little behind him to allow the Prydein archers room to move. Maelbrigt had already felt something dreadful happen, but without knowing specifically what.

"Guthlaf! Hrethel! Advance!" Maelbrigt called to the commanders of the nearest Celidon men, and signalled the Prydein archers to close on their enemy, then ran to join Eadgar and his coterie, who had already taken their place at the front of the Island Treasure-holders' ranks.

Maybe it was the strands of Power bouncing about alerting the Abend, they never quite found out, but the minute Ivain and Swein really began to draw on the power of their respective weapons, they found themselves drawing the beasts of battle like flies to jam. The first time a kokatris rose into the air before him, Ivain thought he would soil himself. It was the most abhorrent thing he had ever seen! Its head was the size of a big dog's but shaped as a cockerel, complete with comb and wattles of bright red but covered in scales, not feathers. Its puny wings were beating furiously to raise it into the air while it hissed furiously at him, serpentine tail lashing about it. Its beady eyes were inflamed, and the wickedly sharp beak snapped reflexively every time it tried to dart in, while the taloned claws scrabbled wildly at the air trying to reach him. And the stench from it!

What jolted him out of his petrified state was the sudden realisation that it was aiming at Eric, not him, although the squint was being well protected by several burly men-at-arms who had formed a shield wall around him.

"Bring them down!" Ivain roared in fury, and saw Swein lift the Arrow aloft and aim it at a kokatris batting its wings not far in front of him. Ivain himself aimed at another and heard Swein yelling with all his might,

"Take aim!"

Ivain counted to three and then bellowed, "Fire!"

As one a thousand arrows rose into the air and headed for clusters of kokatrises, for both the Prydein archers of the first cadre around Ivain and Swein, and the second, had heard them through some devising of the squints. The great bows sang again and another massive volley took flight, goose feathers whistling ear-piercingly in the air as they streaked in unison towards their prey. As the heavy bodies of the kokatrises began to fall to the ground with thuds, Ivain and Swein halted their men and fired a third volley. Yet this brought others of the fell beasts to them. For as the kokatrises died, the DeÁine sent their jaculi to try and distract the dreaded archers.

However the knights' hawks now had a real advantage. They knew instinctively not to feed on the jaculi they had brought down earlier, and so, avoiding the toxic corpses, they had climbed high into the air and rode the thermals in relaxed, gliding, circles until called upon once more by the Knights' whistles. Down they now swooped, seizing the jaculi in their strong talons or breaking their necks with their beaks. And still the kokatrises died, impaled with arrows like cockerels skewered ready for the spit. In a desperate effort to save their beloved lizards, the highborn Sinuti prevailed upon the witches to summon crows, rooks and ravens to drive off the hawks. Yet, in such an empty countryside as Rathlin had become, there were not that many of any of these birds. A few of the smaller buzzards found themselves performing aerial acrobatics with black scavenger birds snapping at their tail feathers, but the bigger hawks like the red kites were too big for even a raven to bother much.

Then suddenly there were no more kokatrises. In ten guided volleys led from the Bow and Arrow they had all been brought down, although the threat was far from over. Prowling up the valley side came the gryphes. Feathered on top and furred beneath, they stalked their prey on feline paws, thick muscular legs ready to administer a fatal blow, or for the predatory beaks to rip and shred.

"What was it with these people that they had such an obsession with fighting birds?" Cwen exclaimed in dismay to Matti.

The two of them were following the others at a more sedate pace, for as yet there was little either of them could do. The Islanders had only just begun to really engage with the main DeÁine force, and Brego and Hugh had decided that the best use of the Shield and Spear would be to get behind the DeÁine army. There they could harass the DeÁine rearguard, or cut down any who tried to flee the battle. But neither of the old leaders wanted to move them too far too soon. It might just be that they would need such defensive weapons if the DeÁine got the upper hand. It made them feel pretty useless, but neither Cwen nor Matti had any battle experience from which to argue otherwise.

Even more displeased was Arthur, who, with some of his cadre of other boys, had been encircled by the men whom Maelbrigt had guarding the two women's squints. Others of the boys were with Ivain and Swein, but Maelbrigt had known that Brego was reluctant to bring Matti and Cwen into the fight more than necessary and so had put Arthur with Daisy and Moss in a last valiant hope that it would curb the lad's ability to get into the fight.

"I can't do nuffin' stuck back here!" the small boy fumed, and someone much older within him stoked the fires of his frustration.

Warwick and his Foresters were now engaged in a vicious fight with the gryphes further down the slope, and to their right Ruari's men were also in the thick of fighting with the Donns' men. Meanwhile, Cwen, Arthur and Matti could just about see the far end of the valley where Brego had now marched his men down, and had all but destroyed the leading slave Seljuqs. Soon the long column of the DeÁine army would be surrounded by a huge elongated horseshoe of Islanders. They were taking casualties, although nothing disastrous so far, yet from his vantage point far away in Ergardia, Hugh could see that their greatest trial was still to come, as the outer slave Seljuqs gave way to the veteran Jundises and they got that bit closer to the Abend and their acolytes. Moreover, in terms of numbers, the vast bulk of this huge DeÁine army was still unscathed and had yet to be deployed in earnest. The Islanders had got nowhere nearing winning yet, and that was starkly illustrated by a sudden and unexpected appearance on the southern valley wall.

Barrax and Eliavres had just that bit more control than Quintillean and Tancostyl in the field – less sheer power in their drawings, but less of the blind battle-rage too. Both had felt the sudden ripping asunder of Anarawd's death on the Power and had paused to try and locate what had gone so very wrong. As Quintillean had gone steaming off up the northern valley side, Barrax had reined in his fury and gone questing on the Power until he discovered the sense of the Scabbard, and the strange emanations of the north-man who was carrying it.

Ruari had rejoined his men, yet as overall leader was forced to remain a little back from them if he was to keep any sort of perspective on how they were doing. He could see Eremon doing a sterling job of leading in Hereman's place, and Thorold and Piran were directing their men with all their veteran competence. Even the recently promoted Instone was doing well, while Breca had the men immediately in front of Ruari formed up and methodically working their way forwards. So the only slight gap in their long fighting front was a small patch further along the left flank where Warwick's men had got a little ahead of his. It was not much of a gap, and Ruari could hardly believe his bad luck when a blast of Power widened it. The Foresters who had survived on the flank of the force, immediately turned and began throwing up wards and charms for all they were worth, yet through the smoking blood strode a tall pale figure who deflected everything they threw at him.

"Sweet Rowan! Not two bloody Abend in one day!" Ruari groaned and prepared to fight once more. He was only too aware that this Abend was wearing the flaming scarlet armour of a full war-mage, and knew too that he had got off lightly the last time, because the only male Abend without such armour had to have been Anarawd, and he had never been known as a fighter. This one, though, looked like he was only too aware of what a proper sword fight was like. *He's never going to fall for any ruse or compound attack*, Ruari mentally sighed, *I'm going to take a real beating here!*

Yet Barrax was different to Anarawd in other ways too. He had no intention of indulging in the egotistic folly of fighting one to one with any Islander. That was just a waste of time when he could accomplish so much more with the Power. He was here for one thing and one thing only – the Scabbard! With a blast of Power he knocked Ruari out and ripped the Scabbard from off his belt. It flew through the air to Barrax's waiting hand like iron-fillings drawn to a magnet, and the war-mage turned on his heels and strode back towards the centre of the DeÁine army while the Foresters' warded arrows bounced off his personal, shimmering shield of Power without doing him any harm at all.

"May you be blessed on the Paths of Purity!" Magda sighed thankfully, as he strode back into their midst. "Such idiocy on Anarawd's behalf! He never could be trusted. You, poppet, are so much better! So much more the proper war-mage!"

Masanae, on the other hand, was less than delighted at Quintillean's reappearance when he staggered back into their lines. She could instantly sense that he was wounded, and all for what? He had not got either the Gorget or the Gauntlet, and there were Barrax, Eliavres and Magda looking so smug with the Scabbard. It was intolerable! Especially when Barrax swiftly went to rejoin Tancostyl and began hammering at the cursed Islanders, using the Scabbard in consort with the Helm to deadly effect. Just at this moment Masanae decided she would happily see Quintillean dead and a new war-mage elevated to their ranks if he could be as useful as Barrax, and not a thorn in her side like Quintillean.

That was very different to how Cwen and Matti were feeling. Cwen knew that Berengar was hurt but still lived because of the affinity Daisy had been able to form with Berengar once he had used the Gorget. Matti, however, had no such reassurances over Ruari. She saw him being blasted by Barrax and go down, but his northern blood rendered him invisible to Moss in the Power. For the briefest instant she had a view along the ridge to see him lying motionless before the fighting between them obscured him from her once more.

"*Nooo!*" she wept. "Oh Ruari, no!" grabbing the rim of the Shield in her horror-stricken state. The Shield and Moss echoed her wishes and suddenly the Shield flamed into life like never before. Matti did not even see or really formulate her thoughts, it just came from her heart, the desire to protect Ruari from being hacked to bits, even if he was dead already. Yet at the leading edge of the Island forces there suddenly appeared a glowing barrier which stretched along a line of hundreds of men, who suddenly found that they could attack out from it, but that the astonished Jundis they had just encountered could make no strike which would penetrate it. As her grief took a stronger hold on her the glowing barrier wavered until Arthur ran up to her and grabbed the edge of her tunic, shaking her.

"No, you gotta stay angry!" he shouted at her, forcing her to see what she had done, and with grim realisation she fought back her tears and focused with all her heart on the thing she wanted most – to drive these monsters back and away from all the people she loved.

# Chapter 17

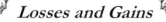

## *Losses and Gains*

### Rathlin: Grian-mhor

With something wavering between fury and exasperation, Masanae summoned two of the most gifted healers to her and Quintillean. Yet as the acolytes tried ever harder to heal the arrow piercings and knife cuts, the worse they seemed to make things.

"Great Dragon of Death, Quintillean! What having you been doing?" she growled through clenched teeth, as she herself tried to find a way of healing at least the worst of his wounds. Every time she aimed the Power at him it skittered around like a ball on polished glass. And where it did come into contact with one of the weeping gashes it smoked, sparked, and burned the flesh around it.

"Stop!" he commanded angrily, his face twisted in pain.

"I shall have to! ...And *you* will have to manage as you *are*!" she riposted angrily. "I should be doing other things this day than acting as your healer!"

She turned on her heels and stamped off, exchanging rolled-eyed glances with Magda, who was also scowling at Quintillean in between directing acolytes. It could have been worse, though, she kept telling herself. If this was all the troops the Islanders could field, then with the overwhelming numbers on their side there was little danger of losing. Admittedly they had lost Anarawd far too easily, but then he had always had that stupid streak in him. No doubt he had gone haring off on some foolish quest of his own – as ever! A new recruit might, like Barrax, turn out to be far more useful.

She cast about her on the Power and then jumped at the feel of something up at the far end of the valley. That was not normal Islander! Someone was using the Power! And it felt like one of those cursed others who had caused them so much grief in the distant past. But that could not possibly be right. All of them had died before the DeÁine had even been summoned home by a furious Emperor, let alone been sent on the Exile. So how had this happened? She prodded at it again. It was a very small sending she now realised, and it was doing nothing but watching. Well let whoever it was watch! They could have a ringside seat to see their fellow countrymen annihilated! And then, when she had time, she would take the weaving apart and teach them a lesson they would remember in the hereafter – if these base creatures even believed in such a thing.

She swept her Power-gaze around the valley. No there were not so very many of them. Then something at the edge of her senses caught her attention. There were ships on the horizon! She quested towards them and felt a laugh bubble up inside her. So the rest of the Souk'ir in New Lochlainn had followed the Tabor and the Dracma! Yes, that was the Chowlai flagship at the fore – who could forget that figurehead? And unless she was very mistaken there were Indiera, Bernien and Inchoo flags flying from other masts too. She spotted the Islanders trying to come around behind them in the valley and laughed again. Let the Islanders try! All that would achieve was them getting trapped between the force she was with and the Souk'ir coming in to land. So maybe today would not be such a disaster – especially if it freed her forever from Quintillean's grasp at the same time.

At the far-right and far-left of the Islanders' force, Sionnachan and Maelbrigt respectively were also about to receive a nasty shock. Magnus' men had taken to the hills and come around the battleground in order to be able to move towards the DeÁine ships. This had now put them well beyond the fighting and they were regrouping, ready to swarm down onto the few men left guarding those ships not already emptied and those out at anchor in the bay. Suddenly Maelbrigt and Sionnachan saw a few of Magnus' men coming haring back towards them gesturing wildly.

"What in the Islands can it be now?" Maelbrigt sighed to Eadgar, as the man far away jumped up and down and gestured furiously towards the coast. Then they saw them – more DeÁine ships!

"Oh sweet Rowan!" Raethun groaned. "Not more!"

"No time to hold back now," Maelbrigt told his four guards grimly. "We must engage with all the Treasures." Which really meant him with the Celidon Foresters, since Matti and Cwen were now trying to do what they could with the Spear and the Shield, although Matti's initial burst of passion had died away and she was once more trying to summon the fire needed to get the Shield to project itself quite so forcefully.

He took a moment to breathe deeply and focus within himself while Eadgar bellowed his orders to the rest on his behalf. Then, beginning to swing the mighty sword in a rhythmic arc, he advanced, senses at the stretch. His Foresters were with him to a man, coming into step with him and chanting softly, but with a steady rhythm, the shortened battle prayer. It was a very risky ploy, for Maelbrigt and Sionnachan had gone over and over how best to use the Sword, and the only really new tactic they could come up with was for all the men to strike in time with Maelbrigt's cuts. This meant that they had to be in time with one another, and that timing was determined by how fast Maelbrigt could move the weight of the Sword, which was nothing like as fast as a normal sword. This would mean that the Foresters would be awfully vulnerable to faster attacks by the DeÁine, for if they were to stay in time with Maelbrigt, they would not be able to stop to parry incoming blows. Everyone of the Foresters had been warned of the immense risk they were taking, for Maelbrigt would not countenance taking any but volunteers with him, yet not one man had taken up the offer to fight elsewhere in the lines.

They reached the men at the rear right of the DeÁine army and the sight, close to, of the lizard-helmed Jundis suddenly ignited a deep anger within Maelbrigt.

*Take our homes, would you?* he thought more than spoke, for it took all his breath to keep up the swings. *Kill our people? ...No! ...No more! ...You* ...he took another mighty pass, *...shall not* ... the tip of the Sword connected with something and severed it without halting a jot, *...get past* ... a Jundis soldier crumpled at his feet *...me!* A head went flying as the Sword severed it with something other than brute force, since the head came off a good foot beyond the Sword's edge. *...Go ...BACK..!* he thought, now finding it almost impossible to walk forward at any sort of brisk pace. He was vaguely aware of Raethun diving in at his feet and castrating a burly DeÁine who had tried to get to him with an upward cut. The DeÁine fell, and Maelbrigt was forced to step on him as he continued in his path down the valley side, and onto its floor.

On the other side Sionnachan saw Maelbrigt begin to move, and then realised why, as a man came tearing up to him with word of what the southernmost men had seen out in the bay. The DeÁine army had kept marching, slowly but inexorably, towards where Brego had the regular Order engaged at the front of the DeÁine, and now the rearmost ranks were coming up to Sionnachan's position. Despite the skirmishes, Sionnachan had been trying to wait to fully engage until the trailing end of the DeÁine army had passed him, to enable them to fully encircle their enemy. Now, though, he realised why Maelbrigt was moving. Even if they encircled these DeÁine, they would only be caught by the others coming up from the beachhead. Better to plough in now and cause some real damage while they could.

He turned and signalled to a watching man and heard the signal being passed. Once more the pipers took up their instruments, and the hills echoed to the drones and grace notes of the pipes. This was no mere cosmetic accompaniment, nor an effort to put heart into wavering troops with jingoistic songs. With the Foresters being the farthest from Brego they were signalling, by what tune they played, a change in plan. Brego would hear it and know that they had seen another threat. He hoped Maelbrigt's Squint had told Sooty, but he still did not trust any of the ancients to turn up and take the time to translate back to normal speech for the black squint.

As the Ergardian sept of Foresters rose from amongst the heather and bracken, and marched purposefully towards the DeÁine, swords and spears glinting, and plaids swinging, Brego heard the pipes.

"A new threat?" he exclaimed in disbelief to Dana, then caught hold of Sooty's paw where the squint rode beside him in his litter. "Was that what you were just trying to tell me? ...Then I must speak to Hugh!"

A moment later the swirl of smoky cloud appeared and then Hugh's face.

"We need you to scry for us!" Brego wasted no time with preambles. "On the coast! What's new? What's Sionnachan signalling 'new danger' to me for?"

Baderon of Sligo was leading the men down on the battlefield on Brego's behalf at the moment, along with the Ergardian ealdormen, but Brego still had men he had not fully engaged with the enemy as yet. He wanted the DeÁine over confident. Not as over confident as they would be now, though, he realised when Hugh looked up from the scrying bowl with his face pale.

"More ships," Hugh said firmly, but with eyes that showed dismay. "They appear to be flying the flags of the Souk'ir."

"Bastard Hounds of the Wild Hunt!" Brego swore, turning in his saddle. "Sound the advance! For everyone!"

The Islanders started to surge forward, but so did the DeÁine.

"Great Maker rot them! They think they've won already!" Brego fumed and loosened his own sword in its scabbard. It was that briefest of delays before he clapped his heels into his destrier's sides which allowed Hugh the chance to suddenly call out,

"No, Brego! Wait!"

Brego spun to the cloud-rimmed circle. "What?"

"There's something wrong! Out there! At sea! ...Sacred Trees! ...They're attacking the DeÁine ships!"

"Come again?" Brego snapped. "Who's attacking the DeÁine ships?"

"The new ships!" Hugh chortled. "Oh my...! The DeÁine flags are coming down! ...Blessed Rowan! They're hoisting makeshift Island flags showing the Rowan! ...They're with us, Brego! Whoever they are they're with *us*!" Then Hugh flickered out of sight before coming back. "Vanadis is going to show me how to get closer to them! I'll be back as soon as possible!" and he was gone.

"Keep the men going!" Brego ordered. "We must let them think we've been panicked by this arrival!"

Out at sea, Will stood on the deck of the flagship and watched with satisfaction as the slaves streamed on board the few manned DeÁine ships and exacted a dreadful revenge for their fate. He had never expected to have much control of these men, and so the best thing had seemed to be to let them be in the leading ships.

Ever since Sioncaet had tottered grey-faced into his cabin, and told him they must take their ships to southern Rathlin, he had been planning this with the ealdormen. They had been well on the way here anyway, but had been wondering where best to land. Even so, had it not been Sioncaet who had told him of the voice in his head telling him to make all haste to Vulinn, he might have questioned it harder. If anyone was going to have the ability to sense the intentions of a malevolent wraith, Will trusted it would be Sioncaet.

Yet he was also now very worried for the small DeÁine minstrel, and had him resting in the luxurious captain's cabin with someone with him at all times. He had been so intense in his insistence that they come this way that Will had been fearful that the Abend had finally found a way to get inside Sioncaet's head, just as had nearly happened to him with Tancostyl. It was only when Sioncaet had become outright frantic, that Will had relented and set sail on the new heading. Then had felt less worried about the source of this information when the sender – whoever it was who was manipulating Sioncaet – calmed down once the ships were moving in the right direction, although his concern for Sioncaet had not abated.

Sometimes it was as though it was not even Sioncaet speaking the words coming out of his mouth. The intonation and use of words were somehow terribly wrong. Even worse, poor Sioncaet himself was becoming increasingly terrified of the voice in his head during his more lucid moments. And if what he was relaying had not been making such sense and proving so accurate, Will would have had Sioncaet heavily sedated for his own good, for he desperately wanted to get his friend to a Forester – Maelbrigt ideally, but anyone half competent with the arcane would have eased his fears.

Now, though, he had rather more immediate and pressing issues to deal with. The vast DeÁine army had very clearly landed already, and from the echoing notes of the pipers drifting down to them, the Island army, however much of it there was, had engaged them.

"Make the signal," he said to Heledd, who was standing behind him with a bundle of flags in her hands, the sisters having insisted that they be allowed to do something useful. A stream of different coloured flags, bunched into groups, ran up a line along the foremast to where they were visible to the other ships. Each company had their own colours, and this was the order in which Will wanted them to engage. It was a simple system and allowed each group to know who was supposed to be in front of them and who behind. Not that a signal was going to make any difference to the two huge ships which the main numbers of slaves were concentrated in. They had already gone inshore to come between the anchored DeÁine ships, had wreaked mayhem amongst the few on board, and had now for the most part swung back on board their original ships with ropes in time to be there when the two ships ground against the makeshift landing stages.

None of the slaves bothered waiting for gangplanks to be run out, they simply swung over the side and swarmed down ropes, or swam ashore. Like a plague of locusts, they swarmed inland and headed for the DeÁine army. In their second wave came Jacinto, heartily glad to be accompanied by Kym and his lance – they seemed to be the only sane people in this seething, enraged crowd! Thank the Trees he had had chance to recover some of his old strength, he vaguely thought, as he forced himself to run as fast as he could to keep up. The old Jacinto would have been in the fore, now he was in the rear, but at least he was not left puffing on the deserted beach like lost baggage. Were Berengar and Esclados here? He blinked the sweat out of his eyes as the midday sun shone in a gloriously clear summer sky and baked them all, then blinked again. Who was *that* up ahead?

To the rear of the DeÁine army had come Barrax, striding through the ranks as his heightened awareness sensed Maelbrigt using the Sword. What was that? He could feel it using the Power, but in a way he had never come across before. Whatever, or whoever, it was, they were doing some serious damage to the troops at the rear, and like the good war-mage that he was, Barrax hated any kind of defeat. This was what he had been born for, he now realised. His blood seemed to be singing in his veins with all the Power he was pulling in through the Scabbard. He had never felt so alive or so invincible! There was no way that this bunch of miserable rebels could win, but while it felt so good to be hurling bolts of Power around, he was more than happy for them to fight to the death, rather than them putting down their weapons and going meekly into slavery.

Quivering with energy, he strode to the rearmost Seljuqs and saw a strange sight. Whose were all these slaves? They were an unruly rabble!

"Mother Seagang!" he swore, as his accompanying acolytes scurried frantically in his wake. "I shall make it my personal pleasure to thrash these Souk'ir afterwards! That's no way to train a Seljuq!"

Then an acolyte behind him bravely wheezed, "Maybe they're throwing raw recruits at the Islanders, oh Great One? They were off on expeditions after all!"

Barrax sniffed, then realised that the acolyte might be right. If the quickest way for the Souk'ir to join them was simply to open up their holds, and expel the newest cull of captives from the breeding grounds far away, then that would explain a lot. They must be very keen not to be left out of the grand return to Lochlainn, Barrax thought with some amusement. Then as the new slaves plunged into the Seljuqs, and began trying to rip them apart with their bare hands, his amusement died a sudden death.

"Volla's balls!" he screamed. "Not *them* you fools!" and aimed a bolt of Power-fire into them, vaporising several dozen.

Coming up behind, Jacinto and Kym's lance saw the blast of Power and nearly tripped over their own feet.

"Flaming Underworlds! What was that?" Kym gulped, even as another blast took out more of the freed slaves.

"Bastard Abend!" Toby said, allowing other slaves to get past him, so that he could try and aim his bow in the right direction.

"You'll never get him from back here," Busby said regretfully. "There's just too many in between us."

"We can't save them except by getting him!" Jacinto said decisively. "Come on!" And he plunged on, now racing for the spot where he had seen the Power-fire come from.

Sionnachan and his men also saw Barrax start to use Power-fire in earnest on the incoming bands of slaves.

"Great Ash guide them to the Summerlands!" McKinley prayed, as he saw another great hole rent in the mass of men.

"That's suicide!" an appalled Anson added.

"Archers! Aim at the DeÁine closest to those new men!" Sionnachan bellowed the order, and led his men off at an angle now. There was an Abend and acolytes down there and that was the Foresters' business if anything was.

Too busy staying alive to take any notice of the wider battlefield, Jacinto was closing on the Abend too. He reckoned that with so many killed that he was nearly there by now. He did not want to think about what his feet were slipping in, and he consciously refused to look down, fearing that he might see the face of someone he would recognise. The slaves were not his friends, he had not known these poor souls for long enough for that, but he could mourn their passing and the loss of life just as they had regained their freedom. Then another of the great monstrous beast that he had seen back in Brychan came lumbering his way, its rider lashing the slaves of the Seljuq onwards. A slave from the ships, still dressed in the rags he had been freed in, spun back to face Jacinto and then died with a rictus scream as a spear appeared through his middle.

Like the snapping of an old belt under strain, something came apart within Jacinto. In his mind he was half in the here and now, and half in the distant past. The memory came unbidden of another man whom he somehow knew was his father dying in front of him just like that. Dying in a fight as those hideous creatures ran him down. With a terrific anger he had never felt before, Jacinto tore into the fray and hacked the rider off his beast. Then in a moment of inspiration, Jacinto hauled himself onto the beast and used the goad, which had luckily caught on the saddle, to force the beast around.

He did not have to turn it far before the Abend came into view. Jacinto stabbed the goad into the beast's armoured rear through a joint in its plates, and felt it catapult forwards. The Abend was in flame-coloured armour, making him visible from far away even in this almighty press, and the charging animal brought them closer at a terrifying speed. Jacinto did not intend to try and stop it, and when he was only a few yards away, he vaulted off as soon as a space appeared. And not a moment too soon! Barrax suddenly spotted the huge edentulous pounding directly at him and drew another bolt of Power to throw at it. The great beast took the bolt straight to its head and went down in a huge spray of blood and fragmented skull. It was Barrax's first mistake, because the splattering blood blinded him to Jacinto's approach, while the would-be Knight had his back to the bleeding animal, and so had a clearer view.

The first the war-mage knew of it was when Jacinto threw himself at him. Jacinto might not have had the bulk he had once had, but he was still a big man by anyone's standards, and the force of him colliding with Barrax was enough to rock the Abend off his feet. He staggered backwards clawing at this new manic. Like Anarawd, he now found that his first instinct was to pull in even more Power, yet as his hand was thrown outwards in the scuffle and a bolt shot upwards into the sky, he also realised that it would not do him any good.

Yet Barrax was not a Monreux for nothing. Unlike Anarawd, he had had his fair share of real fights, even in his teens before entering the Temples, and he had certainly had better training. Wresting himself free from this mad man, he drew his sword and began carefully circling him. The acolytes were giving him room, but all of them were concentrating on looking outwards and trying to fill the gap in their rank which the edentulous had caused. None of them even gave a backwards glance to Barrax to see if he was winning.

*So nice of them to have such faith in me*! Barrax thought irately, if raggedly, as he found his opponent trying all manner of unfamiliar feints and attacks to try to get beyond his guard. He was coping with that, but this man was still never giving him a chance to go on the attack himself. That had to change! Barrax risked getting a wound by stamping his leading foot as he feinted an attack one way, and struck another. He felt his blade connect, and hard!

*Got you, you bastard*! Barrax thought as he fought to redouble his attack. Due to his enhanced lungs he was not breathless in the way that Jacinto was, but the heat of this day was still taking its toll on someone so encased in metal as Barrax was in his armour. The war-mages' plate armour had been designed for standing still and looking magnificent in while directing dozens of acolytes, not getting into the mêlée themselves. Great Lotus, but he was sweating! And he had never craved a drink of cold water so badly in his long life. Then some slaves got in his way, and Barrax blew them apart to be able to see again. Curse the Seagang-rotten Islander! He had somehow avoided the blast and even now was coming at him again, even though he was bleeding badly from a wound in his side. He must free himself of this pestilent creature and return to greater matters!

Jacinto, on the other hand, had no intention of letting Barrax go anywhere. He thought he heard a familiar voice somewhere behind him, and hoped it was Kym dealing with the acolytes, but he was too focused on Barrax to risk turning to look. Then he spotted the Scabbard. It was lashed to Barrax's waist with a normal leather strap, but the thing was glowing with an unearthly white light, and Jacinto realised that part of the trouble was that he was half blinded by it. He had been squinting in the bright sunlight anyway, and so it had not registered initially that he was being dazzled from another point as well. It had to be the DeÁine Treasure! And that now made it imperative that he try to deprive this Abend of it.

He dodged another sword cut, then ducked under another and launched himself bodily at the war-mage. He went not for the throat, as might have been expected, but the Scabbard at Barrax's waist. Seizing it with both hands, he felt the heart-stopping jolts of Power burst through him. He half thought he would die there and then, but the Power he felt was not aimed at him, it was just channelling through him and out beyond him. He stumbled and fell at Barrax's feet, but still hung on to the Scabbard, wrenching it as he fell. Barrax was twisted with him and then, to his horror felt the leather strap holding the Scabbard give way. With a scream of fury he brought his sword up for a killing blow, then struck downwards with all his might.

At the last moment Jacinto rolled, suddenly realising that the Scabbard was free and in his hands. The apoplectic war-mage struck down again and Jacinto rolled again, this time feeling the sword slice into his arm and side as he did so. In desperation Jacinto flung his feet over his head and rolled backwards instead of side to side to try to get a bit more space. A remaining acolyte finally realised that something was wrong, and Jacinto had to dive to one side yet again to avoid her Power-bolt, only to find Barrax coming at him again with his sword, making rapid controlled cuts at him.

Then, as Jacinto put his hand down to try to push himself up from off the ground again, his fingers felt the pommel of a dropped sword. Seizing it he lashed out back at Barrax. It was not any sword move his instructors would ever have recognised, being neither an attack nor a parry, but it was enough to deflect the fatal downwards cut Barrax was making.

It was not enough to free him, though, and Jacinto knew it. He had to get away! He wanted to kill this bastard DeÁine so badly it hurt, but he was still sane enough to know that he must get the Scabbard away from any of the Abend. As Barrax overbalanced and took a jolting step past him, Jacinto got his feet beneath him and took off at a sprint back for the coast. The enraged war-mage pounded in his wake, reeking death and destruction from waves of Power-fire as he passed. Not that either got very far before Jacinto realised that he was never going to be able to outrun this DeÁine. His sides hurt, his arm hurt, and there was a gash on his leg he could not even remember getting which hurt abominably, and was opening further with the effort of running.

As he thought, *I'm not going to make it*, a figure swung into view out of the corner of his eye.

"Stop!" it called in a clear voice. "Leave him, Abend!"

"Sioncaet, no!" Jacinto gasped in horror. The war-mage would surely tear the small minstrel limb from limb.

"It's over!" Sioncaet said, standing still in front of Barrax. "Go home and never return!"

Barrax just laughed and lunged at Sioncaet.

Now it was Jacinto's turn to try to deflect the war-mage. "Hey! Have you forgotten this?" he screamed desperately, waving the Scabbard at Barrax. The war-mage's cut faltered and missed Sioncaet by a hair's breadth. Like Jacinto he was now forced to recognise that the Scabbard took precedence over all others, turning his back on Sioncaet, whom he had registered was hardly even armed except for a small knife.

"Run, Sioncaet!" Jacinto screamed as he took to his heels again, only to trip over a fallen body and go flying. He kept hold of the Scabbard but landed awkwardly. Winded and with his ankle badly twisted, he could only watch the war-mage loom up over him.

Then another figure appeared seemingly out of nowhere to stand over him. That looked like a DeÁine uniform, but why was he protecting him?

"Remember me?" a familiar voice said, but not to Jacinto.

"You?" Barrax answered in surprise. "What are you doing here?"

"Laying my ghosts to rest," Labhran said calmly. "I've lived with the misery of what you made me do for years. Those people never deserved that!"

"What people?" Barrax could not understand what had got into this Donn. He thought he had died, actually, but then who bothered trying to keep track of the Donns? What he could hardly believe was that he now found himself fighting hard with this soldier. Why was he doing this? They were on the same side! Even worse, this manic Donn was fighting with a reckless abandon Barrax had never come up against before.

For Labhran it was as if all the misery of the long years inside New Lochlainn had been lifted from him, and he drew a deep breath, feeling as though it was the first time he had ever felt so light in spirit. This was the acolyte who had done the damage. Had he not stayed so often to watch what Labhran had been ordered to do, then Labhran might have been able to avoid inflicting such terrible and wicked deaths on innocent people. Time and again Barrax had been there, drinking in the scenes of torture. A voyeur, often splattered in red as he was armoured now. Labhran grinned savagely. Time to lay the last, red ghost to rest!

And then it happened. They both struck at once and both swords penetrated deeply, yet Labhran did not pull away but thrust himself harder onto Barrax's sword in order to plunge his own deeper in.

"I'm not afraid to die anymore!" Labhran snarled. "Are you?"

Barrax felt the sword sliding up under his breastplate and into his chest.

"Mother Seagang!" he wailed, as he felt something shift deep inside him.

The stored Power within him exploded outwards along the swords and vaporised his opponent. In the blink of an eye Labhran was gone. That freed Barrax from the swords holding him to the errant Donn, but he found himself feeling terribly faint. His guts felt as though they were sloshing loosely about inside him, and something liquid was running down the inside of his armour on all sides. It felt as though it was only the last vestiges of Power that were holding him together anymore. The world swam about him, and then there was another figure coming at him, raining blow after blow on him in savage, hacking blows.

Will had been hard on Sioncaet and Labhran's heels, horrified at how fast the minstrel could run even when he was clearly far from well. The sudden appearance of a ghostly Master Hugh had told him of the battle ahead, and so they had all disembarked with speed and hurried inland. It had been Labhran's shout as he had torn off after Sioncaet which had alerted Will, and he had been close enough behind him to see Labhran's instant death. *Not even a scrap left for a decent burial for such a hero*! was the thought which ignited Will's rage into the incandescent.

"You miserable bastard!" Will snarled, his heavy sword knocking dents in the polished armour until the joints crimped and opened up to allow him places to stab through. "He was bloody recovering, you *bastard*!" Will howled in blind fury. "He was ready to *live* again! You *fucking* bastard!" And he finally found another gap which allowed him to plunge his sword into Barrax's back, severing his spinal cord. Not that Will realised he was dead straight away. He continued to stab deeply into the war-mage time and again, swearing vengeance with every cut. "Have me and him masquerading as bloody Monreux, eh? Your fucking Donns weren't fit to lick his boots! ...To depths of the Underworld with you! ...I hope the bloody Wild Hunt gnaws your bones dry! ...I curse your rotten soul to eternal torment!"

"He's gone, Will," a sad voice suddenly cut through his rage.

Pausing and panting, Will wiped his steaming brow with the back of his hand, after hauling off his sweat-drenched gauntlets and wiping his hands on his breeches. Sioncaet was standing very still in the midst of all the chaos.

"Whose gone?" Will asked gruffly, stopping to hawk the dust out of his throat and spit in the dirt. "Him?" he gestured to Barrax's bloody corpse. "Bloody good riddance, too!" He drew back his foot and gave the corpse a hefty kick for good measure.

Sioncaet shook his head sadly. "Labhran. ...My good friend. He's gone. I'm glad I'll be gone soon now too. I'm so heartsick of losing all my friends."

Will shook his head, cast about him to make sure that the battle had moved on and that there was no-one about to skewer either of them, then went and enveloped Sioncaet in a hug.

"I know, it bloody hurts, doesn't it! But that doesn't mean you're going to die! Don't you dare think that!"

"But I am," Sioncaet insisted. "I know now why I've lived for so long. All those long years of outliving my families time and again. It was the Power after all! But not the DeÁine Power! The Island one! The voice in my head? It was one of the Islands' ancients! He took refuge in my father, then in me even before I was born, waiting for this day. He knew they'd never look for him amongst one of their own!"

"Oh shit!" Will gasped with dawning horror. "So you mean that he's ...gone?"

"Yes, he's gone," Sioncaet sighed. "Or at least he's going ...soon. And that means that at last I don't have to keep going on and on."

Will could not begin to find an answer that. He was saved from the effort by Jacinto's groan of pain, and Sioncaet breaking free to hurry to Jacinto's side.

"I've got it!" Jacinto croaked weakly. "I've got the Scabbard back!"

Will needed no further urging. He gestured to those Islanders he could see, and sent both Sioncaet and Jacinto back towards the coast with a strong escort, and strict instructions not to let any of the DeÁine get their clammy hands on the Scabbard again! Then he strode on and into the battle again, this day was not done yet and he had an army to lead before he could start counting the cost.

Amongst the Abend they felt the second sheering of the Power which announced an Abend's departure to the Otherworld.

"Barrax?" Magda gasped. "Oh no! Oh, Immaculate Temples, not him!"

Laufrey too looked to her in horror. She had expected to have a long a fruitful partnership with Barrax, maybe one day even leading the Abend as Masanae and Quintillean had done. How could he be gone in such a ridiculously short space of time? Things were not supposed to happen like this! For Masanae it was shocking too, and she looked about for Quintillean. He and Tancostyl were baying like bansithes and were now at the forefront of the fighting, distinguishable by the holes which kept appearing in the Islander army as they blasted men out of existence with the Power. Eliavres was somewhere up there too, but weaving very different signatures on the Power – what they were achieving was beyond her, but then so was most of what the war-mages did.

As Quintillean made another swipe at the Island army and killed half a company of Ergardians, Brego made a decision.

"Time I finished him off!" he muttered to himself, and drew the Knife in his left hand as he took his sword in his right. "You've lived too long, Quintillean!" He turned to his bodyguards. "Guard Sooty! Him before me if necessary! We're going in!" And he heeled his horse into a charge straight for Quintillean.

The heavy war-horse shouldered it way forwards until a blast from Quintillean cleared a way before him. The horse sprang forward and covered the separating ground before Quintillean had chance to form, and throw, another of the Power-fire blasts. Brego's accompanying archers fired furiously at the acolytes and were followed swiftly by more Ergardians, who saw their Grand Master heading into the thickest fighting and were not about to let him go alone. While the others dealt with the acolytes, Brego went straight for Quintillean and struck him with great force as the horse drew level with the mage. It crimped Quintillean's armour at the neck and managed to dent it deeply, but not enough to disable him. Brego struck again at the other side, as the war-mage found himself unable to move his neck and stumbled. Another mighty swipe with the Master's empowered blade finally drew blood, as it bit deeply into Quintillean's neck through the wrecked armour.

Brego drew back his sword to plunge it deep into the mage when Hugh's apparition blinked into being, and the other Grand Master yelled, "No Brego! Not with your sword!"

Brego changed to a cut and kneed his horse to turn again.

"Use the Knife!" Hugh called above the din. "The Knife will take the Power from inside him! Use your sword and you'll kill yourself and all around you! The escaping Power will vaporise you all!"

Brego nodded, let his sword loose to swing by its lanyard and took the Knife hilt in both hands. Coming behind the weakened and reeling war-mage, he raised both hands up high and then, with the advantage of height from his horse's back, plunged the Knife down into the gap he had created in the back of the war-mage's gorget. As the Knife plunged in, a huge explosion ripped out from inside Quintillean. He died shattered into tiny wet fragments, and everyone in that area of the battlefield was knocked off their feet by the blast, but nothing worse. With the DeÁine troops having been closest to him for the most part, they were knocked out, while all but a few Islanders were winded and dazed but generally still conscious. It made a big difference to how quickly they got back on their feet, and the DeÁine here soon found themselves fighting a defensive action as the determined Islanders pressed home the advantage.

Brego himself was thrown from his horse, yet both horse and rider got to their feet quicker than anyone else.

"Thank you, Hugh!" he said, as he staggered to his feet and sheathed the Knife.

"Don't thank me, thank Fin! He screamed like mad at Vanadis to tell me."

"Thank you, Fin! You're a wonderful squint and very brave!" Brego looked around and saw Sooty and his guards standing upright in the midst of hundreds of flattened men. "You too Sooty! I'm not sure what you did, but it certainly worked!"

The black squint chirped with pleasure, and Brego heard an answering chirp through the portal as Fin responded.

Hugh's image swam a little closer to Brego. "Time to tackle the Helm?"

"I think so!"

They scoured the battlefield for Tancostyl, and spotted him further on in the DeÁine ranks. It was encouraging to see that their men were fighting like demons and getting the upper hand against the Donns and the ordinary DeÁine, which explained why Tancostyl was further back than they had expected.

Tancostyl himself was experiencing the new sensation of real fear. What had happened to the others? And that last! For Quintillean to be gone almost defied belief. And something was also very wrong with the Power. He could feel it through the Helm. Pausing to retreat behind his acolytes, he did a swift cast about on the Power and came to a horrifying discovery. The Power they had become so used to siphoning through the enhancers of the Power-rooms in New Lochlainn simply was not there anymore! He swept his search wider and felt an awful shaking somewhere deep inside, the Power itself was flowing as if its current had been diverted or changed in some way. He could not feel the Gauntlet at all, and the Gorget and Scabbard were now not responding to the Helm's call. They should be! He knew that from how it had felt with Barrax using the Scabbard with him guiding that Power through the Helm. Now, though, it was as if it was feeding energy into something else. He was not to know that Jacinto and Sioncaet between them were doing as Berengar and Esclados had done – for Myrddin, deep within Sioncaet, had felt their change and was getting Sioncaet to heal Jacinto's worst and most life-threatening wound with Power drawn through the Scabbard.

*I must get them back!* Tancostyl thought frantically. *If only we can turn them back, then I can get the others to use them if necessary.* It was a measure of his distraction that he had failed to think how many of the Abend were left. Only he and Eliavres of the male Abend remained. The normally unthinkable thought of sharing with the witches was not dismissible in the midst of this disaster, but he had not even got that far. All that mattered was that the Abend survived.

He began ploughing his way back through the ranks of the DeÁine, leaving a frustrated Brego to watch his quarry disappearing out of sight again.

"Sooty! Tell Squint to get Aneirin to tell Maelbrigt to watch for Tancostyl!" Brego suddenly recollected the way he could send an instant warning. "Tell Maelbrigt, Tancostyl is heading straight for him!"

When Aneirin appeared before Maelbrigt to tell him, everyone began looking for the remaining war-mages.

"Is that Eliavres over there?" Tobias suddenly called out, pointing into the distance to something swirling on the Power near to the heart of the DeÁine army.

"I reckon so because that there is more likely to be Tancostyl," Ewan agreed, looking to where Raethun was also pointing in a different direction at the DeÁine's collapsing right flank.

"That's him!" Aneirin confirmed. "Now what you need to do here is... Oh piss and confusion! ...Hey, wait for me!" His spectral form was forced to glide rapidly in the wake of the running Foresters and Squint's litter, who had not waited for Aneirin's elaboration, but were pelting straight for the war-mage.

Squint was hanging on with his paws for grim death as the litter jolted and jostled him about, but still found the breath to tweet madly at Aneirin.

"Alright, alright! I'll tell him!" the ancient said, too bothered by the way everything was spiralling out of his control to worry about standing on his dignity any more. "Maelbrigt! Squint says to let him join with you before you engage Tancostyl! Do you hear me? Wait and link with Squint before you strike the first blow!"

Maelbrigt risked a glance back over his shoulder and gave a curt nod. Then he was slowing down as his Foresters surged around him. He did not need to run anymore because Tancostyl was coming straight at him. He reached deep into himself in the way he found he had been doing earlier with the Sword and then with it towards Squint. There was a momentary jolt as he felt something click into place, almost in the way that a good piece of armour jointed its pieces together, and became something more than the sum of its parts. Suddenly Maelbrigt could feel a surging tide welling up as if behind him, but not in any physical sense he was used to, and a small presence he knew must be Squint.

As Tancostyl stepped out into the space beyond the fighting men, Maelbrigt found that he could actually feel him. He could sense the war-mage's presence with mind-blowing clarity! He felt the swelling of a putrid Power welling up through the Helm, and as it lanced outwards in a blade of Power, he brought the Sword up and parried it with something far more potent than just the pattern-welded metal. Sparks of lightning shot out from the clash as the Powered blades seared one another, and those far above in the valley saw the next exchanges of blows encased in multiple rainbows, as the sunlight was refracted off the crystal-like shards of Power.

For Maelbrigt this enhanced fighting, this ability to feel an opponent beyond the physical, was so alien it was almost throwing him off his stride – almost, but not quite! He saw and felt Tancostyl drawing another blast of Power, and realised the dreadful weakness of the Helm. It could not change the directions of its attacks in the way that the handheld Sword could! While he could strike in any direction he could get the Sword to move into, Tancostyl was hampered by the way that the Power surged out through the Helm's visor. He could angle it up and down, and he could broaden or narrow the spread, but to get anything at an angle required him to turn his head to one side or the other. That meant he was either forced to waggle his head about and lose visual concentration, or do what he was doing, focusing on just cutting across and moving those cuts up and down. Not a problem for sending huge surges out across a battlefield as the Abend had traditionally fought, but potentially lethal for close quarter work!

As another drawing surged up within Tancostyl, Maelbrigt struck. He brought the Sword up and around to strike diagonally at Tancostyl, and there was nothing the war-mage could do to defend himself. The Power-based edge of the Sword, which was projecting over a hand's span beyond the actual metal, sheered its way deep into Tancostyl's armour and was followed by the sharp edge of the pattern-welded blade. The downside was that Maelbrigt now had no defence against the escaping Power leaking out of the Helm. He danced rapidly aside as he tried to wrench the massive Sword out of Tancostyl's shoulder and collarbone, just about avoiding getting his own foot shorn off. The Sword came free, and Maelbrigt took the opportunity to get behind Tancostyl and get the Sword moving again before the war-mage staggered around, pouring blood but swearing viciously.

Maelbrigt deflected the small directed sending of Power which Tancostyl managed to expel, despite having oozed so much involuntarily in his pain. At the same time Raethun did what he did best. He dived in low at Tancostyl's back, and as the war-mage loosed the Power, draining himself in the process, Raethun hamstrung him in the left leg, rolling out of the way before the war-mage even realised what had happened. As Tancostyl swung around and aimed a weak blast of Power in the general direction of Raethun, Maelbrigt was easily able to deflect it, even as Ewan imitated his friend and used his knife on Tancostyl's other leg. Unable to move properly at all now, Tancostyl roared like a wounded bull and pulled ever deeper into the Power. No matter that he was plumbing depths which he had always been warned were dangerous. He was past thinking now and was running on pure instinct. He dredged up what he could and spouted it in a venomous splatter in Maelbrigt's direction.

Maelbrigt brought the Sword low in an arc and deflected most of the sending as he span around, like some highland dancer, lifting the Sword again, and with all his might and will struck again in a downwards sweep. *Not my friends! Not my home! Not our Islands*! he thought, as the Sword seemed to almost tear the air as it descended.

With an explosive crash, the heavy blade went into Tancostyl and, between metal and Power, took his head clean off his body. A fountain of Power shot upwards and dispersed, then the Helm came off the head and rolled away from it, both bowling along the battlefield like balls. The head bounced to a halt against a fallen corpse and lay there in wide-eyed, unseeing paralysis. The Helm, however, rolled further and was seized by an enterprising member of the nearest Jundis. As one of the last survivors of his battalion, he made no attempt to fight, but fled like a man possessed towards the ranks of the DeÁine.

Like a hare with the hounds at his heels, Tobias took off in pursuit. He almost made it too. It was his misfortune for Laufrey to have come in Tancostyl's wake. The witch could sense that Tancostyl was beyond reason, and she correctly feared that he might engage in some foolish action which would cost them the Helm. Seizing it off the flying Jundis warrior, she left him to be cut down by Tobias and took to her heels as well. She fled back through the slain and wounded. Back towards the ships. If the others wanted to stay here and be put to the blade that was their affair. She had no intention of dying here, and Laufrey had always been a survivor.

Yet she had failed to include one person in her calculations. Taise knew Laufrey of old from their time as acolytes, and early on she had sensed her signature on the Power as she had been using it herself to try and heal the worst of the Knights' wounds. It had torn at her to leave the wounded unattended. It went against all her beliefs. But somewhere deep inside herself, she knew that if anyone was going to do something to stop Laufrey, it was going to have to be her. She looked about her and spotted the Gorget. If Laufrey had any sort of DeÁine Power amplifier on her, then she would need something to counter it. With a momentary pause and shudder, Taise clipped the Gorget about her neck. It felt somehow alien and right at the same time, but there was no time to think about that now, she had to get down to where Laufrey was and stop her.

Once on the valley floor in Laufrey's wake in the rear of the DeÁine army, Taise could hardly believe what she was feeling through the Gorget when Tancostyl engaged with Maelbrigt. Tancostyl's signature she recognised with no trouble, but who was this warrior who burned so brightly from within on the Power? Then she felt something familiar, felt an essence more than anything, an essence which she would know anywhere and anytime.

"Maelbrigt!" she found herself screaming in horror and anguish, even though the chances of him hearing her were nil. Her beloved Knight was going head to head with the strongest war-mage left alive, yet echoing down her own connection to the Power she felt Maelbrigt gain the upper hand. She almost wept with relief when she felt Tancostyl depart forever, almost losing sight of the one she was pursuing. Almost, until she saw Laufrey seize the Helm and try to put it on.

It did not fit Laufrey particularly well having been made for a much bigger man, and now it was bent and twisted as well. Taise had a feeling that it would not respond well to trying to draw the female twisting of the Power through it, either. Not that she was that confident of how the Gorget would respond to her. That did not matter. What mattered was stopping Laufrey escaping the field. Hoisting up her skirts, Taise ran for all she was worth. It helped that both of them were now beyond the fighting, although not beyond the fallen, and that slowed Laufrey immensely, while Taise simply skirted the worst of the heaped bodies, being on the edge of the slaughter. As Laufrey finally got to the end of the obstacles to her feet, she risked a brief glance over her shoulder, expecting to see that Magda had sent acolytes after her. Instead she saw Taise run up to within a couple of yards of her. She jumped with surprise. She had not seen this woman for over a decade and had thought her dead.

"Thought I was gone?" Taise voiced Laufrey's thoughts. "You always were too confident, Laufrey. So where do you think you're going with that thing? You can't escape, you know. The ships are in our hands, just look..."

Laufrey's horrified glance took in the way Magnus' men were swarming over the ships, throwing bodies overboard and moving those ships near land further out and away from any stray DeÁine wanting to quit the field's ability to reach. No ship! She had no ship! In panic Laufrey turned and blasted Taise with the Power. Yet the Helm had suffered a terrible battering, and the assault by Maelbrigt using the Island drawings of Power had warped and twisted it in ways beyond the dents and cracks. A twisted worm of Power, half drawn from something deep and dark that Tancostyl had dredged up, corkscrewed in a flash towards Taise. It hit her full on, but the changed Gorget responded in her defence. Laufrey screamed in pain at what was being ripped through her by the Helm, and then screamed even harder, tearing her vocal chords, as the rebound from the Gorget hit her. In a weird crumpling and sucking, the warped Power sucked the life out of her as it slithered back into the depths it had come from.

Like a puppet with her strings cut, Laufrey folded up in a heap and lay still. Taise would have been alright if she had not put the Gorget on around her neck. Had she simply held the Gorget, she could have dropped it when the poisoned twisting of the Power hit, but she had been so scared of doing just that, dropping it and losing it. And she had guessed that she might physically have to get hold of Laufrey, and that would mean having her hands free. So the Gorget had gone on.

Now she felt it burning and tightening. The intent of the Gorget was to protect, and something in that last hit had twisted it so that it had shifted after bouncing the Power back at Laufrey, and now read Taise's DeÁine blood and saw her as an enemy. Sithfrey had already been running after her, and through the Gauntlet he felt the Gorget shift. Now he came dashing up just in time to catch Taise as she collapsed gasping for air.

"Somebody help me!" Sithfrey screamed in despair. His Gauntleted arm was trying to pull him away from Taise, which meant that there was no way he could heal her with it. Across the bloody field he could see a group of Knights tearing towards him, accompanied by one of the squints' litters. Maelbrigt came pounding up, and dropped to his knees in the blood and dust beside Taise.

"Oh my love, why did you do that?" he sobbed. "You'd done enough already!"

Taise could only wheeze at him, but through the connection she had to the Power she saw a new side of Maelbrigt. She could *feel* him! And what she felt as much as saw was a bright presence, a noble and shining force for good. Not some pristine innocence, but something forged and strengthened by living life to the full. She could feel her throat being crushed and her vision disintegrated into flashes. By their sides Squint was going frantic.

"Use the Sword!" Aneirin appeared yelling. "Put the tip against the Gorget and *will* it gone! Squint will help!"

Maelbrigt seized the huge Sword from off Squint's litter, where he had dumped it in order to be able to run faster to get to Taise. Placing the tip against the joint he put no pressure on it, just allowing the weight of the Sword to make contact, and wished with all his heart for Taise to be safe and the Gorget gone. With a sharp crack the Gorget shattered, and even though Maelbrigt tensed his muscles to catch it, the Sword still nicked Taise's neck as it dropped to the ground. In a flash Sithfrey was in, holding the Gauntlet over Taise's neck. The Gauntlet flared and then died.

"What happened?" Maelbrigt asked frantically.

"I don't know," Sithfrey told him, even as Taise took a ragged breath. "It healed the crushed windpipe, but there's something else there. Something left behind that the Gauntlet can't deal with."

"Can you breathe?" Maelbrigt asked gently, lifting Taise's head to place on his knee and then hugging her close to him. Her eyes flickered 'yes', even though she was still working too hard to draw in shallow and noisy breaths to be able to try to speak.

Maelbrigt looked about him as best he could down on the ground. His duty demanded that he return to the fight, yet this was Taise he was holding in his arms, wounded and in need of him too. Raethun's hand squeezed his shoulder.

"It's alright! Stay there! The fighting's too far away from us now for us to join in. It looks like Master Brego and the others are making short work of the rest of the DeÁine."

And indeed Brego, with Hugh's assistance, had lead the Islanders on a bloody but victorious charge at the main DeÁine army. With Hugh watching from on high, Brego had been able to know which way the Donns were shifting their men, and every time they moved he was almost there before them. Matti and Cwen had made it down to the valley floor, and with the loyal and redoubtable Scully and Iago helping them, had formed up a line beyond which the DeÁine could not now retreat. They might try to fire arrows at them. They might try to throw spears or hack with swords. But everything the DeÁine did bounced off the glowing wall without effect, while the Islanders' ripostes hit every time. With Haply and Grimston taking over from Maelbrigt as their personal guides and commanders, Ivain and Swein had led the archers along the valley wall, pouring so many arrows into the hapless DeÁine that at one stage, they had had to send a party out to cut more arrows from the fallen before they could start firing again. Every volley flew in concert and struck a target, the two Treasure holders always focusing their attention on big clusters of men, so that they attacked with maximum effect.

Now they were both resting and allowing the Prydein archers to pick off men one by one, for the Islanders were so intertwined with the remaining DeÁine that they were in danger of impaling their own if they carried on with the massed volleys. The lances of the regular Order were now in their element, fighting hand to hand while watching each others' backs, and this unity made the difference when it came to fighting the Jundises. The DeÁine veterans never thought to help one or two men cut off from the rest regain the protection of the main ranks, and on this scale of fighting, they were losing men fast to this persistent weeding out by the lances.

It also showed how much the DeÁine were used to having the upper hand from the advantage the Power brought them, for even though these DeÁine had not fought with the Abend, they were still used to the acolytes giving them an arcane advantage. To find that gone, and with the shoe on the other foot – so to speak – disconcerted them, and the Sinut Donns in particular. Whole Jundis after Jundis collapsed in the face of the Islanders steady and unified advance, for the Seljuqs of slaves were virtually annihilated by now, the last having been sucked dry by the Abend in a frantic attempt to feed the waning Power in both themselves and the acolytes.

As the sun lowered, and threw long shadows across the depths of the valley while still crowning its tops in bright sunshine, the fighting died down. It did not stop altogether, but there was a natural slowing as the brunt of the clashes ceased. In the heart of the valley, there was a small cluster of Jundises still surrounding the Abend and what few acolytes there were left, and this was surrounded by a shimmering shield of Power. The ancients all stood by their respective Treasure wielders, and Vanadis came to appear by Brego, each opening up more of the cloud-rimmed windows so that the fighters could all see one another.

"What next Master Brego?" Ivain asked.

"Move up," Hugh answered, and Arsaidh's voice could be heard agreeing with him in far off Ergardia. "Get all the Island Treasures closer to the Abend. Then we can think about finishing this once and for all."

# Chapter 18

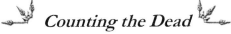 *Counting the Dead*

### Rathlin: Grian-mhor

Amongst the ranks of the Abend there was nothing short of outright panic going on. With only Eliavres left of the male Abend, and the witches having lost their newest recruit, there were just four of the nine left alive. Masanae and Magda especially were shaken to the core. How had this happened? In the course of less than one day, five of the greatest beings on earth had been wiped out as though they were nothing more than the basest slave. It was unheard of. It was inconceivable. It should not have happened!

"What do we do now?" Masanae heard herself saying, even though she was also aware of how feeble and out of control that sounded. Given all the long, long years she had fought and schemed sometimes with, sometimes against Quintillean, his death had shaken her to the very core of her being. For him to suddenly just be gone felt wrong at a level she had never experienced before, almost as if part of herself had died with him.

"We use Nicos," a calm voice said with firmness and authority. The three witches turned to look at Eliavres.

"What?" Helga exclaimed. "Are you mad?"

It showed how badly rattled the two senior witches were that they did not grasp at first what the other two were talking about.

"Well what do you suggest we do?" Eliavres asked pointedly. "Most of our *living* army are dead. So where else would we find replacements to fight for us? It was you three who were so keen to drag Geitla's lifeless corpse with us all this way. You who were so sure we could use Othinn – or whatever he wants to be called in his half-life state!"

"Nicos!" gulped Magda. "Yes, of course!" and she ran to where a silk-draped litter lay on the ground.

Geitla's body had swollen to beyond pregnant size and there was now a visible, glowing presence inside her which nobody needed the Power in order to see. Nicos knelt beside her and now looked up with a cadaverous grin.

"Are you ready? Shall we begin?"

"You've prepared him already?" Magda asked in a panting, breathy voice, which came half from her panic, and half from excitement that she might at last be reunited with the one person she had truly loved.

"Oh yes!" Nicos purred, oblivious to the carnage which surrounded their protected space. "My lord Jolnir is champing at the bit! He'll toss and gore many more for you before this day is out!"

"Then release him" Magda commanded.

"Ah not so fast, my lovely lady," Nicos replied in sultry tones alien to him, but so very familiar in the former acolyte, Othinn. "You must all channel Power into me first before I can release my army!"

"Masanae! Helga! We must feed him Power!" Magda called back.

"Go on," Eliavres said calmly. "I'll take over from you all and hold the shield in place over us. It's not as though I'm going to have to do it for long, and as I've never worked in tandem with you all, I'm more likely to cause problems than help. I can use my Power better back here."

"Yes, yes!" Masanae agreed, pulling Helga with her towards where Magda was.

"Well *I* need more energy first!" the reluctant Helga snarled.

"Then we shall have to use our remaining slaves, and some of the Jundises if necessary!" Masanae declared with more authority than she felt.

Together the three witches allowed their spectral essences to sweep through the remaining household slaves, and then took the outer and most battered of the Jundises too for good measure. As the bodies of the drained fell in untidy piles at the perimeter and crumbled slowly away, the three then placed their hands where Nicos guided them on the recumbent Geitla, and then pumped Power into the being within her. Nicos was chanting and twisting that Power, that much they could feel, but all of them were revolted by the depths to which he was taking that Power and what it seemed to be feeding.

There was a sudden severing of the connection for Masanae and Helga. A harsh cutting off which rebounded and knocked them flying. Magda, though, stayed glued to Nicos' side, and although she no longer touched Geitla, she knelt with a look of absolute ecstasy on her face as she gazed up at something forming in the air above her.

"Othinn! Oh poppet! Oh sweetling! It's been so long!"

The shimmering transformed into a male DeÁine figure, hovering in the air.

"Come to me, my faithful one!" he intoned, and with a shriek Magda was sucked into the Power and disappeared.

"You have your blood sacrifice, my lord!" Nicos screamed in manic triumph. "You see? I promised you I'd do it!"

Masanae and Helga were still picking themselves up off the ground, and could only gape in horror at the death of Magda. But Eliavres was further away and acted. Loosing the shield, he turned and blasted Nicos out of existence.

"Treacherous serpent!" he snarled, then jerked his own sending back quickly as he felt the Jolnir apparition try to snatch at it. "Great Volla! What are you?"

"Better than Volla!" the wraith chortled. "I am Jolnir, Lord of the Isles! Leader of the Wild Hunt! Reaper of Souls! Bringer of the Dead!"

"You're nothing but a self-important acolyte!" Eliavres contradicted him, and was knocked off his feet by a wave of the ghostly hand in response.

"That life is gone!" the Othinn/Jolnir being declared to anyone left listening, for the flesh and blood DeÁine troops took one look at what had been summoned, and decided that they would rather take their chances with the Islanders. They ran like mad from the ghostly being straight into the arms of the surrounding Islanders, who had closed in for the kill. As they were slaughtered, the Jolnir apparition rose into the sky to the height of several men and threw his arms wide.

"Come my pretty ones! Come my invincible army! Together we shall take these Islands once and for all!"

All around, from the bodies of the slain, rose small ghosts. They stood up, looked around, and picked up shimmering weapons, each one a tiny fragment of Power encased in the image of a normal sword or spear. In utter silence the spectres drew up in ranks, and then began to walk calmly towards the frozen Islanders. Nobody could have anticipated this. Every possible use of the Power had been talked over and deliberated upon on the march down through Rathlin, but not once had anyone ever remotely thought that the DeÁine's ultimate weapon might be the raising of the dead – and the entire army at that!

"Sweet Rowan! To see this!" Hugh was appalled. He had heard of such tactics from Arsaidh's old records, but both of them had thought this was something only the ancient Abend could do. They had not really considered that they might have to deal with such a summoning. "Vanadis? Can you not do something? They're more in your world than ours!"

The leader of the ancients was shaking her head in disbelief, then realised what Hugh had said.

"We shall try," she said, but without much confidence and winked out of view in Ergardia to appear again by Brego's side. "Hold fast, don't advance yet," she told him.

"Don't worry! I wasn't going to!" the veteran Master responded. If pulling back would not have broken the circle around the Abend he would have sounded the retreat in a heartbeat. But Brego had meant what he said when he had told everyone that they had to stop the Abend this time. Come what may, they must finish off the last of those who could summon the Power or die in the attempt. Without that, any stray DeÁine became just normal flesh and blood enemies, who could be dealt with by future generations the same as any other threat which might arise.

The six ancients glided forwards and began trying to manipulate the Power to contain this threat. However even the most earthy of Islanders needed no magical powers to see that whatever they were trying wasn't working. Even worse, the moment Vanadis threw her arms up and tried something, she immediately drew Jolnir's attention to her.

"My white queen!" he roared in delight. "My lady, you've come to me at last!" and his spectral figure shot towards her at a frightening speed and enveloped her.

"Cross of Swords!" Maelbrigt gasped as he stood holding Taise's hand. They had brought her with them sharing Squint's litter, while Raethun and Ewan had carried the weight of the Sword for Maelbrigt with Squint helping control the energy. Currently he had it resting point down on the earth, while he stood with Taise's hand clasped to his heart. He was daring to believe that she might recover, albeit slowly, but if this dreadful thing took a hold, then Taise might be condemned to the Underworld forever. That and only that was making him think of engaging this awful enemy.

He looked across to where Matti stood, with Moss beside her. He could feel her trying to form a shield out of the great one resting in front of her, yet as their eyes briefly met he saw her shake her head. She knew what he was asking without words. Could she and Cwen contain this threat? And she knew she could not. Not all the way around. Some might survive close to her, but not all.

Then a big hand closed on Matti's shoulder and squeezed it gently.

"I'm right here! I won't let that thing get you," Will's voice said, and she turned to see him, bloody and battered but unwounded apart from a few minor cuts, and giving her a tight, humourless smile which nonetheless made her inexplicably feel better.

"Where did you spring from?" she asked softly, taking a hand off the Shield to cover and squeeze him back.

"Long story!" he chuckled. "Went into Lochlainn, got an army, came here, kicked some arse! Tell you all about it later – after you've told me what you've been up to!"

Matti could have broken down and cried at that point. As it was she stifled a sob, and felt Will transfer his hand to her other shoulder so that he could pull her tight against him and hug her, even as he held his sword in his other hand.

"We're all in this together," he whispered softly in her ear. "Don't be scared, you're not alone!"

"No, not alone!" she whispered back, and gave Moss' paw a reassuring squeeze as she let go of Will, then put her hand back on the Shield. Why had it taken the world coming to an end to put things right between them? "I just wish I knew what I was supposed to do with this thing!"

Cwen and Daisy were feeling equally at sea. For her it was also comforting to have Berengar appear by her side, and tell her with strained optimism that Esclados might actual survive after Sithfrey had done his best to help. She was not fooled, though. All that would count for very little if they could not stop this fearful summoning. And how far would it go if they failed? Would the whole Islands become a world of wraiths and ghosts? Would Alaiz's children die too? Innocent and unknowing in their beds along with hundreds of thousands more? The entire Islands reduced to being an uninhabitable land infested with ghosts? She shivered involuntarily, and like Matti, fretted over what she could possibly do that would amount to anything remotely likely to stop something as arcane as this.

Swein could just about see the Spear, and he recognised Berengar's pennant planted next to where Cwen must be, even if he could not see the man himself clearly. That was good! At least Cwen would be protected as well as anyone could be against a threat like this. He turned and smiled in

Ivain's direction, then was amazed to see Talorcan's bruised and bloody figure limp up to Ivain on the other side to Tamàs, and put his hand on his lover's back.

"If we're all going to the Underworld then we're bloody well going together!" the scarred Knight said with weak humour, although there was no mistaking the intensity of the feeling behind the words. Having found what he had been looking for all his life, he was not about to lose Ivain now, even if that meant an eternity of suffering to stay close to him.

Swein was not afraid to be alone now, yet he was glad when Warwick appeared beside him and gave him a reassuring nod.

"Do what you can with the Treasures," the head Brychan Forester said calmly, "that's all anyone can ask of you."

Nobody noticed Sioncaet's unsteady figure joining Arthur's small band to the rear of the Islanders' lines. So far the boys had been kept well out of the worst, in part because Maelbrigt had split them into five and allocated each group to a squint. It had not totally protected them, but they had not taken any fatalities either, despite the odd cut and bruise from the eager lads taking on the few who had tried to get to the squints. Piling on four or five to a DeÁine, and fighting with a ferocity none of their enemies expected, the boys' fight so far had been remarkably successful. Now they all clustered around Arthur. None of them knew him well enough to spot that he was speaking differently when he turned to Sioncaet and said,

"They're wavering!"

"I know!" Myrddin said through Sioncaet. "And it's not for want of courage! To have fought these odds and won without it being a pyrrhic victory is a huge achievement."

"That it is," Artoris agreed via Arthur.

"When do we do it?"

"Any time now. I doubt this idiot Othinn will be patient and harvest the whole field of dead before he brings the rest of his force to fight. All I'm waiting for is for him to ope…"

He did not need to finish what he was saying. The apparition of Jolnir was still wrestling with Vanadis with one hand as he swaggered out beyond his expanding ghostly force, then splayed his other hand and placed it on the ground. Whatever he said, the earth gave a reverberating groan and then a great crack appeared in it. As the crack expanded into a chasm, more ghostly figures began to climb up out of the hole.

All around the Islanders began to cry out in horror and fear.

Arthur/Artoris turned to Sioncaet/Myrddin.

"This is it!"

"See you on the other side, I hope!"

"There has to be another side," Artoris said, creasing Arthur's small face into a beaming smile, "we've done our time in torment, that can't be for nothing!"

"On the other side, then! You start them and I'll finish it. Good luck!"

"And to you!" Myrddin wished his old friend.

Acting fully as Arthur, Artoris' spirit turned to the other boys. "Is we gonna let some ghosts stop us now?" he yelled. "Come on, lads! Let's get 'em!" And with that he began running straight towards the widening chasm.

With whoops and hollers the boys broke into a sprint behind him. It took a moment for the rest of the Island force to realise what was going on, for a moment all of them thinking that the high pitched screams were some new venting of the wraiths. And that pause was all it took for the boys to get beyond the Island front line.

"Sweet Rowan! Arthur, no!" Maelbrigt yelled with all his might, swinging the Sword up and beginning to run with it, as he started to get the massive weapon up and moving again, only pausing to slap the rump of the litter horses to send them running away. Ivain and Swein heard his cry and looked towards him, only to see the boys heading straight into the maw of the spectres. With Talorcan holding a shoulder of each as they raised the Bow and Arrow, the three of them also sprang into a run and began a mad dash forwards, the Prydein archers chasing them hot on their heels.

But the greatest change was in Matti and Cwen. Until now there had always been something holding them back just a little. Something within them which could not quite get past the fact that these were flesh and blood people who were being killed, however alien they might look in their gaudy uniforms, strange helms and tattooed faces. As she heard Will say, "Oh shit!" and realised what was happening, Matti found all restraints within her ripe apart.

"*Noooo!*" she screamed in fury and dismay and the Shield at last flamed into an incandescent barrier which rippled with astonishing speed in the boys' wake. Some of them it overtook, but those closest to Arthur were too far ahead already, even with the speed at which it was moving.

For Cwen, too, the final straw was seeing the tiny figures being swept up by ghostly hands and throttled.

"Get ready!" she screamed to her coterie of spear holders, and yanked the massive Spear up so fast that Warren and Mutley had no time to get to her to help. Berengar did, though. He lent his strength to hers, hefting the massive Spear up onto his shoulder and running with her as she advanced with Matti.

"In range!" he panted tersely and she slowed.

"Aim!" Cwen bellowed, and Mutley and Warren relayed the command with their stronger voices.

"*Loose*!" she screamed, bathed in the sun-bright light of the Spear, and threw every ounce of will she had towards Jolnir. The regular spears took flight, every one of them arcing with a unity no normal flight could have achieved. The spears flew in a golden haze straight into the host of ghosts and tore holes in them, even as Ivain and Swein's flight of arrows tore smaller but more plentiful holes from the other side. Maelbrigt's Foresters were now at the edge of the ghostly mêlée, and their co-ordinated sword cuts were having an effect, even though they appeared to be passing through something with no more substance than mist.

"*Again*!" Cwen yelled, as they dashed in, now using their spare spears more like quarterstaffs, as they had done before in hand-to-hand fighting. This time they did nothing more than make collective stabs with them, but every ghost they penetrated winked out of existence.

Yet none of this had saved Arthur, and the distraught Islanders saw the small figure being shaken like a rag doll by Jolnir. Something had the apparition in a fearful rage, and he threw Vanadis and Arthur together and hurled them down to the ground, for the insane Othinn had discovered that his white lady loved the essence contained within the small boy. She never would be his, and in that case he would ensure she and her lover would truly die this time. Nobody needed to see it in detail to know that Arthur could not have survived that fall, even as Vanadis' image winked out of sight, and their rage at that fuelled their resolve and broke all restraints.

Matti's shield-bearers were battering at the wraiths now and trying to force their way forward.

"Aim for that fucking crack in the ground!" Will told her, even as he lopped the arm off a wild-eyed, terrified DeÁine trying to escape the madness whilst protecting her back. "See if your shields can cover it!"

For the crack had stopped expanding as Jolnir had become distracted by Arthur, but the dead from what seemed like all of eternity still continued to pour out of it. Unless the Islander could stop that gateway to this

Underworld of Othinn/Jolnir's creating they had no chance of winning, because as fast as they were culling the ghosts previously harvested by their lord during the great storm of New Year, and sending them to the true hereafter, more came to take their place. And unnoticed by the Islanders, who were distracted by the ghosts before them and Jolnir towering above them, Sioncaet crawled on all fours towards the unnatural chasm.

Ranked around and in between the Bow and Arrow, Warwick's Brychan Foresters were doing sterling work alongside Swein and Ivain's men, planting wands for all they were worth in a rolling barrier which followed every advance that the archers made. Doing likewise with the paired Shield and Spear were Sionnachan's Foresters. Matti's Shield-wall was forcing the wraiths backwards as Cwen's Spear-hedge stabbed at them at every turn, and so it was up to Sionnachan's men to make sure that as the ghosts were squeezed by Maelbrigt fighting opposite them, that there was no bolt hole or escape on their side.

The Ergardian Foresters paused and each took a swig from a small flask of specially infused and incantation-suffused mead. Then they began to sing. This was no light and airy chorus. The deep voices of the men leant the tune solemnity and potency, and the complex harmonies that they began to weave dipped up and down around the main strand of the song.

The strong bass voices seemed to be calling up the very Island earth to their defence. With swords held upright before them – the other way up to when they prayed with the Cross of Swords, but equally as potent – the Foresters marched on the ghostly army climbing out of the ground, singing from the heart and battering the summoning as surely as Matti's Shield-men were doing. Without the Treasures the Foresters could not destroy Jolnir's force, but with them they could contain them while the Treasures did the slaughtering.

*We need to seal that chasm*! Sionnachan thought. *But how*? He allowed his eyes to wander a little off course, even though he kept his singing steady. Where in the Islands were the ancients? He had hoped to see at least one close by. He looked to his right. No sign of Owein or Urien with Cwen and Matti. That was bad! He looked to his left and realised then that something was very wrong, for Peredur and Cynddylan were not there either, and they had resolutely stood by Ivain and Swein so far. Then he spotted the five males right at the edge of the chasm, although Vanadis was missing, desperately trying to do something which involved a lot of swirling Power

336

but which was boiling back up out of the hole every time they tried to force more down it. He caught Owein's eye and signalled that he needed to speak to him immediately. The ancient blinked out from the chasm and reappeared in front of Sionnachan.

"What's wrong?" Sionnachan demanded. "What do you need to be able to seal that thing?"

At that moment Hugh appeared on the Power to join them.

"Yes," he said, "what do you need?"

"More Power! ...I think...?" a distressed Owein answered. "This is nothing we've encountered before. We think it wants a life essence. Some kind of sacrifice. But how and who is anyone's guess."

"Can the Bowl give any more?" Hugh demanded. "We have it linked to all the other Treasures now," and he waved his hand to where Sionnachan suddenly saw that Brego was standing a little apart from the fighting, with the Knife aloft and a steady stream of Power flowing out to the other five Treasures.

"Not unless you can give it even more will and focus," Owein said regretfully. "And half the trouble is that it's a DeÁine summoning. So you can drive it back, but you'll need a DeÁine to seal it I fear. I must go back to the others and try to help," and he disappeared.

Then a small tap came on Sionnachan's arm and he turned to see Sithfrey standing at his elbow holding his Gauntleted arm up.

"We've got this," Sithfrey said meekly. "It's DeÁine, I'm DeÁine. Surely we can seal it?"

"But at what cost to you?" McKinley said from Sionnachan's other side.

"What cost if I don't?" Sithfrey countered. "It's all right, McKinley. I do this willingly because I have to or live hating myself – if any of us could imaginably survive today! Look! The sun is sinking fast. What do you think night will bring if we don't do this now?"

"Then I think we know what we must do here, too," Hugh said with a small smile and disappeared.

In Ergardia he turned to Arsaidh.

"Are you ready?"

"I think so," the elderly head of the Foresters said, patting his pockets which were stuffed with bits of parchment. "I just hope that these survive the change!" He turned to the group of scribes who were clutching writing tablets and looking very miserable. "Now make sure you get all this down!

Every bit! Never mind about me! I've lived long enough as it is. You can mourn me, if you feel you must, later on. Don't miss something vital because you're sniffling over me!"

He wrapped his thick cloak around him and took his staff in one hand and Fin's paw in the other.

"Do you think it will be cold on the other side, Hugh? I do hope not. These old bones do feel it something shocking these days!"

"We'd better find out," Hugh said, taking Fin's other paw. "Give Ivain my message for me, won't you, Aeschere." The Brychan Forester nodded, too choked for words. "Come on then, Fin, let's do it properly this time, eh?"

And together the three of them walked out into the water of the loch and up to the vertical surface of the arch, where the rippling of the Power now made it clear where the Island world ended and the in-between began. With just a fractional pause they took a deep breath and stepped into the beyond. The circle within the arch flamed into gold, obscuring all sight of the trio. What was in no doubt was that the Bowl had instantly stepped up several notches in the amount of Power it was gushing out. The very ground beneath the feet of the scribes began to resonate like a beating drum. In fear they retreated further and further back, trying to write their observations down with shaking hands, for despite being Foresters to a man this was a trial beyond any they had ever prepared for. Only Aeschere stayed at the loch's edge, on his knees chanting the Forester's prayer over and over again, as his tears for Hugh fell into the water.

On Rathlin the surge of Power through the Knife swept over Brego and wrapped itself around him.

"Hello, old friend," Hugh's voice said at his side, then came into view as Arsaidh appeared at the other side.

"So we had to do it after all?" was all Brego said, still holding the Knife, but now pointing straight at Jolnir.

"Yes, but for myself I'm not sorry, only for you two," Arsaidh answered.

"What about Sooty?" Hugh asked, as Fin snuggled himself in between them.

"I had him carried way back when I felt the amount of Power coming through the Knife when we started this time round," Brego replied. "We were the ones who made Daisy change places with Fin, after all. If it had been her with you, then they could have been together back in the Power, but not like this. I still hope the squints might survive. By the way, am I actually dead?"

"Well you'll never enjoy another beef dinner," Arsaidh said with a chuckle, "but dead? No, not exactly. Or at least I don't think so. Not yet, anyway!"

The other Treasure holders felt the great surge in Power and wondered at it but had no time to stop and ponder. It was giving them the edge now, and they were gradually forcing the multitude of ghosts into a more and more condensed space. Will and Matti were surprised to see Sionnachan come hurrying through the lines with McKinley and his men clustered around Sithfrey.

"We're going to try to seal the chasm with the Gauntlet!" Sionnachan said to Matti without preamble. "Get as far forwards as you can and then watch for me! I'm going to get Maelbrigt!" and he gestured that bit further around the fighting. "When I signal, make a run forward and slap the Shield over that monstrous thing."

"It won't cover all over it," warned Will.

"I suspect it will if Sithfrey's idea works," was Sionnachan's parting shot as he hurried on.

He passed on the same message to Cwen as he got to her, and was pleased to hear Berengar catch on instantly.

"A DeÁine weapon to seal a DeÁine creation!" the Brychan Master surmised, and got a terse nod from Sionnachan as they ploughed onwards.

"Then I shall lend you whatever DeÁine will I've got," Berengar told Cwen with a smile, as she flicked a glance his way and saw her give a tight little smile back, even as she projected another stab at the ghostly shades. This shoving at them was making the summonings more aggressive, and they were now constantly trying to reach around below or over the Island weapons' projection. Wraith hands grabbed at anything they could, their mouths screaming silent abuse which no-one could hear, but which everyone understood the intent of, if not the words. These tormented souls would drag them all down to the Underworld with them if they had the chance.

Sionnachan got up to Maelbrigt, and managed to dodge the Sword swings enough to get close and tell him what they planned. Then standing back from Maelbrigt, Raethun, Ewan and Tobias, Sionnachan and McKinley's lance began singing a very different chant to the rest of the Foresters. Raethun and the others heard them and began chanting along with them – not daring to sing and disturb the careful spell but hoping the words had power of their own – and suddenly Maelbrigt was moving forwards through the wraiths, as if creating a tunnel through their press. Sionnachan marched in his wake with a hand on Sithfrey's shoulder, and McKinley and his men brought up the rear with the faithful Eadgar, bleeding from a dozen cuts but still standing and resolute.

At the edge of the chasm they stopped and Maelbrigt slowed the swinging of the Sword.

"Ready?" Sionnachan asked Sithfrey and got a nod. "Go!"

The DeÁine scholar dodged under Maelbrigt's swing and reached up to grab at a wraith with the Gauntlet. To his amazement he managed to catch hold of something. It was not as solid as a real person, but it was definitely something. He hauled it downwards and dropped to his knees to thrust it into the pit. The wraith's mouth opened in a tortured, silent scream as it all but disappeared into the abyss.

Sithfrey was frantically chanting something he had learned as a young student. It was only meant to diffuse Power when something like an experiment had gone wrong, not a summoning of this magnitude, and he was praying with all his might that it would work. But then he had never done anything like this with one of the greatest objects of Power. The Gauntlet radiated a green-tinted, blinding white, and all the press of wraiths still trying to climb out of the pit were halted as if by a glass seal.

"Now!" Sionnachan bellowed, signalling furiously at Matti. Some of his Foresters had gone to her and Will, and had got her closer too. Now she ran forwards with her bearers and flung the Shield onto the chasm. The Shield's energy splashed outwards as it hit Sithfrey's DeÁine one, floating on it like oil on water.

"We need to bond them!" Sionnachan yelled, even though the efforts of the ghosts below were getting more manic with every moment.

He was gesturing frantically to Cwen, and indeed Cwen and Berengar were almost upon them, when another figure appeared out of the chaos. Sioncaet staggered to his feet, picked up Arthur's broken body in his arms, then ran a couple of steps and jumped into the gateway to the Underworld. As he broke through the two shields the light beneath them turned from black and grey to volcanic red. It flamed brilliantly then died to nothing in mere seconds, the wraiths disappearing from view. Even more potently, in the instant Sioncaet's friends cried out in horror at his sacrifice, the apparition of Jolnir/Othinn opened its mouth as if to shriek in sudden agony, yet flashed out of existence before any sound came. The monstrous looming figure had gone.

"Quick! Before any more come up!" yelled Maelbrigt, who was close enough to see fully what had happened.

Cwen and Berengar leapt forwards and plunged the Spear into the two floating shields just as Sithfrey screamed, "Oh Great Lotus I can see them!" and thrust his arm, fingers splayed as if to push at something, deeper into the void to fully submerge the Gauntlet. As the Spear hit the two restraining layers they went solid, melding into a single barrier. At the same time, Maelbrigt in an instant took in the way that Sithfrey was being dragged downwards. Either he would be sucked in and lost, or his falling in would reopen the seal. With one swipe of the Sword Maelbrigt took Sithfrey's arm off at the shoulder and plunged the point of the Sword into the hole which appeared as the rest of the arm sank. Andra, ever inseparable from his friend, pounced on Sithfrey and hauled him backwards to prevent him falling in. Ivain and Swein also thrust the Bow and now inextricably linked Arrow into the remaining gap in the void as Talorcan clasped a hand over each of theirs.

With a massive thump like an earthbound thunder clap, the ground closed. From gateway to the Underworld, to good Island soil, took only the time needed to blink. All that remained was the top two-thirds of the great Sword sticking out of the ground.

Something which sounded like a huge sigh swept over the battlefield, mostly of relief as most of the sad souls whom Othinn had tortured to his will gratefully passed to the great beyond, although a few had faces filled with impotent rage. Moments later silence descended as men looked about them. Every last wraith had gone.

"Blessed Rowan, we did it!" Ivain said hugging Talorcan and Swein. "We've really done it!"

As exhausted soldiers staggered away in the sudden gloom created by the light of the Treasures going out, and natural evening twilight reasserted itself, another, smaller fight was still going on far in the rear of the main battle. As Jolnir had made his appearance above the battlefield, the three remaining Abend had fled from the scene. They needed no telling that any outcome would be catastrophic for them. If, against the odds, the Islanders defeated Jolnir, then they would be hunted down like rabid beasts and killed. If the more likely scenario took place and Jolnir won, then this was still no place for the living to linger. Any hope of going home to Lochlainn was gone for Masanae, as was Helga's dream of ruling the eastern Islands as both queen and witch, and the two women ran with the few remaining fleeing acolytes as fast as they could. Sometimes they played dead to avoid getting caught, other times they ran like the Dragon of Death was breathing its flames at their heels.

Finally they got beyond the piles of DeÁine bodies and any Island soldiers and stopped to draw in gulping breaths.

"Which way?" Helga wheezed.

Masanae's look ought to have frozen her on the spot. "Not with you!" The former leading witch gasped venomously. "From now on I go my own way. You sort yourself out!" And she began heading straight for the boats on the shore, pulling in what little Power she could find after the ghastly maelstrom up in the valley had sucked all to it.

"Those two are ours!" a woman's voice said softly.

Against his wishes, and theirs, Oliver with Lorcan, Bertrand and Friedl had been left to guard Wistan, Heledd and Briezh. Lorcan had taken a pragmatic approach and had walked Wistan off down the coast to look at some of the strange and exotic beasts the DeÁine had left in cages on the beach. However, once he had gone, Oliver and the others had needed little persuasion by Heledd and Briezh to move closer to the fighting. Only Oliver's growing feelings for Heledd stopped him from allowing them all to go and join in the battle. Now he was glad, for here were two of the Abend just walking into their hands! And one of them was Masanae. By the Trees, that witch was going to pay for taking Hamelin's life!

He drew his sword and twirled it in a couple of warm-up strokes, then prowled towards her. Masanae saw him coming and ground her teeth. By Volla's balls, what did it take for these Lotus-forsaken Islanders to wake up and realise that they were beaten? She summoned what Power she could into a small sending. It was not much but it should vaporise this pestilent child out of her way at least. She lifted her arm, and was just about to fling the Power out, when there was a shriek almost down her ear and something barrelled into her, sending her flying.

As she tried to shake the scratching spitting creature off herself, she realised, to her eternal frustration, that it was one of the two she had tried to drag into New Lochlainn and had lost back in Bruighean. Back then she had suspected that Eriu had taken the girls just to spite her. What she had never expected was to find them here! Heledd had a rock in her hands now and was smashing it into the witch's head at every opportunity. Then she heard Oliver shout,

"Move!"

As she lifted her head, his sword whistled down between the two of them and impaled Masanae through the chest. The next thing the two of them knew, they were picking themselves up from off the floor. Masanae could not hold much Power at the moment. Certainly nothing like the amounts Barrax or Tancostyl had had within them when they had been struck down, but it was enough to throw Oliver and Heledd clear of the witch, and she took advantage of it. Struggling to her feet she made a scrambling dash to get away from them, only to run straight onto Bertrand's sword.

"Going somewhere?" he asked in a voice as cold as ice, then twisted the sword in his strong hands. "This is for Saffy, you cold-hearted bitch!"

Masanae turned, piercing agony lancing through her middle, only to have Friedl slice her across the back. She staggered another step and then fell, which only drove Bertrand's sword deeper into her. Barely making it to her hands and knees, she tried to crawl onwards towards the sea, but she only got two jerky moves before the next pain struck. With a spare sword in her hands, Briezh stamped on Masanae's back and then plunged the sword right into her. She did not have the strength to push it all the way in alone, but then her sister's hands clamped over hers, and together they felt it go through and hit the rocky shore.

It fell to Oliver to administer the killing blow. Masanae was half dead already and her life was fading fast. That still was not fast enough for Oliver. He came up beside the sisters who were still leaning on the sword, pining Masanae to the ground, and brought his own blade down to go straight through her neck. There was a whisper of something passing and then the witch's eye glazed over and she lay still.

"That's for Hamelin!" Oliver declared with savage satisfaction, then looked around for the other witch.

Helga had not had it any easier. As she spotted Masanae come under attack, she turned and ran off to the right. She had no idea of where she was running to and she did not get far. She had barely come to where the dunes began to rise from the west end of the beach, when a flurry of sand from above alerted her to movement up there. Looking upwards for tussocks of grass to haul herself up with, instead she saw three kilted and armed women, with another in the Order's black leather fighting gear, sliding towards her down the dune's side.

"Now, now, Helga, you didn't think you'd be allowed to miss the party," the smallest of them said venomously. Nettie had snuck out of Lorne amongst the ranks of the female Foresters, and now stood with Captains Elen and Hawise, and Kayna, who had come across the female Foresters. Denied fighting alongside Maelbrigt once Taise had been wounded, Kayna had been taken with her into the heart of the Celidon Foresters' ranks. There she had spotted the Brychan female companies, and had hurried to them, knowing that they would understand her burning need to make someone suffer for what had been done to her friends.

"Time to pay," Elen said very calmly and drew her dagger.

"You've lived too long already," continued Hawise, as Nettie added, "Did you not think we'd find out what you did?"

Helga tried to back away. What in Great Ama's name were these mad women talking about? Then she felt Masanae's passing and pissed herself in fright. She began staggering backwards, but was too scared to take her eyes off the four in front of her.

Hawise struck first. As the other three went directly towards Helga, she deliberately squatted down and slid on the loose sand to get down faster. Springing to her feet, she plunged her long dagger into the witch's side. Helga had had no time to draw in the Power, so all that happened was that she staggered sideways and felt the most excruciating pain beneath her ribs. Elen was next, feinting at Helga's middle and then stabbing deeply into her other side. With the two knives embedded in her, Helga fell to her knees. Kayna stepped up to her and kicked her hard in the guts, making the witch scream in agony as the knives were brought into contact with other organs. As she tried to hold herself up to ease the pain, Kayna came around behind her and jerked her head back, holding Helga under her chin.

"That was for Taise!" she snarled in Helga's ear, then grabbing hold of it, sliced it off with her knife. "And that was just for the pleasure of hearing you scream!"

Nettie walked up with deliberate calm and stood before the blood-soaked, weeping witch. "But this is for all those unborn children you tormented!" she said, tapping a long and razor-sharp knife on her hand with the detachment of a chef about to chop onions, while Elen and Hawise took hold of Helga's arms. Then she and Kayna exchanged places, Nettie making sure that she had a good hold on the witch's bald head. Having been the Forester to find out Helga's dirty secret from the ancient archives, Nettie had soon incited all of her fellow female Foresters into swearing vengeance against the witches and this one in particular. Yet here and now Nettie did not have the strength to do what came next, but Kayna did, and as long as one of them inflicted retribution that was all that mattered.

"Did you think we wouldn't find out about your perverted beauty secrets?" Nettie snarled in Helga's remaining ear, as Kayna wiped the blood off her hands with sand to get a better grip. "What kind of woman are you that you thought that aborting early foetuses, and then smearing their pulverised and desiccated skin and bones on your face in a paste, would make you stay youthful? How does so much death make any woman beautiful?

"You never gave a moment's thought to the poor slave women who lost their babes before they'd hardly had chance to form. That you used some of them time and again, until they could never have the children they wanted! What made you think you had the right to claim such a thing? And for nothing more than your shallow vanity! Well now you're going to find out how it feels to have your womb ripped out, and cut open while you're still alive!"

As the other three held Helga still, Kayna plunged her knife into her low down and sliced across her. In her screaming agony Helga bit through her tongue, but that did not stop the women. Kayna made another cut and then plunged her hand into the gaping wound. As she made the final slicing cut, Helga gave one last terrified scream and died, the arch torturer unable to stand even a fraction of what she had handed out to so many others during her long reign of terror.

"Pissing weak bitch!" Kayna spat derisively, as she scrubbed her hands clean with sand again. "Master race, my arse!"

"We should have acted to do this a long time ago," Elen said, ever the analytical one.

Hawise went to embrace Nettie. "We did it," she said softly as Nettie hugged her back. "Your unborn cousins are avenged," for the secret Nettie had gone looking for, and then had told all the female Foresters about, had been triggered by the appearance of a lone escaped slave into Brychan, who had been part of her distant family once upon a time. "We can all breathe easy now."

Breathing was not something Eliavres was doing easily. He had taken off across the bracken as soon as he could, and well away from the route Helga and Masanae were taking. He had to get away!

He had had to lie low several times when groups of wounded Islanders came close to him. Wounded they might be, but that did not mean that they would not give up the rest of their lives to take him down with them, and he was realistic enough to know that. And he was equally sane enough to now not to even think about reaching for the Power as he felt Masanae try to do – that would bring the cursed Foresters on his trail faster than dogs after a wounded deer.

As night finally fell on the worst day in DeÁine history, it found Eliavres lying in a sodden bog, but far from the Island army. Tomorrow he would set off west along the coast and look for a boat. No matter that he would be as sick as a dog on the sea, better that than a sword through the gut. He had the ceremonial bracelet tucked in his tunic. He could elevate others to a new Abend – if he ever found any other DeÁine capable of surviving the ceremony that was, and if he ever wanted to share Power again – which was unlikely. He might just be the last ever Abend, but at least he was still alive. He did not care where he went either. As long as it was away from here, and somewhere where they had preferably never even heard of the emperor, that would suit him just fine.

Far off, half a world away, the elderly emperor of the DeÁine watched as the last arrow in the pool of the Imperial Power-room turned to dust. The last of Volla's pieces, except for the two he had, were now all gone. Not just lost as they had been before, but gone forever, and with them a substantial part of his means to tap into the Power. Even worse, that far off strand of the Power now felt totally different. Try as he might he could not reach it, let alone manipulate it.

The elderly Luchaire turned and bowed to the head priest. A message would be sent to the palace for his oldest son. Now there was only one thing left to be done. He picked up the ceremonial obsidian-bladed knife which the priest had pointedly placed on the rim of the pool before him. A knife which had not been used in over two thousand years, and never by one of his family until now. His death at his own hand was the only possible conclusion to this dreadful turn of events. The only one containing even a shred of honour. The shame to be paid for was beyond imagining. The west was lost to the DeÁine.

# Chapter 19

## *Aftermath*

### Rathlin: Mid Grian-mhor, the years 542 & 543

As the dust settled with the night over the battlefield, the weary companies tramped away from the gore and horror of the fallen. Exhausted and wounded though they were, none could face spending a moment longer in that valley. They did not go far, just back to where their last night's camp had been. At least there they could eat and tend their wounds, and here the wise women of Prydein proved their worth many times over. Not only did they help tend all of the seriously wounded, they had already got fires going around the camp and several pots of food heating up on each.

It was not until dawn, which came quickly at the height of summer, that everyone began to look about them for survivors. As the bulk of the army cough, hawked and limped its way back onto its feet, the remaining leaders found one another and retreated to beside a small puddle of a pool nestling near an old, moss-decked and rather stunted oak.

"Where's Maelbrigt?" Sionnachan asked as Raethun came to them.

"He's alive, if rather battered," Raethun confirmed, "but it's Taise."

"Oh no!" Matti sobbed, and felt Will's strong arms pull her close and hold her as she waited to hear the worst.

"It was whatever the DeÁine did to the Power at the end," Raethun tried to explain. "Maelbrigt got the Gorget off her alright, but where it was around her throat the flesh is withering and dying, and it's spreading! He won't leave her side. Eadgar's with him."

"I'll go straight away!" Sionnachan declared and ran off, tugging at the small medicine pouch which he had kept safe throughout the mayhem tucked inside his shirt.

"Master Brego?" Will asked the others.

He stood with Matti in a group made up of Berengar, Cwen and Warwick with five of the Brychan ealdormen, Ivain and Swein with Breca, Thorold, Piran and Instone, and Dana with the ealdormen from Ergardia, while Yaroman had come to represent the Celidon men in Maelbrigt's stead, and Ruari.

"He told me to tell you he thought this might happen," a soft highland voice answered, as Angus walked into their midst. "He and Master Arsaidh discussed it, and felt that it might come to a point where someone human would have to actually be *in* the Bowl to make it give its all. A matter of controlling it, was what Master Arsaidh said."

"But how?" Ruari demanded. "Are they dead?"

"How?" Angus scratched his grizzled beard. "Well I'm no' the man to be giving you all the answers, Master Ruari. All I can tell you is that Master Hugh and Master Arsaidh must have gone into the Bowl in Ergardia first. Then the Knife began pumping out masses of Power and it just swept over Master Brego. But I'm sure I saw the three of them together in it, just for a moment, and that wee squint was with them too."

"So if they're not alive, then maybe they aren't wholly dead either?" Ivain asked hopefully. After all they had been through, it seemed cruel that Hugh would not be around to see him take Prydein back to prosperity.

"Maybe?" Angus admitted. "Just because we haven't seen them since doesn't mean they aren't there."

"Where's Esclados? And Sithfrey?" Swein asked worriedly.

"Esclados is proving remarkably hard to kill," Berengar answered, trying to force some humour into his voice but struggling. "He lost his left arm in the fight with Quintillean. Sithfrey managed to heal the wound in the midst of all that carnage. But of course he in turn is now missing *his* right arm. By some miracle, the fact that it was taken off with the Sword seems to have sealed the wound and prevented him from bleeding to death. And the two of them are sitting side by side, making jokes about fighting side by side so that they have two good arms between them! Andra and Talorcan are keeping them company, although since Talorcan didn't have any assisted healing once he was separated from Sithfrey, he seems to be far more knocked about than they are."

"I spoke with Talorcan this morning," Ivain confirmed. "And I told him he's doing nothing until his wounds stop bleeding! I'm not having him die on me *after* we've won!"

"What's the butcher's bill?" Ruari asked the collected ealdormen in trepidation. "How many did we lose?"

"As best we can reckon at the moment, we lost about a third of the force we brought here," Thorold answered. "Of the rest about a quarter have major wounds and need to rest. Everyone else seems to have some sort of cuts and bruises, but nothing likely to prove life threatening."

"A third!" Berengar shook his head. "Cross of Swords, that's a heavy price!"

Ruari nodded and came to put a consoling hand on his shoulder. "Aye, I know! But it could have been so much worse! Think on that! We took on a force twice our size, and with those amongst them who were practised at using arcane weapons. We had the Island Treasures but no idea how to use them. On that basis we did incredibly well. I know it's no consolation to those families who won't have someone return, and every man lost should be remembered – and will be! But for such a fight? To lose only a third means we were very lucky!"

"What of the Abend?" Cwen asked. "And are there any of the Island Treasures left? I know the Sword still stands in the ground, and the Shield and Spear are gone. But what of the others?" She looked hopefully at Ivain and Swein.

"I'm afraid they're gone too," Swein said apologetically. "When we saw you thrust the Spear in to seal the chasm there was a bit on our side of the seal that seemed weaker. So we fired the Arrow through the Bow. Ivain pulled it, but Talorcan, Tamàs and I were holding on to him at the time. It yanked the Bow out of his hands and the locked Bow and Arrow went into the gap and sealed it."

"So no defence against any new threat from the DeÁine," Cwen sighed sadly.

Swein hurried over and hugged her tight. "Sacred Root and Branch, Cwen! I don't think there are many DeÁine left in this part of the *world*, never mind the Islands! It took them five hundred years to come back after the last time the ancients and our ancestors beat them. I don't think we need to worry about it happening in our lifetimes!"

"Speaking of ancients," Warwick said, looking about him, "have any of you seen even one of them?"

A quick check revealed that nobody had.

"Maybe those machines got overworked in the battle?" Raethun speculated.

"I doubt we'll know until we have time to go and visit Taineire," Ruari agreed, "but that seems more than likely. Either that or they somehow died with the apparitions."

By later that morning Magnus had arrived, bringing the welcome news that it would be possible to sail most of the men home in just two shipments given the number of the DeÁine ships they now had. They also had all of them at their disposal, for only a handful of the liberated slaves from New Lochlainn had survived, and they were too few to crew even one of the big ships needed to cross the southern ocean to their homes. He also brought others with him who were joyfully greeted.

Kayna had a brief and happy reunion with Matti, before hurrying off to Maelbrigt and Taise. Captains Elen and Hawise were returned to their battalions to much rejoicing, while the battered Jacinto was given a joyful reception before being carried off to the healers in Kayna's wake. Meanwhile, Oliver, Bertrand and Friedl had a reunion with the others from Prydein, and were able to confirm for certain that Masanae and Helga were also dead.

Less happy was the exchanged news that both Hamelin and Alaiz were dead. Everyone was saddened that neither would live to raise their children, and Ivain promptly declared to everyone that, Hamelin's children or not, they would be brought up as his and want for nothing. That at least brought smiles to peoples' faces, especially when Swein wryly said he could not imagine Talorcan changing a baby, but that he would dearly wish to be a fly on the wall when it happened!

Rather more concerning was that after much head counting nobody could account for Eliavres.

"Leave him to Magnus' men to find," declared Piran. "He can't have got far without a ship."

"We shall scour the hills and the coves!" Magnus declared. "He won't get far!"

Yet the oddest of meetings was between Berengar and Heledd and Briezh. The Master of Brychan almost passed out at the sight of his sisters appearing out of the Rathlin morning. The last he had known of them they had been safe and sound in northern Brychan.

In a ragged and emotional conversation, the two told him of how they came to fall into Masanae's clutches; and of their rescue, first by Oliver and Labhran's party, and then about joining with Will. However, Berengar had almost the harder part, for he had to break the news of Ben's death at King Edward's hands.

Yet even out of that came some good. The two sisters immediately took to Cwen, welcoming her in a way they might not have done so readily had they seen her as just some woman setting her sights on their beloved brother. Instead, the fact that she and Swein had set out nearly a year ago to bring Edward to justice, all alone if necessary, brought approval and the instant start of friendship. It also made Oliver's entry into the family that much easier. Both he and Heledd were quick to say that they had no idea how permanent their new relationship might become, but after the way Oliver had stormed the temple and brought them out, Berengar was quick to declare he could want for no finer brother-in-law.

What cheered everyone was the discovery that the squints had also all survived, except for Fin, and they were not sure whether he could be classified as dead. Shaken and upset by the overwhelming death and violence, the six were found all huddled together during the night, and now were brought to the meeting and fed as many nuts and pieces of fruit as they could consume, while receiving all the petting they could wish for.

"I think they have to live somewhere together," Matti said firmly. "I shall miss Moss terribly, but she's only known me for a short time. She's known the rest of them for eternity."

"She?" Will queried. "Are you sure?"

"Oh yes! I felt that most strongly," Matti insisted. "And I think you'll find that Dylan is female too. We have three *pairs* of squints!"

Swein looked at Ivain in amazement. "Did you sense that?"

"No," admitted Ivain, "but it would make sense, wouldn't it. With things like the Bow and Arrow, and the Shield and Spear, if you were going to pair them, then any creatures associated with them might be more linked to one another if they were ...well, ...a couple!"

"Then I think that ought to be Ergardia," Warwick suggested. "If they are based near the Bowl, and if Fin is alive within it with the Masters, then they might be able to communicate with one another."

However, most of the details of what would happen in the coming weeks and months were too much for anyone to decide after such an exhausting ordeal. Magnus' men were ready to take the Islanders straight away, but all the leaders declared that they should wait at least one day more. That way there was time to go once more onto the battlefield and finish searching for survivors. Nobody wanted to hurry away and leave even one of their men behind to die alone.

In fact it took two days, because rather more were found than anticipated. They carried them down to the shore this time, and once they had been tended to, were ferried straight out to the waiting ships and settled in hammocks to rest. It did not significantly alter the percentage of men lost, but to find nearly a battalion's worth who had been thought lost did much for morale.

That night Taise succumbed to her dreadful festering injury and died. She went peacefully, but Maelbrigt was inconsolable, rocking her lifeless body in his arms for hours as his tears fell without end. Kayna never left his side, fearful of what he might do in his grief, and Eadgar made sure all knives and swords were well out of reach. They managed to get him on board the ship the next day, but only by taking Taise's body with them. Luckily the Attacotti had found many large barrels in the holds of the Souk'ir's ships, and so she was taken home sealed in one as a makeshift coffin. Sionnachan had asked all the other leaders to join him at Kylesk for some serious talks over how they could run the Islands for the immediate future, but Maelbrigt and Kayna he put on the fastest boat for Celidon. Raethun, Ewan and Tobias were going with them, and along with Eadgar were charged with seeing Taise buried at Maelbrigt's old home, and then bringing him straight on to Lorne. Sionnachan had no illusions that, if left to his own devices, Maelbrigt would sit at Taise's grave and quietly fade away, and he was determined that that at least should not happen.

As Magnus' men picked up more sailors from their home ports, and set about transporting the first wave of soldiers back to their respective home Islands, the leaders sat in the garden where Alaiz was buried, and tried to sort their world back into some kind of order. With Hugh and Brego gone there were huge gaps to fill, and it was not only Ergardia and Prydein which had leadership crises, for no-one had forgotten that Rheged had suffered most and earliest in this harsh fight for freedom. There was also the burning question of what to do about the place they'd all grown up calling New Lochlainn. With the DeÁine driven out there would need to be much work done to set that to rights too.

For days they chewed over what would be best for all – Will in particular being questioned at length as to how things lay in New Lochlainn, since of all of them he was the one who had seen most of that land. And that also brought with it one of the biggest surprises. The Attacotti fighters of the far west had been asked to send representatives along, and to Will's great amazement they asked him to come back and help rebuild their land. Will managed to accept the formal offer gracefully, although with remarkable tact suggested that they all think about it overnight. He would give them his answer in the morning, something which the other leaders applauded since it showed the Rathlin Attacotti that Will, at least, was not grasping whatever he could get for himself.

"Could you cope with living over the mountains in a new home?" Will asked Matti in private that night. "I haven't said yes yet. If you say no, then that's it, because I'm not letting you slip through my fingers again Lady Montrose!"

Her reply was some time in coming, not because of any need to think about it, but because they had both found immense pleasure in discovering a new physical side to their marriage which had never been there before.

"I think that would be lovely," Matti sighed later on. "To be frank, I'm not sure that I could cope with going back and trying to rebuild Montrose. Too many memories, too many ghosts! Let Gerard, Edmund and Osbern have the care of Rheged. At least their homes weren't reduced to burned rubble. I do like the sound of that old Attacotti place, though! What did you say it was called?"

"Wyrdholt," Will rumbled, snuggling that bit closer to her again. Ruari had been right, what an idiot he had been not to see what he had been given in Matti. Now he would not have swopped her for any number of the empty-headed girls he had spent the night with over the years. "A nice place for kids too! Not like Mereholt! We'll take years to take that place apart and discover all the nasties the Abend witches have left behind!"

"Kids?"

"Well it would! Be a nice place for them, that is."

"Nice recovery, Montrose, but you'll have to do better than that to fool me!" She let her fingers trail down his belly and turned to nibble at his ear. "If that's what you want, we'd better practise some more!"

The consultation with the western Attacotti had been seen as vital, because Ruari and Berengar had privately agreed that Magnus was bound to want to take them over too, and yet he had hardly got his own Island sorted out. More to the point, most of the men from New Lochlainn had forgotten, or had diverged from, being Attacotti in the way that the Rathliners still thought of themselves.

"We'll need to tread very carefully," Berengar pondered. "The last thing we want is for Magnus' folk to go in lording it over them. That might lead to the kind of civil war we had after Moytirra in Brychan. Absolutely disastrous!"

"I'm with you there," Ruari agreed. "And I don't want to give that Friseal any chance to say that if Magnus is having Rathlin, then he wants New Lochlainn! Cross of Swords, that would be a bloody disaster! If there was one man I could have wished not to come through the battle, it was him. But he did and he's no more likeable for it, either. No, we must ask the people themselves what they want, although I doubt if they'll know. It's hardly likely, is it, when they've not had the chance to think for themselves in over a generation, but we must make the effort."

Magnus and Raghnall were indeed less than pleased when the new Attacotti were asked, yet Magnus demonstrated his increasing grasp on matters when he accepted it without public complaint, even though he probably fumed in private. Raghnall, though, made very vocal his thoughts on the matter, leading everyone to wish that the jaculi had seen him off and saved them the trouble. In the end, Ivain simply clapped him in chains and sent him on the next ship to Prydein, with orders for him to be kept in a secure place until he came to see sense, and told his clan to find someone else to come to the talks.

"We did not lose so many of your clansmen to bicker over the pickings afterwards," he sternly told the assembled Clan Friseal. "Pick someone who has brains as well as brawn!"

There was also the small matter of the folk of Lowes, Farr and Kinloch. These people had no wish to be ruled by Magnus, and wholeheartedly agreed to have Ivain as their leader.

"I shall be your jarl for now – your elected leader in the way I intend to take the rest of Prydein back to having," Ivain said after accepting their offer. "That means that later, when you've had chance to think more thoroughly, you can decide that you want to be ruled by one of your own leaders, or at least send someone of your own to cast your vote when the time comes for Prydein to elect a new leader. You aren't stuck with me and my descendants forever!"

With those at least temporarily sorted, it was easier to deal with the remaining Islands. Ivain, with Talorcan at his side, would oversee Prydein's recovery and that of Kittermere, while keeping one eye on Rathlin. Nobody pretended that anyone could quite replace Hugh, and Thorold openly declared that while he would happily continue to serve as the second-in-command to whoever led the Order in Prydein, he felt that the job of Grand Master should go to a younger, more energetic man. However, Talorcan was quite firm on the matter that he would not even enter into the election, and rather more surprisingly, so did Oliver.

"I don't have the experience, and I know it!" the young Knight said modestly. "I've a lot more learning to do yet before I'm anything like ready for that kind of role, but I don't want anyone voting for me in a blaze of enthusiasm after us winning such a battle. I doubt that many would vote for me, but there might be some who think that getting away from the old regime associated with Amalric would take place quicker with a complete newcomer like me at the helm. Personally I know that that would be a disaster!"

Somewhat harder to decide was what to do with Rheged. In the end Sionnachan and Ruari came to a workable arrangement. Given Rheged's lack of a regular army, it was vital that the Order be a strong presence there. Ruari would therefore command all of Rheged and Ergardia's regular Order, and undertake, if necessary, to post men on Celidon too. Sionnachan would take command of the Foresters of all three Islands, and likewise try to build them up until they could stand on their own feet again.

That left Berengar with the not inconsiderable task of providing Order men for both halves of Brychan, and Warwick with building the Foresters up there too. Nobody was going to be sitting on their hands for a very long time yet! What everyone wanted, though, was to keep in touch. Having forged such strong links they all feared being isolated once more, and the enormity of the tasks they were facing at least seemed bearable when they knew what the others were doing.

"One year from now!" Ruari declared, as they stood on the quay of Kylesk waiting to board their respective boats. "We shall all meet again on the fifteenth of Grian-mhor next year. Here at Kylesk!"

"Why not make it a couple of days before?" Sionnachan suggested. "Then we can go and lay memorial wreaths on the battlefield on the anniversary. I'm sure many would want us to do that." And so it was agreed.

One year on, the harbour of Kylesk was filled with ships once more. This time, though, there was a festival air about the place. The greatest cause for celebration for many had been the discovery a couple of months after the battle, that they could communicate with Brego, Hugh, and Arsaidh by opening the Bowl up. It had shut down after the battle and none of the Foresters had dared open it again until Sionnachan and the leading Foresters got back. However, it had been the squints who had been the most insistent on it. It was harder now, for there was nobody to translate what the little creatures wanted to say, but Raethun and Ewan were developing into experts on all things squint, with the able assistance of Farrier Armstrong. And the six squints in the real world were positively oozing health now, so it was with considerable delight that they were then able to talk to Fin, even if he could not come through to them. Since then the three disembodied leaders had experimented with the ways beyond, to the extent that Sionnachan had made a special cadre of Foresters to do their bidding, to be led by Aeschere with Tobias as his second.

"If we don't give him someone specific, he'll have our men running all over the place to satisfy his curiosity!" Sionnachan had grumbled of Arsaidh, although with rather more amusement than indignation.

Along with Andra, Sithfrey had become part of that team as soon as he was healed enough. The DeÁine scholar was pleased beyond words that he could still learn from the aged Master, and it aided his recovery more than anything else. As soon as men could be spared, Sionnachan had had a proper preceptory built out of wood at the Bowl, with the promise that one day it would be upgraded in stone. By then the three in the beyond place were sure that there would be other places where they could come through, and at least converse with people. The chapel sites on Celidon and Rathlin were clearly two, and with a bit of experimenting they got the pool on Brychan where the Shield had been found to work as another, causing Warwick to build a shelter over it and promise his own building programme.

The six squints were also in residence at the new Ergardian site, and although there was no sign of small squints yet, the way the six were flourishing had everyone hoping that it might still be possible in the future. Arsaidh's scribes were already combing the ancient archives for all they could find regarding the squints creation to help in the care of the much-loved six.

At the end of this first year that was as far as they had got, but it boded well for the future, for all three masters in the beyond were sure that if they could get a working gateway working on Kittermere, then they could calculate where the lost one on Rheged was.

"I think he's even more infuriating in the beyond than he was alive," Sionnachan groaned, as he nursed a large goblet of wine after the celebration banquet held in the open, under a blessedly clear summer night sky, to accommodate so many. "Now Arsaidh doesn't need to sleep at all!"

Ruari snorted. "Flaming Trees, these days I can't remember what it was like to get a straight eight hours' sleep!"

"Me neither!" Will agreed.

"Yes, but we can all see why you haven't!" Ruari riposted. Wistan had blossomed over the intervening months and was currently running about the hall meeting old friends with normal youthful enthusiasm. However Will and Matti had revealed that he still had dreadful nightmares, which often had them up sometimes several times a night.

It had been decided that they should foster Wistan rather than Ruari. For a start, Matti's constant presence at Wyrdholt, which they could make into a proper home, was infinitely better for the troubled youngster, than having a place with his Uncle Ruari and being constantly on the move. They all also agreed that there was very little in Rheged for Wistan to return to except bad memories. Therefore starting over with the Montrose's had been the obvious path to take. Ruari had half expected to see Matti arriving pregnant, for there were several women who were clearly about to produce a new generation to help with the healing process. However, when he had quietly mentioned it to Will, his old friend had shaken his head.

"It just hasn't happened for us yet. Maybe Matti's just doing too much running around for the moment, I don't know. Or we might have left it too late. Neither of us is exactly in the first flush of youth, are we?"

"Can you cope with that?" asked Ruari, concerned that this fragile new relationship might buckle under a different kind of strain.

However Will grinned. "Oh yes! Neither of us was expecting to just walk into a new home and settle into domestic bliss. And we have Wistan! That's been a joy and a blessing all of its own, watching him come back and start playing with the local lads of his own age. And if Matti ever feels the urge to cuddle a baby we're certainly not short of those!"

The women who had been left behind at Wyrdholt had produced their respective infants in the months following the battle. Yet Taise's two former friends had proven singularly inept at motherhood.

"I had to take over the babies' care within weeks!" Matti was telling a very pregnant Cwen in another part of the banquet hall. "Great Maker, I'm hardly an expert mother, but even I had more of a clue than those two! And do you know what? They just turned their backs on those babies and never looked back. It's tragic that neither of the children were properly formed because of their Powered conception, but they aren't about to die either! Yet it's as if they're too much of a reminder of what their mothers went through – too much to even bear looking at.

"Those two are off helping plough through the documents we have left of the DeÁine's, and although I've offered them several chances to come back and see their children, they never do. It's near miraculous those two little ones have survived, not only because of their fragile state, but because we didn't have anyone else who could wet-nurse them, so it was a case of feeding them goats' milk and praying! It seemed to work though – or there was someone looking out for them in the Summerlands – because they've both thrived."

"Oh that's such good news!" Cwen beamed.

Cwen was glowing despite the trial of carrying her heavy weight around in the hottest months of the year, and with an exceptionally good summer in full flower. Berengar was clearly delighted beyond words at his impending fatherhood, and was pressing Esclados to come and stay with them in a couple of months when the baby was due. The old Knight had surprised them all by deciding that he would follow Talorcan back to Prydein, declaring that he wanted to get to know the son whom he had finally tracked down.

Before his departure Berengar had taken him on one side and told him that if it did not work out, being in such close proximity to Talorcan, then there was always a place for him with them.

"Don't think that just because your fighting days are over that you aren't wanted in Brychan," he told Esclados sternly. "Cwen thinks of you as a second father. You'll always be welcome in our house!"

Yet his new life on Prydein seemed to be working out well. The old Knight was enjoying spoiling Alaiz's twins as their only grandparent, and if his waistline seemed to have expanded even more, then nobody was saying anything about it.

Swein, on the other hand, had gently rejected the offer of a home with Ivain and Talorcan and Esclados, to go back to Brychan with Berengar. Berengar had taken him on as his personal aide, and was more than delighted with the speed at which Swein was learning. Currently he was without a lance, but Berengar was quick to say that as soon as the right combination could be found, that he would be sending Swein out into the field to learn even more. He already had part of one, for Talorcan's lance had been left in limbo by their leader's step down from active service.

Ruari and Sionnachan had agreed that there would be no formal severing of Talorcan's service, leaving the way open for him to return in the future if he found life at court too claustrophobic – something Hugh and Brego had disagreed with, but for once they had been told firmly that the Order was no longer theirs to run. So Ad had been allowed to go with Talorcan as his squire, while Decke had returned to Ergardia as fast as he could, and had taken a position working for one of the Order's priests. Tamàs, as by far the oldest of the lance, had asked for retirement from the field, but also for the chance to go back into New Lochlainn where he had been born. So now he was with Will and Matti, nominally as Wistan's servant and guard, but in reality helping mainly with the orphans who had been taken into care. Barcwith and Galey, however, had expressed a desire to serve alongside Swein, and had moved over to be under Berengar's command.

There had been an awkward reunion between Swein and Jacinto with neither knowing quite what to say. However, over the months they had gradually come to a place where they were firm friends, although they would not be working in close proximity for the foreseeable future. Jacinto had been profoundly apologetic to Berengar and Esclados as well as to Swein, making it clear to his old leader just how sorry he was for the grief he had caused in the past. Esclados, meanwhile, had been most vocal in his delight that his most awkward trainee had turned out to be so fine an example of knighthood. However, Berengar seemed to understand that Esclados' unconditional forgiveness actually made things harder for Jacinto, and so he had been thankful, in that respect if no other, that the old Knight would not be around when they returned to Brychan.

Jacinto now held a post with Ealdorman Allainn in the newest preceptory, which had been created in the old palace of Tokai, and was expected to make captain in the very near future. That had been a tactful posting by Berengar, knowing that the battered and scarred young man needed a fresh start where nobody would recall what a headache he had been to them all only a year or so back. However, it was enlightening to hear Jacinto talk of the awakened memories of his family, for it explained so much of his early behaviour. With that ghost laid to rest, Berengar had high hopes of what Jacinto might also yet achieve.

True to his word, Oliver had formally declared no interest in the vote for a new leader of the Prydein sept. That had gone – with Hugh's belated blessing – to Piran, who was proving an energetic and able new Grand Master for the Island, and had surprised every one of the nobles there by making his first declaration one of an intention to enrol Attacotti into the Order. Strangely, though, not a soul had said a thing against it at the first court gathering, when Talorcan glowered at them from beside Ivain from up on the throne room dais.

So amongst those in the new West Brychan sept were now the three Prydein Knights who had shared the trials of crossing DeÁine territory. Like the Montroses, they had all felt that going back home to Prydein would be unbearable.

"Too many memories of the ones we've lost," Oliver had said sadly. "There isn't a sept in Prydein where I didn't go at some point with Hamelin. And although I'm delighted that Ivain and Talorcan are bringing Alaiz' children up as their own, I'm not sure how I feel about actually seeing them do that when their real father was my best friend."

He, Friedl and Bertrand were here to join in the celebrations, however, having travelled across on the same ship as Will and Matti, although Heledd and Briezh were back at Tokai. Heledd was only weeks away from giving birth, and her sister was watching her like hawk to make sure she did not over do things – in between training that was. Poor Berengar had been horrified to find Briezh announcing her intention to become a female Forester, with her application heartily supported by Elen and Nettie – who herself had been elevated to captain, and was currently adapting to life at Tokai too. Warwick had foreseen that without an enemy on their doorstep, Nettie would need a challenge to expound her considerable energy on, and had set her the challenge of developing a training plan for the large numbers of female recruits to both sides of the Order. A job which Elen reported she was doing with great gusto.

Just at the moment, though, Eldaya was temporarily taking over from where Nettie had left off back at Tokai, and was bombarding Oliver with plentiful good advice as she bounced her robust son on her knee, causing Cwen and Matti to have to rescue the poor young Knight on several occasions, before he wilted under Eldaya's enthusiasm for all things maternal. He beamed with delight every time the matter was mentioned, but there were limits to what even he could cope with! Magnus, against anyone's expectations, was already proving to be a doting father, and was going about telling all and sundry that Eldaya and fatherhood were the best things to ever happen to him.

"Good grief, we'll need more midwives than soldiers if they carry on this way!" Sionnachan laughed with Ruari, when they took a slow stroll around the garden after the others had retired to their quarters.

"Hmmm!"

"What does that mean? 'Hmmm'?"

"Well you and Kayna seem to be ...attached ...these days?"

Sionnachan gave a grimace, but seemed rather happy at the association nonetheless. "Well you know how it is at Lorne..."

Ruari did. Maelbrigt was notable by his absence, although no-one blamed him for not wanting to come back to Rathlin. It had been Kayna who had found something to keep him going. On the way back from burying Taise in the garden of Maelbrigt's old home, she had collected Rob and Jakie from the grange to travel with them. The young boys had been kind and sympathetic, but with the optimism of youth had refused to allow Maelbrigt time to wallow in his grief.

Now Maelbrigt was housed in a small suite of rooms at Lorne and was slowly recovering with the boys, Eadgar, and Kayna to watch over him. Of all of them he had suffered the greatest personal losses, for he also deeply mourned the passing of Labhran and Sioncaet. It had helped him somewhat that Will had written to him filling in the gaps in Sioncaet's life, and the minstrel's long-standing sadness at having lost two families – something which Maelbrigt now understood all too well. However, he also joined with Will in grieving over the loss of Labhran just when he had seemed to have cast off his demons at last.

Yet Sionnachan was determined that such talent and knowledge should not be allowed to moulder, and so he had Maelbrigt taking training classes with the youngest recruits for a few hours on most days, and was slowly increasing the number. If he himself was taken up with the outside activities of the Foresters, he had told Maelbrigt, then he definitely needed someone to make sure that the scholarly aspect was not lost. Of course there were many who had studied under Arsaidh for years who had survived the battle, but everyone was tactfully not mentioning that, nor that those men were quietly doing most of the work. For his part in the whole affair Maelbrigt was owed a lot of leeway.

"Will he recover?" Ruari asked after a companionable silence.

"I think he's already started down that path," Sionnachan said. "He'll never be the same man he was. The loss of Taise cut too deep for that. But by nature he's not a morbid man. It'll take a couple more years yet before he's fully on his feet, and even then I wouldn't dream of asking him to take up any sort of weapon ever again. But he's doing a wonderful job with fostering Rob and Jakie even in the state he's in at the moment.

"Well we're going to need a lot of young recruits, and Will was saying only today that there are a lot of orphans about in New Lochlainn – or West Brychan, as we should now call it. Maelbrigt and I have had a couple of tentative conversations about setting up some proper schools, and a mass fostering system by the Order in all of the Islands, to give these lost children the chance they need. I'm hoping that he might even consent to be a figurehead for the scheme."

"What, and the girls?" Ruari gasped.

"Kayna was rather emphatic on that one," Sionnachan said dryly, making Ruari glad that it was now dusk so that Sionnachan could not see his smirk. Clearly Kayna was not going to change that much even if she was willing to tie herself to the Forester. "She invited Captain Elen over, you know, and she's talking about there being a female force in every sept."

"Flaming Trees!" Ruari groaned. "I don't think I'm quite ready for that yet!"

"Well, you don't have to be, you lucky sod, because I'm the one who has to have them first, because there are already female Foresters from Brychan ready and willing to come and help train more for us in the Ergardian Foresters."

"Best of luck!" Ruari commiserated. "I wouldn't want to get on the wrong side of that Hawise, either! She's a big lass and I bet she could give you a nasty thick ear if roused!"

"Oh she can! Two of my lads won't be making ribald comments again anytime soon!" and the two of them winced at the thought.

"At least I only have Edmund, Gerard and Osbern to contend with," Ruari said thankfully, "and I can take their leg-pulling to make me laugh when nothing else does. Although Jaenberht was enough of a handful already, without this worrying new tendency to keep popping over to Ergardia for a chat with Brego, Hugh and Arsaidh. I swear the four of them are in league with one another!"

The elderly abbot had worked wonders in getting Rheged back on its feet, at least as far as essential things went, by the time Ruari had got back. But there was still much work to do, and Ruari had so much on his plate, he had had to delegate many civil issues permanently to his old friends. A small bright spot for him, which he had passed on to Will and Matti, had been to learn that Gerard's family had come to no harm from harbouring the murderous Ismay. As soon as they could, Gerard and Osbern had ridden for Thorpness and thrown Ismay, spitting and snarling and cursing them roundly, into chains. Yet when Tancostyl had died in the battle, all the light had gone out of her and she had withered and died within days. So while Edmund and Gerard wrestled with the civil government of Rheged, Osbern had now volunteered to become Ruari's aide on the Island, and had saved his sanity with his talent for organising and bureaucracy.

Meanwhile, as Ruari and Sionnachan talked in the garden, up on a balcony of one of the big old houses already being restored to its former glory, Swein and Jacinto shared a flask of wine as they looked out over the sea.

"Did you ever think we'd be doing this?" Jacinto asked in wonder, as the sinking sun mottled the waves in different shades of blues and reds.

"What? You and me and wine in a romantic setting?" Swein said with wry amusement.

Jacinto jumped, then laughed as he realised Swein was teasing him. "Well now you mention it! ...No, actually I was thinking of how close we came to not doing *anything* ever again," he clarified, while at the same time thinking how glad he was in the oddest way to have gone through such turmoil. These days he often found himself giving up thanks that he had not gone on living his life in the old way. And especially that he had not been left in a position to ruin Swein's life as well as his own. "It's little short of a miracle of the kind Andra talks of, that it all came out right in the end."

"Yes it is," Andra's voice came from the gloom of the room, preceding him stepping out onto the balcony to join them bringing more wine. "Sithfrey couldn't face the thought of coming back here, but I felt I had to come. That at least one of us came and said our thanks for surviving."

"Well here's to friendship!" Jacinto declared, touching his wine goblet to the other two.

"And long may it last!" Swein added, clinking goblets back. "Don't forget Andra, you're coming on to stop with us for a few days when you travel back from visiting Matti and Will. We're not losing touch after all we've been through!"

The next day everyone rode south, and on the fifteenth they found themselves standing once more on the battlefield. A rich green sward of grass covered the valley floor, brightly dotted with daisies, buttercups, cornflowers and poppies, and other wild meadow flowers. Nothing remotely hinted at the mayhem and slaughter which had taken place there a year ago. For that they had much to thank the Attacotti for, because Magnus had come back after the winter weather had done its work, and with many of his people, had removed all the weather-stripped bones to the shore. Seven huge cairns now lined up facing the sea, where the bones had been covered with stones, and already they had tiny plants beginning grow on them. The only sign left in the valley was the Sword, still sticking up out of the earth and showing no sign of damage despite having been exposed to all weathers. Around it they placed their wreaths, some made of fresh flowers, but most made up of dried ones so that they would survive the journey to Rathlin from the other Islands.

Ruari, Berengar and Sionnachan each said short pieces, and then everyone joined in the prayer to the Trees. In the silence which followed, they were all suddenly very glad to hear the gurgling chuckle of a baby and another join in. Ivain and Talorcan had brought Little Alaiz and Little Hugh out with them, and now the infants reminded everyone that there was a future. The solemn, formal ranks broke up, and people walked over the grass for a while, sharing individual memories or just silently remembering, before mounting up to ride home.

"We never did find that last DeÁine," Magnus said to Ruari, as they paused for one last glance back down towards the sea as they turned for Kylesk once more. "So many died who didn't deserve to, it doesn't seem right that one of them should survive."

"No, it isn't right," Ruari sighed regretfully.

The Attacotti leader shook his head and heeled his horse after the others, "I do hate loose ends like that. Not knowing one way or the other is always worse."

"That it is," Ruari agreed, "but I suppose it would have been just too neat and tidy to get every last one of them. Life isn't like that, is it? I just hope we never hear of Eliavres or the DeÁine ever again."

Thank you for taking the time to read this series. I hope you have enjoyed it.

If you've enjoyed this book and series you personally (yes, *you*) can make a big difference to what happens next.

Reviews are one of the best ways to get other people to discover my books. I'm an independent author, so I don't have a publisher paying big bucks to spread the word or arrange huge promos in bookstore chains, there's just me and my computer.

But I have something that's actually better than all that corporate money – it's you, my enthusiastic readers. Honest reviews help bring these books to the attention of other readers (although if you think something needs fixing I would really like you to tell me first!). So if you've enjoyed this book, it would mean a great deal to me if you would spend a couple of minutes posting a review on the site where you purchased it.

**About the Author**

L. J. Hutton lives in Worcestershire and writes history, mystery and fantasy novels. If you would like to know more about any of these books you are very welcome to come and visit my online home at www.ljhutton.com

If you would like full colour maps of the ones in the books, they are available via the mailing list.

**Also by L. J. Hutton**:

If you would like to receive the first eBook for free in a new (slightly smaller) fantasy quartet, set in the same world as these books, but in a different location and slightly later in date, then all you need to do is to go to my web page, follow the link, and send me your email. I promise not to bombard you with random mail – this is just to be able to let you know when new books are coming out. Sadly I cannot provide free paperbacks due to the much higher production and distribution costs, but if like me you love holding a real book in your hands, then this new series is also available in paperback.

## Menaced by Magic

A lost soldier, a duchy in peril, and a missing heir who alone can control its only defence. Can a stranger hold the key to everyone's survival?

Modern-day soldier, Mark, wakes up in a strange place only to find he's the double for the lost heir to the Duchy of Palma. Even as he struggles against the intense hatred his double has earned, Mark discovers a new danger is coming, and this one has a potent magical power he has no idea how to combat. How do you fight insane mages whose power you don't even begin to comprehend when they think you've stolen their kingdom? Totally out of his depth, and with no way to return home, Mark must help his new friends fight for the survival of the duchy and its people, or die with them.

I also write mysteries which are sort of urban fantasy and have a paranormal twist. You will get one of these eBooks for free as well when you sign up! And if you love real history too, then look for the first trilogy in my retelling of the Robin Hood legend. The first book is *Crusades* and is available from Amazon.

***Can one man change the fate of thousands? Guy of Gisborne tries, but he needs Robin Hood to succeed!***

Forced to leave their home, cousins Guy and Robin are destined to lead very different lives. While Robin goes with the Templars to the crusades, Guy faces danger on the Welsh border serving brutal sheriff de Braose. Yet a chance meeting with rebel Welsh priest, Tuck, sets Guy on the path of covert righter of wrongs, even before a chance meeting with a prince returns him to Nottingham. And when Robin returns, too, the cousins launch a wider crusade to find justice for the people of Sherwood.

As Robin's spy inside the sheriff's castle, Guy risks being hung – or worse – if caught. Alone and often torn by the decisions he's forced make, Guy must act against the very class he was born into, but once his eyes have been opened to the plight of the ordinary people there's no going back. Yet it will be the infamous events in York in 1190 that will seal the fate of one famous outlaw, his cousin, and a legend!

*Crusades* is the first book in the Guy of Gisborne historical series (previously published as *Much Secret Sorrow*).

If you enjoy Michael Jecks, C. J. Sansom, Nigel Tranter and Bernard Cornwell, long for rich historical detail, or love *Robin of Sherwood,* then you'll love this retelling of the Robin Hood legend.

Printed in Great Britain
by Amazon

41523252R00208